Forthcoming Books by Bradd Hopkins
from

RUSSELL DEAN & CO., PUBLISHERS

The Fourth Corner of the Ninth Room
(Russell Dean & Company, August 1998)

The Morningstar Papers
(Russell Dean & Company, Spring 1999)

Mandelbaum's Donut
(Russell Dean & Company, Fall 1999)

To order additional copies of <u>Navassa</u>, phone
toll free **1-888-438-4115.**

Or write to:
Russell Dean and Company,
P.O. Box 318
Santa Margarita, California 93453

NAVASSA

a novel by
Bradd Hopkins

RUSSELL DEAN & CO, PUBLISHERS
Santa Margarita, California, U.S.A.

NAVASSA

First Printing : February, 1998

Copyright © 1997-1998 by Russell Dean & Company, for Bradd Hopkins.

Published by Russell Dean & Company, Publishers, 22595 K Street, Santa Margarita, California, 93453-0318. All rights reserved. No portion of this book may be reproduced in any form without the express written consent of the publishers.

Library of Congress Cataloging-in-Publication Data.
Hopkins, Bradd
Navassa / Bradd Hopkins p.cm.— (Russell Dean fiction - novel)

ISBN 1-891954-00-8

1. Novel. 2. AIDS I. Title. II. Series. QB981.P425 1997-1998

Russell Dean books are printed on acid-free paper, and meet the guidelines for permanence and durability of the Committee on Production Guidelines for Book Longevity of the Council on Library Resources.
Printed in the United States of America.

DEDICATION

This work is dedicated to Doris Gardner, Letha Coté, and Paul Summers. Thirty years ago they kindled a fire that burst finally into flame. Each will recognize their influence in this work.

Change

Something gathers on the horizon
Distant, yet near.
Like the way birds fly low to the ground before rain,
Or like the subtle change in fog
Just before the sun burns through.
Or like the farmer
Who, greeting dawn from his stoop,
Knows with a primal certainty
That tomorrow
The leaves will turn.

Things are soon to change.

ACKNOWLEDGEMENTS

Nobody ever does anything alone.

I am deeply grateful to my wife Rebecca Hopkins and to Kezia Letzin. Both avidly encouraged and supported the daily efforts necessary to the creation of <u>Navassa</u> by demanding to see the next chapter as soon as it was written. The insightful comments about the manuscript provided by Courtney Cable were a substantial influence on its final form. To my readers Cathy Hudson, Teresa Damas, Jerry James, John and Carol Carson, Norm Hammond and Cindy Winter, Carrie Bassford, Ken McCool, Duncan Osborne, and Gary and Trish Hagerty, I wish to acknowledge my debt and my gratitude.

Thanks also to Zandra Zimmerman, Doug Weissmann, Mike Sisk of the Littlefield, Adams Company, Ray Powers of the Marje Fields Agency, and all of the others who, knowingly and unknowingly pushed, prodded, encouraged and educated me during the course of the labor.

I am particularly indebted to Alan Baughman of Harris-Wolfe and Company for his assistance and support in the production of this work. Finally, the editorial assistance of Brenda Cubbage at Easicritique Literary Services, and the astute comments of Sandra Morgan brought this work to its present form.

NAVASSA

a novel by
Bradd Hopkins

RUSSELL DEAN & CO, Inc., PUBLISHERS
Santa Margarita, California, U.S.A.

AUGURY

Nago Espiridion Uribe was pushing a broom for more money than he had ever made in his life. The place was a tiny island in the Caribbean Sea, a U.S. possession. The year was 1975, but Nago had no concern with time. Numbering years was a white man's thing; something Yanquis did. His people, the Guaymi, did not need such devices.

They paid him ten American dollars a day—for that kind of money he was happy to be the best janitor the world had ever known, and not talk about it. They insisted that he not talk about it—what he did or where he was working—and they paid him in cash money every week. They fed him; they gave him a clean place to sleep, these Gringos, and he was actually saving money for the first time in his life. And now, for the first time in his life, he envisioned a future that was something more than just an existence—a future where he could have some of the things he never thought he'd have. Maybe he could even save enough to find a woman who would have him and never again be forced to settle for the whores in Port-au-Prince. There, American dollars traded for vast sums of the local currency, the Gourde.

Nago thought it was funny that the Gringos didn't want him to talk about being a janitor. As if a janitor had secrets! He began work at seven o'clock each evening. Big secret! Every day they gave him breakfast—all he wanted to eat—when he finished work at seven o'clock in the morning. Mustn't tell! During the day he ate and slept and walked around the island; he was even putting on a little weight. Twice a month, he went into town on the crew boat, for two days, and now he had money for the girls, and for clothes without holes in them.

That Nago had left his home village of Canquintu was unusual for a Guaymi Indian. His people preferred to remain in their small villages along the fringes of the jungle rain forests in northwestern Panama where they had retreated four hundred years earlier to escape the cruelty of the Spanish conquistadors and the alien colonists who followed. There, distrustful of outsiders and isolated by their rugged, inaccessible jungle, his people lived and died in relative peace. In his youth Nago had detested it, this villager's life without challenge, and at the first opportunity he had ventured down river to Changuinola.

He worked for a time on a sugar plantation outside Changuinola, saving enough to book steerage on a tramp freighter bound for Haiti. In Port-au-Prince, he had stumbled on this most lucrative of professions, broom-pushing, thanks to a tip from a casual friend who had grown tired of feeding him.

The only bad thing about this job was the boat ride necessary to come here and to leave. Nago Espiridion Uribe faced it every second week with trepidation and began a vigil two days before each trip, watching the weather, alertly assessing the mood of the changeable sea that surrounded him. Even the gentlest of seas turned him green; a lazy swell with a little chop resulted in a violent illness that was worse than death. Each trip to town was an ordeal. The onset of motion sickness he suffered coincided with the instant the island was lost from view and began to abate only when the coast of Haiti appeared off the bow. In between, the open water was a no-man's-land of gastric rebellion and nearly unendurable nausea. He often wished that the deck hand would shoot him in the head and end his misery.

Still, his discomfort was quickly forgotten in the bars of Port-au-Prince, and the fabulous wages he was being paid repeatedly lured him back to the island for another fortnight as the boat left early every second Monday morning. The alcohol of his weekend debauchery inevitably made the return trip even worse than the going, but thankfully much harder to remember than the sober leg of his journey. His schedule, unlike those of the others who traveled with him, allowed him to sleep the remainder of the day, eat his supper, and generally recover from the indulgences of the weekend before he returned to work at seven in the evening.

Every day after breakfast as he ended his shift, Nago took two bananas from the fruit bowl and tucked them into his shirt as he left the dining hall. Every night, when it came time to clean the room with the monkey cages, he would take the bananas out of his shirt, breaking off small pieces and slipping them to the monkeys. He had never thought to ask permission; the monkeys were fed bananas as part of their daily ration— he'd seen that, so what could it hurt? The monkeys had come to respond to his arrival, waiting at the front of their cages for him to pass by with his treats. He talked to each one for a few moments, told each one how he understood because he too had been in jail once, and the kindness of people had meant a lot to him then. Nago was happy to pass it on to his furry brothers-of-the-heart in their stainless steel cells.

He delighted in their recognition of him; in the responses they made when he entered the room as each competed for his attention and for the first morsel of banana from his brown hand. To him, they were much like small, furry children. He never thought of freeing the monkeys; that would have meant the end of his lucrative job, and, after all, they were only monkeys.

One time, on a Friday, feeling simultaneously frustrated and relieved because his biweekly trip to Port-au-Prince had been canceled due to bad weather, Nago had teased the big one with the gray in his fur. He extended the banana and then withdrew it as the monkey reached for it. He did this several times, until he decided it was time to let the old man have the banana. When he extended his hand and failed to withdraw it, the old man grabbed it as he seized the banana and bit Nago smartly in the soft flesh between his thumb and index finger, drawing a healthy flow of blood and laying him open nicely.

Nago yelped in surprise, leaped backward stumbling and cursing as he fumbled for his handkerchief to staunch the flowing blood. The handkerchief was in the pocket on the same side as his bleeding hand, and he was forced to stain his trousers with blood as he reached into the pocket to retrieve it. His hand throbbed where the monkey's jaw had pierced, and he thought he would do something to the monkey who, in the meantime had prudently retreated to the rear of his cage and was eyeing Nago with great defiance. Nago stuck his broom handle in the cage to poke at the creature, whereupon the monkey promptly grabbed it and started to come at him, hand over hand down the broomstick, screeching in outraged monkey anger. Nago abandoned the broom and quickly retreated out of reach. The monkey dropped the broom; it teetered then tipped over the edge of the cage and rattled to the floor. Nago picked up the broom and looked venomously at the monkey, who retaliated by urinating in Nago's direction from the back of his cage.

"You will get no banana tomorrow, ingrate! See what you have done to my hand!" Nago glared and the old man glared back.

Nago looked for the first aid kit, a hinged, white-enameled steel box hanging on the wall near the door, then decided not to use any supplies from it. If any supplies were discovered to be missing, Nago might have to explain his injury, and how it had happened. That wouldn't do, and so they would think he had stolen the supplies. Either way, he would lose his job. It was better to say nothing and take care of his hand when he was finished with his sweeping and emptying the wastebaskets. He would do an even better job than usual tonight, as sort of insurance. Under his breath he apologized to the Virgin for swearing when the monkey bit him and then resumed his routine.

His hand healed nicely, in spite of the less than antiseptic care it had received. There had been no sign of infection, although Nago watched the wound closely. It just made pushing a broom and swinging a mop a little uncomfortable until the pain went away.

The whores of Port-au-Prince would have to wait even longer than Nago intended, however. The departure of the crew boat two weeks hence would find him in bed with the worst case of the flu he had ever had.

Time passed on the island, and now Christmas was approaching. It was Nago's third Christmas in this place, far from his home, his family, and his village. The holiday was still three months away. It could take nearly that long for Nago Espiridion Uribe to get home, especially if he followed his plan to do it without spending any of the fortune he'd acquired working for the Americans—a fortune that was worth much more at home than it was here.

The Americans were almost finished here on the island. Nago could tell. Non-critical supplies were dwindling and not being replaced. There was less cleaning to do; some of the rooms in the laboratory were empty now, needing only infrequent dusting. The quality of the food was diminishing. Today they were starting to remove the monkeys, and Nago would soon miss the pleasure of smuggling bananas from the mess hall to them.

Not long ago, he'd lost one of the few friends he had made on the island; well, perhaps not really a friend because there had been so little they shared in common. Even so, Doctor Harwiczki—the name tangled Nago's tongue—had always had a friendly word or a kind gesture for the diminutive Guaymi Indian with the brown and steady eyes who kept the laboratory so spotless. Nago had rather liked the old man, fascinated by his balding pate fringed with wispy, fine white hair. It was such a contrast to his own coarse, black locks.

It was sad that the Doctor had been lost in an accident,

Nago thought. It was also a strange mystery that puzzled Nago from time to time. On the ill-fated morning of the Doctor's death in a helicopter crash, Nago watched him climb aboard the helicopter, and then had seen the same machine, days later, undamaged. But he had no way of knowing what had happened after the helicopter vanished from view heading eastward over the azure water on that clear, pleasant morning. Nago did not think the helicopter flew all the way to Minnesota where the Doctor lived. It must have been another helicopter.

The Doctor had told Nago about Minnesota winters one night when he'd been working late enough on his research to actually encounter Nago on his janitorial detail. Nago could not imagine why anybody would live in a place as cold as the Doctor described. It was clear that the Doctor wanted to return there, and was doing so in his mind, since his body must remain here on the island for Nago to speak with it. Nago understood the Doctor's homesickness, though the words the Doctor used were hard to follow.

Nago also understood that the gravy train he had been riding, broom in hand, was soon to be over, and, if the truth were known, he was quietly happy about it. He would return to his village of Canquintu; perhaps even find a woman to marry. If he did not find such a woman, he had sufficient money to visit the prostitutes in Changuinola occasionally. But a wife would be so much better—she would cook for him and wash his clothes and take care of the many children he would give her; she would increase his standing in the village.

He dreamed awake as he monotonously pushed the broom over the same floor in the same routine he'd been performing now for more than three years. In his mind, he could see the open water of Laguna Chiriqui. He could almost feel the sunshine over the open water and the heat, and the relief from the heat as his homecoming launch penetrated the mouth of the muddy Rio Cricamola, moving along the banks overhung with vegetation where it was always cooler than in the middle of the river. Brightly colored birds would shriek from the trees at his arrival. Perhaps he would wave at the people in the small villages along the riverbank as he passed, returning as a champion from the great world adventure. Twenty miles up the river he would leave the launch, and make the easy walk of five miles through the jungle that would bring him finally into his native village of Canquintu: home!

He wondered about his family; who would be changed, who would be the same. Who was married? Had others left during *his absence? How had the children of his sister grown? There was so much he could not know until he returned. It would be a joyous day!*

He would return to the village bearing many presents for his family and friends. He would be a hero in the village for a few days, until all had grown exhausted of the stories of the strange world of the Yanquis, so far away from the reassuring protection of the jungle and their Guaymi culture. Then he would settle into routine village life and take his proper place as a man of substance and means... a life of contentment.

Among the gifts Nago would bring to his village and his people—unknown and unknowable to himself or any of his tribe—was an unwitting surprise. He carried with him the sub-microscopic seeds of lingering death and horror, acquired from the bite of an angry primate during his adventures on that smallish island lost in the blue of the Caribbean Ocean.

> *"It's not your enemies*
> *But your friends*
> *You've got to watch."*
> —Archilochos, 7th century B.C.

> *"...But far out there the little island has its eyes shut tight."*
> —Ranier Maria Rilke
> *The Island I - North Sea*

1

16 July, Present Day

"Is that the island?"

Below the right wing tip of the tightly banking seaplane, Russell Wakefield looked for the first time at a tiny, rugged postage stamp of land in the middle of an azure sea. It jutted five hundred feet from the water as a scraggy green tooth, the remnant of a time of volcanoes and tectonic fissure. No other land was visible in any direction at their altitude of less than a thousand feet.

"That's it. Not much to it, is there?" Major William Curtis Selmack confirmed Wakefield's observation and appended a rhetorical question.

Selmack did not look like a major. His face was pocked like the backside of the moon, the result of a devastating siege of adolescent acne twenty-five years ago. Close-cropped sandy-colored hair receded from the battlefield of his youth. His build was faintly simian; his arms and torso were too long; his legs too short. To camouflage this, he affected a painstakingly erect posture. His facial expressions were open and invited confidence. In a white oxford shirt open at the collar and a maroon windbreaker, he resembled more a businessman at leisure than an Army major. Reeboks and Dockers completed the ensemble; the illusion was his ally. He was on the clock, and Wakefield's state of mind was his primary concern.

The plane buzzed low over a cluster of abandoned buildings that squatted in forlorn solitude, well away from a sandy cove on the island's leeward side. Around the buildings, thick, verdant vegetation grew rampant from every crack and cranny not covered by pavement or foundations. Wakefield recognized the buildings and the cove from the videotape Selmack's boss had given him.

"Can we set her down in that cove by the dock?" Wakefield wanted to get closer. He strained at his window, trying to see more.

"You bet! No going ashore, though. That will have to wait until work begins next week, and then only with proper protective equipment." He stepped forward to the flight deck and spoke to the pilot, pointing past him at the cove with the sandy beach. The pilot nodded and throttled back in preparation for landing. Returning to the passenger space, Selmack fastened his seatbelt and instructed Wakefield to do likewise.

The sleek aircraft dropped in at a steep angle and leveled out over an unruffled sea to set down smoothly amidst a plume of spray. A rooster-tail of seawater arched gracefully from the belly of the craft. There was, of course, no soul on shore to see it. The island was contaminated with unknown amounts of unidentified chemicals. It had been abandoned for nearly twenty years.

The seaplane coasted to a stop. Selmack rose and opened the passenger door. Sunlight streamed in at the low angle of late afternoon. A diamond sparkle on the sea led from the doorway of the plane like a glittering path to the island shore. The hollow slapping of the sea against the sides of the fuselage became audible. He fished a pair of 7x50 binoculars from his briefcase and handed them to Wakefield.

"Take a look."

Wakefield was unable to straighten his tall frame in the low passenger cabin. He hunched over as he rose to approach the open door. He dropped to one knee on the cabin floor and propped his elbows against the doorjamb on either side. He scanned the shoreline with the binoculars. Calm wavelets rippled against a virginal strand. Birds moved among the trees along the shoreline—a good indication. It looked like paradise. In the center of the sandy beach a large sign jutted obscenely from the pristine sand. Wakefield fiddled with the focus knob until he was able to read the black letters on a white field through the binoculars:

**"DO NOT LAND
This island is property of the U.S. Government
Land may contain chemical contamination that is
dangerous to health.
By Order of the United States Government."**

Turning away, he handed the field glasses back to Selmack. "So, you have no idea what's there? It would help a lot if you knew what we could expect..." Wakefield let the invitation to disclosure lie between them like found money.

"Not a clue. It was before my time." Selmack shrugged his shoulders.

"Well, we're going to find out." Wakefield folded himself back into his seat while Selmack gave instructions to the pilot.

BRADD HOPKINS

And when he opened the second seal,
I heard the second beast say, Come and see.
And there went out another horse that was red:
and power was given to him that sat thereon
to take peace from the earth,
and that they should kill one another:
and there was given unto him a great sword."
—The Revelation of St. John the Divine

2

23 November, 1969

Diabolical, destructive, and criminal were not words that General Thomas Martindale would have used to describe the activity his command staff was about to perform. Had he been asked, he would have chosen words like creative, forward-thinking and patriotic. He draped his beribboned dress uniform jacket across the back of his chair and rolled up his sleeves to create a mood of informality.

If he'd been told that the consequence of this black November night would be more than five million deaths, and carry a ninety billion-dollar price tag, he would have discarded such a notion as unrealistically biased and uninformed. He would have ordered his aide out for three large pizzas with extra cheese and two cases of Coors anyway.

"Gentlemen, these are the rules… the *only* rules," he intoned.

He scanned his staff, seated around the conference table in a room on the second floor of the building housing the Chemical, Biological, and Radiological Research Command. Resting his meaty fists on the simulated walnut Formica tabletop, he leaned forward intently, knitting bushy, wild eyebrows into a single, ragged line across his forehead. He was a big man, tall and broad, but his height forgave his heavy build. He was nonetheless intimidating and had played guard for Army in his younger days. A square chin jutted aggressively forward from the plane of his face, giving him a pugnacious appearance even at rest. From this, and partly due to the single-minded determination with which he attacked any problem, he had earned the nickname 'Bulldog' during those college days. The nickname was still with him, to a select group of friends, although he now looked even more like a bulldog than he had in college.

"There is no rank in this room as of right now. All rank is suspended. There is no such thing as a bad idea, or a wild idea, or a stupid idea here. All ideas have equal value, and all voices have equal volume. I urge you to step outside the boundaries of conventional thinking, dream your dreams aloud, relax, and see what happens.

"There will be no put-downs, insults, attacks, or debates on the merits of one idea over another, for now. There will be no reprisals for unbecoming conduct here in this room. If you get drunk and piss in the wastebasket, nobody will interfere, or remember. There is no requirement to produce anything except ideas that bear on the question I will pose. Consider the question alone in your own minds for the time being. Nobody may speak until he has finished his first can of beer."

He turned to a flipchart. The scratching of the marker on the pad was the only sound as he wrote the challenge in large block letters in purple ink, "DESCRIBE THE PERFECT BIOLOGICAL WEAPON." He underlined the word 'perfect' and sat down, leaning back in his chair. Through steepled, pudgy fingers, he swiftly gazed about the room, his glance moving from man to man around the table.

Each man at the conference table looked around uncertainly at the others in silent discomfort. Martindale's behavior was entirely out of character, both for the man and for the military. Several wondered if the general had gone crazy.

The aide appeared shortly with the pizzas and passed a can of cold beer to each officer at the table. Colonel Donald Brockner drained his at a drought, crushed the can in his fist, and set it pointedly on the table before him. True to form, he responded with challenge rather with caution or curiosity. Martindale had anticipated it.

"Why?" Brockner asked bluntly. Brockner was Martindale's operations officer. He was lean and balding. He always looked hungry.

"Because if we can decide here tonight what it is, we're going to build it. How would it work?" Martindale urged.

The anthrax and botulism agents already adapted to germ warfare were fraught with attendant problems familiar to those present. It was time for something new, something better. Something the Russians weren't ready to handle.

The age of bacterial germ warfare was coming to a close. Viral agents were the currency of the future. Soon, they could re-engineer almost anything that had DNA, to modify it selectively to their purposes. It was only necessary to decide how the recombinant DNA technology would be used. What did they want from their virus?

"It would be easy to deliver on target," tentatively offered the next officer, finishing his beer. "We have too many problems with our delivery systems. If they are explosive, they often defeat their effectiveness on delivery. Airborne delivery is too imprecise." The aide wrote "easy delivery" on a second flip chart.

"Easy to manufacture and store," chimed in a captain from logistics, crushing his beer can as he spoke. "Safe to handle." Most of the officers in the room were familiar with the quarantined Building 470 at Fort Detrick, Maryland. Building 470 was seven stories of bacterial contamination too dangerous even to decontaminate. It was a legacy from the post-World War II attempt to manufacture anthrax in war-deployment quantities.

Earlier in the year, President Nixon had ordered the suspension of testing of 'offensive' biological weapons. The command had been forced to quietly relocate its research activities from Maryland to the open reaches of Utah.

They were conducting the efforts here, this night, in the name of 'defensive research'. The general believed that the recent presidential ban on offensive research was temporary. They would ultimately rescind it. Eventually, the President would come to his senses, or a new president would order reinstitution of the research at some future date. By the time that happened the U.S. might be irretrievably behind in its germ warfare capabilities. In Martindale's mind 'defensive research' was a vague term for activities designed to keep America strong.

"Selective," said an officer from G2. "It would only kill or disable those capable of resisting. It would sidestep children, and only affect armed adults. I do not see how we could ever find something like that." He took a bite of pizza, catching a string of cheese with his free hand and dropping it into his mouth. It was after six p.m.; everyone was hungry and the pizzas were going fast. The informality of eating pizza was having the desired effect. The staff officers, men of discipline and rigid bearing, were loosening up. *Except for Brockner, who never loosens up,* Martindale thought.

"Don't tear down your own ideas, either," Martindale admonished the last man to speak. "We do not know that we couldn't find it. We just *think* we couldn't, because we never have."

"It would be non-persistent within the theater of operations. Our troops could move in without protective gear, without danger, quickly, after the use of the agent. They would be vaccinated in advance, for example. I guess it would be even neater if they didn't require vaccination; just walk in. But how could you do that?"

"Detecting it would be hard. It would look like something else, like a bad cold, or food poisoning. If it looked like food poisoning, resources would have to be dedicated to searching out the cause, and trucking in fresh food supplies."

Another man, his second beer empty, laughed. "Food poisoning! Imagine the entire enemy unit lined up in front of the latrines, puking and shitting and waiting for an empty stall. Hardly in a position to offer resistance."

"It would be rapidly fatal or disabling."

"It would be carried in drinking water."

"No, airborne, with a short life span. Allergic to sunlight. That way, we could deliver it at night and waltz in at dawn without firing a shot."

"It would disable first, before causing death, with a period to allow us to administer an antidote if we chose to do so."

"And it would be incurable without the antidote!"

"It would spread without further inoculations beyond the initial delivery point, independently, through the target populations. Highly contagious."

"It would act so quickly that it would overwhelm the doctors and the hospitals, and destroy their medical system's ability to stop it!" Ideas began to flow fast and furious as each officer caught the spirit of the session, keying on the enthusiasm of the others, reflecting and amplifying in a synergy of brain-storming.

The general's aide—a nameless and faceless factotum with a very high security clearance—had three flip charts going simultaneously, and was working at a frenzied pitch as ideas began to bounce about the room with abandon. He scrawled the key concepts across the flip charts, using lulls in the activity to rip off full sheets and tack them up on walls around the room. He felt like a field mouse in a roomful of eagles.

They worked well into the night. The few uneaten pieces of pizza became cold, unappetizing slabs and the beer was getting warm. Martindale had counted on this latter development to provide a natural control on how drunk his officers got, and it was effective. Some had already switched to coffee.

They refined and distilled the ideas that had flown wildly and wantonly about the room at the outset, honing them into a conceptual description of the perfect biological weapon. It would be something that disabled the body's ability to protect itself. A virus could be engineered to sabotage immunities to the germs that abounded in the natural environment, and within the human body itself. A virus, invisible to all but the most sophisticated devices, that could be used to empower normally harmless native microbes to wreak havoc on their hosts. By defeating the immune response, it would cause a wide variability in the manifestation of symptoms. With no two cases of infection precisely alike, it would befuddle the hell out of the enemy's diagnosticians. It would create the need for intensive care of its victims before they died. This would further reduce resources available for aggressive combat.

Transmitted initially by water, or by air, it would subsequently spread through some form of human contact. It would be vulnerable in some key aspect, responding to a single variable that could be controlled to protect unintended targets and friendly troops from its effects. There must be a built-in weak link in the chain of transmission, but not an obvious one.

They hammered the basic concept into a more-or-less finished framework in a remarkably short time. The staff officers of the United States Army Chemical, Biological, and Radiological Research Command adjourned this most unusual of meetings before two a.m. They departed the building for homes, families, and the weekend ahead with a sense of accomplishment.

A light snow fell upon the shoulders of each as he crossed the parking lot to his car. Each man left nothing more substantial than his footprints and tire tracks in the newly fallen snow to mark his participation in the evening's labors. Each man's shadow fell long before him, cast on the unbeaten snow by the brightly lighted building.

The name of the nascent project was in each man's mind. In symbolic memory of that vicious, medieval, armor-breaking weapon—a studded iron ball on a chain attached to a stick—the project that would produce the perfect biological weapon was christened "Morningstar."

The weeks after the meeting were filled with the tedium of finding a starting point. The staff reviewed obscure research in virology with an eye toward finding something that would either fit the bill or be close enough to modify into a more desirable form. Ultimately, a solid senior researcher named Albert Bennington rolled an academic rock and discovered beneath it an unnamed, barely documented virus that appeared too perfect. It existed naturally in African monkeys, but it was known to be transmissible, rarely, to humans.

Martindale issued the appropriate orders. They made plans to acquire the virus from its natural source, a trace incidence in certain Western African monkey populations. Bennington was put in charge of its acquisition and development, given a hefty budget, and ordered to report directly to Martindale. Project Morningstar thus advanced inexorably into its next phase.

*"I made no decisions; I gave no commands.
I was just trying to be a good soldier."*
—Martin Bormann

3

3 August, 1970

Nearly two weeks had passed in this hellhole and Devlin had no idea what was going on with the monkeys. He turned to face the civilian camp just as two hunters emerged from the tent carrying a weakly protesting simian in a cage slung between them. He watched as they lugged it over to the verge of the jungle, and opened the gate. The monkey, apparently dazed, stumbled out of the cage and clumsily made off into the broadleaf plants at the edge of the clearing.

Staff Sergeant Leon Ray Devlin had been yanked out of his 10th Special Forces Unit operating along the Laotian Border in South Viet Nam. Twenty-four hours later he stepped out of a MAC transport onto the red Georgia clay at Fort Benning. A week after that—after a barrage of vaccinations that left his arms tender to the touch, and an operational briefing that raised more questions than it answered—he found himself on a plane with eleven other Green Berets, flying east over the Atlantic toward the flaming crimson band of a sun just below the horizon.

The mission briefing, given by a Major Adams, was to the point: "We will be in country with the high government's knowledge and permission, arranged diplomatically, but they will not officially acknowledge our presence there, or intervene if our situation takes a dump on us. The locals, if we run across any, may be loyal to a guerrilla faction that controls the region where we'll operate. If the guerrillas learn of our presence in the region, they will undoubtedly make things unpleasant.

"Extraction under fire will take at least two hours from the time we radio in our request, if things come to that.

"Hot food and coffee are in the galley aft. Serve yourselves.

Eat and rest. Tomorrow may be a long day, and it may be a while before you see a steak again."

The first day in the jungle passed with agonizing slowness. Three-man patrols moved out every four hours, traversing a two-hour circle around the clearing where Huey UH-1 helicopters had deposited them on the final leg of their flight.

The sun was only a few degrees above the horizon when it gave the first hint of the oppressive heat that would mark the day. The humidity must have been nearly a hundred percent. Devlin found each breath he took required an effort, and its result was damp and unsatisfying. Sweat, unable to evaporate in the saturated air, rolled off his body as he ate his midday rations. He ate because he knew better than to miss any meal in an unknown place, but the heat robbed him of any small pleasure the act might ordinarily have given him.

The patrols started and ended at the silent radio. The radio had been cargo on the first chopper. It sat silently under a tarp at the base of a tall tree, monitoring a frequency that nobody was using. It was manned constantly by anyone who wasn't doing anything else. The tarp was necessary protection against the sudden deluge of rain that hit without warning in the late afternoon, thundering down onto the broadleaf plants in the under story of the jungle so loudly that communication was impossible. It rained violently for about twenty minutes, and then it was over. They could hear again. The drops continued to fall from the higher plants to the leaves below for several minutes, popping as they struck the broad leaves below. Then the heat returned for a final, steaming assault before sundown.

The air was motionless, and the flies bit in spite of the repellent Devlin sprayed on. Malaria pills had been issued, and Devlin had taken his; but malaria was carried by mosquitoes, not by flies. Foraging through the mental archives of an old training class on parasitic jungle diseases, he wondered if any were Tsetse flies, carriers of *Trypanosome Gambienzi,* the microbe that caused African sleeping sickness. He marveled that this obscure and useless piece of information had managed to remain in his brain for so long, unused, yet was suddenly available to him when he needed it. He was sure they were in Africa. The Congo Basin? Maybe. It was only a guess.

Three guards were posted just after dark. The rest of the men hung around the radio, not talking much, just waiting and watchful, sweating, trying to relax as the heat began to abate a little in the still air.

They jumped when the radio, silent as a stone for hours, suddenly spit and hissed like an angry tomcat: "Albert, Albert, this is Bennington Transport. Come in, Albert."

Adams reached for the handset. "This is Albert. Go ahead."

"Albert, Bennington. Are you ready for visitors?"

"Bennington, Albert. The table is set."

Minutes later three Hueys dropped into the clearing, discharged passengers and cargo with an undisciplined racket, and flew off into the night. The pace was casual compared to that of the preceding night. The new arrivals appeared to be civilians. There were eight of them, and they had a raft of gear.

Adams approached the new arrivals while the others watched. One civilian, a tall, slender man, came forward to meet him, and they talked for several minutes. Then Adams turned away, moving back toward the waiting soldiers.

"They're here to catch monkeys," he said simply. His expression was an indecipherable mask. "Guards out, same as last night."

The next morning, Devlin watched as the civilians put up a tent and assembled a number of steel cages along the edge of the clearing. Before noon two of their number went into the jungle, carrying the first of about two dozen cages, and what appeared to be specialized rifles slung over their shoulders. He puzzled over it for a few minutes, his expertise in weaponry challenged by his failure to identify the weapons from a distance. Then it came to him; they were tranquilizer rifles.

The patrol schedule continued as before. At the noon meal of cold K rations, Adams briefed the men who were in camp.

"The tall guy is Bennington; he's in charge. They really are here to catch monkeys. He says he doesn't expect any trouble, and that we're too far away from anything to be worrying much about the political situation. What that political situation is... he's not saying. Nevertheless, we will continue to provide security for their activities.

"Bennington has asked that we keep contact with his people to a minimum; all communication with their group will come through me. If you want to bum a cigarette or accept a candy bar from one of them, see me first. We will eat separately, sleep separately, and shit separately. No contact. No conversation. Is that clear?"

All nodded. The group shot glances at the now forbidden contacts.

A week passed, providing ample time to watch the goings-on at the civilian camp. Each passing day deepened the mystery. The hunters left early, before sunup, with tranquilizer rifles slung over their shoulders. The hunters would bring the monkeys in from the jungle in cages, tranked out and unconscious. Then they took them, one at a time, into a tent. Two of the civilians spent most of their working time in the tent where each monkey was taken. After about two hours, a hand would gesture through the tent flap, summoning the hunters.

Most of the monkeys were released at the edge of the jungle, where they wandered away as if drugged. Occasionally, one or two of the primates were sent to cages on the shady side of the tent. The soldiers who watched the operation soon came to associate the detained monkeys with the arrival of a chopper shortly after dark. Cold flares would be set out on stakes, at the order of Adams. The luckless primates were loaded aboard and taken on a helicopter ride to who-knew-where. The ratio of keepers to rejects seemed to be about one in twenty.

Days dragged, hot, enervating and indistinguishable, until one day the civilians broke down their tent at dusk and the choppers arrived just after dark. While the civilians loaded their equipment into the Hueys, Bennington came over to the soldiers' camp to meet with Adams. It was the closest Devlin had ever been to the man, and the lines in his face told Devlin that he'd substantially underestimated Bennington's age. The man was every bit of fifty, but he moved his lank frame like a much younger man. His eyes were a washed-out blue and he needed a shave. Devlin took a mental snapshot of the sallow face.

"Thanks for your services." He spoke without smiling, meeting Adams' eyes only fleetingly. "Tomorrow, dawn, police up the camp area and collect all traces of our presence and your own. The helicopters will be in after dusk to take you and your men out of here. Don't leave anything behind, not even a gum wrapper."

He turned on his heel, without so much as a handshake, and went to the last Huey, looking around over his shoulder one final time before he boarded. His survey did not include the men he left behind on the ground.

20

"Experience teaches us to be most on our guard to protect liberty when the government's purposes are beneficent."
—Chief Justice Brandeis, Olmstead v. U.S., 1928

4

10 December, 1974

Elmo, the last of Bennington's monkeys, had died the previous night. And not of natural causes.

Richard Elwin turned the battered Plymouth off Utah State Highway 23 onto an unmarked dirt road that headed like a draftsman's line across the flat, open desert for as far as the eye could see, disappearing in the blue distance. The road was poorly maintained, full of washboard and potholes where the first few miles had been oiled sometime in antiquity. Stretches of tire-miring, wind-blown, soft sand merged where the ancient oil job ended. Elwin kept the tires on the old Plymouth under-inflated to spread its weight across a wider base for traversing the sand patches, but he still got stuck occasionally. When that happened, he wound up waiting an hour or so, usually in sweltering heat, until they noticed his late arrival at the security gate and sent a tow-truck to pull him out.

Today, however, his luck held. He barreled through the sand traps with the engine gunned, the tires spinning, the radio blaring, and the rear end of the Plymouth whipsawing like a flag in a stiff breeze. He was glad it wasn't his car. It came with the job. He treated it with disdain, as did the rutted desert road. A cloud of dry salt dust billowed out behind the old road-lizard as Elwin careened up to the gate. A sandblasted sign was posted to the left of the gate: *"Desert Range Experimental Station,"* in plain black letters on a dirty white background.

An MP in khaki stepped from the guard shack. He carried his M16 assault rifle casually, with the muzzle pointed generally downward. A magazine was in the receiver of the weapon, and Elwin knew from his orientation briefing that the ammunition was live. The MP also wore a .45 caliber sidearm in a leather holster with a buttoned-down flap. A second soldier, also armed, waited in the guardhouse, watching.

The guard leaned down toward the window of the Plymouth, peering in, squinting to adjust his eyes to see into the darker interior. "Dr. Elwin," he said. "They called us to expect you. Sorry about the vacation. Go ahead, sir."

Elwin shrugged, and glanced down.

The MP signaled the man in the guard shack and the chain-link gate moved smoothly out of Elwin's path. Elwin scanned right and left as the gate opened, looking down the line of a twelve-foot chain-link fence. Concertina wire ran in three strands at the top straight away in each direction as far as the eye could follow. Nothing moved. For a hundred feet on both sides of the fence, the view was clear of even the sparse native vegetation. The field of smooth, wind-blown sand along the barrier would reveal the slightest disturbance by foot traffic.

The old Plymouth floated through the gate on its spongy suspension and down the dirt road for about a mile, taking the left option at a Y. Five hundred yards from the fence, the Plymouth disappeared. It simply bobbed out of sight, into the sub-grade, camouflaged entrance of a small, underground parking garage. The tunnel entrance had two turns. Elwin swerved first left, then right. He once asked why the entrance was not just a straight shot with a door and was told that the entrance design prevented light from escaping. The entrance was invisible at night from the air and from satellites. A door would have required expensive additions to the ventilation system to handle the auto exhaust in the underground garage—and would still make a visible light signature when it was opened.

Elwin parked the car without removing the keys or locking it. His footsteps echoed off the cool concrete walls as he walked diagonally across the lot to the only door. A half a dozen equally decrepit vehicles were parked haphazardly in the structure. He recognized John Talley's battered old Ford among them, issued with no regard for Talley's preferences. Talley drove a new Buick when he wasn't working.

As Elwin approached the door, he reached down inside his shirt and retrieved a white plastic rectangle with a magnetic strip and no other markings. He inserted the card into an unmarked slot in the door, a buzzer sounded, and the door opened. As he stepped inside, the door closed behind him.

He was in a small concrete room. A second steel door stood directly ahead, some fourteen feet away. The seamless walls were blank except for a single pane of bulletproof mirrored glass and two concave holes about one-half inch in diameter. The holes were widely separated from each other above the mirror panel, near the ceiling. He turned to face the mirror in the wall for visual identification. An unseen guard on the other side pressed a button to open the far door.

Elwin's card was only good for getting *into* this room from either direction. It took the action of the guard behind the mirror to allow him to exit. During his initial employment briefing four years ago, they told him that the two holes were outlets to discharge one of two gases into the room, at the guard's discretion. One gas would cause a quick loss of consciousness; the other was fatal at a breath. Any attempt to force either door would automatically release the latter. It was simple, but effective security. He earnestly hoped the guard was having a good day.

Elwin ambled down the hallway toward John Talley's office, the rancid smell of ancient coffee becoming stronger as he neared the open door. Talley looked up from the bound report he was reading as Elwin entered.

Talley wore his inevitable pastel golf shirt with the little green alligator on the breast. He was an inveterate golfer with a rather good handicap. Elwin thought Talley always looked taller when he was sitting, with his long torso and short legs. He was rounded in the shoulder, generally endomorphic, but not obese. He had a full head of hair and a cookie-brush brown moustache that ended at the corners of his too-small mouth. His lips were full, and his rounded chin receded ever so slightly.

"Home from the wars?" He greeted Elwin without rising.

"It was O.K. Good to get out of this godforsaken desert for a while." Elwin had been hanging out in Cabo San Lucas, fishing, drinking cheap margaritas and reading Michener novels for the last ten days.

Piercing blue eyes sparkled at Talley from under a high, smooth forehead. He was tanned and relaxed, and his white shirt blazed in contrast with his skin. His hair, normally a dusty, nondescript brown, had gained golden highlights due to his exposure to the tropical sun during his vacation days. "I could have stayed another month. The dorado were in a feeding frenzy."

"When we finish the autopsy and tie up some loose ends, you can go back. They're closing the project."

"Really?" Elwin raised his thin eyebrows, tacitly asking for an expanded explanation.

Talley accommodated: "General Martindale was here yesterday with his usual entourage. He said that they won't fund the project past the first of next year. He's convinced we're not going to get anything they can use even if we continue."

"What about all the stuff we've been shipping?" Elwin asked.

"That's over now that Elmo's gone. We've already done the extraction on his blood. The courier was here this morning. When the autopsy's done, there's nothing left for us to do. Martindale said you'll be reassigned to a facility in Colorado, if you want."

"What are you going to do?"

"Something will come along," Talley shrugged his rounded shoulders. The last few months had worn him down; it was apparent in his bearing and corroborated by the dark circles under his eyes. He wasn't playing much golf lately. The mystery of the monkeys' deaths was no closer to being understood than it had been on the morning when they discovered the first one cold in its cage with no apparent cause.

Talley was a topnotch research virologist. He had been on the crest of a breaking wave of research since his work on the T2 virus in the early 1960's. In fact, his work on the T2 had been a springboard to this project. The T2 virus was a readily obtainable, easy-to-study little guy that had provided some valuable insight into how viruses reproduce.

Viewed under an electron microscope, the T2 virus most nearly resembled a golf ball with a tee permanently attached. It used bacteria to reproduce itself, a process that Talley had studied and published. The T2 would attach itself to a passing bacterium, responding to some undetermined biochemical coding on the bacterium's cell wall. It would then insert its golf tee through the cell wall of the bacterium, injecting its entire core of genetic material into the hapless microorganism, much like an animated bulb syringe. Then something that was not yet understood happened inside the single-cell creature. The bacterium's cell wall either dissolved or exploded, releasing between six and eight new T2 viruses. These new viruses were created as the T2 reprogrammed its victim's DNA to replicate more of itself.

It was the first time the process had been observed and documented. The understanding of the mechanism of T2 reproduction threw light into a relatively dark corner of virology, though they only dimly saw the full implications of the research at the time. If they could apply the process with control, it was becoming increasingly apparent that modifying genetic material by introducing foreign genetic material into a healthy cell might actually be possible. If the T2 could do it...

An additional ramification of the work was developing in the field of immunology. What if, for example, they could create a virus that was harmless to humans but selectively attacked one or more pathogens, like swine flu, or bacterial meningitis? Introduce that virus and a human would become permanently immune to the pathogen.

Once the pathogen was gone, the virus would stop reproducing and remain dormant, reactivating only when the pathogen appeared again. It represented a potential end to all bacterial diseases currently preying on human populations.

Shortly after a popular article on Talley's work on the T2 appeared in an article in *Scientific American,* General Thomas R. Martindale telephoned him at the university and requested a meeting at Martindale's office. "Fine," Talley had said, "but I'm in Illinois, and your office is in Idaho Falls."

Talley's connection had been promptly transferred to a secretary who informed him that a ticket was waiting at the United Airlines counter at O'Hare Airport in Chicago. A wire, waiting at Western Union in his name, should cover all expenses. The wire had been for one thousand dollars—a lot of money at the time. The meeting with Martindale followed.

The offer Martindale made was a research scientist's dream come true. Talley was to have a substantial salary, a car, a house, and access to sophisticated laboratory gear to pursue his research. The downside was that he must relocate to a remote area of Utah, hours from the nearest golf course, and that he could not publish any results. The duration of the contract was open-ended, but Martindale implied that there would be plenty of work if results were forthcoming.

Three months later, Talley found himself working as lead research virologist at Desert Range Experimental Station. The nearest decent golf course was two hundred miles away. He found himself, however, living and working in the biggest sand trap he'd ever seen. He'd honed his bunker shots to a fine art by batting balls around the open desert with a pitching wedge after work, knocking a stroke off his handicap.

The work was fascinating, the equipment was state-of-the-art, and he liked his new boss. If he needed something for the laboratory, he had only to ask. Paychecks came regularly, on checks imprinted *"Center for Disease Control, Utah Field Research Office."* Initially, the research involved waterborne disease organisms—typhoid bacteria, among others—with an eye toward finding a virus that would neutralize them without harming people.

Progress was slow and often discouraging. Nonetheless, Talley knew that the benefits of success would be extensive, maybe even Nobel Prize stuff... except he couldn't publish. That fact rankled when he thought about it, so he didn't think about it much. If they really found something and Martindale didn't release it, Talley figured he could always replicate the research elsewhere. Out from under the terms of his present contract, he could publish without restriction. And if Martindale did release any results, keeping the Talley name from being associated with the information would be difficult. Then, in early 1970, Martindale showed up at the laboratory. Without explanation, he directed Talley to change his focus and redirect his attention to a virus of Martindale's choosing: an uncommon virus, found only in a single species of monkey in Africa and in very low distribution in that specific population.

In fact, the virus was only suspected in the population by inference, based on some obscure research by a field biologist named Tyler Skinner that documented symptoms associated with blood chemistry and immune system changes in the monkeys. Talley was charged with developing a way to isolate the virus and cause it to reproduce.

From that point forward, the project gained new vigor. Immediately, technicians and laborers began to work furiously on an unoccupied section of the underground facility at Desert Range Experimental Station. It was modified to accept and isolate large animal cages. They worked around the clock, and the modifications, including quarters and offices for the animal handlers, were complete by July 1970. In late August, the monkeys began to arrive.

Using Skinner's field notes, Talley began looking at the blood of the monkeys. This was a large part of Dick Elwin's role. He was a damned good biochemist with a long suit in mammalian hematology. His diagnostic intuition was uncanny. It had been Elwin's idea to look for antibodies in the monkeys' blood to establish the presence of the viral antigen, and they found them. From the absence of any regular pathogen, and from the unusual character of the antibodies, they inferred the existence of a virus, which they arbitrarily named SK-443. It was an abbreviated composite of Skinner's name and the blood assay batch that finally produced irrefutable results.

After a few more months of painstaking laboratory work, the technicians managed to extract the still unseen virus from the monkey blood and keep it viable in a temperature-controlled matrix of glucose and saline solution specifically formulated for the purpose. The biggest problem had been to find a way to neutralize the antigen, which was inevitably extracted with the virus and continued to kill the viruses in the matrix solution. After some more cerebral hair-tearing, they finally found a protein that would bond with the antigen to neutralize its effects on the virus.

They duly reported their success to General Martindale. He ordered them to produce as much as possible and provide it for shipment to the couriers he periodically sent. The tedious process of its extraction from the blood of the monkeys limited the supply of active virus. The blood had to be kept fresh and warm or the viruses died.

They developed a battery-powered, temperature-controlled courier case to keep the viruses warm and viable. One of Martindale's couriers would arrive within twelve hours of notice to General Martindale and spirit the living viruses off to another research station. That was all the Desert Range researchers could ever discover. Martindale had told them bluntly that it was outside their appropriate realm of concern, and that they had no "need to know". The couriers would not even engage in idle conversation about the weather.

During the assays associated with drawing blood from the monkeys, Elwin began to notice a steady decrease in immunological blood components, and reported this to Talley.

Mean white blood cell counts were also going up across the board in the monkeys. It was faster with some than with others. Once the slope of the curve was detectable, it tended to remain constant. T-cells and macrophages dropped off, ultimately to twenty percent or so of the established levels for healthy monkeys. It wasn't long after the pattern was identified that the first monkey died, and some of the others were showing signs of malaise. This, too, was duly reported to Martindale, accompanied by a request for a good zoological pathologist. The staff veterinarian was out of his depth. The following week, Suzanne Coletti arrived. After brief introductions to the staff she was set up in a vacant office on the opposite side of the blood lab from Elwin's.

Coletti was fresh out of UC Davis with a specialty in veterinary pathology. One of her graduate instructors had worked on the NASA animals during the heyday of the space program, and she'd soaked up his instruction like a sponge.

She was 'California' to the bone—petite, blond and tanned

to a turn with the nicest flashing white teeth Elwin had ever seen. She was long used to being treated as a centerfold with a brain and adopted a businesslike, even brusque, manner in her professional dealings with men, sending any incipient ball-of-fluff approaches into disorderly retreat.

She began the autopsy on the first dead monkey almost before the dust had settled from her trip across the desert access road. Elwin, of course, began immediately working up the blood analysis.

He found the analysis somewhat disturbing. The white blood cell count was in a range that indicated a massive infection, but macrophages, those little enemy-eaters in mammalian blood, were almost entirely absent. They should have been abundant. The few that were present were damaged.

To his great bewilderment, there was no sign of an antigen or any antibodies not usually present in healthy monkey blood—except for the SK-443 antibody. The common antibodies were present at levels slightly higher than he expected. The SK-443 antibodies were not elevated. In fact, they seemed to have dropped off, and were well below their expected baseline values, which ought to have indicated a successfully defeated infection. Yet the monkey was dead.

It was confusing, at best. The physical signs and symptoms that Elmo's handlers had reported contradicted the levels of the various blood components. It was all wrong. And this wrongness was consistent with his findings on all the other monkeys that had died.

Coletti came into Elwin's office from the autopsy, still in her operating gown. She trailed an acrid, medicinal odor of alcohol and formaldehyde. Even in her less-than-flattering lab garb, it was apparent to Elwin that the scenery would be much improved if she stayed on for a while. He wondered briefly if she fooled around, and then dragged his attention back to the professional side of the field.

"What'd you find in the blood?" she asked without preface. She flopped into the only other chair in Elwin's office, fake leather government issue, and leaned forward expectantly.

"Signs of a severe systemic infection, without signs of a severe systemic infection. The white blood cell count was through the roof, but with no apparent cause. Macrophages were well below normal levels and appeared to be functionally impaired. The T-cells are mostly gone. The few that are left are damaged. Other than that, nothing of interest."

Elwin leaned back in his chair. He touched his steepled forefingers thoughtfully to his mouth, the tips of his fingers brushing his thin upper lip. He peered out from under his eyebrows, scowling.

"What did you find?"

"I'm not too sure yet," Coletti said. Her tone was dubious and tentative, and she absently rubbed her knuckles with the palm of her left hand. "There were swollen glands in the lymphatic system. There was widespread, non-specific pathology in most of his systems. Other indicators suggest that, somehow, the germs that a monkey normally harbors turned on this one and killed him. It's like he died from the common cold, but not really. It's more like he died from diseases that he should never have contracted; from the actions of microorganisms which don't even *cause* disease." She sighed. "I've never seen anything like it."

"Let's talk to John. Maybe he'll have some ideas."

"Why don't we wait until he's read our reports. I'm still not quite certain how I need to write this up. It will give us time to think some more about what we've found. And what we didn't find..."

Elwin nodded, unconsciously chewing his lower lip.

"Tomorrow, then."

They still had no answers and the monkeys were still dying—three more during that month. Statistical analysis of their deaths over time produced a standard distribution along a bell curve without regard for their variant ages, suggesting that whatever caused the deaths was related to an event which affected all of the monkeys at essentially the same time.

At first, Talley had been almost certain that some new disease was causing them to waste away—perhaps an infection associated with the abrupt change to life in the laboratory. The monkeys were halfway around the world from their normal habitat, perhaps prey to local microbes for which they had never evolved immunities. Some old, familiar, local microorganism found a target of opportunity and was exploiting it.

He recalled his undergraduate studies of epidemics that raged through the American Indians when they were exposed to European diseases. When he bounced this similarity off the other members of the research team, they asked a simple question: if his hypothesis was true, how did African monkeys survive in American zoos?

Elwin had helpfully pointed out that his blood tests did not bear the theory out. He had found no anomalies in the blood chemistry of any of the monkeys, living or deceased, that indicated a new antigen was present. He had found no pathogens at all in the course of his blood analyses.

"Maybe you need to look harder, or in a different way," Talley told Elwin, masking his peevishness that his theory had been shot down without resorting to any laboratory work to test it. Was he losing his perspective, his scientific detachment?

"I had a professor in grad school who told me I could save hundreds of research hours if I looked first at the most likely, obvious explanation and tried to confirm it before I went galloping off after the obscure," Susan Coletti offered. "The most obvious connection here is the virus you've been working with. Maybe we just don't understand it as well as we *think* we do. Maybe it's changed in some way. Maybe it's simply following a regular course of pathological manifestation we don't have enough experience to recognize. I think we ought to start with SK-443."

"I don't agree," said Talley. "The most obvious place to look, since African monkeys manage to survive in other confined conditions, is here, in this particular zoo: the physical environment they live in."

Elwin cut in. "My blood work shows lower SK-443 antibody levels as the monkeys get sicker, not the increases that you'd expect if SK-443 were causing the infection. How do we explain that? I agree with John. I think we ought to look at the physical environment here."

"I was using that fact to rule out SK-443," commented Talley wryly. "It seems obvious." The daggers he shot at Suzanne with his eyes were not lost on any of them. *Couldn't resist the dig, huh, John?* thought Elwin.

It got frustrating. Their first tactic had been to recheck for anything in the monkeys' environment that might provide a plausible explanation for the puzzle. Humidity and temperature of the monkey house were recorded as a matter of course and had not deviated from the settings recommended by the staff vet. Fruit used to feed the monkeys was checked for pesticide residues. Nothing there. Stressors in the monkeys' environment were reevaluated: noise, lighting, drafts. Social access to other monkeys was limited to visual and audible contact, but these limitations were common in documented research and had not produced die-offs in other monkey populations. Cultures were taken from the ventilation system filters and analyzed: still nothing.

The brainstorming sessions became a part of the daily regimen scheduled every morning to take advantage of fresh minds. Initially, wild ideas were tolerated, even if only to be discarded after deeper analysis. But John Talley, who set the tenor of the meetings, was becoming less tolerant of wide hypothetical ranging afield in search of clues to the answers that still eluded them. And the monkeys kept dying. The findings of each new autopsy and the accompanying blood work remained consistent with those of the first monkey that died—inconclusive.

General Martindale's denial of a request from Talley for more monkeys was the first indication that Martindale might be losing interest in the project. Talley had never asked the General for something and not gotten it before. The full implications of his denied requests were buried in renewed efforts to come to an explanation of why the research animals were dying.

Martindale's recent visit and the news of the cancellation of the project following the death of the last monkey left Richard Elwin and the others feeling like dismal failures. Some weeks later, when Elwin, Talley, and Coletti exited the last time through the deadly room where the unseen guard controlled their futures for a few brief seconds, they felt like kicking cans down the sidewalk.

General Thomas Richard Martindale, Commanding Officer of the Army Chemical, Biological, and Radiological Command, Etiologic Agent Research Command, received a telephone confirmation of the quiet final departure of the three scientists from Desert Range Experimental Station. He ordered the entrance and ventilators of the underground facility to be secured, sealed, bulldozed over with a cover of sand, and planted with native vegetation. *He* knew why the monkeys had died. And he was very pleased about it.

BRADD HOPKINS

> *"Our scientific power has outrun our spiritual power.*
> *We have guided missiles and misguided men."*
> —Martin Luther King, Jr.

5

18 January, 1975

General Martindale woke himself without benefit of an alarm clock at 0530 hours, as he had every day for the past thirty years, rain or shine, holiday or duty day. His fifty-eight-year-old bones protested this early rising a little more with each passing year, but the habit was too ingrained. He would have been even more uncomfortable had he tried to remain in bed once his eyes snapped open.

Mrs. Martindale did not stir as he swung his feet to the floor and padded into the bathroom. There he showered, shaved, and generally made himself ready for the day. The bathroom mirror offered the usual tacit accusations of aging and physical decline it made every day at this time but Martindale dismissed them with a promise to resume jogging next week. The mirror didn't buy it, and neither did Martindale. He donned a bathrobe to shut the mirror up, but it failed to cover the business that was happening under his chin. He ignored it one more time.

He heard Sergeant Thomas, his orderly, in the corridor tap twice at the outer door of the bathroom. Thomas entered with a cup of coffee on a saucer, placing it on the sink counter beside the general officer.

"Good morning, sir. Uniform of the day?"

"Class A, sergeant. Meeting with some folks this morning, all business."

"Yes, sir." Thomas left to lay out the general's uniform, with the fruit salad of medal color bars installed in the correct order and the brass collar emblems shined to a bright luster. The shoes were virtually mirrors as the result of Thomas' ministrations with the buffing cloth.

As he ate his breakfast of poached eggs and rye toast, he thought he definitely wanted his command presence about him this day. It was always a matter for excitement when he could report success to the command group. Given enough such successes, he might be able to add another star to his shoulder boards before his retirement. Martindale drank the last of his orange juice and headed for the office.

At eight-thirty, a security and countermeasures team swept Conference Room C for bugs, finding nothing. They also swept the corridor outside, and the restroom down the hall, again finding nothing. They reported their negative findings to Colonel Don Brockner, who thanked and dismissed them. At nine-thirty, General Martindale entered Conference Room C on the third floor of the headquarters building of the Army CBR Research Command facility outside Idaho Falls. His bearing was all business, and he radiated his authority with a casual skill born of years of command.

He barked, "At ease!" before anyone could come to attention. He took his accustomed chair at the head of the table, facing the door, back-lit by the only window in the room. The room itself was a cut above the normal for Army. Wallpaper adorned its walls instead of cheap wood paneling. Carpet lay on the floor instead of the pandemic vinyl tile. Both extravagances had been justified as sound-deadening measures.

The greetings and semi-formal banter, suspended when he entered, briefly resumed to include him. He looked about the room, making at least eye contact with each of the eight other officers present as he extracted some papers from his briefcase and arranged them in front of him. The officers in Conference Room C fell silent as he opened a manila file.

"Good morning, gentlemen," he said, rising from his seat. "I thank you all for being prompt. I would like to dispense with routine reports this morning to allow more time to discuss Project Morningstar. The remainder of this meeting is classified Top Secret, and no written notes are permitted. You will not discuss any information you receive here outside a secure area, or with anyone not authorized to receive it." It was a ritual incantation that each man could recite by heart, but Martindale never omitted it.

"As most of you know, we closed down research operations at Desert Range Station, ending phase two of Morningstar. Those operations were a success, paving the way for subsequent break-throughs at Plum Island. We successfully isolated and replicated a little creature we're calling SK-443. It shows extremely positive potential for being exactly what Morningstar was supposed to produce."

As all in the room knew, Plum Island, just off the easternmost end of Long Island, New York, was a major laboratory center of the CBR Research Command. Signs identified the building as a veterinary research facility, which was at least partially true—anthrax was a veterinary disease. Plum Island had been the facility that manufactured cultures of live SK-443 virus for continuing development and modification into a weapon at Navassa Island.

The live cultures were delivered to Navassa by two special couriers who had been psychologically evaluated for any loose screws, investigated for evidence of vulnerable behavior, and cleared to the highest level of security classification. There were always two couriers because the live cultures they carried were weapons grade and very dangerous (or very lucrative) if placed in the wrong hands. Each was there to watch the other as part of the Surety Program developed after the second World War as a mechanism to insure no one had access to special weapons without a chaperon. Couriers were qualified to the same technical level, so neither could "buffalo" the other and somehow tamper with the goods. Each was armed. Each was aware of the existence of multiple checkpoints on the journey, but neither knew where they were nor how many. Other armed men monitored both couriers as they strictly followed the precise route mapped in detail to their destination.

Martindale continued. "Construction was completed at Navassa last year. The Plum Island product has been there six months for engineering. Dr. Harwiczki reports that a weakened strain will be available for testing as early as next spring." *How about them apples?* Martindale tried not to smile as the import of his announcement registered on the listeners.

"The testing should run no more than a year, probably. We already know the effects of the full-strength organism from our research. The tests will be used to determine the best delivery system and evaluate the best vectors for maximum effect. Once we have those answers, I'll report directly to the Joint Chiefs of Staff."

"We're using the virus itself?" Colonel Brockner wanted an explanation. "Why not a simulant?" He referred to the established practice of evaluating a bacterial agent's effectiveness by using a non-virulent microorganism that behaved like the nasty one in all other respects.

"There is no simulant for SK-443. We have to test with the

weakened, living virus."

"Then, how do we know that exposure to the weakened SK-443 strain won't confer immunity? How do we know that we won't, in fact, be vaccinating the test populations?" Brockner posed a legitimate question, the single biggest unknown remaining in the research.

"We don't," Martindale countered. "That's one purpose of the testing. If we immunize our own population incidental to the test, how can that be harmful? We do know that the full-strength virus kills in twenty-four hours or less. That's what our enemies will get." Brockner nodded, relinquishing the floor.

"Has the research team at Desert Range been debriefed? Is there any chance of a leak from that quarter?" one of the staff officers queried.

"A debriefing was conducted," General Martindale said. "Those researchers thought, and still think, they were working on a cure for typhoid fever. Their checks came out on Center for Disease Control stationery, addressed for a CDC office that never existed.

"Even if they suspect something, they wouldn't be able to trace anything beyond a nondescript piece of desert on a low-security military research facility. We even removed the road that led to the facility and transplanted a few creosote bushes. Talley's been offered a position at Rocky Flats—which he's sure to turn down. He'll probably try to get back into the University system somewhere where they will fund his research in return for a few post-graduate instructional hours.

"Elwin has the inclination, and enough money rat-holed, to spend the rest of *his* days drinking margaritas somewhere in Mexico. Even if he figured out the true nature of the research, nobody would believe him. *I* wouldn't believe him if he told me!" The general snorted.

"Coletti doesn't know enough to pose any threat to security. She'll probably go back home to Oregon and open a veterinary practice or something. We'll keep tabs on her for a couple of years as a precaution."

"General, can you tell us just what are the effects of SK-443 as it's been developed?" Brockner was now Martindale's "G2," his head executive officer for the functions of Intelligence and Security. He already knew the answer to the question he had just posed. Because Brockner always had the answers—and asked the right questions when he didn't—Martindale had moved him from operations to G-2 several months ago. The man had good instincts.

36

"I can only say that the effects of this particular virus will not be attributable to anything specific. It's highly contagious, with various manifestations in different individuals. One thing I *can* tell you: it's one hundred percent fatal within two days of contracting it. Our best information is that 99.8 percent of all exposures result in acute symptomatic manifestation in the first twenty-four hours after exposure. And, it is invisible to our best microscopic technology. We've never actually *seen* it, ourselves." Only Brockner knew that Martindale had doubled the numbers, underplayed the lethality. The virus was more deadly than any of the others needed to know.

"Jesus!" whispered one of the junior staff officers. Then, louder, "What happens if this stuff gets loose? Do we have an antidote? What kills it?"

"Two things, as a matter of fact." Martindale was grateful the kid had given him his choice of questions to answer. "Temperature and moisture are the critical factors. SK-443 dies if it dries out, and it dies if it's chilled below fifty degrees Fahrenheit."

"But... neither condition can exist in a living human being." This last comment issued, almost subliminally, from Major Dowling.

"That's right, Major."

The room remained silent for a polite moment. Then, Major Cummings, who was responsible for personnel administration and staffing (G1) under Martindale, spoke. "How much longer will we need to keep Bennington at Plum Island?"

"Bennington. Shall we keep him working there on some other project, or ship him out to Navassa to learn what Dr. Harwiczki can teach him about SK-443?" Martindale's question was rhetorical since he'd already made his decision. "It was more or less his lead on Morningstar that made Harwiczki's work possible. I think maybe we should put them together at Navassa and see where it leads. The Morningstar work at Plum Island is essentially over, in any case."

"As you wish, General," Cummings affirmed. "I'll have him transferred before the end of the month, if he'll go. He says he's getting too old for all this. Wants to retire."

"He'll go. His curiosity will see to that. Make him the offer."

"Sir, what kinds of tests should we prepare to run when the weakened strain of SK-443 is ready?" This question came from Major Thomas Dowling, Martindale's new operations officer, who would be expected to conduct, oversee, and document the tests. He was a competent, predictable man, and Martindale didn't particularly like him, but those two qualities of his personality were very necessary for what was to come.

"Tom, I'd like you to remain with me after the meeting to begin our preliminary assessment of that." Martindale looked around the group. "Our testing plans will be discussed with members of this group as soon as they are formulated and finalized. It will be, of course, on a need-to-know basis."

A general discussion about the nuts and bolts of completing the work at Navassa ensued. Questions were carefully phrased to prevent any appearance of being interested beyond the scope of duty—it was the way business was conducted in this Command, and all officers present at this meeting were accustomed to operating under the constraints of circumlocution.

The meeting ended just before noon. As he strode back down the hall from the conference room, Martindale remembered with satisfaction a meeting nearly six years earlier that carried the seed of his current triumph.

> *Oh, what a tangled web we weave*
> *When first we practice to deceive.*
> —Sir Walter Scott, *Marmion*

12 September, 1976

In the early fall of 1976, Albert Bennington arrived at Navassa Island by marine shuttle from Guantanamo Bay. He was met at the pier on the leeward side of the island by a nameless factotum who handled his baggage and took him up a badly rutted road from the pier directly to the administrative center in a bone-jarring jeep ride. He located and introduced himself to Dr. Paulus Harwiczki, the lead researcher at the facility.

"Dr. Harwiczki, it's a pleasure to make your acquaintance. General Martindale sends his regards." Bennington towered over the diminutive Harwiczki by nearly a foot of height. The effect was amplified by a difference in their builds. A bantam Harwiczki assessed the beanpole Bennington.

"Yes, thank you. We were told you were coming." Harwiczki's accent was thicker than any Bennington had ever heard. It was hard to believe the man thought he was speaking English.

Harwiczki didn't appear particularly overjoyed to meet Bennington. Sparse, white hair flew away from his scalp as though he were holding a Van de Graff generator with tens of thousands of volts of static electricity flowing through him to ground. He wore old-world spectacles with round frames perched precariously atop a bulbous, Slavic nose, giving an overall impression of a terribly frightened owl, comical yet serious. His rumpled clothing and wild appearance stood in great contrast to the fastidious, aristocratic Bennington with his tailored suit and polished bearing. They came from different worlds, managing to intersect only through the accident of a common profession.

Bennington went straight to his purpose. "We have a lot to discuss. I'm told you've succeeded in developing a means of producing SK-443 in quantity."

"That is so."

"Perhaps we could discuss it tomorrow?"

"Yes... we shall see. I am curious as to your presence here. They told me little."

"I'm here to learn what you have learned about SK-443, and help you in any way I can."

"How can you help? Do you know what we do here?"

"To a large extent, I'm responsible for what you do here; for what you've been able to do. I supervised the work at Plum Island that produced your raw materials, the basic virus from which you developed a weakened strain for testing."

The tone was a little too pompous and arrogant for Harwiczki's liking, and he struggled to conceal his reaction. "I did not know it was you. As I said, they told me little."

Harwiczki mentally pigeon-holed Bennington as a pompous ass, and wouldn't waste another moment in trying to decide whether or not he liked the fellow—he didn't. Somehow Bennington was not a fellow scientist, notwithstanding his reportedly impeccable credentials. Yet Harwiczki knew he was expected to form a collaborative relationship with the man and did his best to mask his summary judgment with a forced smile.

"We can meet to discuss this further after you have had a tour of our laboratories tomorrow. After lunch." Harwiczki's pique at having to interrupt his regular work regimen for the purpose of showing his new colleague around was poorly masked. It burrowed through his thick accent like a mole to sunlight.

"Very well. Where am I to sleep?"

"Your quarters are ready. I'll have someone show you to them."

In the months that followed this disagreeable introduction, the two virologists acquired a grudging respect for each other. They worked together and managed to be productive in spite of their mutual disaffection with each other as a human beings and colleagues.

At last, in May of 1977, the work was completed; they successfully developed a way of weakening SK-443 without killing it. General Martindale was duly notified and arrived at the island the following day with Colonel Brockner to pounce on the samples. They met the two scientists in Harwiczki's austere office.

"Gentlemen, you and your staff are to be congratulated," Martindale began after the obligatory preliminary greetings. "If the testing succeeds we can close this facility and reassign you to facilities on the mainland where the creature comforts are a little more handy. My compliments for a job well done." He beamed across the six-pack of capped stainless steel cylinders on Harwiczki's desk.

"I am not sure how the virus will test on anything but our monkeys here," Harwiczki said. "We don't know, for example, what it will do to horses. We do know that the full strength strain should kill a human in half a week or less by destroying his immune system. The virus doesn't actually kill, you see—it just paves the way for an opportunistic disease to invade a defenseless immune system. It might help if we knew what species you'll be testing it on."

"I thought you knew, Doctor. We'll be testing its dispersal through domestic water systems on a human population."

At this, Harwiczki's owlish eyes got even rounder behind his spectacles and he shot to his feet like a Canaveral rocket, his hair even more electrified than usual. "You can't do that!" he stormed. "It's too dangerous! It's... It's immoral!"

"Calm down, Doctor. You knew this research was for a biological warfare agent." Martindale was firm and logical. "Will the weakened virus kill people?"

"No. Not if they're healthy to begin with. But it is still immoral to test this thing on unknowing subjects. You can't do this! War is one thing—subjecting an innocent population to such an experiment is something else entirely!"

"Will the weakened strain make anybody ill, Doctor?" Martindale repeated persistently.

"No. It might cause an existing infection to linger a little longer, but it shouldn't make them ill if they're already healthy."

"Then we'll test it," Martindale decided. "We *must* develop information on delivery vectors. We've spent too much time and money to leave the final testing undone."

"I must protest, General. What you propose is fundamentally unethical. The virus should not be tested on human populations for any reason unless they do it voluntarily." Harwiczki was regaining some composure but he was still obviously struggling with his outrage in an attempt to be reasonable and appeal to rational good sense.

"We're not testing the effects of the virus on people, Doctor Harwiczki; only its mechanism of delivery. We need data that tells us precisely how pervasive the agent is in a population when delivered in urban water supplies. And we don't need the population's consent for that. It's a matter of national defense."

"Then I must resign my post if you persist in this folly," Harwiczki declared passionately, drawing himself to as much height as his diminutive frame could muster. "You will receive my resignation in the morning, before you leave." He had seen the suffering in his native Poland inflicted by Nazi butchers in the name of national defense. He saw the same blind nationalism here and it horrified him to the core of his soul.

"I'm sorry you feel that way, Doctor. We will continue to have need of your services; I ask you to reconsider."

"Absolutely out of the question. I will not be a party to this idiocy." Harwiczki stomped out of his own office leaving the General, Colonel Brockner, and Dr. Benning-ton alone.

"He'll talk," Bennington warned. "He'll tell somebody."

"I think not," Martindale said with a finality that made Bennington's blood run even colder than normal.

Harwiczki packed that afternoon. He flew about in a fury, muttering to himself in Polish, flinging his possessions into his luggage with a vengeance. He would not remain on this island or remain associated with this project a minute longer than necessary. He felt betrayed, furious that these imbeciles had subverted his patriotism. A weapon of war was one thing; he'd seen war. He knew its horror and had come to accept the development of biological weapons as a necessary evil. They would never be used, he had convinced himself. But now Martindale and his cronies were planning to expose innocent people to the agent he had developed and reality was beginning to settle in, uncomfortable and heavy. Why not test it on consenting felons or volunteers who would be informed about what they were getting into? The immorality of Martindale was appalling! It was irresponsible—incomprehensibly unethical! Criminal! Heinous! Harwiczki thought.

He stuffed the last of his belongings into his suitcase and returned to his office to write his letter of resignation. As he began to write, he decided that the world must know of this infamy. He finished the letter and made an exact copy, without using carbon, on his electric typewriter.

Collecting the documents remaining in his office that would constitute proof of the immoral actions of Martindale, he looked for a place to hide them. Harwiczki was convinced he would be searched before he would be allowed to leave the island. He wanted a stash he could return to, proof of the allegations he intended to make to the proper authorities. Martindale, this man who had betrayed him so casually, was owed no loyalty and he would, by the hand of Paulus Harwiczki, be exposed for the beast that he was.

He found a tin of coffee at the coffee maker in the hallway outside his office and dumped its contents through his office window. He folded the document copies and stuffed them into the can, together with the copy of his resignation, and sealed the lid. He began to search for a place to hide the can.

Fumbling in his desk for a screwdriver, he removed the screws from the ventilator grill in the wall behind his desk. There was a space in the wooden framing and he managed to shove the can into the wall void. He replaced the grill, being careful to avoid leaving any sign it had been tampered with. He slid the originals into the lining of his briefcase, except for his resignation letter. He turned off the light and went to his quarters. He would leave on the morning boat to Guantanamo. Damn this place; damn Martindale, and that pompous ass Bennington; damn the whole business, he thought.

The following morning at five after eight, Dr. Paulus Harwiczki formally placed his written resignation in Martindale's hands. He stood rigid before the general, firm in his resolve.

"You're sure you won't reconsider, Doctor?" Martindale was solicitous. "We really do need you and there is little danger associated with our proposed testing. No one will be hurt. No one will even know. I really think you are overreacting."

"General, I cannot. I will not. I am returning on the ten o'clock shuttle." Harwiczki remembered too well Hitler's rise to power and the fall of his own native Poland. In his mind, one of the fundamental causes of all the ensuing death and destruction was that not enough people had "overreacted" to the atrocities of the German war machine.

"I was afraid you might not see things our way. I'm sorry. Have a safe trip. Please avail yourself of the helicopter shuttle this morning. There's an empty seat."

Harwiczki turned stiffly, and walked from the room. Martindale picked up the phone.

The ten o'clock helicopter shuttle, a refitted Huey flown by military pilots, lifted off precisely on time. Harwiczki wondered why he had not been searched. Even on normal rotations they always searched every passenger. It seemed unusual, faintly unsettling. He shrugged it off.

Feeling the shuttle lift into the air, he breathed a sigh of relief and began to focus his thoughts on seeing his wife and finding other work in his field. Perhaps he should retire and spend more time on the roses that were his passion. He wondered if Mildred, his wife, was ready for him to be home all the time. Maybe it would drive her nuts. Maybe he shouldn't retire...

He shared the passenger space with two other men. He didn't know them, but he vaguely remembered seeing them from time to time around the island. One, he recalled, was a security guard. The other, who knew? They seemed preoccupied with their own thoughts and Harwiczki was content to be left to his own. The chopper headed out over the open sea. He dozed, lulled by the muffled rhythm of the blades beating the air and the windless, warm sunshine streaming through the windows of the craft.

He was suddenly startled awake by a blast of cold air. He perceived that the cargo door of the Huey was open, barely an instant before hands roughly seized him and hurled him through it. He didn't even have time to scream.

> *"If the perfect weapon is invented,*
> *against which there is no possible defense,*
> *logic dictates that we must use it."*
> —John Goffman

7

18 August, 1977

An August evening would have been balmy anywhere else, but this was San Francisco. The air, rising on the heat of California's San Joaquin Valley, drew in the marine layer, laden with moisture, to create the summer fog for which San Francisco is famous.

Newly promoted Lieutenant Colonel Thomas Dowling, chief of operations for the U.S. Army CBR Command, Research Division, was casually dressed for a night on the town. It really could have been a night on the town if that tight-ass Brockner wasn't tagging along. Still, this was a covert mission, and surety protocol required two of them to complete it. Colonel Brockner wore a tan polyester leisure suit, which reduced their chances of getting anything going with the local female population essentially to zero. Dowling was embarrassed to be seen with him but dared not show it.

They'd rented a car rather than obtaining one from the motor pool at the Presidio. There were two reasons for this. First, the inevitable black-walled tires in the inexhaustible supply of Dodge sedans would be a dead giveaway that the vehicle was government-issue. Secondly, checking a car out of the motor pool would have documented their presence in San Francisco. They chose a Cadillac, and would find a way to bury the extra expense on the vouchers they'd file for travel reimbursement for their "official" trip to Rocky Flats Arsenal in Denver.

They went out a few minutes after midnight. Each had a single drink, enough to leave a faint smell of alcohol on their breath in case they were stopped. They located what they were looking for—a wet-barrel fire hydrant on a large water main in a reasonably secluded location. Beneath the front seat of the Cadillac they carried an adjustable hydrant wrench. On the back seat was a camera bag which—taken together with their dress and the rented car—would mark them as tourists in case anyone got curious. There was a camera in the bag, and several film cans. They did not contain film. They held a weakened strain of SK-443 in specially devised, weighted paper packages, designed to dissolve in water while remaining impervious to the oily, viscous liquid inside.

By three a.m., the streets of the city were nearly deserted. Brockner pulled up next to the fire hydrant they had selected earlier and parked the Caddy precisely where it would screen the hydrant. Both men left the car, looking cautiously but casually around for any prying eyes in the poorly lighted thoroughfare. Brockner fished the camera bag from the back seat while Dowling retrieved the hydrant wrench. Dowling checked to make sure the hydrant was turned off and then removed the cap from one of the outlets. The control valves of wet barrel hydrants are set above ground, and the hydrant barrel itself was filled with water, a perfect open conduit to the water main below.

When Dowling had the hydrant cap removed, Brockner, wearing surgical gloves, inserted half a dozen of the paper cylinders into the barrel, leaning them carefully against the closed valve. He replaced the cap, then gradually cracked the valve open to gently fill the chamber with water. A faintly audible hiss was soft in the air as water surged into the chamber. When the hissing stopped, Brockner knew the chamber was full. At that point, he spun the valve quickly to its fully open position, allowing the capsules to drop down into the buried water main. The entire operation took less than a minute.

They sat in the car for five more minutes—the guaranteed dissolving time of the paper cylinders—then Dowling got out and closed the valve completely, leaving it closed. And thus the weakened strain of SK-443 virus was introduced into the city's water supply.

Five more hydrants were visited that night and treated like the first, hydrants strategically pre-selected based on their location in the water main grid. All in all, it took two men less than two hours to introduce the virus into the water supply of a major American city.

They were not questioned. No one bothered to accost them.

Brockner made a mental note to spend a little time assessing the vulnerability their actions pointed up. Leaving the car at the airport, they took the next flight to Denver where they were already checked into a hotel.

Thirty days later, the test results were on Martindale's desk, and he was pleased. He'd been a little concerned about the molecule-thick protein coating, developed at Navassa to protect the virus from the effects of the chlorine used to keep the city's water system free of microorganisms. The coating was designed to remain intact at pH levels above seven, a level maintained by most municipal water systems to prevent corrosion of the iron water mains.

At pH levels below seven, as found in the human body, for instance, the coating was supposed to dissolve. They weren't sure it would work in the field, or if it did, how well it would work. This was another major purpose of the testing. If it didn't work, the rest of the test would be a bust.

He needn't have worried. The coating worked superbly. The virus flooded the system. No significant or noteworthy increase in emergency room visits had been reported in Bay area hospitals. Martindale knew now that the virus could be delivered successfully to urban populations. In a couple of months, he would have confirmation of one of his other concerns when the city's water temperature dropped as the weather cooled. The viruses should die, leaving the water system pure again. The dead virus would be totally undetectable, as would the fact that it had ever been there in the first place.

Martindale indulged himself for a moment in the fantasy of receiving another star before he retired. It could happen. The Joint Chiefs of Staff would have his report in a few months, and they had been known to reward the development of a new weapons technology with liberal promotion policies. It would definitely fatten those old retirement checks. He could probably count on it.

But one critical factor Martindale failed to include in his calculations: the weakened strain of SK-443, theoretically harmless to a normal population, found as its target a society whose immune systems were already weak from other, unrelated environmental causes. Hundreds of apparently healthy people drank the contaminated water and the virus found perfectly acceptable hosts with immune systems that were no match for it.

BRADD HOPKINS

Shooting the messenger doesn't change the news.
—Anonymous

September, 1981

Dr. Albert Bennington waited in General Thomas Martindale's office. He paced impatiently back and forth in front of the window overlooking the Snake River. Quietly he cursed everything military, especially the air conditioning which was no longer even trying to hold its own against the hot July sun of Idaho Falls. Martindale was late and Bennington suspected it was intentional. Damn the man! Although he'd had no official business with Martindale's people for nearly three years, he'd called Martindale days earlier to request this meeting and the General had more than adequate notice to prepare—he damned well ought to have been on time.

Bennington was older and grayer, a shade more lank and lean, than he'd been when, over a decade ago, he'd entered the African rain forest with a military escort in search of monkeys with specific and unusual ailments. The heat had bothered him then but nothing like it did these days.

He heard a noise at the door, and Martindale entered, followed by Colonel Brockner and two other members of Martindale's staff. The two were introduced as a Colonel Thomas Dowling, Martindale's operations officer, and Dowling's assistant, a Major Malleck.

"Albert! So good to see you! How's your handicap since you retired?" Martindale asked as hands were shaken all around. He referred to Bennington's golf game which had sadly failed to respond to treatment for nearly two decades. This innocent-sounding question also served to clearly mark Bennington's retired status to the two who were unacquainted with the man, a code that meant he was no longer part of the team. Whatever message Bennington was bringing was strictly subject to

Martindale's approval.

"Good enough," Bennington responded curtly. The tactic was transparent and Bennington was more than slightly irked by it. "That's not why I'm here. We have a serious problem."

"We?" said Martindale, blinking pale blue eyes.

"Yes, we. More you than me, actually, but if you don't solve your problem, mine gets worse. I was in Atlanta last week for a symposium at the Center for Disease Control. One of the fellows on staff there is a friend of mine. He's very worried. Frantic, actually. Seems they're tracking cases of a new disease, something they've never seen before. The infection curve—the rate of occurrence of new cases—indicates they might have an epidemic on their hands, and they don't know what's causing it or where it came from." He looked directly at Martindale and blinked just once.

"So?" Martindale wasn't particularly interested. He already had his extra star. Retirement was just around the corner. In the very near future, Brockner would have to deal with any problem. The decision of who would be promoted to fill Martindale's command position on his retirement was already largely made, though Brockner didn't know it yet.

"It's Morningstar, General." Bennington made the declaration flatly, simply.

"Bullshit!" Martindale huffed. "How can you know?"

"I developed it, remember? Who would know better what it will do?" Bennington retorted. "All the symptoms are there; the variable presentations of an immune system gone awry. It's Morningstar, alright."

"How long have they been tracking this new disease?" Martindale asked.

"Almost a year. They think it may have come in from Haiti. There was some speculation about airline flight attendants bringing it in. It seems to be worse in San Francisco. More cases," he clarified.

"It was never in Haiti," Martindale observed pointedly. "It was on the island. How could it have gotten off?"

"I don't know, General."

"And how many people have died from this 'epidemic'?"

"Not many. Not yet. It seems to cause a lingering death. They really don't know for sure. Deaths reported by the medical community at large might be categorized as something else; one or more of the opportunistic diseases, Kaposi's sarcoma or pneumonia, for example. At this stage, it would be hard to identify as a syndrome due to the relative isolation of the medical profession from new information. Only an agency with the oversight capabilities of the CDC would be in a position to detect it this early."

"Albert," Martindale said in a reassuring, almost patronizing tone, "You know as well as I do that Morningstar kills at high efficiency within three days of infection. The immune system is simply stripped away, destroyed. If your patients aren't dying, dying very promptly, then it can't be Morningstar. Q.E.D."

"I've been thinking about that. It may have been degraded by some environmental influence. Or it may be a new strain, a mutation of the weakened stuff that we tested. It's not as virulent as the stuff we made, but the signature is the same." The room was getting even warmer with the added bodies present, and Bennington was starting to perspire freely.

"Christ!" Martindale swore. "If *that* can happen it's going to be *worthless* as a tactical weapon. How can we get confirmation of whether or not we have a problem in our stockpiles?" Martindale directed this latter question to Colonel Dowling, but Bennington spoke before Dowling could answer.

"General, I think you're missing the point. CDC is going to make an official announcement soon... very soon. They're worried as hell. They believe they have an epidemic on their hands, and they know they have no defense. They need major funding—federal funding—to develop a cure. To obtain that funding, they'll go before Congress. They'll submit a report and hold hearings. They can't even *find* the virus, much less identify its vectors. So far, most of the cases have been seen in homosexual men, primarily in San Francisco with a few cases among Haitians.

"General, San Francisco was where we tested SK-443. It may be sexually transmitted, or it may not. They just don't know for sure. Blood, maybe other body fluids, appear to be vectors."

Martindale steepled his hands, leaning back in his office chair. "So, Dr. Bennington... you propose that we should step forward and tell them all about our top secret biological weaponry; how to cure its terrible effects? You propose to just throw away ten years and millions of dollars of research and disembowel a clear tactical lead over our enemies in biological warfare... all because you think our bugs got loose?

"Has it occurred to you that if we do that, and it works, we'd be blamed for every death that's occurred so far? And every death that may occur before the cure could be administered? If we trotted out a cure, we'd be tried and convicted in the media as the cause—even if it isn't our virus. Not to mention the accusations that would fly from the international community about violating the treaty against further development of germ warfare agents. If *that* happened, heads would roll, my dear doctor—and, yours among them. In the interests of National Security, I think we need to wait and see what develops. Going off half-cocked would do more harm than good, don't you think?"

"I don't know what to think," said Bennington, making curious washing movements with his parchment hands, "but it's a safe bet the Joint Chiefs haven't forgotten your presentation to them four years ago when you reported our success. Once CDC releases its information, it's only a matter of time before somebody in Washington figures out what's happened. Then, as you say, heads will roll, anyway. There'll be a lot of embarrassing questions to answer... from some very powerful people."

"Maybe they'll ask questions, but they won't want the cat out of the bag any more than we do. It would violate the 1972 Biological Warfare Convention accords. Nixon was supposed to have closed down these operations officially back in 1969, while we were still engaged in research. We might have a rough time explaining to the public that our research was defensive in nature. They seem to resist understanding the difference between offensive and defensive testing. Such a revelation would call into question the authority and credibility of the Office of the President. They can't afford for it to become a matter of public knowledge any more than we can. Still, Doctor, we really don't know any of this requires action, do we? I want to thank you for coming out here with this important information. Please, keep us posted."

Dr. Bennington was livid at this abrupt dismissal but managed to restrain himself. Mentally shrugging off the insult, he took his cue: time to go. On his way back to the airport he wondered if Martindale would take any protective measures, or if he was, indeed, as complacent and unconcerned as he appeared to be. He was a hard-headed old son of a bitch... there was no telling. Bennington didn't stop sweating until his 727 was airborne at cruising altitude en route to Seattle and the jet engines could spare enough power to drive the plane's air conditioning system.

Shortly after Bennington's departure, General Martindale held a conference with the key staff people who'd been present at the briefing. The consensus was that there was some remote chance that Bennington's analysis was correct... remote at best... but it wouldn't hurt to begin covering their tracks anyway. Martindale ordered a review of the security and surety programs that had been used on Project Morningstar. If questions were going to be asked, he wanted to have the answers in his hands.

Ten days later, Martindale received an early morning call from one of the Joint Chiefs. After his ears stopped burning and he'd collected himself somewhat, he called his orderly and directed the man to arrange a flight to Washington on the next available plane.

BRADD HOPKINS

A new broom sweeps clean.
—Folk saying

9

September, 1981

On the morning following Martindale's return from Washington, Colonel Donald Brockner knocked twice sharply and entered the General's office. His instruction to appear for this meeting had been communicated by telephone the previous afternoon—with great urgency—as Martindale waited at Washington International to board a flight back to Idaho Falls.

Martindale sat quietly at his desk as Brockner entered, and the latter silently observed that his commander had aged visibly since his precipitous departure for Washington. Martindale motioned brusquely for him to take a seat.

"Don, we're in deep shit," he said ominously. Brockner lifted his eyebrows toward his receding hairline and said nothing. The tone of the statement put Brockner's self-preservation system on high alert and his hawk's eyes glittered. At times the old man could be ridiculously transparent. He'd already guessed where Martindale had been these last few days, and confirmed it by bullying the General's orderly. He waited wordlessly for the General to continue.

"I've just met with the Joint Chiefs. The Center for Disease Control in Atlanta is studying a new disease they've found, which, unfortunately, matches the profile of our SK-443 based weapons. Their projections indicate an epidemic, and the Joint Chiefs made the connection between the CDC's new disease and our weapon. They're concerned that the coming epidemic might be attributed to our testing. They know we tested in San Francisco, and that's where the majority of cases are appearing. It's beginning to look as if Bennington was right."

"Good God!"

"Here's the upshot. I've been relieved of command and

55

placed on retirement status effective as of noon today. You are to assume command, and the Joint Chiefs will be in touch. Meanwhile, you are commissioned as damage control. You're to destroy all stocks of SK-443 and take such other measures as may be necessary to 'eliminate the real or perceived threat to the public and to assure that appropriate measures are taken to eliminate any possible connection between the new disease and the operations of the command'."

Martindale read the last words from a sheet of paper, which he then handed across his desk to Brockner. Brockner noted the stamp of classification as *"Top Secret—Restricted Data"* at the top and bottom of the page with the insignia of the Office of the Joint Chiefs of Staff at the top. There was no signature, and further instructions on the sheet directed him to destroy the document upon reading it. He walked over to the shredder in the corner of Martindale's office and inserted the document. The buzzing device promptly reduced it to a small heap of confetti in a large pile of confetti destined for incineration at the end of the week.

"I'm to bury it, then?" asked Brockner.

"Yes. Don, if you do this well, you can write your own ticket to the top. I've talked to the Joint Chiefs and they're blind scared. SK-443 never happened. That's what they want. Here are your promotion orders. Congratulations."

More papers changed hands. Brockner accepted them in a manner as abrupt as that with which they had been presented. He set them aside. "But how are we going to erase the connection with the emergence of the disease in San Francisco? I mean, I can destroy the stockpiles and the documentation. But I can't do anything about the fact that the disease is already spreading through the population. What are we going to do?"

"I'm going to clean out my desk," Martindale said quietly. "I'm sure you'll think of something. *General* Brockner."

The remainder of Brigadier General Brockner's day was spent issuing the necessary instructions to key people in his staff to accomplish the mandates set forth in the shredded orders. That was the easy part; the work would be accomplished within two days simply by implementing a contingency plan already in existence.

That much was clearly expected by the Joint Chiefs; it was a given. Brockner racked his brain for a workable solution to the second part of the critical instruction. Something really creative would be required for that—something that would further cloud the issues involved.

It hit him with Machiavellian simplicity in the middle of his noonday meal. Leaving the greater portion of his luncheon order untouched, he rushed headlong from the Officers' Mess, leaped into his olive drab, government-issue Chevrolet sedan, and sped at breakneck speed across the facility to the incinerators.

The last load from the stockpile had just arrived from the storage bunkers as he skidded to a halt, breathless, and collared the Officer in Charge of the burning operation. He identified himself as the new Commanding General, and shoved the notice of promotion under the startled Lieutenant's nose.

Intimidated by the arrival of the Commanding General at his operation, the young lieutenant saluted and did as instructed. His men, in orange self-contained moonsuits, extracted six paper vials from an olive drab metal case and placed them into an empty, padded case. They passed the case across a deconta-mination line to other moonsuit-protected men, who took them to a device resembling an autoclave where the case's exterior was treated to a charge of ethylene oxide. The case was removed from the sterilization unit by still another team of enlisted men, handed across another decontamination perimeter to the lieu-tenant, who placed it in the trunk of the general's staff car and turned to face the General.

"This is highly irregular, sir," the lieutenant said. "We'll have to clear this with security."

"Lieutenant… Newberry, is it?" He peered at the junior offi-cer's nametag. "Listen carefully to me, Newberry. If you screw up the instructions I'm about to give you, you will be court-mar-shaled. You'll spend the rest of your natural life in Leavenworth breaking rocks, assuming, that is, some outrageous miscarriage of justice occurs and you aren't summarily shot. Make no mis-take of that. Is that clear?"

"Yes, sir!" The lieutenant snapped to attention, rigid and alert.

"Very well. I've never been here. You've never even seen me. This conversation never took place. All stockpiles of SK-443 under your charge were destroyed by incineration, wit-nessed by you, per the directive that you received this morning from me, and your records will reflect that fact.

"I'm acting under the express orders of the Joint Chiefs of Staff. To discover more you'd have to demonstrate a need to know. And because I'm the one you must show proof of that need to, I can tell you right now that you will have no need for further information on this action in order to be able to discharge your duties. Do you have any questions?"

"No, sir!"

"Carry on, Lieutenant!"

"Yes, sir!" The lieutenant snapped a crisp salute, which the departing Brockner ignored.

Back at the headquarters building, the sealed case resting closed before him on the desk, Brockner called a young operative into his office. The man was trustworthy, loyal, and talented—a boy scout in any other organization. The man's name was Bill Selmack.

He issued verbal instructions to Selmack that were as bizarre as the young operative had ever heard in a trade where bizarre was the order of the day. Selmack was to travel, as a tourist or photographer, to a city in a third world African nation Brockner would specify. There he would enter the rain forest. Using rubber gloves to open the case, he was to throw its contents into a river—any river—and return. The simple, cryptic instructions were very clear, although unusual.

Selmack had already learned that the need-to-know doctrine would prevent him discovering anything further about the nature of his assignment. Whatever he was doing, it was clearly in the interests of national security or he wouldn't be doing it. Q.E.D., as the old man was so fond of saying.

What the hell! thought Selmack as he exited the new commander's office with the case under one arm. *The pay's the same...*

> *"Everything in life is somewhere else,*
> *and you get there in a car."*
> —E. B. White, One Man's Meat

10

12 May, Present

Jim Auvil, recently hired by Wakefield Environmental Company as a laborer/roustabout, leaped from Drilling Rig 9 and stalked seventy-five feet across the west Texas prairie to the control box where the driller crew chief, Rob Dawson, waited.

"It's fixed," he reported, nodding toward the loose hydraulic line connection he'd just tightened. A small puddle of hydraulic fluid lay on the plastic sheeting. They were running behind and he hadn't taken the time to throw a shovel full of kitty litter on the puddle; he intended to do it when the next segment was added to the auger.

"Handle that spill before you make a single turn!" The safety engineer, Bud Something-or-Other, was adamant. "We're not about to contaminate our client's site with our own spills." Bud was such a prick—always interfering with the flow of the labor—Auvil had trouble remembering the man's last name.

It was beginning to feel like the promise of a real rotten day for Auvil. The sun hadn't even risen yet when he went a couple of rounds with Sally Ann, his wife, over writing a rubber check to prevent the phone company from disconnecting their service until his paycheck arrived.

He was feeling downright salty when he met the crew out at Site 173. His right front tire had taken a roofing nail on the way, and the tire was noticeably mushy as he pulled up, ten minutes late for work. He knew his spare was flat. Site 173 was six miles from the nearest service station, out in the middle of nowhere. Even if he could get Rob to wait around after work while he pulled the tire and give him a ride to the gas station, he'd still have the problem of getting the tire back to the truck, six miles out where nobody traveled. It was a long walk, especially rolling a tire.

He helped lay out the clear plastic 10-mil sheeting and guided Ryan Williams, the operator, as he backed Unit 9 into place in the center of the plastic barrier. When the stake marked "173" was centered on the tailboard, four feet away from it, Auvil held up a clenched fist to signal Williams to lock up the wheels and engage the hydraulics.

Rig 9 was a hollow core auger rig, small and easy to operate. Its segmented bits were six inches in diameter and six feet long. The inside of each segment was hollow; the outside had a welded-up spiral screw-thread pattern. Each segment locked to the one preceding it with a pilot bolt, following its predecessor down the hole. The auger would cut like a hot knife through butter in the sandy soil they were going to drill into this morning.

Auvil staked out a work area in a square around the drilling rig about fifty feet on a side using yellow barricade tape. They called this bounded area the "Hot Zone", and no one could enter it once the drilling had commenced unless they donned disposable Tyvek chemical protective coveralls, neoprene gloves and carried a respirator, in case the hole was producing chemical contamination.

Lastly, he set up a rudimentary field decontamination station at one corner: two steel wash tubs and some bristle brushes. He furnished it with a live water supply from the tanker that accompanied the rig. Williams tilted the derrick into place, and checked Auvil's "spot"; only two inches off plumb dead center of the stake. *The kid learns quick,* he thought. *Now if he'd only get his shit together at home...*

Bud, the safety engineer, recorded the requisite sniffs with his air sampling instrument at the tip of the auger and near the surface of the ground where drilling would begin. He signaled thumbs up and joined Rob. All the workers withdrew to the location where Rob was manning the remote control. They were seventy-five feet away because there was a minuscule chance of trouble "down hole". The precaution was a pain in the neck—operating remote so far from the rig—but it was company policy for this job. They were, after all, drilling on an abandoned military bombing range.

Auvil knew that each drill site had been surveyed with special detectors to assure that the rigs didn't drill into unexploded ordnance on their way to the specified depth. They were boring for samples to determine if there was any chemical contamination of the soil or the underlying water table. The job was part of a Superfund assessment, but Auvil didn't know that. He also didn't know that this day, which had started bad and gotten worse, wasn't done with him yet.

Three days earlier, just before the rain, two dirt bikes had roared up to a red-flagged stake in the middle of the old bombing range. It was the only thing of interest in a plain of sparse sagebrush and sandy washes. The two kids riding the bikes were both from Abilene High School, and knew they weren't supposed to be there—but the biking was so good it was hard to resist. Jackrabbits were numerous; they never had to search long until they found one to chase on their motorcycles.

While they stopped to stretch, one of the boys pulled a flagged stake from the ground, parrying and thrusting for a few seconds with this makeshift sword. He used it as a swagger stick, tucked it under his arm, and walked a few dozen feet away from the parked bikes to relieve his bladder on a sage bush. As he zipped his trousers, he stuck the stake into the ground, wondering briefly what the number 173 chalked on the stake meant. Probably nothing. Forgetting it, he walked back to his bike and his buddy. They jumped another rabbit before they were a hundred feet from their rest stop.

The rain came that night, heavy and pounding, to wash away all signs of their visit.

On this same bombing range, forty-two years earlier, Major Walter Winslow banked his superannuated B-36 bomber in a sweeping right turn and leveled off at a heading of due north at 10,000 feet. He notified his bombardier that they were commencing their bomb run and opened the bomb bay doors. The bombardier acquired his target in the bombsight's cross hairs— a fifteen-foot square of plywood in the middle of the Texas prairie with painted red stripes on a white background.

To the bombardier, it was of little consequence whether or not he hit the target; the purpose of this run was to find out if the newest modification to the Mark 85 would fix an irritating problem—its tendency to refuse to detonate when it was supposed to. Nonetheless, he adjusted the crosshairs in the bombsight and, at precisely the perfect instant pulled a lever that released the first of two five-hundred pound bombs. A tug on another lever freed the second bomb a moment later. Both bombs dropped toward the target.

The first bomb detonated on impact. The second, true to form, plowed into the soft, sandy dirt at over three hundred miles per hour and came to rest, unexploded, buried four feet below the surface. The Mark 85 detonator failed to function. Winslow would note in the flight log that there was another unfired 500-pound bomb loose on the range, thanks to those idiot engineers at the factory who still couldn't get it right.

He wondered idly if they'd really changed the Mark 85 at all for this run... and why they were still trying to fix the same old detonators that hadn't worked consistently since they'd first been produced. Why didn't they just start from scratch and pitch the troublesome Mark 85s? How hard could it be to build a detonator that worked? He tripped the hydraulic controls to close the bomb bay doors. He dropped his left wing tip, banked left in a smooth, sweeping arc, and took a heading for the landing field.

Rob Dawson moved a lever that opened the hydraulic valve to start the hollow core auger turning, and began to lower the turning drill on cables into the sand. He judged the rate of drilling penetration to be about a foot a minute, which meant that they'd have to hump to add the six foot long sections to the auger as it entered the hole. Normally, in harder strata, they had some time between extending the sections; time to take care of the details related to the business of boring a hole in the planet. When the drilling went easy, they worked so fast that it was often hard to attend to the details.

As the auger cut past the three-foot mark, another hydraulic connection began to leak, spurting out a jet of high-pressure hydraulic fluid each time the line was placed under a load. *Damn that kid! He's just not with it.* Dawson looked around cautiously, but Bud was sitting in his truck, making out the daily safety plan—not watching.

He nodded toward Auvil, pointing to the leak growing larger each time he moved the remote control in his hand. Auvil got the message, picked up the wrench he'd been using earlier, and trotted over to the connection panel at the back of Rig 9. Dawson made every effort to keep the augur turning at a steady rate. If Bud heard any change in the noise level, he might glance up and see that Auvil was in the exclusion zone when the drill was operating. The kid would surely get written up for a safety violation.

Auvil finished tightening the fitting and removed the wrench. The leak stopped. The small amount of fluid remaining was barely noticeable.

He turned toward Dawson with a thumbs-up signal just as the auger passed the four-foot mark and bored into the forty-two year old bomb. The auger jumped in the hole, bucking as it turned. Dawson reversed the control to lift the auger up and away from the obstruction... too late.

The Mark 85 detonator faithfully refused to respond—just as it had failed forty-two years earlier—but the high explosive in the body of the bomb had become unstable and crystallized over the years. It detonated under the pressure of the turning, bucking auger.

Bud looked up from his field notes when the first metallic clanking sound of the auger jumping in its hole reached his ears. He watched the ground swell like a blister, lifting surrealistically underneath Auvil and looked on, amazed, as Rig 9 began to climb into the West Texas sky. Before he could begin to even form a thought the shock wave hit his pickup and the whole world vanished.

BRADD HOPKINS

11

13 May, Present

Russell Wakefield—owner and chief executive officer of Wakefield Environmental, Inc.—parked his white-over-gray Lexus in the reserved space in the parking lot of the modest two-story wood, stone and glass office building that served as the main office of his company. Unwinding his tall frame from the driver's seat, he stepped out and the door closed behind him with a satisfying, quiet 'thunk'. He thumbed the button on the ignition key, locking the vehicle. The alarm system didn't even chirp... it simply began to do its job with neither fanfare nor ostentation, understated, elegant. Wakefield liked that.

He entered his offices through the front entrance and passed the receptionist/secretary, Rosie, who smiled engagingly and greeted him by his Christian name. He always entered through the front entrance. It gave him an opportunity to see what his clients saw when they entered the building. He knew the importance of that first impression and reviewed it daily as a matter of course.

He was an impressive man, himself. He towered six-four and moved with an uncanny grace and fluidity. Slight premature graying at the temples combined with the aquiline cut of his features to give him an air of authority, almost as though he belonged to the aristocracy. His easy Texas drawl destroyed the aristocratic impression, however. The moment he opened his mouth to speak he instantly became "just folks". He knew the effect was amplified by wearing a blue business suit, and he invariably wore one for critical negotiations. His ready smile and easy manner had managed to lull more than one competitor into a false sense of security, gently encouraging them to lower their guard and leave their homework undone. To Wakefield, this was not a ruse—he actually was gentle and easy-going—but he was also shrewd, which made him a devastatingly effective negotiator. Wakefield usually left the most formidable business opponent either speechless in awe while he was being beaten out of a contract, or ruefully feeling that he'd simply acquiesced to his best bowling buddy, good ole' Wakefield.

As he passed through the lobby, his eyes noted and his brain evaluated the meticulously arrayed fans of financial magazines and trade publications on the coffee table. The latest issues were always carefully placed there, but it galled Wakefield if any visitor was forced to wait long enough to pick up one of these papers.

The leaves on the potted plants were shiny and free from dust. The deep Federal-blue leather of the brass-studded straight-backed armchairs was flawless. The carpet was clean and plush, an expensive, dense woolen weave, in a light, full bluish gray. Cherry wood paneling glowed mellow with polish, speaking in whispers of restrained success. The room, by design, smelled like a cabin in the woods—an oddly reassuring, musty mix of pine and wool and faint, sweet wood smoke—the result of a designer air freshener Wakefield had ordered from Europe.

Directly opposite the entranceway, an authentic Navajo rug hung on the wall. Wakefield remembered the purchase of this rug from its maker in an Arizona pueblo. He had not been able to locate the "spirit hole"—an intentional imperfection woven into the rug by its weaver in an effort to avoid offending the gods through any aspiration to perfection. The old woman had pointed it out to him, pleased that he had enough acumen to know the spirit hole was required and that he was unable to locate it without her help. Now, each time Wakefield looked at the rug he saw her old brown face superimposed upon it, the texture and color of a dried fig, her ancient wise black eyes sparkling among the wrinkles.

Coffee was brewed in the hallway alcove. Wakefield stopped and poured a cup. His chief operations officer, Gene Briggs, a wiry west Texas third-generation cowboy with an MBA, emerged from a side office, coffee cup in hand, and greeted him. " 'Morning, Russ!"

Wakefield returned the greeting and entered his office at the end of the hall. His mail was laid out neatly for him on the desk blotter. As he moved around the desk and sat down, his eyes caressed a photograph of Susan, now gone these four years, in ritual greeting. Near it stood a framed photo of his son, Thomas, in his University of Texas A&M football colors.

Wakefield was always amazed at the way the features of his

wife shone through the countenance of their son. His fine facial bone structure and high cheekbones were hers, and the rendering of her features in the gender of her son was simultaneously haunting and reassuring. The image of his son was an open channel to her memory.

Rosie entered with a hot cup of coffee, realized that he already had one, and set the service off on a sideboard.

"Bruce called yesterday after you left," she said brightly. "He said to tell you that the radiation levels were lower than they expected in the samples. You don't need to go up there unless you want to. Everything's under control."

Bruce Parsons was site supervisor for a job Wakefield Environmental was doing in Illinois, boring sampling holes into a low-level radioactive landfill under a Department of Defense Site Assessment and Remediation Contract (SARC). They'd anticipated problems with radiation levels in the dump, closed over twenty years ago on a military facility. Now Parsons was telling him that the problems were not as severe as they'd anticipated—which meant that their expenses would be lower and the company's profits on the job were assured.

It was a great way to start the day! If things continued to go this well it might be possible to leave early for a round of golf.

"See if you can get me a start time out at The Meadows for this afternoon," he directed Rosie. "Then call Warren Stone and invite him to join me there, if you'd be so kind."

Rosie smiled inwardly at his phrasing. He was always coming up with slightly unusual ways of saying 'please'. He was always polite to a fault, like a child who was just learning the skill. Under a rare cloud of rage at some blunder, Wakefield's politeness became painstaking. Rosie had learned over the years that such extremely pointed courtesy meant the sky was about to fall. Today, however, he was in a great mood, as usual.

"Yes, sir. I'll let you know," said Rosie, scooping up the coffee service on her way out the door.

Rosie rang his office just before lunch to confirm a two-thirty tee time and the availability of Warren Stone to join him. Warren had been the company's lawyer as well as Wakefield's personal friend for fifteen years. They golfed together at least once a month. These days, most of their routine business seemed to be done on the back nine.

The morning passed without event. Wakefield spent most of it reading specifications on the new drilling bits he was considering for their hard-rock drilling operations. He left the office and met Stone for a leisurely lunch. They were on their way to the links by two p.m.

Wakefield had just finished a sterling drive from the fifth tee in what promised to be one of his best games ever when Stone's pager went off. Stone shut it off. It toned again with the same number displayed. Stone glanced at it, muttering an oath under his breath. The second page from his office was a code that denoted urgency. The two men broke off their game and headed for the clubhouse.

Stone located a phone and rang his office. He was told to have Wakefield ring his own office—that there was an emergency.

Rosie answered on the first ring. "There's a problem in Abilene," she said when she recognized his voice. "They hit a bomb and one of the drillers is dead. The base commander is fit to be tied and wants you there as soon as possible."

"Who got killed?" Wakefield wanted to know.

"New hire on rig nine," Rosie said. "Rob Dawson, the tool pusher, says he's married, no kids. Rob got hurt, too. He says it's not serious, and he sounded O.K."

"Call Westair and have them heat up the fastest thing they've got. Tell them I'll be there within the hour."

Wakefield replaced the phone on the cradle and turned to find Warren asking the question with his eyebrows.

"Time to earn that fat retainer I pay you," he said to Warren. "Can you leave with me right away for Abilene?"

"You bet," Warren affirmed. "Let me call Teresa and tell her what's going on. What's going on?" Wakefield told him.

Wakefield phoned the office again. "Rosie," he said without preamble, "please tell Briggs to pack a bag and meet me at Westair in forty-five minutes. And call Wallace, let him know what's happening. Call Esterson and have him shut down the other rigs we've got working in Abilene. Give the crews a day off at full pay. Call Diana, and let her know I'm leaving, won't be home. Send my day bag and a clean suit to Westair with Briggs."

"Briggs has already gone home to pack. He'll meet you at the Westair terminal," reported Rosie. "I can't reach Wallace, but I'll keep trying." Wallace handled the company's insurance.

An hour and a half later, Westair's Cessna Citation lifted off the runway and climbed to cruising altitude with Wakefield, Stone, and Briggs aboard, headed west. Briggs had been told of the incident in the lobby of Westair's terminal while they waited for the pilots to complete the pre-flight checks on the small, fast jet.

Each man sat quietly now, immersed in his own thoughts, as the jet raced across the sky at 260 knots, headed for Abilene, two hours away.

Russ Wakefield had worked his way up from the very bottom of the drilling trade to become the owner of one of the most financially successful well drilling companies in the nation. It had taken a raft of hard work, careful management, and luck. The time had long passed when he needed to go to work. He showed up every day because he loved it.

He had hired on summers before he got out of high school to Nolan Drilling, a one-horse water-well drilling outfit as a laborer—a grunt. Nearly two years he'd sweated in the hot Texas sun and frozen in the stiff, cold winds of the panhandle winters, perforating aquifers with men who had been doing just that for decades. He was fascinated by the idea of finding water—cool, clean, clear water under the dusty Texas soil.

During the two years he worked for old man Nolan, he'd earned a solid reputation as a willing hand and as an increasingly knowledgeable worker. Tool pushers wanted him on their crews because he worked like a trooper and his interest carried beyond the paychecks. He always came early and stayed late.

It came to him one day that drilling was what he wanted to do with the rest of his life. He told old man Nolan he wanted to go back to school, to learn everything he could about drilling holes in the ground.

He applied to Texas A & M and was turned down cold. Undaunted, he enrolled in San Antonio Junior College. He cracked the books with a vengeance, never missed the Dean's List, and reapplied to Texas a & M at the end of his first year. He was turned down again. That summer he worked for old man Nolan as a "tool pusher", supervising his own crew on Nolan's Rig 2 at the ripe old age of nineteen.

Fall saw him back in the junior college. He devoured geology, meteorology, chemistry, and archeology with an appetite that amazed his professors, pressing the academic lemon with the same single-minded ardor he was to carry with him throughout his life.

Like a pit bull in his concentration, he never released his grip on a subject until he understood its intricacies and its relationship to other disciplines. His native intelligence had always been there. Directed, it was almost formidable. Calculus fell to his understanding after a siege in which he was victorious primarily by virtue of sheer perseverance; the other studies fell to him as wheat before a scythe. He developed relationships with his professors that were more characteristic of students in universities than in junior colleges.

His third application to Texas A & M was the charm. He was admitted in the fall of 1970 for studies majoring in geology, with minor emphasis on groundwater hydrology. He forgot to file for his 2S student deferment with the local Draft Board, and was promptly drafted into the Army before he finished his first quarter.

In a panic of rising apprehension that life would pass him by before he could live it, he married his high school sweetheart. It was a Texan thing to do. He feared secretly that she would be snapped up by another, more available suitor before he could finish his tour.

After the battery of tests, he was offered his choice of military occupational schools in return for extending his tour of service for one year. He took the bait; Viet Nam was going at a gallop and lots of young American boys were coming home in body bags. Wakefield decided that if Viet Nam was in his future, he was going to carry the biggest guns he could get his hands on. He signed for Army Nuclear Weapons Maintenance School.

Almost before the ink was dry on the bottom of the form he signed, he was shipped bag and baggage to Fort Ord, California for Basic Combat Training. The fact that the west coast was a jumping-off point for Viet Nam was not lost on him. It was clear that the war would not be over before his training was complete.

He detested Basic Combat Training and military life in general. He loathed the military mentality and detested the foggy, wet weather of the central California coastal summers. It seemed to him that he would never be warm again. He hated running everywhere with full field gear and that god-awful boat-anchor M14 rifle. Most of all, Wakefield hated the regimentation. That he understood the need for it did not ease his dislike in the slightest.

He hated the barracks where the windows were kept open all night by order of the Post Commandant. The temperature was kept below 50 degrees, so the bacteria that caused meningitis could not survive the journey from one warm body to another. Recent outbreaks of the disease had killed three recruits during the preceding year and the Drill Instructors were enforcing the directive with vigilance. Now, instead of meningitis, everybody was getting pneumonia and bronchitis from the open windows.

Basic Training ended. Russell Wakefield's name was not called at the final company formation where everybody, still woozy and white-faced from their celebration the night before, received their orders for new duty stations. Most, of course, were assigned to AIT (Advanced Infantry Training) Battalions. A few received orders for artillery school, and a couple of the guys went to Motor Pool. One enviable soul was slated for Redstone Arsenal to become an Ordnance Disposal Technician. Wakefield didn't go anywhere.

After about a week of miserable limbo in the empty barracks waiting for orders, Wakefield was ordered to report to Battalion Headquarters. The sergeant major there told him to move his gear into different quarters to make way for a new batch of recruits coming in. Wakefield was told that his orders were awaiting a security clearance before they could be issued. It would take about two weeks. Meanwhile, he would be assigned as an aid to the sergeant major, Wilbur R. Tucker.

Four months passed with no word on his orders. He had managed to be extremely useful to the sergeant major. Wakefield's role was as a facilitator, negotiator, and inventory expert for Sergeant Major Tucker; he always knew who owed what to whom. As a gesture of thanks, Tucker saw to it that Private Wakefield was promoted to Private First Class Wakefield upon his first eligibility.

Wakefield had use for the extra money his promotion brought; Susan told him she was pregnant. It made him edgy, wanting to be with her, and he searched for ways to get a leave. Reassignment to another post would virtually guarantee one and he was overdue.

Tucker had come to rely on him, and when the relationship was finally on firm ground, Wakefield asked what could be done about his delinquent orders.

"I thought you liked it here working for me," Tucker had growled. "You're too valuable to me here to press anybody for your orders."

Wakefield frowned. "I do, Sergeant Major. It's just that I was supposed to get the training, and I haven't heard a thing from Admin. I've wondered if you haven't had a hand in the delay. I know you've got the juice to do it."

Wakefield knew his bluntness might offend the sergeant major. He was even more concerned about what would happen if some administrative orders clerk found him in the Basic Combat Training unit without orders and decided to ship him out to an infantry unit as an expeditious way of solving the problem. Of this latter concern, however, he said nothing to the sergeant major.

Wakefield knew that this conversation was pressing the relationship he had developed with the non-com. He hoped he hadn't pushed it too far with that last, implying that Tucker had constructively delayed the late orders. Tucker bristled at the implication, and tossed off a half a cup of cold coffee at a gulp. He was livid. He surged to his feet and started around his desk.

"Get the hell out of my goddamned office, you son-of-a-bitch!" roared Tucker, with a voice that had been terrorizing recruits into abject submission for over twenty years.

PFC Wakefield retreated, wondering if the sergeant major was angry enough to really ruin his life. That afternoon, right after colors, PFC Winters, the colonel's driver, caught up with him on the way to the mess hall.

"Sergeant Major Tucker says you report to the Officers' Field Mess for KP at 0430 hours tomorrow. What the hell did you do? He was really pissed." Private First Class Winters was also a first class jerk, and Wakefield knew better than to say anything which might get back to the battalion commander, or, worse yet, the sergeant major.

"I guess I stood up when I should have shut up," replied Wakefield glumly, hoping that this would be as bad as things got. As it turned out, it was the tip of the iceberg.

His KP assignment stretched out over eight days, each starting at four a.m. and ending at ten p.m. Each day was filled with mountains of potatoes to peel, dozens of pots to scrub, and ubiquitous grease traps to clean. Fatigue became the dominant feature of his life. Wakefield kept his mouth shut and did as he was told. On the ninth day, he was summoned from the pots-and-pans detail to the sergeant major's office.

He changed uniforms quickly on the way, but was unable to shower and remove the smells of the kitchen from his person. He arrived at the sergeant major's closed door and knocked twice.

"Enter!" It was a bellow.

Wakefield entered smartly and placed himself three feet in front of the sergeant major's desk, centered, at attention. "PFC Wakefield reporting as ordered," he said. He knew he reeked of onion. He hoped it helped his cause.

"At ease, Wakefield," Tucker snapped. "Captain Ramirez over at the mess says you did a good job."

"Thank you, sergeant major." His tone conveyed just the right measure of contrition and apprehension. Young Wakefield knew better than to use the word "sir" in this situation. Its use was reserved for officers and would offend the sergeant major.

"I found out that an E-4 clerk down at HQ misfiled your orders for school," growled Tucker. "I had his sleeve lightened. Your orders for Nuclear Weapons Training at Sandia Base in Albuquerque will be cut tomorrow. You'll be out of here by the end of the week. I want to thank you for the job you've done for me around here." Tucker rose from his desk and extended his hand.

The orders came as promised. PFC Wakefield shipped out for training at Sandia Base in Albuquerque.

Wakefield snapped back from his reverie as the jet's wheels lowered and locked for landing. The Citation touched down smoothly and taxied to the private terminal. There they were met by a staff car sent by the base commander, and taken to the Hilton. Colonel MacCaffrey would see them at 0700 hours. A car would be in front of the hotel at 0630.

Wakefield checked in and immediately called Davis Esterson, his job foreman for the Abilene job. There was no answer. He left a message on Esterson's machine with the hotel's phone number.

He called Rosie at home to ask if she knew which hospital had admitted Rob Dawson and if she had spoken with Rob's family. The answer was 'no' on both counts. Russ began calling each hospital in the phone book. He hit on the second try and was told that visiting hours were 10:00 to noon and 4:00 p.m. to 6:00 p.m. There was nothing to do but wait until morning. He wolfed down a prime rib sandwich from room service, laid out his morning clothes, and called Stone and Briggs for breakfast arrangements.

BRADD HOPKINS

12

16 May, Present

Dawn came early. Russ Wakefield was groggy from sleep as he hadn't been for years. He showered, dressed, and met Stone and Briggs for breakfast at the hotel restaurant by six.

The coffee helped. The juice and sausage and eggs helped even more. Russ had never responded with politically correct lifestyle changes to the ubiquitous warnings of cholesterol and heart disease. He disdained the fruit and bran muffins offered at the buffet. 'Yuppie food', he called it. Stone ate the Yuppie food from the buffet in spite of Wakefield's pronouncements.

It was decided over breakfast that Briggs would look in on Rob Dawson and engage Davis Esterson for lunch. Wakefield and Stone would meet with Colonel MacCaffrey. They would all meet for lunch to compare notes.

An Air Force staff car wheeled up under the *portecochere* as they stepped outside from the lobby. The driver, in starched fatigues with creases like the blades of straight razors, got out and approached them. "Mr. Wakefield? If you'll come with me, sir." He ushered them into the back seat of the government-issue battleship gray Chevrolet sedan. Warren Stone preceded his employer.

After a quarter-hour drive in silence, the staff car pulled to a stop at the gate of Dyess Air Force Base. a crisply dressed A/P peered in at them, straightened, and saluted with a white-gloved hand. They arrived at MacCaffrey's office in a few minutes and were ushered in.

MacCaffrey, a bird colonel, rose and stepped briskly around his desk to greet them. After handshakes and Stone's introduction to MacCaffrey, he gestured toward two chairs in front of the desk. He retreated behind the desk, where he sat down and leaned forward.

"Sorry to be meeting under these circumstances, gentlemen," he intoned. "Can I get you anything? Coffee, perhaps?" He paused before he continued, allowing them both time to acknowledge his offer and decline. Both visitors were astute enough to recognize the offer as largely pro forma. Otherwise, MacCaffrey would have made it before he seated himself. *The military are a strange lot,* thought Wakefield.

"The incident occurred late yesterday morning," he began. "Your man, Dawson, was taken to Fisher Hospital. Your laborer, Williams, too. Williams was released, Dawson they kept. The one named Auvil was apparently standing on top of a 500-pound bomb when it detonated. They didn't find much of him.

"Your Safety Engineer, Bud Willis, got cold-cocked by the shock wave where he was sitting in the truck. His company has seen to his medical care. They tell me he'll be O.K. Headaches for a while, is all."

The colonel was familiar with Wakefield's practice of hiring his field safety supervisors from specialty companies on a contract basis. It avoided any possible conflicts of interest or confusion of loyalties, and the government usually favored such arrangements for a number of other reasons, as well.

"Our people from the 73rd EOD—that's Explosive Ordnance Disposal—are working with the Air Police to determine exactly what happened. The EOD technicians are actually Army types, posted here on the base since there's no Army facility around. They are useful from time to time when ordnance shows up in places it doesn't belong. Happens more than you might think."

"How could they have hit anything?" Wakefield wanted to know, referring to his drillers. "Each site was supposed to be surveyed with metal detectors and low frequency sound before any marker was placed, before any drilling was begun." The event was beginning to register emotionally on Wakefield. His stomach was rebelling against the breakfast he had consumed. He wondered about Auvil's survivors and wished he knew more about the family of the dead man. Stone remained quietly attentive.

"Our best guess for now is that the drilling crew either moved the set-up point of the rig, or somebody moved the marker. We'll know more in a few hours. I've made arrangements for us to have a look at the site. There's a vehicle waiting."

"I need to make a phone call first, Colonel. Do you have a FAX here?" Rosie would have access to Auvil's employee file.

He needed to know more, not just for the family but also for the non-military OSHA investigation he knew would follow Auvil's death and the injuries to the other employees.

Wakefield made a mental note to have Briggs tighten up his field safety procedures on all his working rigs, so that the inevitable Occupational Safety and Health Administration inspectors would have a favorable impression of the operations being conducted. They would flock like buzzards to a kill. Wakefield knew enough to realize that his crews would be subject to intense scrutiny at all his working locations in the aftermath of an incident such as had occurred here. There was no remedy. The law required him to report the injuries within twenty-four hours. It also required OSHA to investigate.

It was twenty-five minutes by jeep out to Site 173. Conversation was impossible, particularly after the jeep turned off the paved road. It bounced onto a dusty two-wheel track across the open sageland basin. a cloud of alkali dust billowed out behind the rear wheels of the jeep and drifted on the wind. As they slowed on approaching the site, the dust cloud overtook them and all were covered with the gritty powder.

"Sorry, sir", the driver offered sheepishly to Colonel MacCaffrey as they stepped from the halted jeep. MacCaffrey snorted, but did not otherwise acknowledge the apology.

Site 173 was cordoned off. Two Air Police guards were posted in the unlikely event that an unauthorized person happened by. The military investigators were examining the rear end of the drilling rig, which lay on its side some thirty feet from a crater about six feet deep and forty feet in diameter. Twisted and deformed beyond salvage, the vehicle attested mutely to the forces released during the incident the previous day.

As Wakefield and the colonel approached, one of the investigators broke away from the group and moved toward them. He stopped and saluted almost casually. The gesture was answered by a perfunctory wave that would pass as a salute only among friends.

"Terry, this is Russ Wakefield and his counsel, Mr. Stone. This is Terry Cheswick. He's in charge of the investigation." He turned again to Cheswick, who wore Captain's bars and a sheen of perspiration. It was hot even this early in the day, and getting hotter.

"What can you tell us so far?"

"Well, sir," Cheswick began, wiping his brow with a handkerchief, "we compared the survey map of drill sites that you gave us to the center of the crater. The site they were supposed to drill at is right over there." He indicated a spot about fifty feet to their left, well away from the edge of the crater. The investigators had driven a flagged stake into the sand to mark the spot.

"There is no marker there. We checked with the survey crew; they put one out. We found the stake marked '173' at the edge of the crater, there. It was probably lying on the ground at the time of the detonation, since it shows no blast damage. It looks like the stake was moved from its surveyed position before the explosion occurred...and probably before the drilling started. Unless that was so, the stake could not have been found between the point of explosion and the site. It would have been farther out, possibly damaged by the blast.

"From the size, shape, and depth of the crater itself, we think that the explosion was in the range of five hundred pounds of H.E., buried about four feet. The residue analysis will tell us that for sure. We've found some pieces of bomb casing that we will be able to match up to tell us exactly what exploded here."

"Do we have confirmation records that show that the metal detectors and low-frequency sonar tests were done here?" MacCaffrey wanted to know.

"Yes, sir. The records are in the engineers' logs. As a matter of fact, the engineers even used a MAD—that's a Magnetic Anomaly Detector—on this site. They're satisfied that it was clear. Their logs show it clear."

"Very good, Terry," said the Colonel. "Carry on. Let me know right away if you find anything significant or unusual."

MacCaffrey looked at Wakefield and then Stone. He raised his eyebrows to invite questions. Wakefield and Stone looked at each other and Wakefield shook his head. They returned to the jeep and the driver took them back to MacCaffrey's office.

As they entered, MacCaffrey's clerk handed him a note. He read it, stopping to make sure he did not have to respond. He spoke briefly with the clerk. Then he went into his office followed by the others. The clerk brought up the rear.

"Colonel, there is a FAX for Mr. Wakefield." Upon the colonel's nod, he handed the document to its addressee and departed the office. Wakefield glanced at it, fanning through several pages: it was the information he had requested from Rosie about Auvil. There was also information on the other members of the crew on Rig 9. He had not requested it, but was nonetheless grateful to have it.

"What are you gentlemen doing after lunch?" asked MacCaffrey as he laid the note on his desk.

"I thought we'd get back to Houston," said Wakefield. "I

plan to leave my operations supervisor, Briggs, here for a couple of days to put things in order."

"Apparently, somebody wants to see you while you're here. Ever heard of a General Brockner? He's inbound on a MAC flight, due at two forty-five. I have specific instructions to ask you to stay and meet with him."

"Brockner? Don't know him. I suppose he's part of the administrative load for the investigation."

"I don't think so," MacCaffrey said. "My staff and I will do all that's to be done. Besides, Brockner is Army, not Air Force. Means he's not associated with this investigation. No concern to them."

"Of course we can wait."

The Colonel excused himself and left the office to make arrangements for General Brockner's transportation from the landing field. As soon as he left, Stone turned to Wakefield.

"Russ, I need to get back. I have an appointment in the morning I can't duck. I can jump a commercial flight from here. I've seen all I need to see anyway. If they want anything from you, call me before you agree to it."

"Nonsense, Warren," said Wakefield. "Take the charter and I'll catch a commercial flight back tomorrow. It'll work out better for everybody that way."

"Thanks, Russ. Looks like you're not at great legal risk here. Your biggest headaches are going to come from Worker's Compensation, and possibly from some pro forma fines from OSHA, if they can clearly establish their authority here. Bring me anything they give you. Oh, and reassure Auvil's widow, but keep it generic. Don't make any commitments."

"Christ, Warren, that's cold-blooded. I can't just tell her everything's going to be fine and walk out."

"It's business, Russ. Just tell her that... well, tell her that she'll be contacted by your insurance people. Convey your sympathy. And don't visit her alone. Take Briggs, and try to stay until she's contacted a friend or relative. It's not your job to cut the settlement deal."

Wakefield looked away, gazed out the window, dreading the contact with Auvil's widow that he knew must come soon. He vowed to himself that the widow would be taken care of, and that Auvil's kids, if he had any, would not want for a college education.

Colonel MacCaffrey returned to the office and invited them to lunch at the Officers' Mess. Wakefield noted, as he ate, that the mess help was contract labor. KP was no more, and he felt

79

somehow very, very old.

Brigadier General Harris Donald "Don" Brockner arrived on schedule. By three o'clock he and Wakefield were seated in a small conference room adjacent to MacCaffrey's office. Brockner was young for a general, trim and fit. Wakefield read him as a hard charger, purposeful and to the point. He was one of the "New Managers" that the regular Army had held in such disdain in the not-so-distant past.

"So, what can I do for you, General?" Wakefield opened, masking his wariness. Stone had departed an hour ago. He felt naked and vulnerable without his counselor at hand.

"I've got a job for you," Brockner said without preamble. "I want you to assess and remediate a hazardous waste site."

"General, with all due respect, can we talk about it another time? The only reason I'm here is to deal with an accident we had on one of our work sites. I'm a little overwhelmed, and I don't think I'm at my best right now to evaluate a new contract."

"Please, call me Don. It's important for a number of reasons that this meeting should occur now—and here. Whether you accept or reject my offer, our contact is classified. I cannot come to your office and you may not come to mine. We have to meet on neutral turf and keep our contact to a minimum. This regrettable accident you refer to has given us the opportunity to meet with you under circumstances that conform to our requirements."

"You realize I don't have a security clearance?" Wakefield wasn't ready to call the general 'Don' yet.

"But, you do. If that work hadn't already been done, this meeting could not occur." Brockner paused to let the implications of his statement sink in.

Wakefield felt like his mind was mired in molasses. It explained how Brockner had found him here, when he hadn't known he would be here himself. They were watching him—they must have been—and he didn't like it.

"The Army has its own contractors for site remediation. Why not use one of them?"

"Simple. This, as I said, is classified. Highly classified. Army contractors," Brockner explained, "are in an environment where, if something slips, the internal damage could be difficult to control. Since your company does not work regularly for the Army, there is less likelihood of leaks within the organizational structure. Since fewer Army people will know about your work for us, fewer questions will be asked."

"Just what kind of a site is this?" asked Wakefield.

"It's an island. Sensitive research was done there two decades ago under a previous administration. Frankly, the existence of the site could be embarrassing if it became a matter of public knowledge. We want to make things right before anybody discovers they were wrong. The contamination levels, and the contaminants that might be present, are unknown.

"The first phase of the contract I am offering would be to identify the scope and nature of the contamination problem. The second phase of the work would be to assess and propose measures for remediation of the site. The third phase would be to implement those measures, as approved, to clean the site up. You do it all the time."

"I don't think you should continue, General. I don't think it's something Wakefield Environmental can do." Wakefield sensed a political minefield of unknown proportions, and his gut instinct told him to stay clear of this job. The terms and descriptions that Brockner was giving him were circumspect. They offered the illusion of substance without telling anything.

Brockner sensed he was ready to rabbit. He smiled sincerely and leaned forward in his chair. He placed his hands flat on the table.

"Hear me out, Russ. The people who contaminated this site are long gone; the reasons for its existence have long ceased to exist. We need a solid, reliable, and discreet company to close the book once and for all. The only reason this site is unique is that its existence is virtually unknown and we want to keep it that way. Frankly, we're taking enough flak as it is for the known sites."

"What about the EPA? If you're working a site anywhere, they're bound to find out. Once they know, it's a matter of public record."

"This site is unknown to the Environmental Protection Agency. In fact, few people even know the island is part of the United States' domain. No reason to change things in that regard, is there? Besides, given the conditions under which the U.S. holds the island, the EPA would probably have great difficulty establishing its authority there, even if it did find out. The place hasn't officially existed for two decades."

Wakefield looked directly at Brockner.

"Now, how can that be?" he said softly. He flashed mentally on the Marshall Islands—Eniwetok—blown out of existence by thermonuclear testing. *No way, if that's it...*

"Not what you might think," said Brockner. "Listen, I have

to be going." He shoved a nondescript, double-locked briefcase across the table toward Wakefield.

"The combinations are the first four and the last four digits of your social security number. Everything you need to know to make a decision is in there. Read it, and make up your mind. I'll be in touch to get your decision in two weeks. If you decide not to take the contract, I'll send somebody by to pick up the materials. This is for the good of the country, you know. And you're the only one we'd be comfortable with. The contract prices offered reflect that."

General Brockner rose to his feet.

"One last question before you go," said Wakefield, also rising.

"Shoot."

"How did you find me? On what basis was I selected?"

"Easy enough. The Air Force has a lot of this work going on. They have a 'preferred providers' list; contractors who have delivered outstanding services at reasonable cost, consistently. Unofficial and deniable, but it exists. I simply called the man who makes the decisions and asked him who could best do a hypothetical job. He gave me the name of your outfit."

"Colonel Davis signs my Air Force contracts. I can't believe he'd keep such a list."

General Brockner peered out from under his brow at Wakefield. "Don't be obtuse, Russ. I said the man who makes the decisions, not the man who signs the contracts. I doubt your Colonel Davis even knows who he is," he said blithely.

"I must be going. We'll be in touch. Once again, all we have discussed, and the very fact of this meeting, are confidential. Good day. I hope everything works out for you with this current problem." He drummed his manicured nails once in a staccato roll on the Formica table top as he rose, as if to confirm his departure. Wakefield found it a strange gesture. He rose out of politeness as the General left the room.

Wakefield sat down, took a few deep breaths to refocus his thoughts. Whatever was in that briefcase would have to wait. He picked it up and returned to Colonel MacCaffrey's office. MacCaffrey wasn't in, but the colonel's secretary intercepted Wakefield and told him that there was a staff car waiting to take him back to his hotel.

That night he slipped down to the hotel bar alone, for a nightcap. The self-prescribed medication would serve in part to help escape the thoughts of the briefcase the General had given him, as well as to run through a mental rehearsal of the duty which awaited him on the morrow. The briefcase nagged at him but he resisted the temptation to open it for the time being. If it were business, it would occupy his thoughts; he knew he would consider its contents in spite of himself. That wouldn't do. He needed to focus his mind on the present, on the families he must visit in the morning before he returned to Houston.

The idea of death was deeply troubling to him and having to face it with the bereaved family of his employee made him acutely uncomfortable. It wasn't that many years ago that he'd paid the fare on Charon's ferry for his lovely, vital wife. He remembered vividly how inconsolable he had been. It had shattered his life, and it had not given him the words to enable him to be of comfort to others.

Death was a coward, a sneaky knife-fighter which couldn't be overcome in the light of day—only in the long and lonely recurrent nights of grief for the loved ones Death had poached from the gardens of life.

BRADD HOPKINS

"Opportunity can often sway even an honest man."
—Latin Proverb

13

20 May, Present

Wakefield's sister, Diana, had gone to bed. Wakefield entered his study. He picked up the briefcase that Brockner had given him and placed it on his desk. He dialed in the dual combinations Brockner had given him: the first and last four digits of his own social security number. He released the fasteners and raised the lid. Inside was the massive document he had been reading for the last three nights, since his return from Abilene.

It was the contract and a description of work for what he was beginning to call in his mind the Island Project. It was stamped on every page in red ink and half-inch high letters with the word 'Secret'. Each page was serially numbered. He had copy number two of three copies, as the annotations on each page informed him. A cover letter, numbered page one, informed him in no uncertain terms of the consequences of revealing the contents to unauthorized personnel.

He reached into the briefcase and removed a similarly marked videotape. Whoever had marked this stuff was really into rubber stamps. He wondered, with amusement, if the tape would self-destruct after playing. *Your assignment, Mr. Phelps, should you choose to accept it...*

Wakefield slid the videotape into his VCR. It played forward automatically to an aerial view of a lush, green island from a distance of maybe ten miles. It squatted like a mossy-backed terrapin drifting in the electric blue waters.

So that's the island! It was small, almost tiny compared to the Florida Keys where he had vacationed. The Keys were flat; this island had some elevation. Parts of the coast were inaccessible for landing even a small craft.

The window frame of what was probably a helicopter occasionally crept into the edge of the picture. The light seemed to flutter ever so slightly as the distance shortened and the video-tape began to reveal details of the coast. He watched for almost an hour as the video presented first the coastline, then what he took to be key facilities on the island, from the air. They appeared to be long abandoned. He fanned through the documentation to find the map of the facilities he had seen during his reading of the contract documents and began matching the labeled features on the map to what he was seeing on the television screen.

There was a row of long, narrow buildings—dormitories, the map said. Nearby stood a u-shaped, two-story structure that looked like a cheap hotel. This was labeled on the map as housing the dining hall in the center and a recreation hall in one wing. Administrative offices stood across the courtyard formed by the u, in the wing opposite the rec hall.

Several hundred feet to the northwest was another building, bigger than the others, which the documentation listed as the research laboratory. There was a helipad. Down at the shore were a dilapidated dock and a small warehouse. A small steel tank sat near by: diesel fuel storage for the generators that once had provided the power to the complex.

A badly rutted dirt road connected the decrepit dock to the remainder of the compound. It was set well away from the beach and a screen of vegetation hid it from view. All the buildings were a rather dark shade of green. What remained of the roof covering was an indeterminate color. There was a curious absence of windows on all of the structures.

Behind the laboratory, and down a low hill, was what appeared to be a landfill. Some small liquid storage tanks squatted above ground to the northeast of the lab building. The problems would most surely be there. He flagged it in his mind.

Out of curiosity, and then with mounting interest, he had read the documents that accompanied this tape. The contract was the safest and most lucrative he had ever seen. The document was about an inch thick, and seemed to have been boiler-plated in his favor. The basic premise was cost-plus-twenty, with no cap on cost. With Thomas, his son, in college for a while yet, it was an attractive proposition.

Still, he pondered the downside. What if there were something illegal, or at least questionable, about the work being proposed? Why all the secrecy, unless it were to subvert the authority of the Environmental Protection Agency to regulate the site?

If he tried to pull a fast one and the EPA found out about it, he knew he could count on them to hound every job on every contract he might put a pen to. They would inundate his business in a regulatory tsunami of red tape. Good relations with the EPA inspectors, and with OSHA, were one of the foundations of his success. They could not be placed in jeopardy.

What if there were problems with very unique types of contamination with which he wasn't equipped to deal? What about the logistics of working and getting materials to a site, the exact location of which he did not even know?

Wakefield pulled a tablet out of his desk. He started jotting down the questions he wanted answered with solid, rational answers if he were to take the job. The cost-plus-twenty clause answered many of the questions he posed. In that light, the ones he couldn't answer didn't seem too ominous.

BRADD HOPKINS

14

29 May, Present

Two weeks after his meeting with Brockner, a weasel and a raccoon showed up at Wakefield's main office in Houston, unannounced, and asked Rosie for an audience with Wakefield. They wore dark suits and unimaginative, skinny ties over white Oxford shirts. Both were shod in highly shined wing-tips. They did not provide business cards, nor did they observe the usual business amenities. They remained standing even after Rosie offered them a seat. Only a gentle prod from Rosie extracted their names: Smith and Jones. They asked her to tell Wakefield that they were there to pick up General Brockner's documents.

Rosie rang Russ's office, conveyed their message, and was not particularly surprised when he agreed to see the pair. He always saw everybody if it was possible. "Mr. Wakefield will see you right away," she said brightly. "If you'd come with me…" The weasel and the raccoon glanced at each other and followed her wordlessly down the hall.

Rosie was screeching with laughter inside as she showed the unlikely pair into Wakefield's office. They were so serious. To her they looked like caricatures from an illustration in a Beatrix Potter book, or one that Beatrix Potter might have written if she had ever decided to do a children's' story on I.R.S. agents. This thought nearly doubled her over as she opened the door to Wakefield's office, but she managed to mask her mirth with a particularly bright smile as she introduced the pair. She held it in until she was a safe distance down the hall, and then wheeled into the privacy of the ladies' room, where she collapsed in convulsions of laughter.

"Mr. Smith, Mr. Jones. What can I do for you?" Wakefield knew something had gotten to Rosie, but tabled it mentally for later inquiry. He was faintly amused at how much Smith looked like a weasel, and how Jones' sunken eyes with bags under them, set widely apart in a wide, triangular, jowly face, reminded him of a raccoon.

"We're here to pick up the materials placed in your hands by General Brockner at Dyess Air Force Base two weeks ago. Or, in the alternative, to accept your signature on the proposed contact and make arrangements for you to begin work." Smith, the weasel, spoke without preamble in a nasal voice.

"Gentlemen, I've reviewed the documents. I must admit the terms are favorable. Wakefield Environmental is capable of doing the job under the terms set forth. However, I am not prepared to sign the bottom line without a visit to the proposed work site. I cannot proceed without the answers to a few questions I have about the job."

"A visit to the site is impossible until *after* you've signed the contract," said the weasel. "I'm sure you realize that the escape clause in your favor allows you to terminate the work at such time as you might wish, at any stage of completion of service on the contract. Presumably, this covers a situation where you do not wish to proceed after inspecting the site."

"Fair enough," admitted Wakefield. "Still, the site visit alone would incur an unknown, but substantial, expense. Since we're dealing with unknowns my people would require full Level A protection. That's not inexpensive, and I haven't been able to factor in transportation and staging costs, since I haven't a clue where the site is located."

"I was told the General made it clear to you that the precise location of the site would remain unknown to you. There is a further constraint of contract prohibiting any methods or devices that would enable you to discover the location, even while you are working there. It is a condition of the job."

"I was told no such thing," countered Wakefield with some irritation "How, then, am I to get workers and equipment to a place that I cannot be allowed to know the whereabouts of?" His brain winced at ending the sentence with a preposition, but he was convinced that his meaning was clear.

"You will stage at a designated location, and we will do the rest. Allow two days between the arrival of your equipment in staging and its delivery on site."

"What about medical care for the workers? What if somebody requires urgent care? We can't wait two days if one of my people gets hurt."

"The contract allows you to take what measures you deem necessary, and bill back all costs. We would expect you to be reasonable."

"What if we disagree about what's reasonable?" It was a reasonable question.

"You will be given the maximum latitude in that regard. We don't even want to see justifications on anything, any single item, under ten percent of the monthly pay-outs. Obviously, if something extreme comes up, we want you to run it by our contract administrator. He would hold an absolute veto power, which he would be instructed not to use except as a last resort. At that juncture, we would expect you to activate your bail-out option."

The taxpayers have incredibly deep pockets. These guys were giving him carte blanche.

"Who will be this contract administrator you refer to?" Wakefield felt his grammar deteriorating before his eyes, evaporating like a puddle of gasoline on a hot day.

"We have a competent person in mind. You will meet him during the site evaluation if you accept our offer."

"There's a matter of carrying expenses on a job for which, at this point, I cannot estimate scale. I have nothing on which to base any projections. While Wakefield Environmental does have some depth of financial reserve, the scenario you are painting suggests that it might be compromised before the first pay-out occurs." *Let's see how serious you guys really are.*

"We are prepared to advance $100,000 against the first month's operating expenses once the contract has been signed. We realize that there are unusual circumstances surrounding performance. The contract administrator can authorize a cash draw any time you can convince him that it's appropriate."

They're definitely serious! Where's the catch?

As if reading his mind, Jones, the raccoon, interceded for the first time. "The real issue here is the security of your operations. We recognize that it's an expensive component of the contract, and we are able and willing to pay for it.

"We will provide security personnel for all on site work. All of your people involved in the work will require security clearances and background investigations. You provide us a list; we pay to have it done to our satisfaction. If we say no to anybody, you lay them off. Even if they've been with you for twenty years."

"That's pretty stiff, don't you think?" Wakefield wondered briefly if any of his staff had skeletons in their closets that wouldn't pass muster. "Can't we just reassign any such people elsewhere in the company?"

"Sorry. They might see more than we want, just working here. Employees talk to each other. You may, however, bill back severance pay and placement costs for any such people as a matter of contract. You may, if you choose, rehire them at the conclusion of your work for us."

Wakefield didn't like being told whom he couldn't hire or retain, simply on the principle of the thing, but it was clear that they would not budge on the issue.

Wakefield tacked in a new direction, but it was an important question. "You do understand that if Wakefield Environmental signs the contract, we will conduct all operations in accordance with all pertinent federal laws, regardless of whether or not there is clear federal jurisdiction over the site? I refer specifically to matters of employee safety and health."

"Of course. We wouldn't have it any other way." The weasel was back in the driver's seat.

"Gentlemen, may I have twenty-four hours to make my decision? I want to pass this by my key people in the morning tomorrow, and I'll have my answer ready by tomorrow after lunch. I have not discussed this with anybody yet, and I'm inclined to see how my folks react before I commit them."

"Very well, Mr. Wakefield. We will accept either an executed contract, or all contract documentation in your possession at one p.m. tomorrow."

The weasel and the raccoon rose to leave, making no effort toward a cordial conclusion of a business meeting; they simply walked out of the office.

Wakefield shrugged, shook his head, and punched Rosie's number into the phone. "Rosie, please call everybody in for a very important meeting tomorrow morning at eight. I want all my regional operations chiefs here, even if they have to charter flights. Don't accept any excuses; they *must* be here. Also, ask Warren Stone to come by the house around eight tonight. Tell him it's very important, and cannot be postponed or delayed."

"Yes, sir. Can I tell them why?" The question was partly to the point, partly fishing. Little went on at Wakefield Environmental that Rosie didn't scoop, and now she was in the dark as much as anybody except Wakefield himself. Whatever it was, it was big. Flying in the regional bosses by charter would cost a bundle.

"Just tell them to be here. They will all be told at the same time."

"Yes, sir."

"Thanks. That's it." Wakefield broke the connection, and Rosie immediately turned to the task of executing his instructions, to see to the details of assembling the five men from all

92

corners of the country in less than twenty hours. Undaunted by the task, Rosie suppressed a giggle as the weasel and the raccoon passed her desk on their way out the door.

Supper that evening in the Wakefield house was tense at best. Diana knew when her brother was agonizing over a major business decision, and all the classic signs were there. The meal was silent. He hadn't touched the single bourbon on the rocks that was his custom before dinner. His answers to questions about the day seemed like recorded messages designed to provide only the appearance of communication. His attention was elsewhere. He pushed his food aimlessly around his plate, and glanced often at his watch.

At 8:10, the doorbell range, and he answered it. She recognized Warren Stone, her brother's friend and attorney for Wakefield Environmental, Inc. He was immediately ushered into the study and the study doors were closed. She wondered what was cooking, but remained tolerant of her ignorance. She knew with certainty born of a childhood with the child and nearly a decade with the man that she would have the whole story sooner or later. She could afford to be patient.

Diana had come to take care of Thomas and the house some months before Susan died. It filled a void in her life, created recently when her husband and two daughters had been killed by a freight train at one of the last remaining unsignalled grade crossings in Texas.

From that point forward, it seemed that there was nothing pressing in her life, and she doted on young Thomas with the earnest attention of a widowed aunt. She found a certain solace in her return to her care-taking role for her younger brother, Russell. Russ had been a basket case, grieving silently, angry and frustrated at his helplessness against Susan's illness. The household existed at that time under a black shroud of familial grief and loss that had only recently begun to lift.

Russ had been quietly inconsolable as he watched Susan struggle hopelessly in a losing situation. Somewhere, she had picked up chronic hepatitis. Nobody could say where, but there it was. It appeared to be controllable by persistent medication, and there was no reason not to expect her to live a long and full life.

Then, when Thomas was fifteen, she caught pneumonia. The drugs used to control the hepatitis were incompatible with the drugs required to combat her pneumonia. By that apparently inconsequential shortfall of medicinal compatibility, her fate was sealed.

The hep medications were discontinued to treat the pneumonia. Just as the pneumonia was beginning to come under control, the hepatitis would flare up. The pneumonia treatment was halted in order to stop the hepatitis, and the pneumonia reestablished itself with a vengeance. Caught like a Ping-Pong ball between the competing diseases, Susan lost ground with each change in medications. For four months she battled like a trooper, then died a week before her thirty-eighth birthday.

Somehow, Diana had never gotten around to leaving after Susan's death. It suited her and her brother that she remained to take care of the widower and his growing son. She had come to derive a certain satisfaction from her importance in both their lives, and it was a comfortable life for her.

Eventually, she knew, her brother would meet someone, and she would have to make other living arrangements. For now, however, he wasn't showing much initiative in that regard. Instead, he poured his energy into the company.

Behind the closed door of the study, Wakefield poured copious doses of straight Kentucky bourbon over ice into two Old Fashioned glasses and handed one to Warren Stone.

"What's this all about?" Stone asked after a preliminary sip.

Wakefield, still standing, set his drink down on a coaster. He opened the briefcase and gestured at the contents.

"I have a proposal in there that could make my retirement a fashionable place to be, something well beyond comfortable. I'm going to bounce it off my key people tomorrow morning and I need to come to a decision before noon. I want you to have a look at it, and tell me where the sand traps are."

"That's too fast, Russ," Stone scowled. He glanced at the document package in the briefcase; it was almost two inches thick. "Why didn't you bring me in on this sooner?"

"The job is highly classified, a remediation contract for a military facility offshore. The Army, actually. I didn't feel comfortable sharing it with anybody until I decided that it was something we might want to do. You're the only person other than me who's seen it."

"Does this have anything to do with that guy who saw you at Dyess when we were there with MacCaffrey?" Stone asked.

"That's who gave me the package and made the offer, yes," Wakefield answered.

"Interesting. Look, I can't give you a real good assessment based on the time we have right now. There's just too much there."

"Most of it is garbage, boilerplate," explained Wakefield. "But it appears that the boilerplate is largely in my favor. There's an entire section on security requirements and performance, which is procedural rather than contractually significant. I've highlighted the sections that I want you to take a look at."

"Let's do it." Stone took another drink, then set the glass aside.

Two hours later, Stone closed the document. He looked at Wakefield and smiled a tired smile, and stood. He walked over to the bar caddie and poured himself his second drink of the evening, took a sip, and returned to his chair, where he sat and leaned back. His sleeves were falling. He had removed his coat and rolled them above the elbows two hours earlier. His tie hung knotted but loose at his collar. He pinched the bridge of his nose, massaging it with his thumb and forefinger before he spoke.

"Well, unless there's something you're not showing me, this is the safest contract I've ever seen. No attorney in his right mind would ever give such advantages to a contractor. Those advantages are reasonably secure in the wording and the intent. The profit margin—and the guarantees—make it a virtual gold mine. The way it's written, you have sufficient latitude to bankrupt the federal government if you choose to... and if they weren't broke already." Stone did not smile when he said this. "I don't see how you can lose, and, frankly, I'm a little envious."

"You're reasonably certain that there are no flies in the ointment?"

"I'm never certain of *anything,* but this is about the closest I've ever come. I was worried at first by the very nature of the thing. Nobody writes a contract like this unless they expect to ignore it. But, if they do, you can back out with impunity... and a hefty profit! The security thing essentially means that they don't want a lawsuit and are liable to interpret and honor the contract terms in your favor to prevent that from happening. As I said, I think this is a gold mine, and you'll be counting your cash by the pound. They must trust your integrity more than their own mother's love."

"Take it?"

"Take it! I'll send you a bill—a *big* one—now that you can afford it." Warren slugged down the dregs of watery bourbon that remained in his glass and rose to leave.

"Thanks, Warren. I really appreciate your helping with this on such short notice." Wakefield rose, as Stone picked up his coat and headed for the door.

The next morning, Russell Wakefield arrived at the office at 7:30 a.m. and found Rosie brewing coffee in the conference room. There was a tray of Danish and a bowl of fruit on the sideboard, together with orange juice and apple juice in iced pitchers. The conference table was arranged to accommodate eight in addition to himself and he realized that the count was perfect, for he wanted Rosie, Gene Briggs, and Hector Ayala, his corporate Safety Director present in addition to his five regional directors. Yet he hadn't told Rosie his intentions, and he wondered how she knew.

"Why nine, Rosie?" he asked of her back, which was all he could see while her front side was engaged in arranging coffee cups on the sideboard.

Rosie glanced at him over her shoulder. "The meeting was rather suddenly called. If you need to add anybody at the last minute, the meeting need not be disturbed to set a new place. The table holds twelve comfortably."

"I'd like you to be here this morning. Have somebody stand in for you at reception, one of the yard men."

"Thanks, Russ. What's it all about, anyway?" Rosie would never have asked had not the invitation she had just received implicitly given her additional license.

"Hang in there, Rosie! I only want to explain it once." Russ smiled at her warmly. "I'll want your thoughts on what we'll be discussing. Your 'sense' of it as well."

"Happy to oblige."

Some of the field business unit managers began to arrive, greeting Wakefield and Rosie informally, helping themselves to coffee and pastries and juice. These were men who shared a bond of doing the same job for the same company and the banter between them was that of old acquaintances long separated, yet aware of by some indirect knowledge of developments in each others lives. "How's the new baby, Walt?" and "Hey, Hector, whatever happened on that Iowa job?" and "Did you ever finish rebuilding that old MG?" There seemed to be a tacit agreement among those present to avoid discussing the purpose of this unusual meeting.

Walter Rodgers had flown in from Redmond, Washington. He ran Wakefield Environmental's Northwest business unit, encompassing its Washington, Oregon, Idaho, Colorado, Montana and Utah operations. The Southwest business unit was comprised of California, Arizona, New Mexico, and Nevada. It was headed by Cooper Black, now on his second Danish.

Davis Esterson, who had been delayed in Midland/Odessa by weather, ran the Central division. Even though he was based at the Houston Office down the hall from Wakefield, he had been in west Texas since the beginning of the week.

Amos Roman, the oldest of the group, ran the Eastern office. His flight was due within the hour. The Northeast business unit was the fastest growing division in the company. Al Smith headed it. Between them, they directed the efforts of nearly three thousand employees and created jobs for thousands more. Hector Ayala came in, followed by Gene Briggs and Rosie, just before starting time.

Most of the men in the room had been hand picked for their jobs by Wakefield personally, based on personal and business acquaintanceship. They were all well drillers first and by trade; they became managers only if they showed aptitude.

The company's emphasis on environmental assessment and remediation was relatively new. It arose in the early seventies, when Wakefield realized that there would be a huge demand for environmental evaluation and chemical clean-up services in the coming decades. Drilling skills were only part of the picture, but these would give a strong leg up in the developing market.

Given his education in what later came to be called environmental science and his avocation as a well driller, the timing was perfect for a corporate marriage of the two disciplines, over which Wakefield officiated. He had anticipated a market that he was in a unique position to exploit. The business took off like a rocket sled.

In the early days of his success, he nearly succumbed to the classic mistake of businesses that encounter too much success too quickly. He nearly went belly up when he found the business extended beyond its cash flow and its fiscal reserves. He fell back in the nick of time, regrouped and restructured, and emerged from the trial as the undisputed leader in the field. His company now provided one-stop shopping for clients with sites contaminated by hazardous chemicals. Wakefield Environmental furnished a cradle-to-grave management of hazardous waste sites, and there were literally hundreds of thousands of such sites across the nation. Everything from leaking underground fuel tanks contaminating the groundwater under service stations to government hazardous waste disposal sites that were no longer deemed acceptable risks. With the new wave of environmental consciousness sweeping the country, the demand for his services became enormous.

There were urban dumps where discarded toxins concentrated in the voids of the covered landfill. There were mass graves of leaking fifty-five gallon drums containing all manner of particularly nasty stuff. There were industrial deposits of deadly chemicals that had been spilled, fenced, and never cleaned up because it would have been hard on the bottom line. There were aquifers and water basins loaded with ethyl benzene and deadly dioxin.

Industrial slobs, ignorant citizens, and unconcerned governments of the industrial revolution's last days assured unparalleled job security for the employees of Wakefield Environmental, Inc.

The military establishment, particularly the Air Force, proved to be the company's bread and butter. Decades of arrogant military disregard for sparse local and state waste management laws under the Sovereign Agency Doctrine had created hazardous waste sites at virtually every military installation in the nation.

Now, a ground swell of public awareness and editorial outcry had activated a flurry of catch-up legislation mandating a cleaner world. It was time to pay the piper, and Wakefield Environmental was playing the right music. Wakefield Environmental would have a bushel of business for years to come. But, conscious of their beginnings, they still drilled an occasional water well for a private citizen.

From the beginning, Wakefield had noted anyone he happened to meet who seemed to be particularly competent in the field, and he hired them away from the competition as his needs dictated. The company's compensation package, and more importantly, his own management style, operated to prevent the reverse from happening to him. Wakefield Environmental never lost a manager to a headhunter.

Wakefield called the meeting to order by welcoming everyone and thanking them for coming. Nobody wore a tie. Wakefield had a finely tuned sense of propriety and ties would be expected when meeting with clients, but here in the fold, comfort took precedence over formality and everyone dressed informally. Wakefield held a secret belief that ties cut blood circulation to the brain and impaired clear thinking, though he'd wear one whenever convention dictated. But he never made a business decision while wearing a tie.

"We have been offered an interesting piece of business," Wakefield began, "and I wanted all of you to hear about it together. If we take it, things will be wild and crazy for a while, and I need your buy-in before we proceed.

"Some of you might be away from home for quite a while if we accept this contract. We can't handle the job by hiring new managers; it will take your experience to make it work. The new guys we do have to hire may wind up filling in for you at your own business units while you're occupied with this job. If you've got an up-and-coming that you think might be ready and want to test him with some responsibility, this may be the opportunity."

Wakefield briefly described the salient elements of the contract to the group, and enumerated some of the blind spots as well. He urged them to consider the knowns, and to tolerate the ambiguity of the unknowns, justifying the latter course by explaining the escape clause in the contract. Amos Roman came in quietly, looking a little road weary, but forcing alertness. Wakefield acknowledged his arrival with a glance and a nod, and continued.

"There's one last thing before I open this up to general discussion. If any one of you has anything in your background that might interfere with obtaining a security clearance, I need to know about it. See me privately before you go back to your own business units if there is any question at all on this matter."

General discussion followed; the issue was pro'd and con'd to death by some very sharp and seasoned minds. In the end, they reached a consensus: they'd do it.

15

30 May, Present

Weasel and Raccoon arrived soon after Wakefield returned from a long lunch with Amos Roman and Gene Briggs. During the meal, Amos was apprised of the material he had missed because of his late arrival. To the old mossy-backed driller, it was just another job. The younger managers delighted in ribbing Roman—asking him how he'd ever learned to drill before there was any dirt—to which his laconic response was inevitably a derisive snort. Briggs had come in from Midland-Odessa just before noon and also needed a briefing.

They returned to the office together slightly after one p.m. Rosie announced the arrival of Messrs. Smith and Jones, and Wakefield asked Briggs to sit in. Amos wandered away to find the others and catch up on corporate gossip.

Following the obligatory round of greetings and introductions, Wakefield announced that he was prepared to sign the contract documents.

"There are a couple of other things we forgot to mention yesterday," said Weasel. The glances exchanged between Briggs and Wakefield were not missed by either of the two government agents. Weasel continued.

"First, we want you, Mr. Wakefield, to assume direct field supervision of the operations your company will be conducting on the basis of the agreement we sign today. It is a matter of covenant, and we may not proceed without your agreement in this regard."

"Agreed," said Wakefield. *There go my Sundays...*

"Second, you will stage all personnel, equipment, and material at McDill Air Force Base, in Tampa. A lay-down yard will be established there suitable to your needs. All transportation will stage from there. Workers will travel by marine transport vessel to and from the site; your key managers will have access to helicopters."

"That should be no problem," agreed Wakefield.

"Moreover, you will make no attempt to determine the precise location of the work site, and you will specifically instruct all workers to that effect. Here is a copy of the personnel transport procedures you will use. Please take a moment to read it."

Wakefield accepted a single page document that described the procedures; they seemed rather elaborate. All watches and any compasses would be confiscated during air or marine travel from McDill; the watches to be returned to their owners at their destination. Compasses would be returned to the shore base. If workers were transported by sea, they would be kept below decks until the vessel was out of sight of land. Vessel masters would be required to sign non-disclosure agreements with criminal penalties for violation. A number of other procedures imbedded in the document made it clear that they did not want anybody to locate the island. That was all right with Wakefield. It really didn't matter where the island was located. If medical care was a reasonable distance away, he could get some folks on-site for emergency care and stabilization if anyone was badly injured or became seriously ill. Wakefield looked up from the document and found Weasel waiting.

"You must sign that before we proceed," Weasel said, blinking repeatedly as if expecting a blow.

Wakefield fished a pen from the top drawer of his desk, signed and dated the sheet at the bottom, and proffered it to Weasel. Weasel handed him an unsigned copy and stuffed the signed one in his briefcase.

"Anything else?" asked Wakefield.

"Nothing but your signature on the contract. I have a cashier's check for you when that's done and instructions for beginning your work."

Wakefield signed without ceremony and accepted the check. *One hundred thousand dollars. Already in the black!* He smiled inwardly, but was careful not to show his delight.

Weasel said, "Your staging area is ready and waiting in Tampa. Contact Major Selmack, who will be your liaison for the entire job. Here is his number." Weasel handed him a card. Wakefield recognized the 305 area code. Selmack was already in Florida.

"We would like you to begin assessment operations on the job site thirty days from today. Selmack is your contact for all further action on this contract. Thank you, Mr. Wakefield, and we'll be on our way."

Wakefield rose, and they shook hands, but only because

Wakefield offered it. *These government types are something else.*

When they were gone, Wakefield handed the card to Briggs. "Call this guy. Get down to Tampa and let me know what you've got and what you need. You're in charge of our new shore base. I'll have an operational game plan to you by the end of the week, but basically, we'll go in with three level A teams and full offshore support. Plan on three-week rotations for the work crews; we'll work out the details later."

"Color me gone," Briggs replied, his west Texas twang familiar and reassuring to Wakefield's ear. "I'll get back to you as soon as I know anything." He vanished out the door and went to his office where his bags from Midland-Odessa sat in a corner behind the door, still packed.

At forty-two, Briggs was unmarried, which gave him a valuable mobility. He had the unmistakable, exaggerated skinniness of a slender man who spends a lot of time on horseback. He was slightly bowlegged. His narrow face and pointed features gave him the look of a mosquito. He was loyal and smart as a whip, soft spoken and effective. He'd been with Wakefield almost from the start.

Wakefield buzzed Rosie. "Get 'em in here! There's work to be done," he said, referring to the managers who were scattered about the building killing time and making phone calls to their respective business units while they waited for the contract rituals to be completed.

They spent the remainder of the afternoon and early evening hammering out a basic plan of operations and settling the details of the personnel changes necessary to free up the key people Wakefield wanted to have working on the job. Their early discussions were hampered by not having a name for the job, but by the end of the day one had evolved: the 'Island Job'. The whole organization swung into gear, doing what it was designed to do, with remarkably little confusion and dissonance.

BRADD HOPKINS

> *Up spake an old sailor*
> *Who had sailed the Spanish Main*
> *"Pray, put in to yonder port*
> *For I fear a hurricane.*
> *Last night the moon had a golden ring;*
> *Tonight, no moon we see."*
> —Henry Wadsworth Longfellow
> *The Wreck of the Hesperus*

16

21 August, Present

Two hundred miles east of Honduras the sub-tropical jet stream shifted to the south, and the several hundred square miles of the Caribbean Sea went dead calm. High pressure hovered and the sun blazed down on an unruffled, oily sea.

As the air heated and rose slowly across this vast expanse of open water, a slight lowering of barometric pressure would have been measurable, if there had been anyone there who cared to observe it. As more warm air drifted laterally into this local depression, it was further heated and rose, slightly faster than the air before it.

Imperceptibly, it began to form a broad-based column as the Coriolis effect imparted a slight counterclockwise spin to the rising air mass. Virtually undetectable at first, centripetal force from the spin of the rising air created even more lowering of the isobaric pressure in the region, and more warm air was drawn into the convection.

As the moisture-laden warm air rose to higher, cooler elevations, water vapor began to condense into visible clouds, adding additional mass and density to the growing momentum. The motion of the clouds as they turned counterclockwise on the convection was not yet perceptible from the surface. Only a satellite photograph showed the motion and the development of the pinwheel cloud structure to those who watched the satellites.

The pinwheel was interpreted by the National Weather Service analysts in Coral Gables, Florida, as the beginning of a tropical storm. It would be watched casually for the next twenty-four hours, then reevaluated when that time had elapsed.

Twenty-four hours later, the winds were whirling at gale force. By late afternoon, they passed the arbitrary demarcation of velocity—sixty-three miles per hour—that defined the disturbance as a "storm" on the Beaufort Scale. The hollow core of the broad, squat column of whirling air and moisture was clearly visible from the satellite. The tropical storm began to move eastward, and was given a name.

On the third day, the sub-tropical jet stream track veered back northward twenty thousand feet above the wind-whipped surface. It began to influence the motion of the air mass, much as the push of an invisible hand might increase the rotational velocity of a rotating drum. The storm began to move northward, as if running from the effects of the jet stream. Wind speeds increased and passed the arbitrary velocity that changed the storm's characterization to hurricane.

Thus Cedric was born. He turned and took a bearing for a smallish island where, in the not-so-distant past, forces of a different nature had been set in motion. Cedric would change many people's lives in many different ways as he lived out his own brief, violent existence. One of those people was named Russell Wakefield.

> *"Heavy and high buckled the sea.*
> *A cloud tall and straight has gathered...*
> *Forewarning of thunder, lightning, and wind.*
> *What we don't expect comes fearfully."*
> —Archilochos, 7th century B.C.

17

21 August, Present

They had been working at the island for over three weeks. The crystal blue water that had greeted them, and the island itself, set like a rough emerald on the line between sea and sky, were no more.

Now, the island was the barnacled back of a gray whale squatting in the surly onslaught of torrential rains from a dirty gray sky. The sea, no longer gem-like and sparkling, roiled and foamed as winds whipped it into angry froth.

Cedric was still eight hours away by the best guess of the National Weather Service as interpreted by the skipper of the *Gulf Star,* the only person there who knew the precise location of the island where she lay at anchor. Cedric had called ahead with high seas and driving, beating rains and thunder to warn of his coming.

It had been Briggs' idea to stage all initial entry and assessment operations off an anchored barge, and it was working well so far. Wakefield watched with binoculars from the bridge of the support vessel, the M/V *Gulf Star.* A 175-foot "mud boat", the *Gulf Star* was normally used for hauling crews and drilling mud to offshore oil platforms. Now, it was doing duty for berthing and mess, as well as coordination and communication functions for the operation. They had installed a helipad on the after deck with contract welders from the Tampa area hired by Briggs. A silver Aero Spatial sat idle on the helipad, lashed down against the vessel's heaving motion.

The motor vessel *Gulf Star* was leased with master and four crewmen, on contract from its owners in New Orleans for thirty dollars per foot per day. The barge was flat-rated at eight hundred a day; Wakefield could feel the meter running as he watched the first day's operations. He still hadn't made the mental adjustment that would allow him to see the profit rather than the expense, and had to consciously remind himself of that fact.

The barge had been set without incident at a three-point anchor in a leeward bay at the island, just off the old dock and warehouse. When they first arrived at the island, the cove had seemed snug and protected, a shallow bite out of the coastline on the sheltered side of the island. Now the barge was straining at its moorings.

It had arrived ready to go, having been fitted out at what they were coming to call Tampa Shore base for the job it was to do. In Tampa, Briggs had one of his people fabricate a long floating ramp, similar to those used in boat marinas, which was affixed to the "dirty" side of the barge.

At the other end of the barge—the "clean" end—a portable building had been anchored to weld points in the steel deck. The building housed the laboratory and sheltered the technicians who evaluated the results of the sampling being done to determine the type and nature of any chemical contamination present.

At the dirty end, a second building provided a combination of shower facilities, laundry, storage, and locker space for the three entry teams. The space amidships between the two structures was an organized confusion of air manifold packs, cable spools, pumps, heaters, dryers, spare parts, compressors, and virtually anything else that might be needed and could be stored outdoors. Everything was tied, bolted or welded down. The bargemen systematically checked the anchors to make sure they would hold secure against the coming weather.

As he watched the activity on the barge from the bridge of the *Gulf Star,* he heard the helicopter start up. He turned to look aft and almost bumped into Captain Mihailish, the master of the vessel.

"Oh! Excuse me. Hello Skipper. Where's the helicopter going?" queried Wakefield.

"We're in for a blow. I sent him to land before it gets dark. If it gets thick, I don't want that beastie on my afterdeck, no matter how well it's tied down. Neither does the pilot."

They both turned to watch the Orange entry team, in fully encapsulating chemical protective suits making its way down the ramp, which swayed and plunged roughly in the choppy water. The four men of team Orange, bright yellow dots at this distance, were on their way to an aluminum landing craft which would ferry them back to the barge for ritual decontamination after their foray ashore.

The Blue team had returned an hour earlier. Their instruments had found nothing, which was expected. The inter-tidal zone and the beach were not areas likely to hold contamination; nonetheless, their assessment was necessary to rule out the possibility.

On the Blue team's return, they had tried to disembark the landing craft by dropping the bow gate onto the float platform Briggs had designed. The technique had not worked. The swells, even in the relatively calm water of the cove, created too much conflicting movement between the barge and the landing craft.

The lowered bow gate would rise above the platform and then slam down onto it forcefully The landing craft danced on the waves with greater mobility than the ponderous barge, which moved hardly at all. The configuration had a high potential for breaking bones, especially in view of the restrictions on vision and movement imposed by the level A 'moon suits' worn by the entry teams. Now, under the direction and scrutiny of Hector Ayala, Orange team boarded the landing craft over its starboard rail. It was still a cumbersome operation in the suits, but at least the direction of motion on the disparate vessels was along the same axis, less violent, and safer.

Wakefield watched them land. The pier itself was unusable. Damaged by previous storms, it was in a state of decay and disrepair and not to be trusted.

Using air-sampling instruments over the two weeks, they had expanded the demarcation line of safe area. It now included a large concrete slab that remained near the foot of the old pier, and part of the beach road to the old recreation hall. From their beachhead at the crumbling concrete slab, monitoring operations had expanded the safe area to include the office complex Wakefield had first seen on Brockner's videotape. Wakefield could hear the routine communications of the radio-equipped entry teams. Things sounded good so far, but it was time to pull back and wait out the storm.

Orange team turned a few shovels full of sand at the high tide line and checked for contamination. They found nothing obvious, and captured some samples for more sophisticated analysis at the floating lab on the barge.

The voice of Hector Ayala, supervising the entry of the level A teams, came on the radio.

"Orange team leader, this is Safety." Ayala used Incident

Command System protocols for his communications. Key players were designated by function in clear, predefined roles, not by name or corporate position. Authority was conveyed by his assigned position within the Incident Command System rather than his rank in the Wakefield Environmental organization.

"Go ahead, Safety, for Orange team leader."

"Time to pull out. Your air time is at its limit for safe exit from the area."

Ayala was referring to the bottled air supplies in the self-contained breathing apparatus worn inside each of the totally encapsulating chemical protective suits. Although they were using air bottles rated for one hour, they had only a few minutes to work before they had to be extracted.

A supply of bottled pressurized air was retained as a safety factor to allow them time to exit the area and be decontaminated while remaining inside the suits. If something went wrong, this margin might just save a life or prevent an injury. The suits were fitted with connection ports for umbilical air, with attachment hoses hooked to a bank of air cylinders on the landing craft. They were on the clock for air supplies until they were back aboard it.

"Safety, this is Orange team. We copy. We are exiting the hot zone."

Wakefield watched from the bridge as the team, in pairs because Ayala was using the 'buddy system', moved back toward the landing craft at the beach. The operation was going smoothly so far, despite the rising wind and rain. It looked as though they had some good people on the entry teams. They moved in the slow and deliberate manner that was second nature to anyone with experience in level A suits, much like astronauts.

They looked like Pilsbury doughboys, or Michelin Men, with their suits capturing the pressure of their exhaled air. The slight positive pressure this created inside the suit was additional insurance against the intrusion of unwanted gases or liquid contaminants they might encounter.

As the last man of Orange team stepped up onto the old breakwater, Wakefield watched in horror as a freak gust of the rising wind caught the ballooning protective suit like a sail. It slammed the man down backwards off the seawall.

Hector saw it, too, from his vantage on the barge off shore, and knew the man was hurt. It was confirmed when he remained down. The radio in the wheelhouse of the *Gulf Star* crackled as he called for the paramedics who were berthed somewhere on board the vessel.

"Gulf Star, Gulf Star, this is Safety! We have a man down on the entry crew. Get the medics onto the beach!"

"We saw it, Safety. The medics are being alerted right now." Captain Mihailish was already at the microphone.

Wakefield threw on his oilskins, grabbed a portable radio from its charger on the bridge, and made his way hastily to the stern of the *Gulf Star,* where a Zodiac was being loaded with medical and rescue equipment. He approached one of the frantically working paramedics.

"I'm going in with you," he yelled over the wind.

The medic hesitated, then nodded, and gestured him into the rubber inflatable. Its outboard motor was already idling strongly. He tossed Wakefield a personal flotation device, which Wakefield donned. The seas were surprisingly violent as Wakefield climbed aboard the little rubber craft, and he nearly pitched headlong into the transom before he could get a grip against the surge. The *Gulf Star* was standing at anchor in deeper water, well off the shallow draft barge, out of the cove's protection.

The medics jumped in and cast off, moving as fast as was safe across the churning water toward the beach. The bottom of the Zodiac pounded irregularly against the crests of the waves, jarring Wakefield's eyeteeth. The rain whipped his face. He lowered his chin to his chest and turned away from the stinging, driving spray.

They landed roughly, met by the remaining members of the Orange team. Wakefield followed the medics up the beach, lugging his fair share of the equipment they had brought. He ordered Orange team to return to the barge immediately. They reached the injured man, and began their work as darkness approached.

Wakefield did not flinch as they cut away the five thousand dollar protective suit the man was wearing with bandage shears. They cut the straps of his breathing apparatus and removed the air bottle from the man's back.

He was conscious and alert, soaked in perspiration despite the cold wind. He complained that he had landed on his back with his air tank directly behind his spine, and couldn't feel his legs.

The lead medic looked up at Wakefield. "We can't take him back to the ship across the rough water. He may have a broken back, and the ride might paralyze him for life, or even kill him."

"Well, we can't get the chopper in here in this weather. What about getting him inside one of the old buildings and out of the weather, at least?" Wakefield had to shout to be heard against the howling wind. It seemed to blow his words away before they could be heard.

"Where are they?"

"About a quarter mile up that road!" shouted Wakefield. He gestured toward a muddy track that crawled up a short hill to disappear into the overgrowth.

"Are they safe?" This was the first time ashore here for the medics. They knew there was potential danger on the island, but had no idea to what degree they might be at risk.

"Better than here!" hollered Wakefield over the storm. It would mean entering an area that had not yet been declared safe, but Wakefield had assessed the risks. So far, during three weeks of work, the sampling teams had not discovered one iota of contamination any more hazardous than old, weathered diesel fuel. Furthermore, they would be moving into the buildings that had served as habitation during the island's occupation. These areas had substantially less likelihood of containing dangerous residual contamination than, say, the laboratories. Also, it had been a long time since any new contaminants had been added to the risk—time for nature to do a little detoxification where it may have been necessary.

The bottom line was that if they didn't take shelter, they would all be at greater risk from the storm than from anything they were apt to find in the old recreation hall. Nothing was a sure thing; you assessed the risks and played the odds.

"Let's go!" Wakefield shouted, gesturing toward the old road.

"We'll get him on a backboard," responded the medic. "We'll have to carry him."

Wakefield momentarily regretted having sent Orange team back, but there was nothing to be done for it. The medics strapped the injured man onto the backboard and placed him in a Stokes basket, a tubular steel and wire mesh rescue carrier designed for moving non-ambulatory patients during rescue.

By the time they'd carried the man up the hill on the muddy road and reached the old recreation center, Wakefield was very clear in his own mind that he wasn't as young anymore as he used to be. As they kicked in a door and entered the old building, dripping with rainwater and covered to the knees in mud, the cessation of the wind and rain provided a sudden and welcome calm.

They found a relatively dry spot on the windward side of the recreation hall and they set down their patient. The plaster on

NAVASSA

the old walls was greenish and crumbling. The open, empty room smelled musty and dank. Every noise echoed hollowly, even above the howling wind and drumming rain outside.

"Find the driest spot and make him comfortable. I'll contact the ship," Wakefield instructed the medics unnecessarily.

"Not a chance!" the skipper told him when he radioed to ask about getting back aboard the *Gulf Star.* "The storm's really getting bad. We're pulling the hook and heading for deeper water, to ride her out under power. We'll come back in for you when the blow's over. The hurricane's turned, and it's headed straight for the island. You'll just have to sit it out. Your man, Ayala, barely managed to pull the barge crew off. It may not last the night at its moorings."

There was no need to tell the medics and the injured man the news; they had heard everything. The medics went about the task of setting an IV up for the injured man.

"Mr. Wakefield," said one, "we'll need drinking water. You might see if you can find something to catch some rainwater."

It was nearly dark and difficult to see inside the old hall. Wakefield hastened to find some sort of container to catch the rainwater, falling in wind-driven sheets with amazing force. He was unable to locate anything even remotely resembling an intact container, and returned to inform the medics. One emptied a plastic bottle of the saline IV solution it contained, and stuck it outside under a stream of runoff from the dilapidated roof. He rinsed the bottle, then let it fill and replaced the cap.

"It'll have to do..." he said wryly, looking at the others. Wakefield was struck with the absurdity of anyone being thirsty in the midst of the plentiful downpour of the storm, but did not smile.

Dawn arrived without fanfare, barely distinguishable from the blackness of the night. The full force of the hurricane had hit the island around two in the morning, and Wakefield had thought the roof would blow off. Somehow, it held.

He had waited in the darkness for the period of surrealistic calm that he'd heard described by people who had been at the eye of a hurricane. It never happened. The wind persisted, whistling around the eaves, banging a door somewhere in earshot, without abating. They were cold and wet and very hungry, but as the pitch of the night moved imperceptibly to gray it appeared that they were going to survive.

The medics took turns throughout the night watching and tending to their patient. As the night progressed, their murmured conversations assumed a worried tone. They began checking the patient more frequently, evidenced by the occasional flash of a diagnostic light in the darkness. They'd used up their last bag of saline solution in the IV kit and the patient was going into shock.

One of the medics scrambled over to Wakefield.

"Unless we get him out of here, he might not make it," he said in hushed tones to Wakefield. He fought to keep his teeth from chattering as he explained; they were all cold and wet.

"He apparently received a blow to the cervical spine when he fell. He's been going into neurogenic shock since before midnight. We didn't catch it. The cervical collar we installed prevented further injury, but the injury itself had already occurred. It's messing with his ability to regulate his peripheral circulation. He's getting colder, and real shocky. We're starting to get a drop in his blood pressure, which means he's in serious trouble. We've got no way to keep him warm."

"We can't leave. Nobody can come to us. Do the best you can."

"It's just damn frustrating, sir. He'd be fine if we could have gotten him to a doctor right away. As it is, I'm not sure he'll make it."

"Don't blame yourself. This storm can't last forever, and he's not gone, yet... do whatever you can."

The medic nodded and went back to his patient. The other medic stripped to his underwear and crawled under the flimsy paper blankets covering the injured man in an attempt to warm him with his own body heat.

The light was better now, but it remained gray and angry outside. Wakefield got up from where he had been trying unsuccessfully to sleep and began to move around, to stop the shivering and work the stiffness from his bones. He decided to do a little exploring.

He walked to the door at the end of the great hall and opened it. It led to a corridor with doors along each side. Offices. He entered each one, and looked around. There was no furniture, just an occasional wood packing crate, and not much of anything else. Rain penetrated the rotting roof here and there, dripping from the ceiling into black puddles on the floor with an eerie 'ploit' sound that echoed down the barren corridor. Debris hung from the rotted ceiling and littered the floor, along with shards of glass from windows shattered during earlier storms. Vegetation had gained a foothold at the base of those windows that had been broken long enough for windblown dust and leaves to settle and accumulate. Vines crawled through the

NAVASSA

empty windows like slithering green snakes. The feeling of the place was of long absence of its occupants, of desolate deterioration and disrepair. And mold. The smell of mold was everywhere.

He wandered into an office that was larger than the rest and walked over to a window. In this room all the windows were intact; it seemed to be protected from the force of the storm raging outside by its orientation toward an interior courtyard formed by the wings of the building.

The decay was tangible in the air. The stark sense of forlorn abandonment in the empty rooms began to play on his thoughts. He gazed out into the gray rain and wondered if it was worth it. He thought of Susan, and of Thomas, of how little time he had spent with them, and how little he would see of Tom now that he was in college.

It seemed that in his efforts to provide well for them he had failed to provide the one thing they most sorely needed—the presence of a participating father and husband. It had been work, always work. When he looked up from the work, his beloved wife was lost to him forever, and the kid was in college.

He loved Thomas with an intensity that he could never express; an intensity that included, in some fashion, the love for his wife that could now no longer be shared with her. He thought of Thomas who so much resembled his Susan it made his heart ache and who was now his only hope for some small degree of immortality through grandchildren. Where had life gone?

He shook himself and moved brusquely away from the window to leave the room. This place was depressing. It invited thoughts of isolation, and feelings of despair.

As he turned away, he glimpsed what appeared to be a rusted coffee can, exposed in a wall where the rotting plaster had molded and crumbled away from an old ventilation screen. Remembering his need of the previous evening for some sort of a container, he retrieved it.

It was sealed with a tight-fitting metal lid and seemed sound enough to hold water. He shook it. Something rustled inside. He moved into an adjacent office where he sat on an old packing crate and wrestled the lid free.

There were papers inside, old and stained, starting to deteriorate from the bleach that made them white over a decade past. He began reading a memo typed on official U.S. Army government stationery.

It was dated May 7, 1977, addressed to a General Thomas Martindale from a Doctor Paulus Harwiczki.

115

As he read in the dim light of the open window, his blood chilled and his heart surged with adrenaline shock. He quickly replaced the papers and the lid on the can. Any desire for further exploration of the facility evaporated. He returned hurriedly, the coffee can under his arm, to the desolate refectory hall where his companions waited, in ignorance of his horror. He tried to regain his composure, tried to deny the conclusion that had immediately leapt to his mind. If the memo were true, they could be in great danger—and there was no reason to believe that it wasn't.

18

23 August, Present

The *Gulf Star* moved back into the shallow cove that evening. The radio, mute now for almost twenty-four hours, abruptly crackled with a hail from the *Gulf Star* as Mihailish, the vessel's master, asked Wakefield how they had fared. He was surprised to learn that the injured man was dead. He sent a launch and party ashore instantly to retrieve the castaways on the island and recover the body.

The members of the landing party were sobered to learn that Avery Douglas, the Orange team fellow, had died. They brought sandwiches and hot coffee for the three remaining men, who numbly wolfed the chow down while Douglas' body was zipped into a black bag and covered with a canvas, to be carried down the muddy jeep road to the waiting launch.

The sun blazed from a sky of clear and transparent blue as the launch cut the glassy water on the return trip to the *Gulf Star*. Wakefield and the medics shivered uncontrollably as the warmth of the rays penetrated and began to warm their cold bodies. It seemed as if the weather was intent on making them forget its wanton misbehavior of the previous twenty-four hours, as if the sun burned brighter in an apology for its absence during the storm.

Back aboard the *Gulf Star*, showered and nearly normal again, Wakefield made arrangements to fly home the following morning. After briefing Hector Ayala with the details of the accident, he retired to his cabin where he re-read the memorandum from the coffee can and the additional documents that had been stowed there.

As he absorbed the full implications of the documents he began to grow sick. This island had been a germ warfare research facility. What if... what if there were still microorganisms around? What if his men started getting sick from germs their bodies had never seen before? What if *he* had caught something during his unprotected overnight stay in the facility? As the full potential of the information began to emerge in his whirling mind, he stumbled into the private head in his cabin, and was violently ill.

Pale and numb, he took the crumbling documents to the copier in the signal room and made copies of the originals. These he placed in plastic covers, and inserted into a manila 9 x 12 envelope. As he left the signal room, he ran straight into Bill Selmack. Although Selmack had left his major's rank ashore and was "Bill" to everyone aboard, Russ Wakefield hadn't forgotten why he was there.

Selmack's unremarkable face was covered with residual scars from what must have been a horrible bout with acne in his youth. Every visible inch of it was pocked and cratered like the surface of the moon. He had an athletic, almost simian build, and had learned early in life to stand erect and move crisply. Slow movements and slouching amplified the simian look to the point that it had drawn ridicule from his schoolmates as a youth.

The man had a ready and engaging smile that instantly set people at ease, and a bright, friendly, masculine voice that made others listen to his words. In Wakefield's mind, however, he was still an unknown quantity.

"Russ! You feel O.K.?" he asked with concern, noticing the pallor and lack of animation of Wakefield's face. "You look like hell." He did not add that Wakefield smelled like hell, too; he fairly reeked of having been ill.

Wakefield took a deep breath and tried to pull himself together. "I'm fine. Just tired from that business last night." He wondered if the tremor he felt in his voice showed through the mask of friendliness that he had assumed for Selmack's benefit. Selmack was the last person Wakefield wanted to know what was in the brown envelope he carried.

"Must have been rough," Selmack offered sympathetically.

"It was," Wakefield attested. "I'm heading in tomorrow, if we can fly."

"Probably not a bad idea. Who's going to run the show while you're gone?" It was a matter of concern to Selmack as liaison and general agent of the clients, Wakefield realized.

"I hadn't thought of it," Wakefield answered lamely. He realized his mistake and tried to minimize it. "I'll have Amos Roman come out on the return flight from Tampa Shorebase. He's a good man. You'll like him. Old mossy-back. Meanwhile, Hector can handle things."

"Good. Listen, take care of yourself. Get some sleep. You

really *do* look like hell."

Wakefield returned to his cabin and breathed a sigh of relief when he'd locked the door behind him. He put the manila envelope into his briefcase and lay down on the bed, trying to calm his mind enough to get some rest. He tried closing his eyes, but it didn't seem to be working. He was exhausted, and yet his mind wouldn't let go of the terrible matter of the island's historic use.

He understood clearly now Brockner's seemingly paranoid insistence on security measures, which he had previously viewed as mostly *pro forma,* a puzzling by-product of military paranoia. He also knew that he had to move very carefully in acquiring the information necessary to evaluate the job in its new light. If he simply pulled out when everything was going so well, the death of Douglas notwithstanding, it would raise questions...

He needed to talk to Warren Stone very badly.

The French-made Aero Spatial arrived an hour after dawn the following morning, setting down smoothly on the stern of the *Gulf Star,* its three-bladed rotor remarkably quiet and stable. Wakefield ran quickly across the pad, beneath the whirling blades, crossed in front of the pilot, and climbed in. He buckled his seat belt, donned the headset and adjusted its volume as he nodded to the pilot. They lifted smoothly from the helipad, the pilot's hand barely moving on the controls. Wakefield kept his briefcase on his lap.

"How did you fare in the storm?" Wakefield asked the pilot once they were safely airborne and moving across the water.

"Got out in the nick of time," answered the pilot. "The storm missed Guantanamo completely. The bird stayed warm and dry."

Guantanamo! The island is near Cuba, within easy range! Wakefield thought. He peered at the pilot to see if he had realized his slip. Apparently not. He knew the pilot was military, despite the Hawaiian-print shirt and designer sunglasses he wore. To leave the flying to civilians would have been to compromise the great dark and guarded secret of the location of the island.

"That's nice. I really appreciate being able to leave so soon after the storm."

"No problem. Couldn't ask for better flying weather." They were blazing along at three thousand feet, at an air speed of just over a hundred and twenty knots. Their heading was 45 degrees by the compass. Wakefield could read the instruments from his seat beside the pilot.

"What happened to the storm?" Wakefield wanted to know.

"It just kept moving east. Hit a few places, just nicked Port-au-Prince, but missed most of the inhabited ones. Good that it did, too. It would have been a killer if it had moved onto the mainland."

"How does this helicopter handle?" asked Wakefield, anxious to keep the conversation alive while the pilot was talkative. Pilots loved to talk about their aircraft. "She feels smooth as silk."

"Nice, generally. She can be tricky as hell on landings, especially on uneven surfaces in crosswinds. The belly shape is rounded, and it reacts strongly to reflected rotor down draft when it gets close to the ground. Gotta' watch her then. It'll push her sideways just before touch-down."

Wakefield nodded and murmured acknowledgment, but was at a loss for further comment. As if sensing his desire to keep chatting, the pilot spoke again.

"In the pocket at the side of your seat, you will find a black shroud on a headband. Please put it on for the remainder of the flight."

Wakefield looked at him.

"Sorry, my instructions . . . " the pilot answered the unspoken question without returning the glance or making eye contact. Instead, his eyes searched the instrument panel as if he were looking for a serious malfunction, then returned with equal concentration to the sea below them, and then scanned instinctively the airspace around them. Wakefield saw how it was. He donned the shroud.

Wakefield spent the rest of the flight to Tampa Shore base in a darkened world with his eyes behind a densely woven, light fabric shroud, hearing the beat of the rotors and the whine of the engine. He saw only the subtle flicker of light in his peripheral vision as the blade movement cut the sunshine. Conversation seemed to be blocked by the simple mechanism of the shroud. Wakefield felt as if he were a bird in a covered cage.

When the pilot finally instructed him to remove the shroud, Tampa was in sight ahead of them. They were coming in from the southeast.

19

24 August, Present

General Brockner's home phone in Idaho Falls rang at 3:30 a.m., but it was well after breakfast where the call originated. The duty officer at command headquarters had the military operator patch the call through to Brockner's residence when it came in off the satellite network. Brockner snapped awake when he heard Major Selmack's voice.

"This is not a secure line, Major. What is it?"

"Wakefield knows something."

"What? How can that be?"

Selmack described the events of the preceding two days at the island. He gave an assessment of Wakefield's behavior after coming back aboard the *Gulf Star.*

"How can you be so sure? Maybe he was upset because of losing that guy. He seemed to be upset at Dyess when I talked to him there. Same situation."

Selmack didn't bother to mention that he had excelled in kinesics, the interpretation of body language and gesture, during his academy days. All operatives received the class, but few equaled Selmack in native skill. He was convinced that Wakefield's behavior marked an internal emotional event substantially more significant than the death of an employee.

"I don't think so, sir," Selmack replied deferentially. "I think he was worried beyond that. He left a few minutes ago, three days before his scheduled rotation."

"He's gone?" Worry edged into Brockner's voice.

"Yes, sir," replied Selmack. "He choppered out a few minutes ago." Selmack was getting tired of telling this idiot everything twice, but kept it from his voice.

"Why didn't you stop him, damn it? If he *does* know something we can't let him tell the world! Why didn't you hold him there where you could find out what he does know?"

"If he only suspects, and I'd stopped him, he would have

confirmation. This way is better." *What an arrogant asshole,* Selmack thought to himself. He ran his right hand through his thinning hair as his left hand gripped the handset tighter.

"Where's he headed?"

"The signalman heard him make reservations for Houston Hobby from Tampa. I think he's headed home."

"We've got to find out what he knows."

"I'll take care of that from this end," said Selmack. "I'll keep you posted."

"Do that, Major. Don't do anything drastic without checking with me first."

"Yes, sir. Just the usual, for now."

"Thank you, Major." Brockner hung up the receiver.

Selmack depressed the cradle button and redialed the satellite access code, then the number of his operations office chief. He ordered a tail from Hobby Field in Houston to be in place when Wakefield deplaned, and phone taps to be placed on Wakefield's office and residence.

"Put Brian Olmstead in charge and have him call me here. I can't do it myself; Wakefield knows me. Tell Brian that he can use whatever resources he needs. I'm giving this Priority One.

"Ask Brian if he can get the house bugged before Wakefield gets back," continued Selmack into the receiver. "We need to know what he tells his sister."

Selmack put the phone down and stepped outside the communications room, waving to the signalman standing down the companionway, waiting to return to his post. He'd thrown the man out brusquely only minutes before. Now he flashed him a copy of the winning, easy Selmack smile.

"Sorry. It was critical, and I needed to make sure it remained confidential. Thanks for not making a fuss." The smile came again, and the signalman thought that maybe he'd over-reacted in feeling hostility when Bill had suddenly ejected him from his domain.

"It surprised me, Bill. That's all."

"How do you take your coffee? I'll fetch you up a cup from the galley. My way of saying thanks."

> *Everybody's talkin' 'bout them worrisome bugs*
> *But ain't nobody doin' nothin' about 'em.*
> —Lacy Dalton

24 August, Present

Russ Wakefield knew he was back in Houston, and that it was late August, before he left the plane. As he approached the forward door of the Boeing 737-300 that had flown him there from Tampa, the heat and humidity combination that only southeast Texas can generate hit him like a wall. The bugs were bad this year—the worst anybody could remember, everybody was saying—but it was good to be home.

Gripping his briefcase, he walked up the accordion gangway and into the terminal, heading straight for baggage claim and ground level where Diana would be waiting for him. He had called her by air phone as soon as the plane was airborne out of Tampa and given her his scheduled arrival time and flight number.

Down the concourse, he spotted a bank of phones, and stopped, fishing in his trousers for change. He found a quarter and dialed Warren Stone's office.

Across the corridor, a clean-cut college student wearing jeans and a Dallas Cowboys sleeveless sweatshirt watched him closely without appearing to look directly at him. The kid was sipping a huge coke from a waxed paper cup. As Wakefield began to dial, the kid ambled slowly up to the phone bank and picked up a receiver of the phone next to Wakefield's. He, too, fished for change, but more slowly, holding his coke in one hand while he searched one pocket, then shifting the coke to his other hand in order to look in his other pocket. Wakefield ignored him as Stone's receptionist answered the phone.

"Bixler, Messer, Stone, and Yamata," she said brightly.

"This is Russ Wakefield," he said, confirming what the college student already knew. "Can I talk to Warren?"

"I'm sorry, Mr. Wakefield. Mr. Stone is still out to lunch." Wakefield glanced at his watch. It read two twenty-five. *A little long on the old lunch hour, Warren?* "Would you please have him call me at home as soon as he comes in? It's important."

"Yes, sir. I'll tell him. Would you care to speak with anyone else?"

"No, thanks. Please just have him call me. He has the number."

Wakefield hung the phone in its cradle and walked on down the corridor without glancing back. Had he glanced back, he would have seen the college student making a phone call of his own.

The college kid, who was actually thirty-two years old and long since graduated from college, punched in a number with a speed born of familiar use.

"Olmstead," answered a voice at the other end.

"Our boy is in town. Went straight for a pay phone, called somebody named Warren. The number was 345-88 and I missed the last two numbers, 'cause he turned away from me."

"Good work. That only leaves us less than ninety nine numbers to check for a Warren." There was no sarcasm in Olmstead's voice. This was better information than he could have hoped for. Tracking down the last two digits would be a piece of cake.

"It's somebody he calls often; he didn't look the number up. Check his old phone bills."

"Sometimes the short way is the long way," Olmstead intoned philosophically. Ma Bell, he knew from experience, wasn't all that cooperative, even when you flashed a badge and uttered the magic words 'A matter of National Security . . . '

"Come on in and change clothes." He broke the connection.

Wakefield reached the curb and spotted the idling Lexus, double-parked. They had discovered that it saved a lot of hassle if Diana didn't meet him at the arrival gate, but rather spent her energies trying to time a curbside pick-up so that the airport gendarmes did not get too upset. Mostly, it worked well.

He leaned down into the passenger side window and greeted her fondly. She had a knack for looking cool and crisp, even in this wretched, wilting heat. She was slender, svelte, and leggy and was often mistaken for much younger than her forty-six years. She wore her currently blond hair in a Julia Roberts cut, short and simple, casually elegant.

Her coloring allowed her to change hair color easily, which she did at a whim. Then, just when he became used to blond, she went jet black. Her large hazel eyes had just enough yellow in them to get away with it. The effect was exotic. Wakefield wondered that she had never remarried, but had never questioned her directly about it. She had never offered an explanation.

She was in no single feature pretty, but her triangular face, classic cheek bones, and a nose slightly too large for her face combined into a composite that was uniquely handsome and sexy at the same time. He threw his bag and briefcase into the back seat of the Lexus, and climbed into the passenger seat in front.

"I didn't expect you back until Saturday," she offered, flashing him a smile of even white teeth—the dentist called them 'cute teeth'—as she dropped the lever into drive and moved off from her illegal parking place. "Everything O.K.?"

"Guy got killed."

"Oh, Russ . . . " Diana's tone was sympathetic. "How awful! Who was it?" Her voice lowered as she realized it could be somebody she knew. "Not one of the company guys . . .?"

"No . . . no! New hire for the Island job. It's been a bad year." Wakefield sighed, thinking back to the Dyess Air Force Base incident. He shook it off. They drove north on Highway 35 for a few minutes, toward downtown. Wakefield preferred flying into Hobby Field, even though Houston Intercontinental was closer to home by half an hour. Hobby had personality.

"Your son is home. He says he has someone he wants you to meet." Diana passed the information on with mock nonchalance.

Wakefield turned toward his sister, raising his eyebrows. "Have you met her?" he asked. This was good news. Secretly, he had been a little worried about Thomas, although never seriously enough to give it voice. There had not been a flurry of dating and no parade of coeds when Thomas discovered girls. Other things, little things, insignificant alone but worrisome when taken together, had fueled his unspoken concern. He inevitably dismissed the concern when he applied his conscious mind to it. He had chalked it up to Thomas' restrained nature.

"No. Thomas is being really secretive. He won't even tell me her name until they come out on Saturday. I'm dying of curiosity!"

"Why aren't they staying at the house? We're not prudes. We know how things are with his crowd today."

"They're staying with friends. She must be special for him to make such a deal of it. I guess we'll just have to wait and see."

As they neared their driveway, Wakefield noticed a delivery van parked across the street from their house. *Odd time for a van to be here...* Then, he noticed that the left front tire was flat, and gave it no further thought. The unassuming, drab sedan that had been following the Lexus since it left the airport did not even turn down the street and drive by the house. There was no need.

As pleased as she was to have him home a few days early, Diana sensed that there was more to his withdrawn demeanor than the death of a worker. She wondered if there were other problems with the job that he wasn't telling her. She knew that eventually he would tell her what was going on, and so bided her time. She keyed the electronic garage door opener, and the door moved up and away.

21

25 August, Present

"Dad, this is Roger."

Russ Wakefield's weekend had gone from bad to worse, and capped a bad week as well. On the night of his return, he had told Diana over coffee in the wee hours of the morning about the man's death on the island. She had comforted and reassured him, wondering what was eating at him at some even deeper level that he was not sharing. They finally called it a night and left for their respective bedrooms, leaving the coffee service for morning. Wakefield fell into an exhausted sleep, with a sense of safety at being home.

Early the following morning, as he sipped freshly squeezed orange juice on the patio in his bathrobe, he made his decision. His mind was clearest in the early morning, and the terrace behind the house was his favorite place to think. The sunlight soaked through the chill; small birds were calling and flitting briskly about the yard. The air was cool and satisfying to breathe. By noon, the birds would be still and the air stultifying. Diana joined him on the terrace, taking a seat with a mug of freshly brewed coffee in her hand. He nodded to her in familiar greeting, sipped his orange juice, and spoke.

"You remember what I told you last night about the night I spent on the Island when the man died?"

Diana nodded, then looked directly into his eyes.

"There's more. And I think maybe it's even dangerous to share it with you."

"Nonsense, Russ. We can share anything. You know that."

"I found something when I was roaming in the old offices. I don't think anybody was supposed to find it, and it scares the hell out of me. I brought it home. It's in my briefcase. I need to know what you think. Wait here while I get it."

He returned to the patio with his briefcase, opened it and removed some papers, handing them to Diana. He had brought with him her reading glasses. These were new accessories for her; only recently had she realized that her arms were no longer of sufficient length to read a printed page. He sat close to her while she read, looking over her shoulder as though the words would change if only he could read them enough times.

She finished reading and looked up at her brother, removing her glasses. "I don't get it. It's just a resignation letter from some doctor with an unpronounceable name. He objects to testing something, SK-443, on human populations. Why does it scare you? We don't even know what SK-443 is."

"It's some kind of a weapon. It must be. A chemical agent, perhaps. Look at the letterhead. Army Chemical, Biological, Radiological Command. If the doctor felt strongly enough about it to resign over the possibility of testing it, it was serious.

"What if there is contamination at the island? What if we are being exposed to some unknown agent during the clean-up, something we can't detect? Something we're not even looking for? Agent Orange or worse . . . "

"Why don't you call that guy, what's his name? Brockman? The one who hired you. Why don't you ask him what it is, and if there's any danger?"

"Brockner. You read the document that was attached to the letter. The doctor was worried that they would test it, no, that they *intended* to test it, on human populations. What if they did! Brockner isn't going to cop to it."

"So, what are you going to do?"

"I'm going to pass it by Warren Stone on Monday morning and see what he thinks. It's all I can think of to do right now. Meanwhile, when are the kids coming?" The third document, the one that described SK-443, remained inside the briefcase. Wakefield gathered up the others his sister had been reading and slipped them into the briefcase.

"One o'clock. Thomas seemed nervous. I can't wait to meet this girl he seems to have gotten so serious about!"

"I'll fire up the barbie. Let's forget about the island and just enjoy the kids."

Outside, in an unmarked van with a flat tire down the block, a man named Osborne sipped lukewarm coffee from a thermos bottle filled the night before. It was barely warm enough to be palatable, but it was better than nothing. He wondered why he wasn't picking up any noises in his headset from the sophisticated listening devices he had placed in every room of the house. *Damn! They're outside! How could I have forgotten to bug the patio?*

Minutes after one o'clock, Thomas came out onto the patio where his father was setting coals in the barbecue. Diana was at the grocery store, looking for some last minute items, when Thomas arrived. He let himself in and found his father on the patio, poking at coals in the red brick barbecue pit with one hand, holding a bag of charcoal under his other arm.

"Thomas! I'm happy you could come! Its good to see you." Wakefield set down the bag of charcoal and turned to embrace his son.

Hugging did not come easily to him. His family, and particularly his father, had rarely expressed affection physically. It was, in the final analysis, his nearly adult child who had taught him to hug by tacitly insisting on it when they greeted. His hug was awkward, but sincere. It terminated with a flurry of pats on his son's back that somehow restored his masculinity after the tenderness of the hug.

He set Thomas at arms' length and looked at him, seeing a handsome young man with striking, intense blue eyes and sandy hair. He already had most of his father's height, arranged on the finer bone structure influenced by his mother's genes. Susan had often said the eyes were his father's eyes, and they changed color with mood, going from the normal vibrant blue to gunmetal gray in anger or pain. At this moment, they were somewhere in between.

"So where's this girl you're so anxious to have us meet?"

Something passed quickly across the vibrant blue eyes, so fleetingly that Wakefield would have missed it if he hadn't been looking right at them. Thomas took a deep breath and looked back over his shoulder at the patio door.

"Dad, this is Roger," he said, as a good-looking young man stepped out of the doorway, looking apprehensive and ready to bolt back the way he had come.

Wakefield stared uncomprehendingly at the young man, then at Thomas, then repeated the looks as the reality of Thomas' introduction began to sink in. Wakefield absent-mindedly picked up the poker from the barbecue.

"I thought . . . I mean . . . Do you mean . . . ?" Wakefield snapped his mouth shut as he realized nothing coherent was coming out of it. He looked dumbly at his son and poked absently at the coals.

"Dad, I'm gay." Thomas spoke the words gently, matter-of-factly, without drama or affect.

Wakefield's brain went into high gear, examining and discarding hypothetical explanations for his son's behavior while his mind tried simultaneously to deny and to accept the words he had just heard. At some deep and subconscious level he knew that his relationship with his son would be profoundly influenced by the way he handled the disclosure.

"I need to sit down for a minute," he said lamely, and stood rooted as he was. Thomas came to him and took the poker from his hand, ushering him to a chair at the table, and nodding at Roger to take a seat. Wakefield sat, then looked up at Thomas.

"I guess we'd better talk," he said lamely. The litany of denial in his mind continued. *It's a stage he's going through. How can he possibly know for a fact he's gay? Who is this Roger person, has he seduced my son? What could I have done to him that queered his mind? Maybe I can convince him to get counseling . . . I'll pay for it! How long has this been going on? Why didn't I see the signs? Thomas doesn't look gay. Hell, he played football. Maybe I didn't hear him right. This is not a joke. Where's Diana? Where the hell is Diana!*

He took a deep breath, then exhaled slowly, throttling back his mind to a manageable speed, trying to find the switch labeled 'rational' in his behavioral circuits.

"Have you told your aunt?" he asked, finally.

"No, Dad. I wanted to tell you first. I think she suspects, but I haven't told her."

"Christ, Thomas, are you sure?"

"Yes, Dad. I'm sure," Thomas said with exaggerated patience. Some of his friends had asked the same question on receiving the news, as if to suggest he had not already completed the process that brought him to the truth about himself. It was not something one announced without being absolutely sure about it. He always marveled that people did not realize this and always required reassurance that the issues had been examined.

"Have you thought about how this will impact your life? Can you even begin to imagine what a difficult way you say you've chosen?"

"Dad, you're using all of the clichés. This is me. I'm still your son. I still love you and Aunt Diana. It's important that you accept this new information about me without rejecting me. Or Roger. This doesn't change things. I was gay before I decided I had to tell you. Nothing's changed, except now you know."

Wakefield struggled with the news. His mind suddenly turned from the issue, and he glared venomously at Roger, who felt an instant of terror at the mayhem embodied in the look and tried hard not to look at the poker Wakefield had held moments ago. Then the look was gone.

Diana came through the patio door at that moment, silken ears of fresh sweet corn jutting out of the shopping bag she carried. She took in the scene at a glance, and understood that she needed to be a calming influence. She set the bag of groceries aside, and went to her brother.

The steaks were perfectly done, largely due to Wakefield's single-minded attention to their preparation, and the meal was as pleasant as could be expected. Wakefield the Father had leaned rather heavily into the bourbon while they cooked, and was almost, but not quite, affable as he allowed himself to assess this person called Roger that his son had brought home.

Diana let the bourbon go down without censure. She knew that Russ was a friendly drunk, and a little friendliness, even if alcohol-induced, would ease the tension that had been nearly palpable since Thomas dropped his bombshell. Her own feelings would wait for later analysis; just now she was needed as ombudsman for the interchange that was taking place. In her mind, Thomas' sexual orientation changed nothing. She fervently hoped that Russ would feel the same when everything shook out.

Through an easy fuzziness of thought, Wakefield concentrated on the externals of the situation. His buzz enabled his mind to ignore the internal turmoil he knew would emerge when the buzz wore off. Roger seemed like a nice enough kid, in college like his son. Damn it, he didn't look gay! He carried on an intelligent, if reserved, conversation. In other circumstances Wakefield would have had little trouble liking the young man. He restrained himself to a veneer of civil politeness for the time being.

Thomas was too wise to hang around long after they finished eating. He activated a carefully planned escape excuse, and left with Roger shortly after the strawberry shortcake, suggesting that he would stop by on the following day and they could have a talk about things. Roger was visibly relieved to be going, but Thomas could sense his father's dismay and confusion beneath the cordial front and felt saddened. His aunt was unreadable, but predictably calm and unruffled.

After they departed, Diana sat quietly with her brother on the patio, not speaking, as he continued to drink himself quietly into a stupor. With a sense of timing born of years of caring, she escorted an unprotesting Russ to an early bedtime just before he lost his ability to walk.

22

27 August, Present

Warren Stone found the two hours between eight a.m. when he arrived at his office and ten a.m. when his office opened were the most productive hours of his workday. There were no secretaries, no partners, no clients, and no phone calls. Only a few clients knew that he consistently arrived at the office two hours early, and Russ Wakefield was among that group.

Russ had called him Sunday evening, still in some discomfort from his debacle the night before, and arranged to meet first thing Monday before the office opened. There had been an ominous sense of urgency about Wakefield's call, and he had refused to discuss the matter of his concern over the phone, which was unusual.

Still, Russ was a personal friend and Wakefield Environmental, Inc. was a good client. Stone had acquiesced and agreed to the meeting, mildly irritated that his 'quiet time' was forfeit. He arrived a little earlier than usual to make coffee, which he did not drink but which he knew Russ would enjoy.

Wakefield arrived at three minutes of eight, briefcase in hand and after greeting the two went into Stone's office. As Stone poured coffee he opened the discussion.

"Russ," he said, "It's good to see you. What brings you here so early in the day?"

"Two things, really," answered Wakefield. "First, we've had an accidental death on the island job, a man named Douglas. I thought you should know the details in case anything comes up. I'd like to get that out of the way before we go into the other."

"That's two this year, Russ," observed Stone ruefully. "Are your safety programs in place and working?"

"This was a fluke, Warren. The weather came up, and prevented Douglas from getting the treatment he needed." Wakefield explained the details of the accident.

"You'll probably be sued anyway. They will allege that there were insufficient safety controls being used, that the workers should have been immediately evacuated to wait out the storm in safety, and that a paramedic team was insufficient medical support for the situation; you should have had a physician's assistant. They will allege that Wakefield Environmental was negligent. And they'll probably win, given the climate in the courts today. Have you talked to Bob Wallace about this yet?" Stone knew Wallace handled Wakefield's insurance; they had worked together to handle the claim when Jim Auvil had been killed at Dyess Air Base earlier in the year.

"Later today. I just got back Friday night."

"That's all you can do for now. What's this second issue you wanted to discuss?"

Wakefield took a deep breath. "I found this stuff hidden in a wall in an office on the island the night Douglas died. I need to know what to do about it." He handed a sheaf of papers from his briefcase across the desk to Stone. "Read it."

Stone read, first skimming the pages, then slowing to read more carefully. Wakefield waited patiently. He had given Warren the entire set of documents, not holding back the description of the SK-443 research as he had from Diana.

Warren Stone looked up, finished with the reading. He peered at Wakefield over his reading glasses. "Who knows about this?"

"Diana knows part of it. Nobody else."

"Do you have the originals? These are obviously copies."

"Yes. They're in my safe at home. They're pretty fragile."

"May I have copies of these?"

"Of course."

Stone vanished into the hallway and Wakefield heard the copier warming up. Moments later, Stone returned to the office and handed the papers to Wakefield, keeping a sheaf for himself. He sat down and pressed his thumb and forefinger to the bridge of his nose, sliding his glasses down to make room.

"Do you know what you've got here?" Stone queried after a moment, gesturing at the papers.

"Well, it seems to me that maybe my workers are being exposed to something on the island that could harm them. I don't have a clue as to what it is. I've been thinking about calling Brockner to ask him for more information about it."

"You're kidding! That's all you see? Incidentally, don't call Brockner under *any* circumstances."

"What else could there be?"

"You really don't see it? Russ, did you read these documents? Do you understand why the guy who wrote them resigned? What are the symptoms of SK-443 exposure?"

"They vary. They're different in every individual, since the stuff attacks the immune system . . . "

It hit him like a freight train. For the second time in as many days he grappled with an overwhelming urge toward denial. Stone watched him come through it on the other side.

"AIDS. Jesus Christ! AIDS?" he breathed. He looked at Warren. "Is it possible?" Wakefield couldn't believe he hadn't already made the connection; he'd been too worried about his workers and himself to think clearly, to capture the broader picture as Warren had done.

"If the testing that...what's his name?...Harwiczki! — describes did indeed occur, it's more than just possible. It's the biggest cover-up in the history of the world!" Stone exclaimed.

"The time line is right," he continued after a thoughtful pause. "Before 1980, nobody had heard of the AIDS virus, and these documents are dated in 1977. Suddenly, in epidemic proportions, it's running through the population like wildfire. Not in third world countries but in the most advanced industrial nation in the world. It blindsided the medical establishment, and it caught the civilian government unprepared. There is no precedent.

"The theories of its origin have been lame and conflicting at best. One theory said 'Monkeys in Africa', but the U.S. has far outstripped Africa in its incidence of early cases. The statistics actually suggest it was imported into Africa, rather than endemic. One theory said 'Genetic mutation of existing virus', but they've been unable to locate a precursor. Another early report said it came out of Haiti, something about flight attendants bringing it to the states. If so, why hasn't Haiti itself had the most severe impact from the disease?

"No, Russ, it's been my experience that in most cases the explanation which covers the greatest number of facts is usually closest to the truth. We have no proof beyond the fragile copies in your office, but my best guess is that the AIDS virus was manufactured by these idiots as a biological weapon and somehow found its way into the population. Probably it was intentionally introduced to test its effects or something. All this, of course, would fall into the category of Wild Hypothecation given what little we can actually prove right now."

"I can't believe that the government . . . "

"It wasn't the government," Stone interrupted him. "It was some *people* in the government. Brockner may have been involved. Was probably involved," he corrected his thought.

"Then why hire somebody to clean up the site? Why not just let it lie?"

"Great camouflage, Russ; a clean site proves several things when you think about it. It proves you're conscientious. It proves that there is no danger there. And it makes it more difficult to find evidence, if that's what you're looking for. It suggests that you're trying to make amends for what your predecessors may have done. Most importantly, it destroys any evidence and makes the specifics of the whole business deniable. Do you even know where the site is located? I seem to remember some security provisions in the contract . . . "

"All I know is that it's a little over four hours flight time from Tampa, and about two hours by helicopter from a military air base. Guantanamo, I think. My pilot let it slip that's where he'd weathered out Cedric. We flew a heading of 45 degrees from the island until the pilot made me put on a shroud. After that, it may have changed."

"All that tells us is that it's not more than four hours. They could have flown in circles for three and a half. Still, it gives us more to work with than I thought we had."

"The boat operators and pilots must know. The skipper of the *Gulf Star* has to know."

"I'm sure he does. But what do you know about him? Do you even know his real name?"

"I see what you mean . . . Say, is it possible that we—I— could have been exposed to it on the island?"

"Possible, but not probable. Actually, I doubt it very much. I doubt there is any living trace of unmodified SK-443 anywhere."

"Why? I mean, you just said it might be AIDS, which means it's still around. What makes you say that it doesn't exist?"

"If I had developed a weapon like this, and subsequently it was released in a population which, in turn, developed symptoms, I'd damn sure see to it that all traces of it were destroyed. You might not be able to get it out of the population, but you could certainly eliminate any connection that might be made between your weapon and the population's symptoms by destroying the weapon and concealing the fact that it had ever been present.

"Sanitize the situation. Then all you'd have to do would be to sit by quietly while somebody else deals with the problem. It would be all you *could* do. Even if you had developed a cure in conjunction with the weapon, you couldn't release it without implicating yourself. You wouldn't even dare to nudge the research in the right direction."

"What happened? Did they screw up, or have an accident? How do you suppose the stuff got loose? You mean they may have a cure?"

The battery of questions posed by Wakefield all had the same answer, for the present.

"That's anybody's guess, Russ. They tend to be really careful, but who knows? All it would take would be one simple act of stupidity."

Stone was trying to remember a case he had read, a lawsuit that involved biological weapons testing in San Francisco, but it had been too long since the reading. The facts were simply not available to his memory. He resolved to look it up after Wakefield left.

"So what do we do now?"

"You go about your day as though nothing were different. I'm going to make some discreet inquiries and see what I can learn. There's really not enough here for any action without corroboration. We need to find someone who knows what happened, and get them to talk. The hard part is finding them. They'll probably be ready to talk, if we can get to them. If somebody knew about this, they've been carrying a carload of guilt around for nearly two decades. They'll welcome the chance to unload, assuming we can find them and press the right buttons. You're sure Diana is the only person who knows about the documents other than us?"

Wakefield nodded in the affirmative.

"Then we have all the aces, and we can control the game. Do not contact Brockner, or anybody else. Tell Diana to keep quiet. Call me after lunch."

"O.K. Listen, Warren, should we be scared?" Wakefield wanted an assessment.

"For now, be careful. I'll let you know by the end of the day if we should be scared. Just to be on the safe side, why don't you get tested for AIDS? Get a complete physical, and blood work. It'll put your mind at ease, and it may become important later."

The implications of Stone's recommendation were not lost on Wakefield and he met Stone's eyes with a silent question.

"It's just a precaution," Stone said, casually. "To establish that you don't have it as of this date."

"Thanks, Warren." Wakefield was not mollified. "I'll call you after noon." Wakefield rose, shook Stone's hand, and left the office. His head reeled from the conversation he had just

137

had. He did not know what to do next, or where to go, and sat quietly in the Lexus for nearly twenty minutes before driving off.

Across the street from the offices of Bixler, Messer, Stone, and Yamata, in a vacant office on the third floor of the building, the college student who had met Wakefield at the airport on Friday snapped a reel off a tape machine, and removed his headset. He placed the seven-inch reel of tape into a special pouch, sealed it, and carried it into an adjacent room, where an even younger-looking man in a gray flannel business suit waited.

"Get this to General Brockner," he said, handing the pouch to the man. "Quick!"

23

27 August, Present

As Wakefield drove toward home, his mind calmed and he thought of a thousand things he should have discussed with Warren. He wanted Warren's thoughts, for example, on yanking his work crews off the Island. To allow them to continue working in light of this new information might be placing them in jeopardy, but to yank them now would tip his hand to Brockner. He decided to swing by the office and check in. He must pull the workers off the island until he knew more. He took some comfort in the fact that the precautions they were taking to prevent chemical exposures would probably protect them somewhat from biological risks as well.

Rosie greeted him as he entered through the front door, again making the subconscious inspection of the lobby to feel the impression it would make on clients. The familiarity of the act and Rosie's greeting were both reassuring.

"Russ! Good morning! I didn't know you were coming! I thought you were still at the island."

"Got in Friday night. How are things going?"

"Real quiet with you and Gene gone so much. All of the divisions are quiet; business as usual. How's the island job going?"

Rosie did not miss the shadow that flickered across Wakefield's eyes for an instant but knew better than to question his response.

"Fine."

Anything but! Rosie translated mentally.

"Well, not really. We lost a man."

"I know," said Rosie. "Hector called. You want me to call Bob Wallace?"

"Please."

"I'll bring in some coffee as soon as I brew fresh. You look a little peaked."

"Thanks, Rosie. Would you get me Gene Briggs on the line at Tampa Shorebase?"

"Yes, sir." The coffee could wait. "It's almost noon there, and he may be out to lunch."

"Try." An idea was forming that would solve at least some of his problems. Two minutes after he sat down at his desk, Rosie buzzed him and announced Briggs on line two. Wakefield picked up the handset.

"Gene, how are you? How's everything going?"

"Fine, boss. What can I do for you?"

"Gene, this is going to sound weird, but I need you to bear with me and not ask any questions." Wakefield waited for confirmation, then continued. "I want to find a way of keeping our crews off the island without it seeming unusual. Some sort of problem that doesn't get anybody too worried, one that only interferes with their landing. Any ideas?"

"I suppose we could have trouble with the air supplies, or the pumps on the barge at the decontamination side. Hector's out there; why don't you check with him?"

"I can't talk to Hector without going through Captain Mihailish on the *Gulf Star,* which I don't want to do. The stop-work order must not be seen as coming from me."

"Chief, I don't get it. If I call Hector and tell him to stop work, it'll amount to the same thing."

"Send the instruction by courier. Grab somebody you can trust and give him a note to hand-deliver on normal crew rotation. Make it look like a random discovery of an unsafe condition. Just get things shut down."

"Is tomorrow too late? I'm scheduled to relieve Hector tomorrow morning."

"That's perfect! Why didn't you say so right off? Can you handle shutting down the job?"

"Sure. Of course. I can find something to honk about, and stall things until it gets corrected. Mind telling me why?"

"I can't, Gene. You've got to trust me for a while. Just keep it believable and away from any association with me. Selmack can't know this is my doing."

"Consider it done. Anything else?"

"No, Gene. I'll get back to you as soon as I can. Thanks." Wakefield broke the connection and breathed a sigh of relief. It was after one o'clock. He dialed Warren Stone's private number. Stone was on by the second ring.

"Warren. I've got them shutting down the job at the island. Nothing that seems to come from me; just mechanical trouble.

Briggs is taking care of it. Any news?"

"Good, Russ. Briggs has been with you a long time. Good. I found Harwiczki. He's buried in a cemetery in White Bear Lake, just outside St. Paul, Minnesota. There's a Mildred Harwiczki still in the phone book there."

"How in the world did you get that information so fast?" Wakefield was incredulous.

"We counselors have to be pretty good at finding people who don't want to be found; when they aren't hiding, it's a cake-walk. Also, Martindale, the other name on the documentation, is retired U.S. Army. He lives somewhere in Tucson. I've got Sylvia working on it."

Stone referred to Sylvia Bixler, one of the partners of Bixler, Messer, Stone and Yamata. Wakefield had met her in passing, a vague memory from any of a half dozen parties and functions he had attended, and remembered her as attractive, but a bit austere. She had a very quick, incisive mind, he recalled.

"My God, Warren, are you sure that's wise?"

"Don't worry, Russ. She doesn't have a clue about why. She'll be a model of discretion in her inquiries. I owe her a big one for this, and she'll not hesitate to collect quid pro quo. She's already nailed me for a fancy lunch. Still, she's good. She worked her way through law school as an investigator for the D.A.'s office, mostly skip-tracing. I'll bet we have that address before closing time today."

"What should I be doing now?" Wakefield had not yet managed to acquire a solid sense of Warren's strategy, but so far everything seemed logical.

"Nothing to do while we gather information. Let's get together tomorrow, my office, same time. Meanwhile, go home, have a nice supper, and try to relax."

"In the morning then. See you in the morning . . ."

Wakefield spent the remainder of the afternoon going through an in-basket that was piled high with things that required his attention, things that had been accumulating while he was away at the island. The quarterly reports from the business units were in and looked generally good.

He fell comfortably into the routine of running the company, and his mind gratefully edged away from the terrible secret he had brought with him to Houston. There was the perennial solicitation from a securities law firm that wanted him to take Wakefield Environmental public and offered to handle the initial issue of stock. The letter assured him, as usual, that he stood to net a bundle if he'd only sign on the bottom line and give them the green flag. That they would make a bundle, too, was implicit in their solicitation.

Just after four p.m., the phone rang. Rosie announced Briggs.

"Gene, hello. This is Russ."

"They're shutting down the job," said Briggs without preamble. "I thought you'd want to know."

"I thought you weren't going out until tomorrow. You didn't get Hector to do it, did you?"

"No, sir. Hector called me, ship to shore, just a few minutes ago. Said that Major Selmack had ordered the crews in. Something about budget problems. Hector says it sounded lame, but he's complying. Russ, what the hell's going on?"

"I honestly don't know. You didn't talk with Hector about closing down?" This last question was unnecessary, and Wakefield regretted it immediately. Gene had never failed to follow an instruction to the letter.

"Absolutely not."

"Then I'm as surprised as you are. Have Hector tell Selmack to give me a call first thing in the morning. Meanwhile, follow his lead."

"Yes sir. Hector says they're coming in tomorrow. Everybody."

"O.K. Listen, Gene, keep me posted. See if you can get a line on what this is all about."

"You bet, chief. I'll call you if I learn anything."

"Thanks, Gene. Talk to you in the morning."

Almost at the instant Wakefield cradled the receiver the phone rang again. This time, Rosie announced that General Brockner was on the line. Wakefield punched the button that opened the line while his mind wondered at Brockner's call. He wasn't using intermediaries this time.

"Good afternoon, General. What can I do for you?"

"We've got a small problem, Russ. Not at your end; something internal, but it affects our relationship. We may even have to close the job for a while."

"What is it, General?"

"I'm sending a plane for you tomorrow morning. We need to meet; I can't discuss it over the phone. There will be a Cessna 310 at the private terminal at Houston Hobby tomorrow at eight o'clock. A Captain Bradshaw will pick you up."

"Should I bring anything? Do you need to look at the records?"

NAVASSA

"Yes. Bring everything. Ledgers and logs, personnel rosters, everything. We may have had a security breach."

"General, are there any budget problems with the job?" Wakefield was smart enough to ask the first question a businessman would ask faced with the threat of job closure. It was the first question Brockner would expect.

"No, not at all. This is a security matter. Why do you ask?"

"That's usually where problems occur, in my experience. Just thought I'd fish a little."

Wakefield marveled at his own competence at duplicity. Innocence of knowledge virtually oozed from his tone. His concern over money and job funding were typical contractor responses to the situation. He believed Brockner had bought it. The fact that the dog's head was barking while the back end was doing something else was not lost on him. They'd told Briggs it was budget problems, and now Brockner was howling 'security breach'. The disingenuous nature of the two conflicting stories gave him pause.

"Save your speculations for tomorrow," Brockner said brusquely. "I'll fill you in completely when we meet. Don't worry; this won't cost you a cent. We'll pick up the tab for any delays."

"I'll be there, General. Anything else?"

"No. Have a safe trip." The General hung up.

Wakefield buzzed Rosie. It was almost closing time.

"Rosie, can you stay late today? Something's come up, and I need your help."

"Certainly. What do you need?"

"How long will it take to assemble and copy all records that pertain to the island job? I'll help."

"About two hours, I think."

"I'll be right out. Let's get started."

"Four, if you help," said Rosie.

Forgiveness is easier to get than permission.
—Anonymous

24

27 August, Present

General Donald Brockner swore under his breath as he punched the button on the reel-to-reel Akai tape machine that shut off the device. He had heard enough, and almost regretted the orders he must now issue. He rang his clerk and had his G2, Colonel Bill Malleck, summoned to his office. Times had changed since that old fart Martindale had retired, he reflected briefly, and Malleck was the only other member of his command staff who knew the whole story of Martindale's blunder fifteen years earlier. His companion during the San Francisco testing, Major Thomas Dowling had died of cancer half a decade back. Brockner now ran a tighter ship. Nobody was told anything they didn't specifically need to know.

Malleck was in his office in moments, looking, as always, like a recruiting poster model.

"Bill, this business with Wakefield has gone sour," Brockner informed him without preamble. "The son-of-a-bitch has documents, and he's given copies to his attorney, a man named Warren Stone. I don't know where he got them, but he's not going to let it alone. He's also told his sister."

"How long ago? How much do they have?"

"His attorney found out this morning. They don't have any solid proof, yet, but they have a hell of a springboard into an investigation. We can't let that happen."

"I've got Olmstead and Osborne in Houston right now, as you know. I'll put them on it."

"Use Selmack, too," Brockner ordered. "I want him to get dirty on this one. If he hadn't let Wakefield off the island, things would never have gotten out of hand."

"Selmack's still on the island. Can he be moved into position quickly enough?"

"He can be in Houston by sundown today. When we finish here, I'm pulling everything off the island."

Malleck raised his eyebrows, and looked at his commanding officer. "That's going to raise a flap," he observed.

"Wakefield will never know it's been done. I'm calling him in for a meeting first thing tomorrow. He'll be in the air and under our control before he can learn about that attorney of his. I'll have him bring all records of the operation along. I'll give him some song and dance about a security problem. If we move quickly, we can nip this thing in the bud. That means the attorney must be removed tonight. Make absolutely sure that your people recover all the documents that he has. Timing is everything. Clean it up."

"Jesus, Don, I could use a little more time to plan things."

"You should have planned for this weeks ago. You're supposed to cover all contingencies with plans. I assumed you had done so."

"Only in a general way. Who could have anticipated the way this situation has developed?" *You bastard! If this queers, you're going to hang me, aren't you?* Malleck's face gave no hint of the unpleasant conclusion he had just drawn, and he looked at Brockner with an air of apparent concern.

Brockner ignored the rationalization, and changed his tack. "Let's concentrate on damage control for now, Bill. Get your people moving on it. I'll get Selmack into Houston by dark, and you take him from there. Keep me posted on your progress."

Malleck had already decided that progress meant taking Wakefield out before he could get on the plane Brockner was sending. It was the best insurance he could hope to provide for himself in light of Brockner's clear intent to pin the whole mess on him. Malleck knew that in certain situations, it was easier to get forgiveness than permission. Wakefield would never get on that plane. Osborne could set it up and save them all a lot of trouble. Osborne had special skills.

"Yes, sir." Malleck's attention was already elsewhere, and he parroted the words to mollify his commander.

"Oh, and listen to this tape. There are details on it you need to know." Brockner handed the seven-inch reel across his desk to Malleck. He turned away as Malleck left to gaze briefly out the window, across the Snake River toward downtown Idaho Falls. Autumn was coming, always short here. And after that, winter. Always long.

146

NAVASSA

Matt Osborne glanced intermittently at the small, highly specialized transmitter beside him on the front seat of the rented Buick as he drove slowly around the suburban residential neighborhood near Russ Wakefield's house.

He had parked at the curb in front of that house earlier in the day and let the machine walk through the frequencies commonly used by garage door opener remote control units until the door of Wakefield's empty garage opened. He locked in the frequency and tested the setting by closing the door on command from the transmitter. The drive through the neighborhood now, with the transmitter operating, was to ensure that no other doors in range of the transmitter would operate on the same frequency as Wakefield's. Random transmissions of that nature could cost him his life.

To an observer, his slow cruise would appear to be that of a person in an unfamiliar neighborhood looking for an address. He systematically queried every garage within a quarter mile of the Wakefield house. He found only one within his search area operating at the Wakefield frequency, which made his job substantially easier. He noted the address. He noted mentally the location of the power drop to the house, left front corner, against his necessary visit after midnight. Satisfied, he returned to his room at a small motel three miles away where he programmed a small receiver to accept the frequency he'd identified at Wakefield's garage.

Then he went out for a sandwich, first making sure that the receiver was isolated from any random transmissions and that its power source was deactivated. He returned, showered, set his alarm clock, and crawled into bed to get what sleep he could. He would be up late tonight, and he wanted to be fresh to complete the last elements of his task.

Wearing civilian clothes, Major William Selmack was met by Brian Olmstead at Houston Intercontinental Airport when his Tampa flight arrived at 5:45 local time. Olmstead briefed him on the situation and the status of operations up to the moment. He conveyed the orders he had received earlier from Malleck. Selmack did not like the orders one bit. They hadn't done things this way since the mid-1970s, and it seemed to Selmack that there must be a better way.

Still, orders were orders. He was in no position to back out. It was clear that either Brockner or Malleck wanted him tangled up in the messy end of things; otherwise, why not simply let Olmstead do the job? He knew how Brockner's mind worked. It

147

was probably Brockner's way of letting him know that allowing Wakefield to leave the island hadn't been such a great strategy...

"He's working late tonight, which is perfect for us," Olmstead was saying. "It's supposed to look like a burglary he interrupted in progress. There are documents to recover, and there's no telling where they are. You will have to get that information from him before you take care of the other business. And you'll have to make sure you've gotten them all. Every scrap.

"There's a case in the back seat with everything I could think of that you might need. Take a look and see if there's anything else you want."

"You're not assisting?"

"Malleck said you go in alone." Olmstead hated wet work, and tried to keep his voice from revealing his relief that he wouldn't be getting involved. "I'll drive you to the airport after. You're booked as Peter DeVries to Salt Lake City, eleven-fifteen departure tomorrow morning. Ticket's at the counter. You can stay with me tonight. I'm at the Sheraton."

Selmack reached into the back seat and retrieved the case, set it on his lap, and released the catches. He pawed through its contents, taking a silent inventory. It contained everything he would need.

It was twenty minutes after six when Olmstead dropped him off in front of the building where Warren Stone labored late, catching up on the work that he had postponed while he was gathering information on the people named in Wakefield's documents.

Bill Selmack stood briefly at the curb, the attaché case dangling from his left hand, gathering his thoughts and his resolve before he entered the building. *I'm getting too old for this shit.* He turned and entered the building.

Warren Stone looked up from the briefs scattered across his desk at an indistinct noise to find a moderately tall, sandy-haired man in a burgundy windbreaker standing in the doorway of his office. The man entered, closing the door behind him.

"We're closed," Stone said. "Everybody's gone home." He was working in his shirtsleeves, as was his custom. The cuffs were rolled neatly to mid-forearm. The blinds were drawn closed against the glare of the low afternoon sun, two hours away from setting.

"Are you Warren Stone?" The smile was easy and engaging as the man eased into the room and sat down in a chair across the desk from Stone. He placed a case across his lap and began dialing in the combination of first one latch, then the other.

"Yes, I am. Can I help you?" Stone was irritated by the man's rudeness, by the insolence of his bearing.

"Mr. Stone, I need some information I believe you have."

"Who are you? I'm extremely busy just now, but I'm sure we could help you in the morning."

"Name's Bill Selmack. I just got into town and I'm in kind of a hurry." Again came the self-deprecating smile. "Do you know Russ Wakefield?" He glanced up from his manipulations with the case.

Stone immediately became cautious. "Yes..." he admitted guardedly, laying down his pencil. "He's a client. What is the nature of your business?"

Selmack opened the case on his lap and paused. "Mr. Wakefield has some documents that belong to me. I understand he has given you copies, and I need them back. I also need you to tell me what, precisely, he told you and what actions you have taken with regard to the information in those documents." Behind the raised lid of the case, he deftly donned a pair of surgical gloves as he spoke.

Stone went livid, but restrained his voice. "That is absolutely outrageous! I'll have to ask you to leave immediately. I don't know who you are, but you can just get the hell out of here!" Stone rose abruptly to come around the desk and found himself staring into the barrel of a handgun. He'd seen enough movies to recognize the silencer on the muzzle, and he froze. Selmack did not rise, merely moving his hand to keep the weapon trained on Stone's chest. Stone was a man who fought his battles with words and paper and intellect. The deadly looking handgun took him immediately out of his league.

"Sit down, Mr. Stone." Selmack drew back the hammer in a fashion designed to punctuate his command with the click of the cocking mechanism. Stone realized the man meant what he said, sensing that he would pull the trigger without hesitation if Stone moved suddenly. Something about the man—his cold reptilian gaze and surrealistically casual demeanor—immediately convinced Stone of the man's willingness to do exactly as he said he would.

Stone remained standing, at the corner of his desk. His heart was racing and he felt weak in the knees. He regained a semblance of composure and backed cautiously, slowly to his chair. He sat, placing his hands on the desk, never taking his eyes off the gun. Once he was seated, Selmack rose, placed the case on his empty chair, and hoisted a thigh up onto the corner of

Stone's desk. He leaned forward, the gun casually, almost carelessly, covering Stone.

"What do you want?" Stone tried to keep the tremor from his voice, but failed. He was scared. This man in his office was clearly dangerous; Stone thought it best to give him whatever he wanted and pray that he left without violence. He mentally reviewed the man's description for his report to the police. It was all he could do. Five-eleven, medium-length, sandy hair, piercing blue eyes . . . and a face that looked like a bombing range. Something about the man put Stone in mind of a chimpanzee.

Selmack lashed out with the barrel of the gun and cracked Stone smartly across the temple with the speed of a lightening bolt. Stone felt a lance of pain shoot through him and couldn't remember for the life of him where it came from. In the wake of the pain a funny numbness remained, and some flashbulbs going off behind his eyes. The room swam, then re-focussed.

"You're not paying attention, asshole," the man was saying, almost gently. "This will go easier on both of us if you give me your undivided attention. You will cooperate and answer my questions. There are no other options. It's not negotiable, counselor."

"What do you want?" Stone heard himself say.

"I want all the copies of everything Wakefield gave you. I want all your notes. I want everything you have that has anything to do with the discussion you and Wakefield had the other day. And I want you, when you've provided me with these items, to devise a way of convincing me that you have held nothing back."

"But why . . . " Stone began. Selmack struck him sharply again with the gun barrel, this time on the chin. He moved so quickly Stone never saw him; Stone only felt the pain.

"You're not a very quick study, are you?" Selmack smiled engagingly, patronizingly. "I get so *damned* tired of repeating myself. Is that going to be necessary, or can you remember what it is I asked you for only a second ago? Try real hard."

"In my drawer," Stone mumbled. His jaw hurt like hell and was beginning to swell. Selmack hit him again, and Stone almost blacked out from the pain. Selmack used the opportunity to quickly cinch both of Stone's hands to the arms of his office chair with plastic friction ties from his case.

"Which goddamn drawer? You're really trying my patience."

"Top . . . right." Stone had trouble finding the words and

sending them out his mouth, but they were intelligible when they finally emerged. He abandoned any thought beyond cooperating with his tormentor and concentrated on that. It was difficult, finding the information in the fog of pain Selmack's blows had created. *Just stop the blows, just let this be over.*

Selmack rummaged through the right-hand drawer and extracted everything in it, dumping the papers and files into the top half of the open case on Stone's desk. He turned to Stone.

"What else?"

"Notes. On a pad under the stack on the right." Stone nodded toward the right location. A few drops of blood spattered from his hair onto the papers in front of him. His temple had been lacerated by Selmack's first blow and was bleeding profusely. Blood streamed down his face and neck and soaked into his shirt collar. The drops of blood were bright, red on the white of the paper.

Selmack retrieved the note pad, scanned it. "What else?"

"Nothing. That's everything." It hurt to talk.

"Anything in the wastebasket?" queried Selmack conversationally, dumping it over on the floor.

Stone shook his head from side to side. Selmack hit him again, this time with the flat of his hand on the bruised and swelling side of Stone's jaw. The pain was excruciating. Stone screamed. Selmack wiped the blood from his hand on Stone's white shirt.

He went to his case and removed an elastic band, which he knotted around Stone's left arm. He took a charged syringe from the case, and Stone's eyes got big.

"Something for the pain?" offered Selmack brightly. "You'll love this stuff! It's one hundred percent USDA guaranteed to make your troubles go bye-bye. Let me help." He smiled the exaggerated smile of a lunatic at full moon.

Stone mutely shook his head from side to side. His eyes bulged and his head rebelled against the motion with even more pain. He struggled, but his arms remained immobilized by the plastic ties.

Selmack thumped a vein on Stone's arm and deftly inserted the needle, released the constricting band. He taped the needle in place, circling the entire arm of the chair and Stone's arm as well with a roll of tape. This done, he depressed the plunger of the syringe part way, injecting half the reservoir's contents into Stone's arm.

Stone groaned with profound relief as the drug took effect. The pain lifted like a fog when sunshine burns through. He felt absolutely, overwhelmingly rosy and cooperative. Selmack wasn't going to hurt him any more: hell, he was a pretty good guy and he had a great smile. They could be buddies. He wanted to thank his buddy for relieving the pain, but that could wait. There was no hurry. Selmack was asking questions and he was answering them, without effort, almost as if he wasn't even participating in the answers. It was enough just to sit here, all pain banished, his mind clear as a bell. He knew the secrets of the universe. He understood the meaning of life, and appreciated the beauty of the human condition. Subterfuge was so *unnecessary...*

Warren Stone was still appreciating the beauty of the human condition when Selmack was finally convinced he had all there was to be had. Selmack depressed the plunger of the syringe to inject the remainder of the drug for a fatal dose, then placed the silenced .22 caliber revolver to the base of Stone's skull and pulled the trigger. There was a muffled 'zip' sound as Stone's body jerked from the shot.

The special low power of the powder charge in the round, further dissipated by the silencer, gave the bullet enough velocity to enter the brain, but not enough to penetrate the skull and exit. The bullet simply bounced around inside Stone's skull until its energy was spent. Stone's body slumped quietly over his work; he was irretrievably dead in a fraction of a second.

Selmack reached into Stone's pocket and removed his wallet. There were three hundred and thirty-two dollars in the bill compartment. He extracted the money and stuffed it into his own pocket. He threw the wallet onto the desk near Stone's head.

Selmack checked himself for bloodstains, packed up his case with the Navassa papers and his paraphernalia. He locked Stone's office door behind him and calmly walked out of the building. Olmstead swung up to the curb as he appeared at the front door and Selmack entered the car. He removed the surgical gloves he had been wearing and stuffed them into his case.

"It's done. I'm taking the papers to Brockner myself," he said quietly, coldly, in a way that warned Olmstead not to interfere. They drove back to Olmstead's hotel room where both men went wordlessly to bed and slept the dreamless sleep of deep exhaustion they'd come to associate with the conclusion of wet operations. The release from the incredible tension of the operations inevitably affected them like a powerful drug.

In another part of the city, Osborne awoke moments before

his alarm went off, verified the time, and deactivated the alarm before it could ring. He had always had, as long as he could remember, an internal sense of time almost as precise as the mechanical devices on which it was based.

He dressed in dark clothing and collected the components of the device he would assemble at the last possible moment, checked his tools, and loaded everything into the front seat of the Buick. He gave the room a once-over to make sure that no personal traces were left behind. He wiped the tab on the room key to clean off any fingerprints and likewise wiped the door-knobs, the shower handles, and the flush knob on the toilet. Leaving the key on the nightstand, he locked the door and left.

The streets were deserted as Osborne drove to his first stop: the house with the garage door opener on Wakefield's frequency. He parked around the corner on the street and went to the front left corner of the house where the power came in. Wearing gloves, he cut the seal with diagonal pliers and removed the electric meter. He applied insulating tape to the electrical pin contacts and reinstalled the meter. He replaced the damaged seal in a fashion that would serve to conceal his tampering from the casual observer.

Osborne let himself into the garage through the back door, which he found conveniently unlocked and pulled a spring-loaded center punch from his pocket. He applied the punch to the driver's side window of the Volvo parked there, pressed, and was rewarded by the disintegration of the tempered glass in the opening. It was a remarkably quiet event, marked only by a gentle 'thump' as the punch released. It would wake nobody. He fished around in the center console, using a small flashlight, searching for the door operator control. Nothing. He looked up, and there it was, clipped to the visor. He removed it, shoved it in his pocket, and repeated the procedure with the second car parked in the garage.

Next, he traced the power from the door opener receiver unit, unplugged it, and cut away the plug end. He smiled to himself as he envisioned the puzzlement of the unsuspecting occupants of that house when they'd discover his sabotage in the morning—probably after over-sleeping. They'd be unable to leave for work because their garage door wouldn't open; they would wonder at the curiously specialized nature of the vandalism, and wonder why the power was out. By the time they'd figured out what he'd done, Osborne would be a thousand miles away. They would probably never know why he had done it.

Returning to the Buick, he drove to Wakefield's home. He

picked the lock on the side door of Wakefield's garage and entered. Moving with rehearsed precision in the near darkness, he completed the assembly of all the components he'd brought. They included five pounds of plastic explosive, the receiver programmed with the garage door opener frequency, a delay timer pre-set to seventy five seconds, a battery pack, and a radio-remote arming detonator that connected to the receiver. He hid the entire assembly in among the fishing nets, boxes of old photographs, storm windows and other paraphernalia stored in the rafters above the parking stalls. He flipped a switch on the assembly; an amber-colored LED glowed faintly. The device was now armed.

It was just past four in the morning when Osborne finished his work. He slipped out quietly, locking the door behind him, and headed for a Denny's he had spotted earlier for coffee and an early breakfast. His own flight wasn't until 9:20. He had plenty of time. He dropped the two garage door controllers into the Dumpster behind the restaurant before he entered its brightly-lit interior. He took a seat at the counter and ordered a hearty breakfast.

25

28 August, Present

Russ Wakefield finished dressing and followed his nose into the kitchen. The smell of freshly brewed coffee drew him like a magnet. Diana, scrambling eggs at the stove, felt him enter the spacious kitchen. She intercepted him at the coffeepot with a clean cup. It was six thirty a.m. He was due at the airport in an hour.

"When will you be back?" she inquired "We've still got that business about Thomas to discuss."

He winced involuntarily. "That . . ." Wakefield sat at the table by the bay window that looked out on the back yard lawn. It needed mowing. "A couple of days at worst, I guess. I don't know what Brockner has on his mind, but I don't see how it could take very long."

"You know, he's still the same person. You still love him. You don't need to be all in a fuss about this."

"I don't want to discuss it." Wakefield declared flatly, in a tone forgivable only by a sibling. Diana backed off and changed the subject.

"How did your meeting with Warren go yesterday? What did he think about the documents? Does he think there's any danger?"

Wakefield avoided all three questions in a voice that was conciliatory. He regretted his abruptness of a moment before. Diana deserved better. "He's still checking things out. We'll have a better idea when I get back."

"Your overnight bag is in the hallway. I packed it for you last night. There's clean shirts and socks for two days. Your passport is in the side pocket." Wakefield never left town without his passport. If international business came up, he certainly didn't want to return to Houston for it.

"Thanks Diana. How would I ever make it without you dotting my 'i's' and crossing my 't's' while I sleep?"

"You wouldn't, and you're welcome." She was still smarting a little from his earlier brusqueness about the Thomas question.

Diana sat a plate in front of him, and poured orange juice. The eggs were done perfectly to Wakefield's taste, scrambled slowly, 'without violence', in butter over low heat. He dug in with a will, knowing that they had better leave soon if they were to make it to the private terminal at Hobby Field. Highway 35 could be wretched if they caught it at morning rush hour. They left the lights on in their hasty departure to meet the plane Brockner was sending for him. Diana drove, and would return home with the Lexus so as not to leave it in the parking lot while Wakefield was away.

Diana dropped her brother off, tripped the trunk lever and watched him remove a box of papers from the trunk. He set it on the curb and walked around the car to the driver's side. He returned with his load to the open window.

"No point in waiting," he said. "I'll call you and let you know when I'm coming in as soon as I find out. I'm sorry about the Thomas thing. You don't deserve that kind of treatment, Sis," he smiled.

"I understand. It's just that you're making things harder for yourself than they need to be." She smiled as she pulled away from the curb and headed for home, but the smile faded a little as she thought of what she would do when she got there. She wanted to call Thomas before he returned to school, maybe talk with him alone before her brother returned and try to understand what her nephew was going through. She bit her lower lip as she turned north onto Highway 35, lost in thought.

As they arrived at the terminal, Matt Osborne was waking up in a rented Buick behind Denny's Restaurant a few blocks from the Wakefield house.

"Shit!"

Osborne started suddenly awake and instantly knew he'd dozed off. It was almost seven thirty and he had intended to drive by Wakefield's house at six forty-five to arm the detonator he had placed there earlier. He had not armed it earlier because he had not wanted the charge to remain armed any longer than was absolutely necessary. It was a matter of safety and precision. He knew there were only two types of people who worked with explosives: the meticulously cautious and the dead.

He started the engine, turned on the windshield wipers to remove the heavy dew and switched the defroster on full to clear the fogged windows. He wiped a hole in the fogged window so he could see enough to get moving and flew out of the parking lot toward Wakefield's house. Malleck would gut him if he screwed this up.

Osborne slowed as he turned onto Wakefield's street, activating the transmitter that armed the detonator in Wakefield's garage as he passed the house. Unseen in the rafters of the garage, the faint amber light on the device winked out and a red LED came on. He could see that house lights were on behind the closed draperies, and breathed a sign of relief. He parked down the block to confirm the detonation he knew would occur when Wakefield opened his garage door to drive to the airport.

He nearly missed seeing the returning Lexus almost an hour later because he was watching the garage door and not the street. On her way home, Diana had been caught in the notorious snarl of traffic that stacked up on Highway 35 every morning. Horrified, Osborne watched the door roll up and away. A lone occupant drove the car *into* the open garage, when he had expected to see the garage door open, and the garage explode. Helplessly, he watched the door swing shut. Then, before his eyes the garage disintegrated in a fiery orange ball and a mushroom of black smoke roiled into the clear morning sky.

Dreading the explanation Malleck would demand, Osborne started the car and drove slowly away down the street. He was gone minutes before the keen of the first sirens rose in the distance.

Russ Wakefield hung around the terminal for nearly an hour, waiting for the Cessna 310 to show up. He had no means of contacting Brockner to find out why the plane was delayed. When he finally decided to wait no longer, he fished out a quarter and called home for Diana to return and pick him up. There was no answer. He let it ring for almost a minute before he hung up and called his office. Rosie answered: "Wakefield Environmental. Can I help you?"

"Rosie, this is Russ. Listen, I'm stuck at the private terminal at Hobby. Can you have Davis send a yardman out to pick me up and take me home?" He referred to Davis Esterson, who had been running the main office since the Island Job began.

"Right away, Mr. Wakefield. Anything else? I thought you were off to meet that General about the Island Job."

"No plane. No explanation. No communication." Wakefield shrugged, even though Rosie could not see it. "I'll wait at home. I have some personal business to take care of today."

"We'll get a yardman there for you. Driving time."

"Thanks, Rosie."

Diana turned the Lexus into the driveway and keyed the garage door opener, triggering the timing mechanism attached to the detonator in the rafters of the garage. The timer began ticking off the seconds quietly, inexorably.

She pulled the car into the garage, shut off the engine, and keyed the opener control again. The garage door rolled shut, and the garage interior light came on automatically. She opened the back door of the car and retrieved her purse, turned, and walked to the kitchen door, thinking about what she would say to Thomas and what he might say to her. Russ would come around, she was sure. Thomas was too dear to him for it to be otherwise.

The timer in the detonator assembly reached zero and sent a signal through the squib, firing its small actuating charge, which in turn detonated five pounds of plastic explosive in the rafters of the garage. The shock wave and fireball slammed into Diana from behind, propelling her across the kitchen with tremendous force as it disintegrated the garage. She was slammed into the wall and died instantly, without pain.

Just after eight that morning, Olmstead and Selmack were jarred awake by the insistent ringing of the telephone. Selmack, the senior man, answered. It was Colonel Malleck, and he was boiling.

"You guys have got to get out to Wakefield's place!" he commanded urgently. "Osborne says he set everything, but he screwed up and armed it too late. It took out the sister, but Wakefield wasn't with her. It's up to you guys to find him, finish the job."

"Jesus Christ! Sir."

26

Afternoon, 28 August, Present

Fire engines were visible on the street as Wakefield's driver made the turn and Wakefield realized with a sinking horror that they were parked in front of his house. Their approach to the house was stopped by charged hose lines snaking across the street like canvas spaghetti.

Wakefield left the pickup truck at a bound, running toward the barricade tape that surrounded his lot. Men moved about. Smoke drifted up from the pile of rubble that was formerly his garage. He could see the charred remains of his Lexus and his sister's car smashed down at the top, their twisted, blackened remains almost unrecognizable in the smoking ruin. The kitchen was obscenely exposed to view, like the back of a dollhouse, charred and littered with debris. Water was everywhere. The grass was soggy underfoot as he crossed the barricade line toward the house. Firemen were dragging hose lines from the seldom-used front door.

His sister was nowhere to be seen. He looked frantically about, searching the crowd of onlookers and casting about the scene for any sign of her. He did not feel the gentle hand on his shoulder until it became strong enough to forcibly whirl him about to face its owner.

"Hang on buddy! You're not supposed to be here. Get back across the line."

He turned and faced the fireman who had accosted him. "This is my house! Where's my sister?"

"Just a second, sir," the fireman said, relaxing his grip and turning. Wakefield caught a glimpse of his eyes as he turned, and felt dread at what they implied. "Captain! I got the owner here!" the fireman called over his shoulder. An officer trotted over and the fireman returned gratefully to his work.

"I'm Captain Rutledge. You're the owner?"

"Yes. Where's my sister? What happened?"

Some firemen moved by, carrying a ladder. The two had to step out of the way. "Let's move out of the work area, sir, and I'll explain what's happened. Step over here, please. What is your name, sir?"

"Wakefield. Russ Wakefield. I live here. What happened?"

"It looks as though there was an explosion in the garage; possibly natural gas judging from the way the walls are blown outward from the top. There was a fire from the explosion. We'll know more in an hour or so when our investigators have had a chance to look through it." The Captain said something into his portable radio that Wakefield couldn't hear over the thunderous noise of the diesel powered fire engines. "Who lived here with you?"

"Nobody. My sister! Where's my sister!"

"She's been taken away, Mr. Wakefield. She didn't make it. I'm sorry."

Wakefield stared incredulously at the fireman as the information seeped past his conscious defenses.

"God . . . oh, God . . . " Wakefield put his face into his hands and sat down numbly on the running board of the fire engine. His knees threatened to fail him. "No . . . no . . oh, God, no . . . "

"Come over here and sit down in the Commander's car, Mr. Wakefield." The Captain took his elbow. He was solicitous, but oddly stiff and formal. "Somebody will be right here to talk to you."

Wakefield let himself be ushered toward a parked Chevy Suburban, looking up to avoid falling over the hoses laying about on the ground. As they walked around the front of the fire engine, Wakefield looked about and spotted a car parked at the curb a hundred feet away. There were two men in it. His eyes widened as he recognized Bill Selmack in the passenger seat. At the same instant Selmack saw him, his face registering surprise and amazement. He turned frantically to the man driving and said something, gesturing wildly. The man leaned forward slightly and engaged the starter.

Wakefield made the connection in a nanosecond; Selmack was responsible for this, for Diana . . . Without conscious thought, Wakefield broke free of the fire captain, seized a fireman's pick-headed axe leaning against the front bumper of the fire engine, and rushed toward the car. The sedan's wheels spun. Its tires smoked and screeched as the car shot away from the curb, straight toward him as he tried to block its escape.

Wakefield swung the axe like a baseball bat at the windshield as he leaped aside. The blade imbedded itself into the glass as the car roared past, yanking the handle from Wakefield's hand and spinning him around. Off balance, he hit the ground hard. A sharp pain lanced through the wrist of his right hand, which he'd used to break his fall. Then he was up and running after the vehicle as it sped past his own pickup truck and driver, bouncing over the charged fire hose in the street.

He stopped, winded and wide-eyed near his truck as the sedan sped away, hopelessly out of reach. He turned and looked back to see the firemen gesturing, pointing at him and waving at two police officers who were at the scene. The police began to run in Wakefield's direction, unsnapping their sidearm holster flaps.

Wakefield leaped for the door of the pickup truck and flung it open.

"Get us out of here!" he bellowed at his driver. The yardman, who had seen the whole affair, hesitated, frightened and confused at his boss's sudden, violent loss of reason. His muscles froze as he tried desperately to understand his part in what was going on.

"*Now!*" Wakefield shrieked.

The yardman shoved the truck into reverse and backed down the street in the direction they had come, whipping backward into a driveway when they had put a reasonable distance between themselves and the two police officers in foot pursuit. The officers abandoned their foot chase and ran for their patrol car.

"Punch it! Let's *go!*" Wakefield yelled at his driver. The pickup truck shot forward out of the driveway at breakneck speed and cut right at the first street. Wakefield ordered the man to make several more turns at random, then had him pull to the side of the road.

"Get out," he ordered. "Get back to the shop and tell Rosie and Davis what's happened. Thanks for getting us out of there, but you don't need to get involved in this."

The yardman left the truck gratefully. Wakefield slid across the bench seat and belted himself in. He pulled away from the curb and drove, not knowing where he was headed beyond evading the pursuit. Then he decided he'd better talk to Warren Stone and turned the truck toward downtown Houston, choosing small surface streets over the quicker freeway routes. It would take longer but at least he would stand a better chance of getting there. He rolled down the window, felt an unexpected dampness on his cheeks, and realized he'd been crying.

BRADD HOPKINS

> *"Grief teaches the steadiest minds to waver."*
> —Sophocles

27

Late P.M., 28 August, Present

Wakefield's mind adamantly refused to look at the appalling reality that had just been presented to it. The gatekeeper of his brain slammed the portals shut against the flood of grief and denial that threatened to rush out and incapacitate him, allowing his conscious mind to protect him by beginning an analysis of what everything meant. He needed to talk with Stone; he desperately needed to talk to Stone. As he wheeled the truck numbly in the general direction of downtown Houston, his mind danced around the grief, trying to understand it without succumbing to it.

As he drove, his thoughts went straight to the presence of Selmack in the car at his burned out home. What did it mean?

Selmack was working for Brockner. He'd been at the island when Wakefield departed the previous Friday. He must be involved with the fire, somehow, else why would he be here, in Houston?

Brockner's plane had never arrived! Perhaps it had never been sent. If *that* were true, then the flight had been a ruse to get him out of the house so that they could do what they did to Diana. Or maybe just to assure that he left the house. But, *why*?

His mind shied away from the feelings that were there, just below the surface. He consciously assisted it; it would not do to release what he knew was boiling there. *Not now.* But, why would they be after Diana?

They'd left early for the airport, to beat the traffic. Diana had returned home; he had not, and hadn't planned to be back for at least two days.

Why would they attack Diana unless . . . ! The explosion and fire had been intended to get both of them, and he'd escaped only because Diana drove him to the airport a little early. She'd been caught when she returned alone! Of course! Why send a plane to pick up someone who would be too dead to travel! A wave of fear rolled through his mind. *They were trying to kill him!*

What was he doing thinking like this? There must be some explanation for the fire, some rational reason for Selmack's presence in Houston. Why had he reacted the way he did, and attacked Selmack? Why had Selmack fled upon seeing him, even before the attack began? He was upset and confused, he acknowledged to himself as he parked in front of Stone's building. He was being paranoid, not thinking clearly. Stone could help.

He dropped a quarter in the parking meter and entered the building, headed for the elevator, punched the button for the third floor, and waited. When the door opened the elevator car was full. Uniformed policemen filled the elevator car, along with a couple of men in plain clothes who were also, obviously, cops. They exited, walking past Wakefield into the lobby. They carried cases and camera equipment and were talking seriously among themselves. Wakefield recalled now that there had been a plethora of patrol cars parked in front of the building as he entered, a fact that had not consciously registered through the veil of near-hysteria and unrecognized shock. His single-minded purpose had been to find Warren Stone, and he had looked neither left nor right on his way into the ground floor lobby.

There were more cops in the hallway when he got off on the third floor where Stone's offices were located. He went in to the receptionist's desk; more police officers plugged about in the waiting room, gathering their gear. Wakefield waited until they left. The receptionist was pale and her makeup was unsalvageable. She had been crying. Wakefield was puzzled by it, but had more pressing concerns than curiosity.

"I need to see Warren Stone. Tell him it's Russ Wakefield, and it's urgent."

The receptionist visibly sagged and began to cry quietly, lowering her head into her hands.

Sylvia Bixler had entered the waiting lobby at that moment and quickly ascertained that Shirley was unable to speak. "I'll handle this, Shirley. Mr. Wakefield? Please follow me..."

She recognized Wakefield as a client of the firm, and he seemed distraught. She made eye contact with him and saw that he recognized her as well. He saw a tall, slender redhead in a tailored, melon-colored designer suit, by Donna Karan if Wakefield had cared. She seemed more relaxed than Wakefield remembered from the occasional cocktail parties they had both attended sometime in the distant past, but she was clearly upset about something. She regarded him almost with suspicion. Wakefield looked about the receptionist's office in puzzlement as Sylvia turned purposefully to stride back down the hall, gesturing for Wakefield to follow.

They went into her office and she closed the door. It was spacious, cool, well-lit with light from the northern windows, done tastefully and elegantly understated in shades of dove and forest green, with cherry wood accents and wainscoting. Wakefield did not so much notice the decor as passively allow it to soothe his battered psyche. She pointed to a chair, moving around the desk to her seat.

"What are you doing here, Mr. Wakefield?"

"I need to see Warren. It's important."

"You realize that you're wanted by the police?"

"*What?*" Wakefield was incredulous.

"I overheard it on a police radio while the police were here. 'BOL Russell Wakefield', it said. 'Be on the lookout' for. It was an all-points bulletin. I didn't think they still did that; not since Broderick Crawford retired. They want to question you about the death of your sister." She watched him intently, but without apprehension, as he absorbed the information.

This third party confirmation of his sister's death was too much for Wakefield. His denial defenses crumbled. He broke down, crying into his hands in great throaty cathartic sobs, trying all the while to regain control of his emotions and not having much success. Sylvia waited patiently, saying nothing. Wakefield finally straightened, and looked at her with red-rimmed eyes. Impassively, she handed him a box of tissues, which she produced from her desk.

"I'm sorry, Mr. Wakefield." Her voice was sincere, but tense in its tone.

"I need to see Warren," he said, gratefully accepting both the tissues and her aplomb, embarrassed that he was sniffling like a child.

"Warren is dead, Mr. Wakefield. He was murdered here, last night."

"Oh, God . . . Oh, my God! How? . . . When . . . ?"

"What about your sister?"

Wakefield winced, gathered himself, and spoke. "There was a fire. I was at the airport, but the plane didn't come, so I went home. There was a fire and she was already gone." He stifled a wave of sorrow that threatened to bring more uncontrollable sobbing. "I'm in trouble. I think they want to kill me, too."

"Who, Mr. Wakefield? Who wants to kill you?"

"Brockner. The Army. A guy named Selmack. I don't know."

"Why?"

"I think I have information. I think that's why Warren was killed. It can't be coincidence. I think they wanted to kill both of us, Diana and me, but I wasn't there."

"Does this have anything to do with the research I was doing for Warren yesterday?"

"I think so." Wakefield was beginning to recapture some composure in response to her matter-of-fact questions. He was still frightened and confused, but managed to answer her, somewhat lamely.

"You'd better tell me everything."

"It's all in the documents in Warren's office. Warren thought it was..." Wakefield stopped, hesitating. She looked at him inquiringly. She raised her head slightly to encourage him to continue.

"You could be in danger if I continue. Everybody I have told about this is dead."

"We don't know that the two facts are related. You're upset. Why don't tell me the whole story and I'll see what I can do to help?"

"We need the stuff from Warren's office," said Wakefield. "It's all there."

"His office has been sealed by the police," Sylvia informed him. "They have been collecting evidence all morning, since Shirley found him. Let me go check. I'll see if they will release the papers in his office. I'll tell them that I need them to prepare a filing. What do they look like?"

Wakefield described the letterhead on the document copies, official and military looking, and the dates sometime in the seventies. She left the room and Wakefield wondered if she believed him or would use the opportunity afforded by her absence to call the authorities. She was gone several minutes. If she was going to betray him, she had ample time. He really didn't care, he told himself. *I have to trust somebody.*

She brought steaming coffee when she returned and handed him a cup. It was hot, and black, and Wakefield accepted it gratefully.

"No documents," she reported flatly. "The police let me in and I looked. There are no documents like the ones you described." Again, she was watching him closely. "Did you keep any copies?"

"I have the originals. In my safe, at home."

"That's out, for now. Look, just tell me everything you can remember. You've got to trust somebody." Wakefield was struck by how precisely her last declaration matched his own thought of moments ago. He decided to tell her everything, starting at the beginning.

A little more than two hours later, he finished. Sylvia had listened patiently, interrupting occasionally for clarification on a point now and again. She jotted occasional notes on a legal pad and had keyed a hidden tape recorder at the onset of the conversation.

Sylvia reached for the phone and ordered out for sandwiches. "I need some time to think this over," she said. "Meanwhile, let's eat something. You do realize how unbelievable the whole story sounds, don't you? Bear with me if I remain skeptical. I really do have your interests at heart, but I must retain a healthy skepticism to be objective.

"If what you've told me is true, the only hard proof of it lies in your safe at home. Without proof, we can't even go to the press with this, which would provide you with some degree of protection. It's substantially more difficult to assassinate someone if they're in the media limelight.

"We need more information. You don't dare go back home for a few days until we get this sorted out. Can you send a relative with the combination to your safe to retrieve the documents?"

"Maybe. Thomas, my son. He's in town, staying with friends." Wakefield thought momentarily about the 'friends', and banished the additional pain caused by the thought. "I won't put him at risk. Will they try to get him, too?"

"I doubt it. I think things are over at your residence. I doubt they're even watching it, after what you told me about Selmack being there. Get in touch with Thomas and have him call me. Give me the safe combination for him. I'll have him go through the Fire Department and ask to remove personal effects. It may work. It depends on the status of their investigation.

"Meanwhile, I want you to check into a hotel for tonight. Lay low, and call me with the number when you have it. Use room service, and don't go out for anything. I'll see what I can find out regarding your status with the police, and let you know when I call. Please keep this meeting confidential; the last thing I need is to be arrested for harboring a fugitive. Please do not forget that is your status until we find out more."

Wakefield sat unmoving, and Sylvia, even though she understood his tacit plea, had to nudge him gently toward the door. "Don't worry, we'll get this ironed out. I'm so sorry about Diana. We met at one of Warren's parties a few years back and I always enjoyed her. She was special. Go now, rest, and don't forget to call me."

She returned to her chair behind the desk when he left and pivoted away from the desk to gaze absently out over the city of Houston. She wrestled with her duties to society in conflict with her duties to her firm's client. The client won. *For now,* she thought. *What have I gotten myself into?*

Russell Wakefield returned to the truck and retrieved the overnight bag he had brought from the airport. He removed the records from the island job from the truck bed and stowed them out of the weather on the passenger seat. He decided that the truck itself was too great a liability, with the words "Wakefield Environmental, Inc." blazoned across each side. He opted, instead, for the relative anonymity of a walk of twelve blocks or so to the Four Seasons.

It was the only hotel in the area with which he was acquainted, having put up numerous clients there in the course of his business operations. The doorman was off somewhere as he walked under the *portecochere* and into the plush lobby, straight for the concierge's desk. He knew the day concierge from past arrangements, and the concierge recognized him immediately. Wakefield remembered that Rosie called the concierge "Immaculate Max".

"Mr. Wakefield! So nice to see you."

"Max. Listen, Max, I need a quiet room for a couple of days. Can you fix me up?"

"Of course, sir. Billing to the company?"

"Yes."

Max palmed the bell on the counter and a uniformed bellman appeared as if by magic, materializing at Wakefield's side. He took the overnight bag, and looked inquiringly at Max.

"Please take Mr. Wakefield to room 433," he directed, handing the bell man a brass key. He turned to Wakefield.

"Enjoy your stay, Mr. Wakefield. If you need anything, ring 222."

"Thanks, Max," said Wakefield, and turned almost obediently to follow the porter.

Wakefield was ushered into a spacious room, and the bellman moved to the window and began to open the drapes. "Leave it," Wakefield instructed. "I'm going to make a couple of calls and then take a nap." He handed the bellman a five-dollar bill, which the man pocketed.

"Thank you, sir. Please don't hesitate to call if you need anything." As he left the room, he hung a "Do Not Disturb" sign on the door.

Wakefield sat on the edge of the bed, trying to ignore the overwhelming fatigue that washed over him. He leaned his head back onto the pillow. *Just for a minute. I've got to call Thomas, and I've got to let Sylvia know where I'm staying. Just for a minute. . .*

He awoke with a start, disoriented and sore all over, as if he'd been beaten with a rubber hose truncheon. He looked around the room, and gradually, creeping on its hands and knees, awareness of his circumstances returned to him. His mouth was dry, and he was as hungry as he could ever remember being. He had not even removed his shoes. There was no telling how long he had slept. He called room service and ordered a sandwich and a pot of coffee. He found the room key on the sideboard where the bell man had left it and picked up the ice bucket. He stepped into the hall and tried to figure out which way to turn to find an ice machine. One way seemed as good as the other, and he shuffled painfully off down the hallway in search of ice and a soft drink.

He finally found a machine, bought two cans of Seven-Up with some change he found in his pocket, and filled his bucket with ice from the adjacent machine.

As he turned down the hallway to return to his room, he spied a uniformed police officer standing outside the open door of his room. The officer's back was to him, and he slipped back around the corner out of sight, his heart in his throat. He set the ice and soft drinks on the carpet and headed for the stairwell he'd passed moments before. Reaching the ground floor, he crossed the lobby, trying hard to be invisible, and went outside to the doorman, who also recognized him and greeted him by name. It was dark outside; he'd slept at least the whole day.

"Sid," he said without preamble, "I need your help. There's a hundred in it for you if you can get me a rental car here in five minutes and keep it quiet."

The doorman raised his eyebrows. "I can do it in three, Mr. Wakefield. We keep them here for our guests."

Wakefield produced the hundred-dollar bill that he kept tucked behind his driver's license in his wallet. "Make it happen, man! Bill the car to my room. Here's the key."

Sid made a phone call to the garage and a car appeared in moments. Sid ushered Wakefield to the open door, and held it while Wakefield slid into the driver's seat. "Thanks, Sid. The less said about this the better."

"I don't know anything, Mr. Wakefield. Haven't seen you all day."

Wakefield pulled out of the driveway and headed for the freeway. He jumped on Highway 57 north out of Houston, stopping into a drive-through burger joint for coffee and food. He ordered two large cups of water, with ice, as well. These he drank in great relief, feeling the cold water inside all the way to his stomach. Back on the highway, the miles rolled away underneath his humming tires. He put himself on autopilot, and finally had time to think.

> *"Weeping may endure for a night,*
> *but joy cometh in the morning."*
> —Bible, Psalms 30:5

28

29 August, Present

Wakefield drove northward through the night and into the early morning darkness. He took some small comfort in the incessant hum of the tires on the roadway eating up miles toward nowhere, and the cool wind in his face. He held the sedan at the speed limit, and checked his rear-view mirror frequently for red lights or suspicious cars. He stopped for gas at an all night station around four in the morning and continued until after sun-up, when he wheeled into a diner for breakfast, then drove some more. Gradually, he reasoned out the meaning of the events of the last few days. He tried to assess what was happening to him.

Diana was dead. Warren was dead. He was on the run, a possible suspect in his sister's death, and possibly Warren's as well. He was sitting on top of what might be the biggest cover-up the world had ever known. People had been killed for less—substantially less. They were trying to kill him, and he was scared. In order to survive, he had to understand their motives, their intent. What was driving them? More importantly, what would stop them?

Selmack had been at his home when he returned from the airport unexpectedly. Selmack should have been at the island. Brockner was shutting the job down. Selmack worked for Brockner. If Selmack was in Houston, it was at Brockner's direction. If Selmack was at his house, it could only mean that he knew something was going to happen. If Brockner had sent a plane for him, Selmack would have known that he, Wakefield, wouldn't be there to catch it.

The inescapable conclusion of this line of thought: Selmack

had been there to confirm the kill! In retrospect, it struck him: Brockner's office was somewhere in Utah! He had picked that much up from Selmack while they were working together at the island. A Cessna 310 didn't have nearly enough range to take him from Houston to Utah. Brockner would have told him to take a commercial flight if they were meeting at Brockner's office. The flight had been a ploy, and now Wakefield ruefully wondered how he had failed to question it.

But why kill Diana? Had the bomb been meant for him? Or had it been meant to eliminate both of them in a single stroke? Wakefield knew it had to be a bomb. The Captain at the fire had said it was probably a natural gas explosion, but the house was all electric, one of those Medallion homes that gave him a rate break for staying all electric.

His last hypothesis, that both he and Diana were the targets, seemed to be the most logical one. Brockner must have planned it, since he had obviously never sent the plane, believing that Wakefield would not be there to board it. The entire complex of events virtually proved to Wakefield that Stone's hypothesis about it being AIDS was right, or at least that Brockner was covering up something so dreadful that he would kill to protect the secret. But how could they have known that it was important to kill Diana, or Warren, to keep their secret under wraps, unless...

Of course! They'd bugged the house! They must have. They had selectively eliminated anyone that he had told of his discovery that night on the island where Douglas had died. Warren Stone's office must have been bugged, too. Had he been followed, and the followers noted his visit to Stone? Probably, but the really important thing to them would be to find out who he had told, and how much. The only way to do that was by electronic eavesdropping. But when could they have done it? The only reason to eavesdrop hadn't even been in existence until he had left the island with Harwiczki's letter of protest and resignation. That meant that the bugs had to have been placed before he had arrived home from the island! And that, in turn, meant that there was a strong organization behind the activities.

His mind suddenly recalled the van with the flat tire he had noticed as he and Diana had pulled into their driveway the night of his return from the island. Was it possible? This was a bigger operation mounted against him that he had first thought, and he would do well not to underestimate them again. These guys were playing hardball, for keeps.

There was too much coincidence for the deaths not to be related. And the killings were too well timed to have been random acts of violence. It was hard to believe. This was the stuff cloak and dagger mysteries were made of, not the type of thing environmental drilling contractors had to deal with. Still, all the indicators pointed to an effective, efficient, disciplined, and directed effort to eliminate any person who had even the slightest knowledge of the contents of the Harwiczki documents, and the events that had occurred fifteen years past on a small island somewhere in the Caribbean.

A plan started to form in his mind, and there were some details that needed attention. He wheeled over at the next opportunity to make a phone call. He dialed his office from a public telephone booth, keying in his credit card number from memory. It was long distance; he'd really put some miles on during the night.

Rosie answered.

"Where have you been!" she shrieked when he identified himself. "Oh, Mr. Wakefield, I'm so sorry about Diana," she sympathized, her voice breaking with tremor. "And poor Mr. Stone. Are you all right? It's all over the news. Where are you?"

"Thank you, Rosie. I'm O.K., just upset. I want you to take care of some things for me. I'll be back soon, just as soon as I get a few things ironed out."

"Tony, the yardman I sent to drive you home yesterday, said you went crazy; that you attacked a car, and the police chased you. He was really upset. Davis gave him the day off. They notified us they found the truck outside Warren's office, and it's been impounded." Wakefield knew she was asking for an explanation, or at least some reassurance, but he realized he couldn't provide either without confirming her worst fears.

"It's too complicated to explain," he offered lamely.

"What can I do to help?"

"Call my son, Thomas, and have him make the necessary funeral arrangements for Diana. Have Thomas call Warren's office and ask for Sylvia Bixler. She'll help with the arrangements."

"Certainly, Mr. Wakefield, but don't you want to call them yourself?"

"That's not possible, Rosie. Just call them, O.K.? I can't come home now, as much as I might want to. Thomas is going to have to take care of everything."

"Yes, sir, I'll do it. Is there anything else?"

"Rosie, I may be away for a while. Davis Esterson is to take charge in my absence. Please let him know that. I know that it's a lot of responsibility to give you to inform him. I should make the appointment more formal, but I cannot speak with him myself. Just do it."

"What about the island job, Mr. Wakefield? Everybody is in a flap, and the job is at a standstill. Nobody knows what to do next. Davis wants to talk to you."

"Tell Davis to pull everything out as quickly as possible, and not to resume work under any circumstances. The contract allows us to do that. Make sure Davis talks it over with Gene Briggs, first. That's all I can tell you."

"Yes, sir. Is there anything else?"

"Yes. Help Thomas handle my personal affairs while I'm away. Make sure the bills get paid. Get with Sylvia Bixler of Warren Stone's firm, introduce Thomas to her, and have her draw up any necessary papers. Put Thomas up somewhere in Houston. I'll call back and get his phone number in a couple of days. Oh, and arrange for a wire transfer of five thousand dollars to the biggest branch of our bank in St. Louis, for release on my signature. Do it right away. I haven't much money."

"When will you be back?"

"I don't know, Rosie. I just don't know. Thanks for everything." Wakefield hung up.

Next, he dialed Sylvia Bixler's number, and was transferred through by the receptionist. He hoped the line wasn't being monitored, but there was no choice.

"Sylvia," he said simply, without naming himself. "I'm going to Minnesota."

Major William Malleck knocked smartly at the door of General Brockner's office.

"Come!" Malleck entered and reported without preface.

"General, we've got a line on Wakefield. He used his credit card to pay for two phone calls. They originated in Arkansas, at a public phone. He called his office and the office of that attorney who was involved."

This information had a price; they had been forced to officially admit their interest in Wakefield as a matter of 'National Security' to obtain the cooperation of the company which held Wakefield's phone credit card account. It had been a calculated risk, but it had paid off, at least marginally.

"Do we know what he said?"

"No, sir. I had the taps removed immediately on execution of the sanctions as a precaution."

"God damn it, man! Put them back on! This gives us nothing."

"Yes, sir. Right away."

Malleck left. General Brockner leaned back in his chair, gazing thoughtfully out the window. *Why Arkansas? Is it a destination, or just a point along the way to somewhere else? Where is he going? Another call location or two would help me make a better guess. It can't be Harwiczki; from the earlier conversations we taped, it's clear that Wakefield knows Harwiczki is dead. If that idiot Malleck hadn't dropped the phone taps, I might know by now.*

The sole intent of Wakefield's stop was to get some rest, but the bar attached to the Howard Johnson's beckoned, drew him in with an irresistible force, waylaying him after check-in on the way to his room. *One quick one,* he had thought to himself, *to help me sleep.* He pulled up on a leatherette barstool, reassured somehow by the rows of liquor bottles on display behind the bar, and by the dimness of the interior. It felt safe, anonymous. He ordered a drink, dropping a twenty on the bar.

It helped. It took the edge off, and it led to another, and then several. Nearly blind drunk, he stumbled to his room, assisted by the desk clerk who had been called by the bartender after closing time. He was unable to buy more liquor at the bar, and unable to hold the glass if he could have. The helpful clerk dumped him unceremoniously on the queen bed, leaving him fully clothed, shoes still on and laced. He was passed out cold before the clerk could slip out and back to the front desk.

The following morning, late, with his mind fogged and his mouth foul, he phoned a liquor store, and had two bottles of bourbon delivered. He just didn't care any more; let the police find him. The pain kept coming. The visions of Diana broken and bleeding dragged it from the depths of his psyche. Only in stupor and unconsciousness, his conscious mind besotted and poisoned with alcohol, could he find respite. His sense of loss was overwhelming, unbearable. Diana! His beautiful Susan! He'd lost everybody who meant something in his life.

The wanton, self-indulgent bath of alcohol and self-pity he was drawing in his emotional bathtub was interrupted unpleasantly before he could truly immerse himself in it. The desk clerk nearly killed him pounding insistently on the door to ask for payment for the coming night's stay. Wakefield told him to put it on the card until further notice, and leave him the hell alone.

Some time later, days as it turned out, he rose from his stupor and didn't call the liquor store that delivered. He sobered slowly, painfully, his shaking hands tilting glasses of foul tasting tap water to his dehydrated lips. He slept again, and awoke sober, with a mouth full of cotton.

Diana came into his mind, and he cried, quietly, for hours. And when the crying stopped, he could care again.

29

5 September, Present

The roses were gone. Their remnant hips were orange dots in the slanting, late afternoon sunshine. It was one of those crisp, brittle autumn days that seems to spatter sunshine about the landscape like sparks from a cosmic welding torch. The colors were extravagant in the spacious garden to the rear of the Harwiczki residence in White Bear Lake, Minnesota.

Mrs. Irena Harwiczki, aged some seventy-seven years but still spry and alert, apologized for the condition of her garden to the young man who waited expectantly for her to pour the tea. From her perspective, he was young. If she had asked him, he would have said he was older, much older, than he wanted to be.

Just because it was rural Minnesota, and he had listened to scores of Norwegian farmer jokes during his college days, Wakefield had expected a comfortably overweight woman in a print dress with a thick accent. He couldn't have been farther from the mark. She was slender, in tailored tweeds of a classic cut. A snow white collared blouse opened at her neck. She moved with the ease of a person half her years. There was no quaver in her voice; it was clear, well modulated, and free of brogue. What few wrinkles she possessed were badges of character, somehow assets; she had remarkable skin.

"I just don't seem to have the time it takes to keep things up anymore," she was saying. "Oh, the neighbor boy comes over on Saturdays and does a little, but he has less regard for the Mister's roses than he does for his pay. You should have seen the garden before the Mister passed on; he had a passion for Old World roses. It was so beautiful it would bring tears to your eyes. The Marschal Neal would bloom nearly all summer, with the sweetest scent. It was quite sulky until the Mister moved it over here where it could keep its feet dry." She gestured toward a rangy, ancient rose bush that should have been trellised, but wasn't. It lay about the ground like the auburn hair of a drowned mermaid awash on the tide. The few leaves that remained were the color of rust.

"Do you like the tea?" she asked solicitously after his first precautionary sip. "I make it this time of year with the hips from the Mister's roses. It's full of vitamins, the books say."

"It's lovely, Mrs. Harwiczki," Russell Wakefield said, saucering the cup as he spoke. "You have a lovely garden here. I imagine it's particularly lovely in the spring. I want to thank you for seeing me." She didn't seem to mind that he'd laid on the "lovelies" a little thick.

"Thank you, young man," she said graciously. "Now, you wanted to know about the Mister." Wakefield felt anything but young.

"Anything you can tell me, ma'am. What he did for the government, and how he came to pass on. Anything you remember."

"May I ask why?" She cocked her head engagingly, peering at him from under her lightly raised eyebrow, with the glittering eyes of an inquisitive bird.

"I'm looking for the people who may have worked with him. There is some new information that we need to get to them, concerning the nature of the research he was involved with."

It was truthful, as far as it went. She accepted the vagueness of the explanation more from the fact that it was offered than from any substance it carried. "Do you know who any of them were?"

"The Mister didn't talk much to me about his work. I think it was secret, or some such thing. He was very brilliant in his field, you know. He was a virologist," she proclaimed proudly.

"Yes, I have been told."

"He worked for a man called Martingale, or something like that, doing biological research. He only mentioned him a few times, and wasn't particularly fond of the man, I gathered. I never met him, but I met a nice young Colonel who came personally to bring the news about the Mister. We had tea in this very garden, but it was much nicer then."

"Do you remember his name?"

"It was Brockner. Colonel Brockner. Nice young man. He looked very dapper in his uniform. He was rather serious, but I suppose that's because he had come to tell me that the Mister had passed on. He was concerned that they didn't have all of the Mister's notes, and asked me to look for them while he waited. He stayed until my friend Molly came."

"When was this? Do you remember a date?"

"One never forgets the date one's husband dies. It was May

NAVASSA

8, 1977, that the plane crashed. The Colonel Brockner arrived two days later, on the tenth." Wakefield suppressed a gasp at her words, and the hair on the back of his neck bristled. The date of Harwiczki's death was the day after the doctor had written the memo that had thrust Wakefield's life into turmoil! Trying to control his tone and keep his demeanor relaxed and casual, he pressed on.

"What did he say?"

"Only that the Mister had been killed in a plane crash out over the ocean, and they had been unable to recover the body, although they tried very hard. He's buried at the cemetery north of town, but he's not really there, having been lost at sea and everything. We had a service and put up a stone anyway."

"Was there anybody else that you can recall? Anybody who might have worked with your husband?"

"There was a fellow, an associate researcher, named Bennington. The Mister came as close to despising the man as he ever did anyone in our twenty-nine years of marriage. He would rant about the man if you got him on the subject. He thought the man was an arrogant charlatan. Had no use for him at all. His last letter was about the man, almost entirely; about how the man was taking credit for the Mister's success on the research project."

"Do you know where he was working then?" asked Wakefield.

"An island somewhere. It was all very hush-hush. He would fly to Florida, and I wouldn't see him for six weeks or so, then he would be home for two weeks and then back to the island. They paid him very well, but I missed him when he was away. He said it wouldn't be long, but it was nearly three years. Would you like more tea? Oh, yes! I recall once that he brought me a wood carving once. It was a monkey. He said it was from Haiti. I threw it out, years ago. It was actually quite ugly, and I had plenty of other things to help me remember the Mister. These roses—these were his passion," she reflected reminiscently. A far-away look had come into her eyes. Her gaze spanned decades.

"Do you have any of the letters he sent you? While he was working on the Island, I mean."

"I would have kept them for years, but when I came back from the Mister's funeral, they were gone. The house had been burglarized, and they were in a jewelry box that was stolen. I'm sorry."

"I can't thank you enough for talking with me today, Mrs.

Harwiczki," said Wakefield. "I hope it hasn't been too much of a burden. I really should be going."

"No burden at all, young man. It has been my pleasure. It's nice to remember my Paulus from time to time."

He left her there, in the garden, lost in a reverie of remembrance for a man who was fifteen years departed. Wakefield wondered if he would ever come to a point in his life where he could talk of Susan—or of Diana!—fondly and quietly, without tears and anger, as Mrs. Harwiczki had of her 'Mister'. He hoped so, but couldn't imagine it.

Driving away from the Harwiczki home, Wakefield stopped along the edge of White Bear Lake, the town's namesake, and used a pay telephone in front of a bait store at the water's edge. It was after six p.m., and Sylvia should be home by now. The phone rang four times, then her answering machine kicked on. Wakefield was about to hang up when Sylvia's living voice, breathless, broke into the recorded message.

"Hello. This is Sylvia Bixler. Just a second while I shut off the machine." The recorded message suddenly ceased mid-sentence. Wakefield identified himself.

"How are you doing?" she asked, cautiously, fishing.

"I've just been with Mrs. Harwiczki," he said. "She confirmed that Dr. Harwiczki died the day after he wrote that letter; the day after he resigned his post. I think the bastards killed him."

"You don't know that, Russ. Still, I'll admit that it is an interesting coincidence. What else?"

"She said he was a virologist working for Martindale, and that she was told of her husband's death by Colonel Brockner, of Martindale's staff, so Brockner knew about it. Brockner appears to have picked up a promotion since then."

"What are you going to do now?"

"I'm going to look up Martindale and see what he's got to say. Have you located him yet?"

"He's retired, in Tucson," said Sylvia. "I had the devil's own time getting the information; they are not inclined to give out the whereabouts of retired generals over the phone. I had to lie. I gave them a song and dance about being a niece of his, just back from several years in Europe. The records clerk bought it, but I had to kiss a little ass." Wakefield was momentarily startled, taken aback by her choice of phrase. Then he wondered how else she could have expressed the idea so succinctly. She gave him Martindale's address in Tucson, and Wakefield jotted it down.

NAVASSA

"Why don't you let a private investigator check it out?" she suggested. "Then you could come back to Houston and take care of business. There's a lot of business to take care of..."

"What's going on in Houston?" he asked.

"They still want you for questioning, and your flight has them looking harder. You're their best suspect. They've discovered the connection between you and Warren. They want to talk to you about that, too. They say you've fled the state, and there has been a federal officer assigned to work with the Houston police on your case. I've managed to convince them that my handling of your affairs is routine and incidental, after Warren's death, and that my client-attorney relationship is exclusively with Thomas. He's a fine, young man, incidentally. Anyway, I'm sure they have gone out on the wire with a request to stop and detain. If I were you, I wouldn't even get pulled over for a tail light violation."

"I'll be careful. Is the federal officer named Selmack?"

"No, not that. Something else, I don't remember. When will you call again?"

"A couple of days. So you're sure the authorities don't have any idea that you're helping me?"

"If they did, I'd be before the bar in a wink. I don't think they suspect. I have to admit I'm not all that comfortable with our relationship in that regard. Why don't you come in and talk with the local police. It's their investigation. You could clear things up in a few days and return to a normal life."

"I need proof before I do that. I'll never get proof if I'm in custody, and they're not likely to take my word for it. As you said, they need a suspect. Besides, I am not certain that the people who are trying to kill me wouldn't be able to waltz in and grab me from the Houston police if I turned myself in. I really don't have a choice. Thanks for helping me, Sylvia."

"Russ? One more thing. The funeral was beautiful. Thomas coordinated it. I thought you'd like to know. The kid's disturbed about your absence. He was a basket case for a week about Diana's death."

Wakefield felt a twinge, but stayed away from the feelings. "Thanks, Sylvia. Thanks . . . "

Wakefield terminated the connection and headed south for the St. Paul/Minneapolis Airport. There, he turned in the rental car he'd picked up when he fled the hotel in Houston, realizing that the bill would be horrendous since he'd used the car point-to-point and not returned it to its original source. He entered the terminal and bought a ticket for Tucson on the next available

181

flight, using his credit card.

The clerk at the car rental counter where Wakefield had dropped the keys and paperwork for the rental car punched up the identification number of the vehicle as a matter of course in accepting the vehicle's return. The file was flagged with special instructions. She called her supervisor immediately. Less than an hour later, she was interviewed by two men in blue suits— from the Army Security Agency, they said.

Simultaneously, two other agents were interviewing a ticket clerk in St. Paul. They showed a picture of the fugitive they were seeking, and the clerk made a positive identification. The fugitive had purchased a ticket to Tucson, via Denver, they were told. The computer confirmed that he had boarded.

In less than two hours after the ticket was purchased, the information was in Brockner's hands. He ordered Major Malleck to get agents in place at the Tucson Air Terminal, to instruct them to intercept Wakefield and maintain surveil-lance—only surveillance—until he could bring in Selmack and Olmstead to handle the matter. Brockner was gratified.

I've got you now, you slippery sonofabitch

30

6 September, Present

Tucson was balmy. The heat of the day lingered, mixing pleasantly with the coolness of the newly arrived night air. The smell of the desert was all around, an interesting, subtle synthesis of dry grass and creosote. Tall stark mountains thrust against the sky north of the city, and a filling moon hovered dangerously close to the lower mountains toward the east. In the gently sloping basin at the foot of the mountain ranges, Tucson lay arrayed in lights, sparkling in the clear desert air.

Two local agents were waiting near the gate at Tucson International Airport when Wakefield deplaned well after dark. They made no effort to detain him. Rather, they followed at a discrete distance as he approached the car rental counter and made arrangements for a vehicle.

When Wakefield exited the terminal, they identified themselves to the clerk, obtained the license number, make, and model of Wakefield's rental car, and arranged a delay so that they could bring up their own car in time to be waiting when his arrived. This was the best class of excitement for the two field office agents. In Tucson; they rarely got a chance to do anything so interesting as tailing a fugitive.

Wakefield left the terminal and headed for the foothills north of Tucson via a back road that the lot attendant had described to him. The attendant marked the route on a complimentary map, and explained that Davis-Monthan Air Force Base was smack in the middle of any easy route from the airport to the city's core. The route was simple enough—Valencia to Kolb, Kolb to Tanque Verde, then left onto Sabino Canyon to River road, then look for the signs to Canyon Ranch—and it took Wakefield across long, straight stretches of unlighted roadways with little traffic at this time of night.

The trailing agents were forced to drop well back after the first turn, but managed to keep the rented car's tail lights in view as they passed through the graveyard of superannuated military jet fighters that lined both sides of Kolb where it traversed through the Air Force base. This was cake, and the agents were impressed with themselves.

The agents were nearly half a mile behind their quarry when he turned unexpectedly right onto Tanque Verde, and his tail lights were lost in the in the bustle of the busy thoroughfare. Wakefield hated airline food, and he'd developed a ravenous appetite during the flight. Unaware that he was being followed, he turned immediately into the first restaurant parking lot that presented itself, looking for something to eat. The trailing agents didn't see the move. They motored blithely past the restaurant, searching the traffic ahead of them for some sign of the white Cutlass Cierra Wakefield was driving. They searched for over an hour, and finally, with a great degree of chagrin, reported to their operations supervisor that they had lost contact.

Wakefield ordered and ate. The fatigue of the day's travel caught up with him as he finished his supper. Martindale could wait until morning. He checked into a nearby motel and fell into a fitful, exhausted sleep before the engine of his car was cool.

"Lost him! What do you mean, they lost him!" General Brockner thundered at the operations supervisor of the Phoenix field office. "You tell those assholes to pack some warm clothes! They're going to the Aleutians!"

The bluster was for show; Brockner knew precisely where Wakefield was heading. Still, it wouldn't do to let the incompetence of the surveillance team go unpunished, and Brockner knew he would have to follow up with a perfunctory, wrist-slapping letter-to-the-file. And, actually, it might work out for the best. He now had two unwilling witnesses to the fact that the trail was lost. It would be harder to connect anything to his own operatives, if it ever came to that.

The real problem was that by the time he could get Selmack and Olmstead mobilized and on their way, the last commercial flight westbound would have already left Houston. Their departure would have to be postponed until early the following morning. It meant a nine-thirty arrival in Tucson. Probably, it meant they would have to take Wakefield at Martindale's home.

The real risk was that Wakefield could conceivably get in, get to the retired general, and get out before Selmack and Olmstead could get there. There was no risk from the old general; he had a vested interest in keeping the whole Navassa thing under wraps, and Brockner doubted that Wakefield had the sophistication to force it from him. It was just uneconomical and worrisome.

With Wakefield at liberty, the secret of Martindale's colossal blunder was in some danger of being revealed. This, of course, would implicate him, Brockner, and his career would be over. If they missed him at the general's house, additional man-hours would then need to be spent in finding Wakefield and carrying out the sanction.

BRADD HOPKINS

> *"Ask not for whom the bell tolls..."*
> —John Donne

31

7 September, Present

The long dawn shadows of the saguaros, sentinels of the desert, cast low by the rising sun, were visibly shortening as Russell Wakefield made his way through the coolness of the morning to the security gate at Canyon Ranch. Cactus wrens flitted and chirped in the branches of a Palo Verde tree opposite the gatehouse as he stopped the car in front of the striped barrier arm and greeted the guard on duty there.

There was money inside the gate. The wealth of retired attorneys, doctors, corporate executives, and shipping magnates was subtly concealed by the unadorned high desert landscape, but it was there if you looked. It was there in the manned gatehouse, in the immaculately groomed and casually natural face of the desert. It was there in the Ralph Lauren and Versace labels inside the collars of the early morning joggers with their designer water bottles. It was manifest in the pristine, reserved silence of the paved, curbed residential streets. It lurked in the closed, air conditioned garages where Mercedes, BMWs, and an occasional Bentley stayed comfortably cool against the time when they might be needed by their owners in the heat of the day.

"I'm here to see General Martindale," he told the security guard.

"Yes, sir. Is he expecting you?"

"Not exactly, but it's important that I see him."

"Your name, sir?"

Wakefield gave his name, and the guard turned to a phone extension. He dialed three numbers, and spoke briefly into the mouthpiece when it was answered. He hung up the phone and turned to Wakefield.

"I'm sorry, sir. The General does not know you, and does not wish to see visitors. Perhaps if you could call later and make an appointment . . . You may turn around through the gate, but you must leave."

"Tell him it's about General Brockner. Tell him that it's a matter of life and death."

"I'm sorry, sir. The General was quite clear. No visitors."

"Thank you for checking. I'll come back later," said Wakefield with mock cordiality, masking with his most unctuous smile his desire to rip the smug, self-important guard limb from limb. The gate arm swung upward, out of his path.

Wakefield contained his frustration, and resisted the temptation to simply keep going once the guard opened the gate to enable him to turn around. That would only attract attention and might get the police involved.

As he drove back up the hill, he realized that even though there was a guarded gate, the remainder of the area was completely unfenced! All he had to do was park the car and walk in unimpeded by any barrier! He pulled the car around a bend in the access road, parked, and headed across the open desert a few hundred feet to the nearest paved road in the enclave where he began what he hoped appeared to be a casual search for the street address Sylvia had given him.

He found it quickly: a low, adobe motif with no windows facing the street. It was aloof from other houses in the tract, private by distance as well as by design. A matronly housekeeper in white answered his knock at the door. She eyed him suspiciously without speaking

"I'm here to see General Martindale," said Wakefield. "It's very important."

"I'm sorry," the housekeeper said politely. "The General is not seeing anyone today." As she started easing the door shut, Wakefield surprised himself by shoving a foot between the door and the jamb, pushing back powerfully to force the door open. The housekeeper screamed and scuffled to close the door with remarkable strength.

"Louisa! Let him enter!" The voice was not loud, but it carried a commanding tone. Louisa, wide-eyed and apprehensive, backed away from the door as Wakefield looked up to see an old, heavyset man with watery blue eyes set in a pale and deeply shadowed face. The man wore a white terry bathrobe, from which jutted spindly, fish-belly-white legs terminating in worn, run-over lounging slippers. One hand remained loosely held in a bulging pocket of the man's garment.

"Who are you and what do you want?" said the man with the

same compelling tone he'd used on Louisa earlier. Wakefield found himself answering almost involuntarily as he straightened to face the man.

"My name is Russell Wakefield. I must talk with you. In private. About SK-443." Wakefield had suddenly dredged up the number from his memory of the Harwiczki papers. The man visibly stiffened and Wakefield knew he was on target.

"Join me for breakfast, Mr. Wakefield. We can talk on the terrace." He issued the necessary instructions to Louisa and turned to lead the way through the house and outside, to an east facing, shaded terrace. The view of the desert peaks in the near distance was ruggedly spectacular. The early morning shadows delineated the deep canyons sharply, and the sun bathed the exposed ridges in an orangey golden glow. Sabino Canyon, to the north, was a ragged black slash through the rose-colored mountain face.

They were barely seated when Louisa appeared with coffee service and orange juice. The old General waved the housekeeper away with a parchment claw and poured cordially himself, then looked directly at Wakefield with unblinking, watery blue eyes.

"SK-443?" In the morning light, the General's pale, gray face was seamed with deep, flaccid wrinkles, and he had a wattle at his throat. He had the jowls of an aging bulldog. He looked haunted, somehow. His shoulders stooped, as if bearing some immeasurable burden, but his eyes were alert in their deep sockets, watching Wakefield intently.

"I found a letter of resignation and a letter documenting your research and intent to test SK-443, both from Dr. Harwiczki. I know that there has been a massive cover-up, and I know that you're one of the key players."

"Just who the hell do you think you are, bursting into my home and making slanderous insinuations?" Martindale snarled, menacingly. "What basis do you have for your wild and unfounded accusations?"

"I have original documents protesting your plans to test a biological agent on the population of San Francisco. I have evidence that shows the author of the documents died the day after he created them. I believe you had him killed. I believe you have set loose a terrible disease in the world, and that you may know how to cure it."

"Dr. Harwiczki died in an unfortunate plane crash," Martindale said sardonically. "You're fishing, shooting at shadows. What is your real purpose coming here? This is all ancient history, and well documented. Are you a damned journalist? You've got to have balls the size of watermelons to even be here, if you are."

"The documents clearly name you as being responsible. And, no, I'm not a journalist. I'm a man who has lost his sister, his best friend, and Lord knows who else. I've got people hunting me like an animal, and thousands of people are dying because you have a secret."

"Where did you find the papers you claim to have?"

"On an island in the Caribbean, working for General Brockner on an environmental clean-up. Brockner and his people killed my sister and my best friend. They are now trying to kill me. I'm scared shitless. I have nothing to lose, and I want some answers. I have proof that will put you in prison for the rest of your life—if they don't rip you limb from limb in the streets first. I want the whistle blown to call off the dogs."

Martindale removed his hand from the pocket of his bathrobe, extracting a .45 caliber automatic pistol. He laid it on the table between them. He sat very still, and was silent for a long time.

Then he spoke: "That's not possible. We killed Harwiczki, and there were no such papers." Wakefield was stunned by the man's casual statement of incrimination, the matter-of-fact admission to murder. It began to worry him. It was too easy.

"I do not carry this for self defense," the general stated, gesturing weakly toward the pistol. "I carry it against the moment when I shall find the courage to put a bullet in my own brain. Your wife and your friend are inconsequential, measured against the number of deaths I've caused, and there is no end to it. I'm retired, in quiet disgrace, for a twist of fate that turned the triumph of my life, the pinnacle of my career, into an abyss of death and dishonor. Mr. Wakefield, I'm the man who gave the world the greatest plague it has ever seen. Do you have any idea what a burden that is? My own death would give me the last great pleasure I could hope for on this earth, and I'm too great a coward to do the deed myself."

"You are wallowing in self pity, general," Wakefield observed coldly. "Cut the crap. You must come forward, tell what you know. At least, you must tell me."

"That is not possible, Mr. Wakefield. There are others who know what happened. They would go to any lengths to suppress such revelations; they are powerful, and their careers and lives hang in the balance. There are even some people who believe that the disease is a blessing, and will ultimately purify the race.

They will eliminate even the *slightest* threat of their exposure. You, yourself, are as good as dead."

"Who are they, General? Who else knows?"

"They..."

The crockery orange juice pitcher on the table exploded in front of them, followed by the report of a rifle in the distance. Wakefield leaped from his chair, tripping in his haste, and sprawled out on the terrace as a second shot rang out. He heard a 'thunk' sound in the wall above his head, followed by a third report. He grabbed the pistol from the table where it lay, wet with orange juice, and returned an ineffectual shot in the general direction of the rifle fire.

The general had toppled backwards in his chair, a double stain of bright red blood soaking through his white bathrobe and spreading rapidly across his chest. Wakefield moved to the general's head, keeping low. The general clearly had only moments to live. He clutched weakly at Wakefield's shirt, staining it with blood, and pulled him closer, speaking with great effort in a wet voice. Frothy blood gurgled at the corner of his mouth as he spoke.

"Richard Elwin knows. Elwin. In Mexico, where we haven't bothered him because he kept his mouth shut. In Cabo San Lucas. Elwin. God, have mercy."

"The island, General. What was the name of the island?"

"Navassa." The General's body went limp. Another round thumped into the wall behind Wakefield, spurring him into action.

He scrambled across the terrace and into the house the way he'd come, bowling Louisa over as he ran. With the house between him and the unseen assailant, he sprinted up the steep hill, through the saguaro and Palo Verde to the roadway above where he'd left the car. As he crested the edge of the roadway, a figure moved near the car, raising a rifle. Wakefield snapped off a shot instinctively, catching the man in the shoulder, spinning him around. The rifle flew from his grasp, clattered across the pavement.

Wakefield leaped for the car, threw the pistol on the seat, and fumbled for the keys in a panic. The engine started. He dropped the lever into gear and floored the accelerator, peeling away from the curb and down the hill. Gravel sprayed from his spinning tires.

His breath came in great gasps, and his body trembled as he drove, trying to recover his wits and his wind... trying to find the balance between his need for headlong flight and a sane

191

speed for the public roadway. He found it just in time.

Two patrol cars raced past him going the opposite direction, just as he managed to get his speed down to an unremarkable rate. He headed eastward, away from town. He had no goal in mind except to put as much distance as possible between himself and his pursuers.

> *"Nothing in life is so exhilarating
> as to be shot at without result."*
> —Winston Churchill

32

9 September, Present

The airport was out of the question. As he listened to the radio in his rented car, it informed him the main roads were also dangerous. He ditched the car, described on the air right down to its license plate number. The Tucson Police were looking for a murderer—and they had a name. Russell Wakefield, of Houston, had entered the house of retired Army General Thomas Martindale and cold-bloodedly shot him in the chest while he was eating his breakfast. The housekeeper, once over her hysterics, had clearly identified him from a photo line-up and reported that she'd seen him run from the house with a gun in his hand. Forensics had the bullet from the General's body, and two others dug from the walls of the house. In twenty-four hours, the official ballistics report and the General's autopsy would show that the general had died from a rifle shot, not a pistol. In the meantime, there was a murderer at liberty in Tucson, armed and dangerous.

It was further known that he was a fugitive from federal authorities, who were augmenting the Tucson city police in the search, lead by a federal officer named Jack Selmack. A federal officer named Olmstead had been wounded in an attempt to bring down the desperate fugitive, and was in stable condition at Desert General Hospital. The exact nature of the felon's federal offense remained unknown, "in the interests of national security".

The manhunt was on. The authorities threw a net around the entire city and began to draw it tighter.

The rental car was found abandoned in a hotel parking lot, just after noon, with fresh bloodstains on the seat. The desk clerk remembered the man from his check-in late the previous evening, and said he had an insane look in his eye. Investigators found a bloody shirt in the wastebasket in his room.

Wakefield listened to the early broadcasts of the breaking news in his hotel room as he showered and washed off the blood General Martindale had smeared on him. He quickly realized that leaving Tucson by any normal means was out of the question. He was at a loss as to what to do next. His hands shook as he washed, and he jumped at small noises outside that were merely the sounds of Tucson going about its business of the day.

He walked from the hotel room with Martindale's gun in his bag and a clean suit of clothes on his back. He went into a corner convenience store and bought a bag full of non-perishable food and bottled water. By back alleys and side paths, he found his way back into the desert, to a thick stand of Palo Verde trees in the bottom of Tanque Verde Wash.

The clearing he found in the thicket was littered with garbage from its use before by transients. He moved into the peripheral bushes and lay down on the sparse, dry grass at the foot of a gnarled bush to wait, to think. He hoped his hiding place was sufficiently out of character for him that the search would concentrate in other, more likely spots. He hunkered down.

The afternoon wore on. Even in the shade of the thicket, the heat grew stifling. He drank water from his bottle but was too uncomfortable, too miserably hot, to eat anything. He was wryly amused at the circumstance he was in...here he was, the owner of a successful, nationwide corporation, cowering like a terrified jackrabbit in the Arizona desert, wanted by federal authorities for a murder or murders he hadn't committed. Worse, people hunted him; people who would shoot him dead before they called out a warning. They not only had a vested, compelling interest in seeing him dead, they also had behind them the full force of authority and tremendous resources at their disposal to accomplish their goal. If they found him, they'd kill him in a heartbeat, and somebody would probably get a medal. His crime against them was far more serious than murder. He knew too much.

He allowed his mind to wander over the painful memories of his sister's death and cried into his hands at his loss. There was so much he'd wanted to say to her, so much he wanted her to know about the way he adored her. He felt as though a part of his physical body had been ripped away, and the ghost pain was unbearable. The catharsis of his grief exhausted him. As the sun lowered in the western sky, leaving some relief from the swel-

NAVASSA

:ering afternoon heat of the desert wash, he slipped into a dead and dreamless sleep.

He woke well after dark, disoriented. For a few frantic seconds his mind would not tell him where he was. The night was still warm, but now pleasantly so, and he was groggy and ill-rested. A world-class headache pounded away behind his eyes. He picked up his bag and walked toward the lighted sign of a gasoline station a few hundred yards away. He found a pay phone and dialed San Diego information for the number of Cooper Black, his regional manager for the western region of Wakefield Environmental, Inc. The phone rang half a dozen times before a sleepy voice answered.

"Hello? Do you realize it's after midnight?" Cooper's voice was irritated and muffled, but recognizable.

"Cooper?"

"Yes. Who is this?"

"Russ Wakefield."

"Good grief! Where are you?" Black was instantly fully awake.

"Tucson. Listen, Coop', I need you to do something for me... and keep it to yourself."

"Anything, Russ. What in the hell is going on?"

"It would take all night to explain, and you still wouldn't believe it. Got a pad and pencil handy?"

"You bet. Just a second . . . O.K., shoot."

"Pull one of your guys who likes to hunt, somebody with a brain who can keep his mouth shut, and buy him a couple of shotguns, in nice cases. Buy him everything he needs for two people to go dove hunting, one outfit in size 42 chest, long, 38-inch waist. Put him and the gear on a plane and send him to Tucson on the earliest flight you can get him on.

"Then call the Jeep dealership in Tucson, and buy a four-wheel drive Cherokee, which he can pick up when he arrives. Light colored, with air conditioning. Tell him to drive it east on Tanque Verde Street until he comes to the Phillips Station, and to park there by the phone booth and wait."

"That package will cost around twenty-five thousand dollars, Russ. Isn't that a bit pricey for a dove hunting trip?" Black had been keeping a tally in his head. It was second nature to him. It was unlike Wakefield to rely on his regional managers for his vacation arrangements.

"Does it sound like I'm going dove hunting? I'm in some serious trouble here, and this will help get me out of it."

"Can't you go to the authorities? Russ, look, I know about

195

Houston. I'm sorry. The police there are getting edgy, according to Davis Esterson. You can't run forever."

"I can run for *now*. Coop, not a word to anybody, O.K.? You've got to trust me, that I know what I'm doing."

"I always have. Consider it done."

"Thanks, Coop. I have to go."

33

11 September, Present

Wakefield watched from the scrub creosote bushes as the white Cherokee with the paper license plates of a newly purchased vehicle pulled up near the Phillips Station and parked. He continued to watch as the driver waited, grew bored, and bought a soft drink from a machine. The station was situated on a corner, with a long expanse of approaching roadway visible in all directions. Wakefield watched for two hours, to make sure that the same car did not pass the intersection twice. Finally, he walked up to the driver, approaching from the open desert.

"Do you work for Wakefield Environmental?" he asked. He was instinctively checking the man's clothing for untoward bulges. His own hand clutched the paper bag that concealed Martindale's .45 ACP from casual view.

"Yes."

"I'm Russ Wakefield. Let's go."

In the closed cab of the vehicle, it was apparent that Wakefield had been too long without a bath. His face was stubbled with three days' growth of beard and his clothing reeked of old, dry sweat. He was dusty, dirty, and haggard, with a wild look in his eyes—eyes that burned with the alertness of a hunted animal. The driver rolled down the window despite the fact that the air conditioning was going flat out.

Seated in the driver's seat, the man asked cautiously "How do I know you're who you say you are?"

"Cooper Black sent you. You have the necessary equipment to go dove hunting. You bought this jeep yesterday, and were told to come here and wait. Does that satisfy you?"

"The Jeep is leased. Mr. Black set it up. Where to, Mr. Wakefield?" The man keyed the ignition and the engine roared to life. Wakefield switched the air conditioning lower and turned on the radio, tuning to a local station.

"Turn right, and keep going. What's your name?"

"Rob Dawson."

"How long have you been working for Cooper?"

"Less than a year. Before that, I worked for Davis Esterson and Gene Briggs in west Texas. I'm a tool pusher. We had an accident, out at Dyess Air Force Base, and I got hurt. When I came back to work, I asked for a transfer. The company sent me to California."

"I know all about that. It wasn't your fault." Wakefield reflected on the coincidence that had put this man in the Jeep with him, of all the employees that could have been selected. His own problems with Brockner had started as the result of the accident to which Dawson referred.

"Are we really going dove hunting, sir? None of this makes any sense to me."

"I'm going to Mexico. You're going back to San Diego when I get across the border. Meanwhile, we're two hunters, going dove hunting in Mexico. There will be roadblocks, and I can't get through alone."

"We can't, Mr. Wakefield. We can't go dove hunting."

The words brought Wakefield up short. He looked intently at Dawson. "What do you mean?"

"What I mean is, if you don't have permits for these guns, we'll never be allowed to cross the border. The Mexicans don't like guns; their people aren't allowed to have them. With their history of revolutions, it takes more effort to get a hunting permit than it does to get a building permit in California. There are two sure ways to get a one-way ticket to a Mexican jail: guns and drugs. We can't be carrying either."

The news came on the radio at that instant, and Wakefield turned up the volume. He was no longer the lead story, but the second item was a recap of the older news about the Martindale murder and a report that the suspect was still at large. He flipped the radio off when the story was finished.

"They're talking about me," he said to Dawson, whose eyes widened. Dawson gripped the steering wheel tighter, and concentrated intently on the deserted road. "I'm innocent," continued Wakefield, "but I can't prove it, yet. Beyond that, the less you know, the better."

The road ended abruptly near a golf course. Dawson stopped the Jeep and they changed into the hunting attire Dawson had stowed in the back. Wakefield kicked a hole in the soft sand at the road shoulder and buried the clothes he'd been living in for the last three days.

When they re-entered the vehicle, Dawson spoke: "Listen,

Mr. Wakefield, I think aiding a fugitive is a crime. This is really dangerous, and I don't like it one bit. Wakefield Environmental's been real good to me, but I don't want to go to jail."

"I've got a forty-five in my bag. If anything happens, tell them that when you found out I was wanted, you tried to leave and I threatened you with it. Cooper will take care of you. Call him if anything goes wrong. Now, let's do some four-wheeling."

They left the pavement, following a dirt track along the base of the mountains south and east of Tucson. They selected a turn at each junction that kept them heading generally south. The going was easy on the hard, rocky ridges where they bounced along at a good pace, but not quite fast enough to raise a dust cloud. The sand in the bottoms of the intervening arroyos that drained the mountains was another matter. The soft, beach-like sand in these places challenged both the Cherokee and the driving skills of Rob Dawson.

They nearly got stuck several times. After two hours moving across the desert terrain, they cut Interstate 10, several miles south and east of Tucson. The roadblocks were behind them. They fueled at the Interstate. Wakefield bought a North American Atlas, groceries, and a case of bottled water. And, much to Dawson's unspoken relief, a stick of deodorant.

He used a pay phone to call Sylvia Bixler.

"I saw Martindale," he informed her without prologue. "He's dead."

"Well, he was older. That's too bad."

"No, no, I mean somebody shot him. While I was there. The Police think I did it. I've been hiding in the desert for three days. Selmack's working with them. And if you believe the radio, I put a bullet into a federal officer."

"Did you?"

"I shot somebody. I don't know who it was."

"Russ! Can you *hear* yourself? Where did you get a gun? Why did you shoot somebody, and you don't even know who?" Her grammar was collapsing in her confusion and she gathered her intellect about her like a shield. "You'd better start from the beginning."

Wakefield began a narration of the events that had transpired since his last telephone call to his attorney, made from Minnesota at the airport. Sylvia listened quietly, and remained quiet when he'd finished.

He endured the silence as long as he could, then spoke into the mouthpiece: "Well?"

199

"Russ, I can't help you any more. You need a good criminal attorney. I'm a civil litigator. This is out of my league."

"Sylvia, I need you! You can't back away from me now! I mean, please, don't back off this thing just because it looks bad right now. You're my only friendly connection. Everybody else is trying to shoot me or put me in jail. Help me get out of this mess."

"Where are you right now?"

"At a gas station on Interstate 10, east of Tucson."

"Turn yourself in. It's that simple. Ask for protective custody."

"Forget it, Sylvia! Protective custody is still custody. If I'm locked up now, I'll never be able to get proof of Brockner's activities and the government's part in all this. Chances are, the Feds would be in on it within the hour and the local police would politely hand me over to Selmack. If that happens, I don't have a chance in hell of remaining alive long enough to be heard. These guys aren't playing by the rules... they play for *keeps*. No way!" Resolve suffused the tone of his voice.

"Where are you going, now?"

"Martindale mentioned a man named Elwin as he died. I'm going to look him up."

"Where?"

"I'll call you in a few days. See if you can't get the heat off me. Your friend, or anybody who can do it. I'm in trouble here, and I'm damned tired of hiding. Sylvia, I'm frightened in a way that I've never been frightened before."

"If I can get you some representation, will you come in?"

"Not until I see Elwin. Take care of yourself, Sylvia. Call you soon."

"Russ!" He had broken the connection. She still didn't know where he was going.

Dawson had been waiting at a discrete distance. Wakefield took him in tow as he headed for the parked Cherokee. They jumped on the Interstate eastbound for a few miles, then caught highway 83 south toward Nogales, on the secondary highway through the mountains. Along the route, Wakefield had Dawson leave the road and drive up into a desert canyon a few hundred feet. He removed all the weapons and ammunition from the Cherokee, packed the stuff in a triple thickness of garbage bags, and buried the package at the foot of a distinctive rock formation. He was surprised to find moisture under the surface where he dug, and completed the backfill of his hole by spreading a layer of dry sand to camouflage the disturbance of the soil.

They returned to the roadway and continued south. Dawson secretly breathed a sigh of relief that the guns were gone. In less

200

than two hours, after buying Mexican auto insurance on Dawson's advice and obtaining a tourist card, they crossed the border at Nogales into Mexico.

Wakefield let Dawson off, making sure he could get a bus back to Tucson to catch a flight. He thanked him and headed south into the Sonora Desert, bound for the ferry the maps in the North American Atlas showed crossing to Baja California from Guaymas.

Less than two hours' drive south, just north of Hermosillo, he was flagged into a roadblock by what appeared to be uniformed teenagers with automatic weapons. They were Federalistas, and they searched his car thoroughly, allowing other cars to pass unmolested. He was held at gunpoint while they completed their fruitless search. Wakefield asked the leader, who spoke a smattering of English, why his Cherokee had been singled out for a complete search.

"You are dress' as a hunter, Señor. Maybe you have guns."

"No guns," said Wakefield, happily. He thanked his protective angel that he had not succumbed to the temptation to stow the .45 pistol under his seat. It had been buried along with the shotguns.

"You may go."

BRADD HOPKINS

34

14 September, Present

The endless expanse of Sonoran Desert was days behind, and the ferry ride from Guaymas to Santa Rosalia on the southern Baja Peninsula was uneventful. He relaxed as he drove the remaining distance along the eastern coast of the Baja Peninsula. On his left, the Sea of Cortez danced with blue light in the sunshine. On the right, bizarre-looking cacti and desert plants grew along the rocky hillsides where the road had been cut. Baja California had an unfinished look to it. The roadway cuts spilled rocks onto the pot-holed pavement here and there, and an occasional ruin, on closer examination, proved to be an unfinished structure that had been abandoned before completion. Small altars, wooden crosses ornamented with plastic flowers and a hubcap or two, sprouted occasionally from the roadside at particularly bad curves.

Wakefield munched on candy bars and potato chips from his car-seat stash, a warm soft drink between his knees, as he motored unhurriedly along DF1. It was great to feel safe at last, and he tried not to dwell overly long on the situation he had left behind. As he approached his destination, boats became plentiful off the coast. Day fishers full of American tourists were hammering the Dorado as they moved into the Sea of Cortez in their annual migration.

When he arrived in Cabo San Lucas, he still had a substantial part of the five thousand dollars he'd picked up—seemingly a hundred years ago—in St. Louis. He used a part of these funds to pay for a hotel room on the beach. The weather was delightful and he decided to rest a day before beginning his inquiries.

No one had heard of Richard Elwin. A search of the phone book was fruitless. He asked at the post office, searched in bars where Americans hung out, and on the street. He questioned cab drivers, bank tellers, anyone who looked like they'd been there longer than he had, to no avail. He came to regret the fact that he'd never learned to speak Spanish, but the desk clerk at the hotel taught him enough to ask after Elwin in the native language.

"¿Conoce ustéd a un hombre Americano que se llama Richard Elwin?" He repeated the phrase like a litany to every inhabitant he met along the streets, muddy from recent rains, and in the shops clogged with American wives shopping while their husbands fished, and in the bars, repeatedly watching as bartenders shook their heads from side to side. He would deal with a positive response when he got one, for the one phrase represented the limits of his linguistic knowledge.

On Friday morning, his third day in Cabo, he called Sylvia. Telmex was working fine. Since Telmex, the phones in Mexico had been largely demystified, and his connection went through flawlessly, albeit operator-assisted.

"Sylvia, Russ. When was your last vacation?"

"Russ! What's that got to do with anything? Where are you? Everybody's worried sick!"

"How about meeting me in Cabo San Lucas? We can talk about what to do with me."

"I don't know if that's such a good idea. I'm not sure I can get away… and I'm not sure I'd come there even if I could. Did you find Elwin? Last time we talked, you seemed to think he had the key." Sylvia converted the conversation to the germane, which, in her view, did not include traveling to Mexico.

"I haven't been able to find him. Not a clue. This place is much bigger than I thought. Still, I'm not ready to give up. Martindale seemed pretty sure he was down here."

"So, what are you going to do now? The local authorities decided to issue a warrant for your arrest for your sister's murder; in view of your recent activities in Tucson, they felt it was the least they could do. It was clearly a bomb that killed Diana, incidentally. I have a copy of the investigation report and a friend at the D.A.'s office is keeping me posted on the case on the Q.T."

"So, I stay here for a while. They can't know where I am, unless you tell them."

"I don't know *where* you are, Russ. Trust me on that." Her tone inferred that she would appreciate it if he would trust her on all matters of his fugitive status and its ultimate resolution, but he wasn't yet ready for that. "I'm beginning to think I don't know *who* you are. What will you do?" she repeated.

"I'm going fishing."

It had occurred to him that if Richard Elwin were indeed in

Cabo San Lucas, it might take months to find him. He planned to find a private lodging and dig in for the long haul.

"I'll call you in a couple of days."

Wakefield had indeed decided to go fishing, to set aside the immersion of the past days and just relax. He got a name and directions to the Embarcadero from the desk clerk at the hotel, who assured him he would get a better deal if he mentioned the clerk's name to the charter operator, a man named Xavier. He pronounced it "hav-yerr", with a brief roll to the final 'r'. The clerk hobbled through the directions in a mixed dialect that butchered both languages, but managed to convey the communication. "Xavier es berry good fishermon," the clerk told him. "He spics Inglés muy bueno. You get many feeshes. I tell him you come mañana. His boat es *Dama Suerte, Lady Luck.*"

Dawn the following day found Wakefield at the docks, looking for the *Dama Suerte*. When he managed to find the craft, it was nicer than he'd expected. A heavy-set man with a moustache was working on some gear on the deck. Wakefield ascertained that the man was indeed Xavier, and was invited to board. On mention of the hotel clerk's name, the man laughed.

"I hope you did not tip him, Mr. Wakefield. He will get his bonus from me for the referral." The man had astoundingly white teeth, flashing like beacons from the dark and weathered skin of his face. Wakefield liked him instantly. His English was nearly flawless, almost elegant, with only the barest trace of an accent. He had the barrel chest and stocky build that bespoke Indian genes somewhere in his heredity. His frame was overlaid with a thin layer of fat that attested to a life that took moderate pleasure in the physical things. The man had an air about him, a friendly and trusting indulgence that resonated with Wakefield's psyche.

"I did, but no matter. He says you always catch fish, so it's worth it."

"He exaggerates. It is called 'fishing' not 'catching'. But we do quite well as a rule."

"Do I need anything, Xavier? Before we leave?"

"Nothing, Mr. Wakefield. I have aboard everything you will need for a nice day on the water. Beer, or hard liquor, if you like. The bar is fully stocked. Everything is provided; you have only to relax and enjoy yourself. My single, exorbitant price includes everything." The teeth flashed transiently as he smiled at his own humor.

Xavier cast off the lines and the *Dama Suerte* headed out of the small boat harbor for the fishing banks. Wakefield mixed a Tequila Sunrise, heavy on the orange juice, and stood, sipping occasionally, beside Xavier on the flying bridge. He was content to let the coastline fade astern and watch the sun come up off the port bow. He sobered for a moment as the Grenadine he'd splashed into the drink reminded him of the growing red stain on General Martindale's terry bathrobe on that fateful morning in Tucson, seeping red blood into the spattered orange juice. It seemed like a hundred years ago, in somebody else's life. He tried to shake the association free of his mind.

"You're on vacation, Señor Wakefield?"

"Not exactly," offered Wakefield abstractly. "Call me Russ."

"I ask because Americans usually fish together, and you are alone." Xavier let the comment lie there. Wakefield remained silent. Xavier shrugged and concentrated on his heading at the wheel.

Finally, after an hour of silence, he spoke. "What kind of fish do you want to catch today?" he asked.

"Anything. Let's fish for something where we can drift."

"Bueno." Xavier took a new heading and the vessel motored on for several more minutes, generally parallel to the coastline and less than two miles from land. Wakefield watched him as he switched on the depth-finder and made some adjustments in his heading. He peered over the windscreen to look discerningly at the water, then glanced back at the depth finder as he corrected his course. Satisfied, Xavier throttled down and shut off the engines. The silence took a new form; the peaceful lapping of the waves and an occasional creak from the rocking vessel were the only sounds. Wordlessly, both men climbed down to the aft deck and Xavier began rigging the tackle while Wakefield mixed another Sunrise.

"Want one?"

"Why not." Xavier shrugged.

Wakefield appreciated the silent acquiescence to his mood that Xavier had perceptively made. He liked the man even more than when they'd met, only a couple of hours past. He made no demands.

They started catching fish—lots of fish. No sooner was the hook at the depth Xavier recommended than a fish struck on the line. Xavier said they were jacks, called *"toros"* locally, due to their characteristic fierce fight on the hook. The excitement of the sport aroused Wakefield out of his thoughts, forcing his attentions to the activity at hand. He found himself smiling for the first time in what seemed like weeks, then laughing aloud with each strike and set of the hook, with each breath-taking, reel-burning run of these two-foot long animated torpedoes as the pleasure of the moment overtook him. Xavier fished beside him. Between them, they were hauling in the entire Pacific Ocean.

As they drifted closer to the shore, the species of fish they caught changed. When they stumbled on a school of corvina feeding along the shore in relatively shallow water, the flurry began anew.

Xavier kept only the largest of certain species, mostly corvina. The jacks, and others, were dispatched back into the depths from whence they came. Xavier told him that the jacks cooked up like shoe leather, but the corvina would make a meal as good as sea bass. Corvina were getting harder to find, Xavier explained, because of the gillnetters. Because they schooled at a consistent depth along the shore, the nets were extremely effective. The populations were being decimated.

Late mid-morning, there was a lull in the fishing. Xavier broke out ham sandwiches. Wakefield was ravenous and ate with a will. He found that his arms were sore from hauling in the feisty jacks, some of which went to thirty pounds. They popped canned, icy beers after eating, and sat on the after deck, drifting, out of sight of land. Xavier toasted their catch, and they struck their beer cans together. They sat, sipping silently, looking out across the water, until finally Xavier spoke.

"I think you have trouble, Russ," commented Xavier. "It is none of my business, but if there is any way I can help, you have only to ask."

"Is it that obvious?"

"Yes. You are sad, and you are angry."

"I am looking for a man. I haven't been able to find him, and I needed a rest from the looking. You've already helped."

"Who is this man? I know many people in Cabo San Lucas. In Los Cabos."

"He is an American. I think he's lived here for many years. I don't know what he looks like, but his name is Richard Elwin."

Xavier looked up from his beer can, lapping his upper lip with his lower in a brief, curious movement. "I think I know this man. He is called Señor Ricardo. He has lived here many years. He has a sadness and anger about him much like your own. Older than yours," Xavier appended.

"How can I find him?"

"He keeps a boat near my own, the *Mariposa Negra*. He fishes often, and he drinks a lot. I think he lives in Todos Santos."

BRADD HOPKINS

"Sometimes I sits and thinks, an' sometimes I jus' sits."
—Pogo

35

19 September, Present

Brassy Mariachi music thumped into the sunny street like a continuous ragged belch from the black, open maw of *La Paloma Cantina* in Todos Santos. This was not an "American" bar, here on a side street off the main thoroughfare, but a watering hole for the natives. There were none of the unessential amenities demanded by the foreigners. It was simple and to the point, a place to forget the world outside for an hour, an afternoon, or a lifetime. Flies hummed and buzzed mindlessly in the merciless heat of mid-day, attracted by the smell of stale beer.

Wakefield entered, and conversations stopped as all heads turned to see who had invaded their refuge. It was dark inside, but still oppressively warm. Wakefield's mind flashed onto a scene from some long forgotten spaghetti western, drawing numerous parallels, as he approached the bartender. The only thing missing was the ringing of steel spurs on the tile floor as he walked to the bar.

"*¿ Conoce ustéd un hombre Americano que se llama Richard Elwin? ¿Señor Ricardo?*"

The bartender's black eyes scrutinized him from beneath bushy dark eyebrows as he polished a plastic mug with the dirtiest rag Wakefield had seen outside a service station.

"*Si,*" said the man cautiously.

Wakefield out-waited the man, who ultimately began a rhythmic staccato of explanation that ended abruptly when Wakefield flagged him down, gesturing with both hands.

"*No hablo Español.*" It was the second phrase he'd learned.

The bartender stopped polishing and peered at him again. "Sometime he come here."

"When?"

"Afternoon, sometime."

"Do you know where he lives?"

"No." The man was clearly lying. If Elwin had been here even a few years, everybody would know where he lived. Todos Santos wasn't exactly a metropolis.

Wakefield ordered a Tecate. He had come to appreciate its smoky flavor while drinking with Xavier aboard the *Dama Suerte*. Ensconcing himself in one of the darker corners of the dingy bar, he hunkered down to wait. The bartender ignored him, limiting his attentions to the delivery of an occasional beer throughout the afternoon and evening. No other American entered the bar, but the locals came and went in a steady stream. Inevitably, they would glance unobtrusively in his direction and converse quietly with the bartender. It was clear that the word of his vigil was getting out. Elwin never showed.

Wakefield managed to get himself fed using words he had picked up in Texas at Mexican restaurants. "Taco" and "enchilada" got him a satisfying meal as he waited for Elwin to wander in. He wondered briefly if eating the fresh lettuce on the taco would carry the price of stomach disorder at a later time, but didn't worry enough to let it interfere with his supper. Everybody always said not to drink the water, to eat only peeled fruit in Mexico, and by those admonitions the lettuce on the taco was suspect. The place looked pretty clean, actually, except for the foul-looking rag the bartender used to polish the glasses. He cleaned his plate, thinking *'In for a penny, in for a pound'*.

Late in the evening, he paid his tab, tipped the laconic bartender extravagantly, and left to find a hotel room. He had noticed a hotel a few blocks away on his arrival in Todos Santos. The bartender took his money and said, cryptically, "Mañana." Wakefield was unsure whether it was an invitation to return tomorrow, or if it meant that Elwin would come in tomorrow, but the tone of the bartender told him there would be no clarification, even if he were to ask.

Mañana it was. On the following day, Wakefield returned for lunch and began his Tecate vigil at La Paloma Cantina. As he finished the last of his plate, mopping up the vestigial sauce from a brace of enchiladas with a fat, homemade tortilla, an American entered the bar.

He was tall, slender, with nut-brown skin and sun-bleached hair hanging down his neck. A sandy moustache adorned his upper lip. He appeared to be about Wakefield's age. He moved with an easy, careless grace, wordlessly accepting a cold can of Tecate from the bartender as he passed the bar on his way across the dark room to Wakefield's table. He sat down without invitation, looking directly at Wakefield with piercing blue eyes.

"You're looking for me. What do you want?" He drank long and deeply from his can, then leaned forward. "Who are you?"

"My name is Russ Wakefield. If you're Richard Elwin, I'd like to talk to you about General Martindale."

"Never heard of him. I was never in the Army." The man got up as if to leave.

"Please, this is important," said Wakefield. "I've got to talk to you."

"But I don't have to talk to *you*," the man said matter-of-factly. "See you around."

"Are you Richard Elwin?" Wakefield asked in desperation. He couldn't allow the man to leave, but had no idea how to stop him. Then it came. "I know about SK-443."

The man hesitated, then turned to face Wakefield. He appeared to blanche underneath his nut-brown tan. "Pardon me?"

"Are you Richard Elwin?"

"And if I am . . . ?"

"Listen," said Wakefield earnestly, "I'm in trouble and I need your help. Please, just sit down and let me explain. If there is nothing to this, it will only take a few minutes."

"Not here." Wrinkles arched across the man's high, clear forehead. He was thinking, hard and fast.

"Where, then?"

"I have a boat. Do you fish?" The man was trying to appear casual, but Wakefield sensed an underlying tension. He was anxious to leave. His eyes darted about the room, as if expecting someone to enter, as if looking for an unfamiliar face among the half a dozen or so locals eating and drinking in the cantina. Wakefield identified the man's feeling. It was fear.

"I fish."

"Then we will go fishing tomorrow morning. Meet me at the small boat harbor in the Marina at Cabo San Lucas. My boat is the *Mariposa Negra*. She's a forty-two foot Post Sport Fisher, slip eighteen. Six a.m."

"I'll be there."

The man left, making purposefully for the door in long strides, and vanished into the brightly sunlit street. Wakefield half rose from his chair to follow, and then sank back into it, letting him depart. They were clearly going to play by Elwin's rules, or he wasn't going to play at all. Following the man would only foul things up.

BRADD HOPKINS

36

20 September, Present

The *Mariposa Negra* churned quietly out of Cabo San Lucas marina the following morning with two lone figures silhouetted on the flying bridge against the brightening eastern sky. Richard Elwin had patted Wakefield down as he came aboard the vessel, uncomfortably asking for leave to do so, but nonetheless searching deftly and efficiently for a concealed weapon. Thereafter, he'd remained wordless until they were well away from land. He shut down the engines, then lifted the hatch cover on the after-deck and vanished into the engine compartment with a screwdriver. He emerged in several minutes, opened a storage compartment under a seat, and took out two fishing rigs. He passed one to Wakefield. "Fish," he said laconically.

Wakefield was writhing internally with ill-concealed anxiety. Elwin baited his hook and dropped the line over the rail, playing line by hand off the oversized saltwater reel. "Thirty feet, " he advised Wakefield.

"Xavier told me about you," Elwin opened at last. "I ran into him this morning at the fuel dock. He says you have a problem. He also said you truly do like to fish." Xavier had also said other things, which Elwin didn't mention but which had influenced his willingness to listen further to Wakefield.

"Tell me what it is that brings you all the way to Cabo San Lucas, looking for Richard Elwin," Elwin invited.

Wakefield dropped the line over the gunwale, remembering the depth Xavier had used. Elwin watched him intently.

"It's a long story, and I don't know quite where to begin. I got your name from General Martindale. He's dead, by the way." Wakefield was edgy, observing Elwin's response to the announcement of Martindale's death. He had no way of knowing what the relationship between the two of them had been and didn't want to tip his hand prematurely, or offend Elwin, or seem to be a friend of Martindale's, if Elwin was an enemy.

Wakefield remained cautiously aware that he knew nothing of Elwin's agenda. They were too far from land for him to survive if Elwin decided to throw him overboard.

"The old bastard. How did he die? Tell me everything, with as much detail as you can remember."

"He was shot in the chest with a high powered rifle while he was pouring coffee for me." Wakefield watched again, intently and thought he saw a shadow pass across Elwin's face.

"Why were you having coffee with the general?"

Wakefield wondered silently that Elwin had not asked who had fired the shot. It was a logical question, under the circumstances . . . unless you already knew the answer. Winding in his drift-line, he began at the beginning, with Brockner's offer of a contract.

Elwin did not interrupt, or ask any questions, throughout the long discourse. It was as if he already knew everything and wanted to see how much information Wakefield possessed. Beyond the indignant resignation letter of Dr. Harwiczki, and Harwiczki's written description of SK-443 that Wakefield had found in the wall of the laboratory on some unknown island named Navassa, Wakefield really didn't know anything. But his sister and his attorney were dead less than a month, and he, himself, had been a target of assassins, and was now a fugitive from the law as well. Martindale, who may have had some of the answers, was dead before he could tell what he knew.

In view of what he did know, Wakefield had a well-reasoned working hypothesis of the facts in the matter, but Elwin did not say so immediately.

Wakefield concluded his epic with their meeting the day before in Todos Santos, and looked expectantly at Elwin. It had taken several hours.

"So what do you want from me?" Elwin asked pointedly.

"I want to know what you know about the whole situation. I hope to find enough truth in what I believe you can tell me to get the spooks off my back and resume a more or less normal life, eventually. I want to go home to Houston, and see my son. I want to clear my name of the charges filed against me in Tucson, and in Houston. Damn it, man, I want my *life* back!"

"It may be too late," said Elwin. "It probably *is* too late."

"I've got to try. My only chance lies with what you may know. Please, tell me."

"I need to think about everything you've told me. We can 'fish' again tomorrow, if you like."

"I need to know now!"

NAVASSA

"No, you don't. The Mexicans have a saying, 'Mañana'. Most Americans think it means 'tomorrow', but it doesn't. It means 'not today'... there's a difference." He looked directly into Wakefield's eyes and said, "Mañana."

Suppressing an overwhelming urge to strangle Elwin, to choke him lifeless and beat his head repeatedly against the teak planks of the deck, Wakefield said, "Mañana." He shrugged not because he felt like shrugging, but because Elwin needed to see it.

Elwin disappeared below deck, down the hatch to the dark maw of the engine compartment, and reinstalled the positive lead to the starter for each of the diesels. Wakefield watched through the hatch as he worked, repairing his earlier sabotage. When Elwin finished, and reemerged on deck, Wakefield asked simply, "Why?"

"I didn't know who you were. If you had thrown me overboard, I would prefer that you remained adrift without power until somebody came along to tow you in, and maybe ask some embarrassing questions about where I'd gotten to."

He switched on the key and pressed first one button, then its twin, on the console of the open bridge. The engines roared to life and Elwin throttled up the *Mariposa Negra,* taking a course heading for Cabo San Lucas in the slanting rays of the afternoon sun.

BRADD HOPKINS

37

23 September, Present

Sylvia had acquiesced, finally. Wakefield called her on the phone after his first meeting with Richard Elwin aboard the *Mariposa Negra,* enthusiastically telling her that he expected to get the answers he needed. He wanted her to hear what Elwin had to say, so she could help with the battle plan to get his life back. Against her better judgement, she had taken a week off and flown to Cabo San Lucas, expecting to meet with Elwin. That was not to be.

Elwin had stalled against additional meetings to discuss SK-443, much to Wakefield's dismay. Oddly, he continued taking Wakefield out fishing every day until Sylvia arrived. Then, when Wakefield had urged the meeting with Sylvia, Elwin had said no emphatically, and vanished. The *Mariposa Negra* remained in her slip, which told Wakefield that Elwin was still in the neighborhood, but he was nowhere to be found.

Wakefield had readily taken to lounging on the beach afternoons outside El Presidente with Sylvia, who—after her initial ire subsided under repeated apologies from Wakefield—decided to make the best of things and treat the trip as a working vacation. She'd checked into the El Presidente, promising Wakefield that he would receive a whopping expense bill for her services. After all, as counsel for Wakefield Environmental, Inc., she had much to discuss with him. And she would do it on a beach chair, if it were all the same to him.

It was all the same to him, until he met her on the sand in front of El Presidente that first day for a work session. She carried a briefcase, and wore a bikini that was remarkably brief, as well. Outside the context of her office, and minus her usual austere business suit, she was strikingly beautiful. Wakefield felt the fleetest of twinges in the pit of his stomach as he realized that the slender, shapely woman walking down the beach toward him—on the longest legs he had ever seen—was indeed his attorney, and not a vision from some long-forgotten dream. She was not as pale overall as he had anticipated, which suggested to him that her coppery red hair was an affectation. Her skin actually held the faintest cast of an olive tone, not apparent when she was fully clothed. It gave her an exotic aura that Wakefield found fascinating because he could not pin it down. There was only one way to confirm his theory about the red hair, and he admitted to himself that he would probably never know. Somehow he managed to regain his composure by the time he rose to greet her and usher her to a sunning chaise next to his own.

She told him she hadn't reviewed the books from the island job. They were in the hands of the Houston Police, who found them in the company pickup Wakefield abandoned after he'd used it to escape from the scene of his sister's death, just where he'd left it, parked outside Warren Stone's office on the day of his murder. Wakefield had totally forgotten the box full of records Brockner had asked him to prepare for their meeting, left on the seat of the pickup.

In the hands of the investigators, that find had been enough to get a search warrant for the business offices of Wakefield Environmental. They had made a shambles of everything during their search, taking not only all records related to the ones they'd found in what they were calling the 'getaway vehicle', but "pretty much anything else they damn well wanted", as Rosie had phrased it. She'd called Sylvia Bixler's office while the search was in progress, asking for help, but the authorities were gone by the time Sylvia had gotten there.

Sylvia admitted co-opting Rosie as an inside set of eyes and ears, in part to see to Thomas' needs and in part as an unofficial conduit from Wakefield Environmental to her desk. It was not normal practice, she confessed guiltily, but in view of the circumstances, it did appear to be in Wakefield's interests. Davis Esterson was doing fine at the helm. Thomas had taken a leave from the university and was working with Esterson, learning the ropes. Gene Briggs had successfully extricated the crews from the Island Job, and Thomas had been a major help in the coordination of their reassignments and reallocations to the various regional divisions of Wakefield Environmental, Inc.

"He's a good man," Sylvia said, speaking of Wakefield's son. "He took Diana's death hard, but he's rallied. He's a quick study, and very perceptive. Esterson is delighted to have him around. He's doing a good job."

Wakefield was thrown momentarily by Sylvia's reference to

her son as a man; he'd never thought of Thomas in that light. He frowned involuntarily as he thought of the last time that he'd seen his son. He was gratified that Thomas was doing well in the context of the company—he'd always wanted his son to follow in his footsteps—*but not on Tinkerbell feet.* He realized his thought issued from a prejudice he hadn't known he harbored. It was a small step towards acceptance.

On Sylvia's instructions, Thomas had returned to the fire-ravaged home as soon as possible and opened the floor safe. There were only negotiable securities and a few odds and ends of legal documentation to be retrieved... he found no sign of any memoranda from or by a Dr. Harwiczki. He had reported to Sylvia that, even though the floors were covered with ashes and debris from the fire, he'd found the combination dial of the safe had been wiped clean. That observation, circumstantial evidence that somebody might have opened the safe before Thomas arrived, was the pivotal factor in Sylvia's decision to remain silent toward the authorities. It also meant that the only physical proof that the documents had ever existed was in the form of the copies made by Warren Stone that fateful morning, which Wakefield had carried in his overnight bag. It was not much, but better than nothing.

"Get Thomas' opinion on the proposal from that outfit in New York that wants Wakefield Environmental to go public," he said, suddenly. "I'd like to know what he thinks of the idea."

"He found the proposal in your office, and came straight to me," Sylvia said. "He was worried. He thought you might be planning to do that when he found their offer, and he wanted to make sure you hadn't set the wheels in motion. He seemed relieved that nothing had been done. I think he'd be strongly opposed to the idea, but I'll ask him, if you want."

"I'd like his thoughts . . . "

They went to dinner together that night. Wakefield enjoyed her company immensely. She was daring in her choice of fare from the unfamiliar items on the menu, not resorting, as Wakefield had, to the familiar items available in Mexican restaurants in the states. Rather, she seemed to search for the most unfamiliar items on the menu, ordering for adventure. Her sense of humor was dry and perceptive, slanted to the absurd quip. She had a marvelous laugh, throaty and sincere.

The work sessions continued during the day, and the dinners together followed every evening, in a familiar, but by no means monotonous, pattern. Gradually, Wakefield gleaned some details of her personal life from their conversations. The most important of these, Wakefield was surprised to realize, was that she was essentially unattached.

She, too, was warming to Wakefield. While acting as the pillar of business acumen during their daily work sessions, she was revealing more and more of herself to him when the day's business was put aside. She seemed to be able to demarcate the line between business and social intercourse clearly in her own mind, and refused to cross it in either direction without a clear transition.

On the fourth night of her stay in Cabo San Lucas, Wakefield kissed her goodnight at the door to her room in El Presidente. While the first kiss was seemingly innocent, the second was less so. There was no third.

"No." Gently, firmly she pushed him away. "No. I'm not going to do anything that would make it harder to defend you when the time comes," she said. "As much as I might want to..." She took a deep breath and sighed, smoothing her slacks with a curious, brushing gesture.

"Russ, you've become special, but there are just too many things happening right now, too much confusion, to add to it by getting emotionally involved. Let's wait until we can explore this thing without the burden of all the excess baggage you're dealing with. Let's give it a chance. Let's wait and explore it when you're not running and I'm not worried sick about you."

"You're right. I got a little carried away. I'm actually kind of surprised that I've come to feel this way about you in so short a time. I feel like a kid."

"Well, you're not. That much I'm sure of. It's just that the timing is all wrong. It won't always be . . . "

Wakefield broke his remaining contact with her. He did feel like a kid. She made him weak in the knees. *That perfume...!* She smelled right, and now, he knew, she *tasted* right. Shaken to some basic and vital depth, he said goodnight, and returned to his room. Thoughts of Susan haunted him, and he chastised himself for the shallowness he had demonstrated in becoming interested in Sylvia. Far into the night, his troubled mind examined this unwelcome guilt as he sat staring at the walls. It had been a long time... how many years was it, now? Maybe it was time to let Susan go, and allow himself to love again.

Finally he fell asleep, but did not sleep well. He dreamed he was a dog. He had a steak in his mouth, and the other dogs were chasing him, snarling and snapping at his heels. He ran and ran, and kept on running... his feet pounded a rhythm against the heavy planks of a dock... there was nowhere to go to avoid the snapping, snarling curs at his heels except to the end of the dock, and into the black water.

His feet beat against the wooden planks with renewed effort. With a final burst of speed, he plunged headfirst into the darkness at the end of the dock.

BRADD HOPKINS

"There are truths which can kill a nation."
—Jean Giraudoux, *Electra.*

38

25 September, Present

The dogs chasing him down the dock faded, first into formless gray shapes and then into black awareness. His pounding footfalls on the dock gave way to a real pounding in the waking world. Somebody was knocking quietly but insistently at the door of his hotel room.

He reached out and snapped on the light on the nightstand as he rose and padded to the door.

"Who is it?"

"It's me... Richard! Let me in!" The man sounded breathless.

"Just a second." Wakefield grabbed his pants from the back of a bedside chair and struggled into them, hopping and stumbling toward the door as he dressed. He disengaged the deadbolt, allowing Elwin to nearly fall into the room, and closed the door behind his untoward guest. Wakefield's mind was still fuzzy around the edges, interrupted as it was from his dreaming sleep. He glanced at the digital clock glowing redly on the corner of the nightstand; it was 4:05 a.m.

"What in the hell are you doing here, at this time of night?" he demanded of Elwin. He reached for the light switch, turning on the overhead lamp. Elwin was wild in the eye, panicked.

"There's a *bomb* on my boat! I found a frigging bomb!" he declared breathlessly. He was beside himself, oozing an indescribable combination of anger and fear, gesturing forcefully, but disjointedly. He flung himself into a chair, sprawled momentarily, then leaped up and began pacing back and forth across the room in his excitement, talking almost as if to himself. Occasionally he glared at Wakefield, who sat mutely and wide-eyed on the edge of the bed.

"I *knew* something like this would happen," he wailed in

agitation. "I knew it as soon as you told me Martindale was dead. The old man kept them off me for years. Told them that I'd be quiet if they'd just leave me alone. I figured Brockner had forgotten me, but that's all changed now, thanks to you!" The last words escaped his lips as a hiss.

"They won't stop now 'til I'm dead," he continued. "They want to kill you, and now they want to kill me! Why did you have to come here?" He was almost whining, childlike in his chagrin.

"Sit down, Richard," advised Wakefield. "Just take it easy and let's get this straight. If there's a bomb, why didn't I hear it go off? The harbor is close enough. I would have heard it."

"It didn't explode! *It's still there!*" howled Elwin, looking at Wakefield as if he were the densest person the world had ever known. "I found it when I was looking for anything that might not be right on the boat. It's in the engine compartment, wired to the batteries, with a cute little electronic timer! Near as I can tell, it's set to go off two hours after I turn on the ignition key. God damn them! God damn them, anyway!" he ranted.

"Can you disconnect it?"

"Would you like to try?" snarled Elwin sarcastically. "It's probably set to go off immediately if it loses power. What *really* pisses me off is that my life here is over. Finis. Kaput."

"You're not dead yet. You can go somewhere else."

"I like it here. I live here!"

"Richard. You've got to tell me what this is all about."

"You can't do anything. The only reason you're even alive is that you've been lucky. These guys are good at what they do."

"My luck can't hold forever, Richard. Tell me what we're up against. Maybe we can help each other."

"Fat chance. But, if they're after me, I've got nothing to lose by letting you in on our little secret, I guess."

Wakefield leaned forward on the bed, saying nothing. Elwin sat down. "O.K." he sighed in resignation. "What do you want to know?"

"Everything. In great detail. All of it."

Elwin took a deep breath, expelled it in a great sigh. "O.K. Fifteen years ago, I went to work for General Martindale. It was a secret place in Utah, near the Nevada border, in the desert. Desert Range Experimental Station, it was called. I worked with a guy named John Talley, a real smart guy, doing leading edge research in virology. Basically, we were looking for vaccinations against germ warfare agents; typhoid, anthrax, bubonic plague. Nasty stuff we knew the Russians had.

"Then, one fine day, Martindale ships us a bunch of monkeys from Africa, and we began extracting microorganisms—viruses, actually—from their blood. There was no reason to be interested that I could see, because they weren't sick. Lots of viruses live in all kinds of animals without doing any harm. Anyway, after a while, the monkeys started dying. First a few, then more and more of them. We couldn't isolate what was causing it, 'though we tore out our hair by the roots trying. The real puzzle was that, as the monkeys got sicker, the antibodies for the virus we were looking for actually *decreased* in their blood. We expected them to increase, as with any other infection."

"SK-443?"

"Yeah. We named it that. Later, they started calling it SIV, Simian Immunovirus. They should have gotten better, but they kept on dying. Antibodies are the things your body produces when it fights infections. When the battle's over, the antibody levels fall off—they decrease, because they're no longer needed. These monkeys were producing zero antibodies when they finally died, inferentially at the peak of infection. It was exactly backwards from what we expected, and it drove us to distraction."

"Us?"

"Me and Talley. And this cute little vet named Suzanne Coletti. I got her down here for a romp when Desert Range dried up, but she got bored.

"Anyway, we were shipping infected blood to somewhere, right up until the last monkey died. I didn't figure out until later where it was going."

"Where was it going?"

"Plum Island. It's in New York, off the end of Long Island. The Army had a germ warfare facility there, but it's billed as a veterinary research facility. Top Secret, and all that. I figured out later that they were refining SK-443 there, supercharging it, if you see what I'm saying.

"Well, when the last monkey died, Martindale shut down the job in Utah. Just furloughed the lot of us and bulldozed the site. I had plenty of money; I came here to Cabo to see how long I could make it last without working. Talley went to work at Rocky Flats, in Colorado. Coletti opened a private veterinary practice somewhere up in Oregon. I got one letter from her after she left here, then nothing.

"I stayed down here for a couple of years, then AIDS hit the newspapers. CDC said they had an epidemic, but it took them almost three years to name it. Remember the early rumors that said it came from African monkeys? Well, they were right. Right away, I snapped to the monkeys and the research we did at Desert Range. The symptoms the monkeys presented were AIDS; we just didn't call it that.

"I went looking for Martindale, and we talked. The upshot was that, yes, somehow the virus had escaped from their island research facility. Actually, that's not quite true. They tested it on San Francisco."

Wakefield was incredulous, but held his tongue. He wished to do nothing to interfere with the torrent of information pouring from the agitated Elwin.

"Martindale was on his way out, in major hot water, and a staffer of his, your General Brockner, was in line for the post. The Joint Chiefs were in a frenzy, he told me, and I'd better vanish and stay vanished. He said if I told anybody what I knew, he wouldn't give a quarter for my chances of staying alive for a week. He said that when they finally did find me, if it didn't look like I would spill the beans, they might leave me alone, especially if it meant they'd have to operate in a foreign country.

"It's been kind of an armed truce since then; an 'I know they know I know' kind of thing, but so far they've left me alone... until now. I don't go back to the states anymore. I keep to myself down here. Life's O.K., and I stopped being bored when I bought the *Mariposa Negra*.

"Now, from what you've told me, it's clear they didn't simply lose it from the island. They *intentionally* dumped it on an unsuspecting population. You're sitting on an information bomb that could blow the good old U.S. of A. into a scandal the likes of which the world has never seen."

"Why would they use a germ warfare agent on their own civilian population?" Wakefield demanded. He wasn't willing to believe it. Nobody could be that evil.

"I've been thinking about that. I *do* keep informed down here; it's just that the news is a little late in arriving, a little stale. Actually, it's nothing new, testing the germ agents on civilian populations. They've done it before, lots of times, with lots of little critters. They've been doing it since the Second World War. Some guy actually wrote a book about it, but it was glossed over as unsubstantiated, raving speculation from a left-wing environmental militant commie bastard and nobody read it. I personally think that *nobody* wanted to know about it, because then they would have had to do something. People aren't really interested in much that doesn't bear directly on their 'three hots and a flop', and the program listings in their current copy of the *TV Guide*. Sad, but true." He shrugged.

"Still, in this case, something went wildly, unpredictably wrong. I've managed to figure out what it could have been, what probably happened, if you want to know."

"I want to know," Wakefield urged, struggling to keep the excitement out of his voice. This was what he'd been waiting for.

"Well, most of the early agents were bacterial, and they tested them with what they called 'simulants'—bugs that behave in the environment like the bad ones but aren't all that dangerous. But when the research on genetically engineered viruses was ready for testing, there *were* no simulants for the virus and they had to figure out another way to do the testing. So, when they do these tests, they do them with a weakened strain of the real virus. It's the same idea as the polio vaccine, which is actually an inert form of the polio virus.

"A major part of the research, actually, would have to be devoted to developing something with all of the characteristics of the virus, but without its virulence. For testing, you see. They can't kill people with their testing, see, or somebody would notice. But nobody notices if there is a particularly bad strain of Swine Flu going around this year. Nobody notices if family doctors see a few more cases of whooping cough than they're accustomed to, for a little while. In the absence of an associated cause, it's read as nothing more than a fluke, an increase that is essentially within the normal statistical variation for the disease."

"What disease? AIDS? You're losing me."

"*Any* disease. The rate of new cases of any disease may go up slightly, even testing a weakened strain that's not supposed to make anybody sick. But who can explain it unless they're looking for that precise set of symptoms? Then the increase takes on a whole new meaning. Otherwise, it's just a random variation."

Wakefield pinched the bridge of his nose, massaging it with his thumb and forefinger. "So, if I understand you, some people *do* get sick when they conduct tests with weakened strains, but it's masked unless you know the specific illness to look for..."

"Precisely, or at least close enough. So here's what I figure must have happened: They tested the weakened strain of SK-443 on San Francisco..."

"Wait a minute. How do you know it was San Francisco?"

"Inference, buddy, inference." Elwin bestowed on Wakefield a 'You're too dumb to live' look, and rolled his eyes back before going on.

"It's where the highest number of cases per capita were first recorded. It's where AIDS showed up first. It has a large enough population so that statistical deviations would be relatively easy to detect. It has two, different, mutually isolated water supplies. Lots of reasons." Wakefield nodded in polite apology for his dunderheadedness and encouraged Elwin to continue.

"So, they tested in San Francisco. And what they failed to factor in was that there is a large segment of the population there that already had compromised immune systems. The bug took off like wildfire, with much greater effect than they'd projected."

"Compromised immune systems?"

"Yeah. Street druggies. Gays. They tend to use drugs. They're particularly notorious for abusing amyl nitrite. They're called 'poppers'. They say it heightens and prolongs orgasm. What's coming to light is that it also decreases immune response with repeated uses over time. Last month, I saw the first published indication that KS—Kaposi's sarcoma— in AIDS patients is directly linked to the use of amyl. People who have AIDS don't get KS unless they've been popping. And that's not all. Other street drugs, like cocaine or heroin, tend to lower the user's general health and may interfere directly with the immune system. That explains why intravenous drug users are also part of the affected population, due to the fact that they share needles. So, there's the increased exposure from dirty needles, and their health is bad to begin with. It explains some other things, too, which I'll get to in a minute.

"Not only do we have the assaults of these life-style elements chipping away at the immune response, but they're probably cumulative with other environmental assaults that are now known to affect immune system response, and probably with a bunch of other factors we don't even suspect yet. Any one factor alone, no problem. But mix them together and the effect is amplified, compounded. Synergistic."

"Environmental assaults?"

"Sure. Listen, you don't need a degree in toxicology to know that some things in the environment hurt people. Not just toxic contamination, although that's a factor, but things like, oh... the infamous ozone hole that has been developing over the poles, for example. The ultraviolet light that is getting through it is known to weaken immune systems. And regular things that we do every day. Some guy at Stanford did some research—I think it was Stanford—and discovered that, statistically, every person in the United States has styrene stored in their fat. Not just most of them; one hundred percent of his samples had detectable amounts. What does styrene do to you metabolically? Immunologically? I don't know. But it's there, and it wasn't there fifty years ago. Comes from drinking hot beverages from

Styrofoam cups, and eating burgers from Styrofoam boxes.

"Everything from household insecticides, to food preservatives, to gasoline, to bathroom tile cleaners might, and probably does, have some effect on the immune system. But we haven't proved it yet. In most cases we haven't even asked the right questions. What happens to mom's immune system if she sniffs her washday bleach every day for thirty years? What happens if she does this in conjunction with spraying for ants on a weekly basis, and eating fruit ripened to color by ethylene chemical treatments and protected from bugs by tetraethyl pyrophosphate sprays while it's in the fields, and filling her station wagon's gas tank up at the self-service pumps without wearing an organic vapor respirator and neoprene gloves to guard against the benzene content of the motor fuel? That's only the tip of the iceberg, but you get the idea."

Elwin was on a roll that had become a tirade. Now he stopped, caught his breath and collected his thoughts.

"In a nutshell, they dumped a *potential* illness on a population that was predisposed to get sick from it," he said in summation.

"How can you be so certain?" Wakefield was skeptical. "It's a hypothesis. There's no proof." He was fishing, looking for something he could take to the bank... hard proof.

"It's a helluva lot more than a hypothesis. There's a bomb in my boat, and that's no hypothesis! And tell me, my skeptical friend, have you been keeping your life insurance paid since you got clued in? Somebody has a lot to lose if you can prove what has been going on. You can't prove anything if you're dead."

"So, where's the proof?"

"Some of it is in the statistics, part of it. It's in the politics. Some of it is in the science. And some of it is in classified government files."

"What do you mean?" The room was beginning to lighten with the coming dawn. Wakefield turned out the light at the bedside. Elwin sat down and leaned forward.

"The AIDS virus, HTLV-III, is a retro virus. Retroviruses don't kill people. At least, no naturally occurring retro does. It's never been seen. Now, out of the blue, here's a retrovirus that *does* kill people. The odds of it being a random mutation are ridiculously minuscule. The odds of it being a managed genetic modification are substantially greater. The technology for recombinant DNA was emerging twenty years ago. Somebody *made* HTLV-III, probably from the SIV, the Simian Immunovirus, which is very similar, and found in African monkeys.

"And I think I helped..." Elwin sighed, shaking his head

slowly from side to side. He went on explaining.

"Back in the early eighties, nineteen eighty two or nineteen eighty three, the Center for Disease Control was projecting four million cases by the turn of the decade. They were screaming 'major epidemic, one hundred percent fatal' from the rooftops. They put the fear of God into Congress. They managed to secure major funding from the federal government for AIDS-related research. The Surgeon General went on national television in an educational series that was superficially to educate the public about AIDS, but at the root of it, it was designed to bolster public support for the funding. All was well and good. The funding came, and the government made AIDS a disabling disease... which had the effect of entitling all the people who had been diagnosed with it to welfare disability payments. It was the least they could do. Free money for the victims.

"Well, the turn of the decade came and went, and the four million cases of AIDS never materialized. It went to about a million cases, and the curve leveled out. Not that anybody noticed. They refocussed the public's attention to AIDS migration into the heterosexual population, making sure the taxpayers remained sufficiently terrified to keep their purse strings loose. The folks that were seeing the original prophesy fall short were not about to point it out. Their funding might dry up. The general public just forgot. It's something they're very good at."

"So? People are still dying..."

"Yes, but the point is, the epidemic did not go tangential. That is statistically significant, because it means the initial projections were wrong. Inferentially, this could be taken to mean that the numbers represent a single exposure to a population, an event. Not characteristic of the progress of disease through a population where the infection was being continually transmitted and re-transmitted throughout that population in ever-increasing numbers. Think about how smallpox decimated the American Indians; *that's* a tangential infection curve! It's different from the curve AIDS has produced. This, in turn, suggests that most of the people who are going to get AIDS have already gotten it, and had already been exposed by the time the initial projections were made.

"Some guy at Berkeley snapped to the statistical anomaly— Duesberg was his name—and he wrote an analysis of the statistics that suggested this was indeed the case. He pretty much laid the whole thing out."

"So?"

"So that was politically inconvenient, for a number of obvious reasons. If AIDS *was* closer to an event than a process, somebody might start looking for the event. And they might find it, or at least begin suspecting such an event had occurred. Also, if Duesberg was right, it meant that the early projections of the National Institute of Health were wrong, and the NIH had just made a two-billion dollar mistake. It would mean also that AIDS was essentially not something that happened to you, but rather, something you did to yourself, by making lifestyle choices that included known risk factors, most of which are illegal. That, in turn, would call into question the massive financial aid programs and disability payments being made to anybody with an AIDS diagnosis who asked for them. Such a possibility was too embarrassing and too expensive to contemplate.

"Also, these massive medical cost supports are essential. The government is sympathetic, finally, but one real, driving reason is that if the information *you* have gets out, wrongful death lawsuits would jam the courts and probably bankrupt the government.

"Anyway, Duesberg, a level-headed scientist until this time, was branded a crackpot. He was thwarted from publishing in this country by the interested powers, but the British College of Surgeons published his work. This guy is credible; he's a Fellow with the National Institute of Sciences. Still, the NIH yanked his grant, and essentially ground further research in this direction to a halt. The political message was clear and concise; 'Continue looking in this corner, and we will no longer support your efforts'. Every researcher knows that in order to be funded, you'll do much better if your hypothesis tends to support the official opinion. If the opinion is 'We think celery causes colon cancer', then it's politically incorrect to conduct research that might suggest celery *prevents* colon cancer, and the research simply will not be funded because the premise is preposterous in the eyes of the funding agency. And you don't get any funding for research unless you tell them what you're looking for...and give them some reason to believe you'll find it."

Elwin had calmed substantially since his tempestuous arrival in Wakefield's room and now peered out from baggy, haunted eyes at Wakefield. An indifferent sun peeked through the blinds, and both men looked out the window at the impossible purple-blue of the Pacific Ocean.

"Listen," Elwin said, finally. "I'm zonked. I've got to get some sleep. We'll have to talk later." He made as if to depart.

"Why don't you sleep here a while?" offered Wakefield. "You can't sleep on the boat, and it's probably not wise to go

231

back up to Todos Santos. I've got a hundred things to do today, and you can use the room. I may have an idea that will take the heat off us while we figure out what to do, but we can talk about it after you've rested. I don't think you'd be wise to go back to your house, under the circumstances, and you certainly don't want to sleep on the *Mariposa*."

"I think you're right. Why not? I'll stay here, if you're sure you don't mind..." Elwin acquiesced. "Watch yourself today..."

Wakefield donned a clean shirt, ordering his hands to stop shaking as he buttoned it. He let himself out of the room, placed a 'Do Not Disturb' sign on the doorknob as he left. He wondered if Sylvia was up yet. They had much to discuss, particularly if the plan growing in his mind proved viable. He was frightened, again. If they'd found Elwin, they'd found him as well. He could assume that they would be imaginative in their attempts on his own life.

39

25 September, Present

Hovering in the lobby near the hotel restaurant, Wakefield waited for Sylvia to come in for breakfast. Meanwhile, he began to lay the groundwork for the plan that was emerging in his mind.

Telmex came through again. Wakefield successfully placed a long distance call to an old acquaintance of his, Herbert Hutchinson, in Taos, New Mexico, and he'd obtained the number by dialing information long distance to boot!

Herb was home. He answered the phone after his wife, Daphne, came into his office to tell him of the call. He admitted to himself that he was puzzled that Russell Wakefield should call him, more or less out of the blue. They hadn't spoken since their tenth year high school reunion several years past.

"Hello, Russ! To what do I owe this honor?" They had been great friends during their school days, but their paths had diverged at graduation. While Wakefield built his well drilling business, Herb had gone into journalism and now had several adventure/suspense novels to his credit.

"Hello, Herb. Listen, I want to know if you're still writing."

"Of course I am," answered Herb. "It's what I do."

"I've got a story for you. Interested?"

"I'm always interested in a story. Something juicy, I hope."

"The juiciest," Wakefield affirmed, trying to keep the enthusiasm in his voice and the rancor out of it.

"Well, what is it? Should I take notes?"

"Not now, Herb. I want to come to Taos and give it to you in person."

"'Curiouser and curiouser, said Alice'," Hutchinson quoted. "By all means, come ahead. I'll be hanging around here tickling my keyboard for a few more days. Come on out and stay a while. You'll like it here." Herb gave him driving instructions from Taos to his home some distance outside the old town.

"I'll be there as soon as I can make it. Herb, don't mention this to anyone, please."

"Aha! Cloak and dagger stuff!" Herb chortled. "I love it." Wakefield could see the image of Hutchinson, his face surrounded by a great orb of peppery beard, looking for all of the world like an Amish farmer. His eyes glinted and sparkled engagingly beneath a vast expanse of wrinkled forehead; his smile was always easy, quick, and alive. And the mind behind those eyes was formidable.

"It's not what you think," said Wakefield. "But give me your word that no one will know of my visit. This is serious, Herb. Very serious."

"You got it, pal. See ya when you get here! You're on your own from the airport, but I look forward to seeing you."

As he completed his airline booking from Los Cabos International Airport to Albuquerque, Sylvia sailed into the lobby, casually elegant and stunning in her sweats and headband. She smiled warmly, with a hint of . . . what was it—mischief? . . . as he caught her eye. They merged at the entrance to the dining room, entered together, and exchanged small talk until the maitre d' found them a table. Wakefield held her chair as she seated herself, then took the chair at her left elbow.

"I didn't think anybody did that anymore," she commented, referring to the historic courtesy he had shown her.

"It seemed like the right thing to do," Wakefield responded.

"It was," she smiled.

Their waiter appeared and poured steaming Mexican coffee, wafting redolent of cinnamon, for each, then took their orders. Wakefield pointed at menu items without trying to read the native tongue. Sylvia read her order passably from the Spanish side of the menu. She would need work on rolling the 'r's if she ever decided to go native herself, but Wakefield found it engaging, nonetheless.

"Sylvia," he began earnestly when the waiter had departed, "Elwin came to my room last night. He told me a lot, and it's clear that there's been a huge cover-up. He believes that the AIDS thing was a product of testing a biological weapon, and he makes a logical case for it, based on what he knows. Still, we've no hard proof. And they are still trying to kill us. Elwin, too."

"Come on, Russ. Aren't you carrying this paranoia thing a bit long on the road?" As nice a guy as he was, Sylvia was having difficulty believing that Wakefield's life was really in danger. Yes, he was in trouble, but he could clear everything up if he would just return with her to Houston and explain a couple of coincidental accidents. She started to tell him so, one more time, but he interrupted her.

In a low voice that was almost a whisper, Wakefield said, "Elwin found a bomb on his boat."

Sylvia stopped chewing and looked at Wakefield in stark disbelief. "A bomb?" was all she could manage through a mouthful of *chorizo con huevos.*

"Yes, a bomb. It's still there. He says it's set to detonate two hours after the engines are turned on. He says that they know he knows about the conspiracy, and now that he's talked to me they won't let him alone. He had sort of a gentleman's agreement with Martindale, but Martindale is dead now, and all bets are off. If they're after him, they're darn sure after me."

"Have you seen the bomb?"

"Always the skeptic," Wakefield said, shaking his head. "No, I haven't actually seen it. But I've seen Elwin, and he's in a panic about it. I believe him."

"So, where do you go from here? How long do you propose to keep on running from the authorities? There is the matter of your two outstanding arrest warrants for murder. As your attorney, I have to advise you that the longer you avoid coming to terms with the authorities, the harder it will be to defend you." She donned her professional face like a mask. The woman he'd started this breakfast with was no longer to be seen. She was all business now. He decided not to divulge the details of his plan to her if he could avoid it.

"I want you to do some things for me. I'm going to New Mexico at noon today. I booked a flight under an assumed name, paying with cash. I'll be back sometime tomorrow. I want you to stay here until I get back and a couple of days afterward. Then, things should become clear. Will you do that?"

"Yes. Where are you going?"

"It's better you don't know. Now, before I go, I need your guarantee that my estate is in order. The business will transfer to Thomas' ownership on my demise, which, if Brockner's thugs have their way, is imminent. Thomas gets ownership of my estate, with Esterson running things for three years as general manager, then transferring the helm to Thomas. Thomas is to be supported by the business until he becomes twenty-eight years of age, then he is to receive a quarter of the stock. And set up a blind trust for me. Is that all in place and bolted down? Have I signed everything I need to sign?"

"Yes."

"Good. Thank you, Sylvia. I have to go now. I have a plane

to catch. See you late tomorrow, or the next day. Please trust that I'm doing the right thing."

"I trust that you *believe* you're doing the right thing. I'm beginning to think you're nuts, but you don't seem nuts when we talk. I'll spend three more days here, and then I want you to come back to the States with me when I go."

"We'll talk about that when I get back. Meanwhile, say 'Have a nice flight, Russ!'"

"Have a nice flight, Russ."

He bent and kissed her. The professional Sylvia was uncomfortable, but a part of her responded, lingering beyond the limits of simple friendship, and far beyond those of her status as his legal counsel. Wakefield was torn, momentarily, wanting more than anything to forget the flight and take her back upstairs. He pulled away.

"Also, Sylvia, don't mention the bomb Elwin found to anybody. If they find out we're onto the fact that they've planted it, they'll be forced to try something else."

He left her there at the table and went to his room, where Elwin was sleeping as if pole-axed. He woke Elwin up.

"Can you get your hands on a good powerful outboard motor?" he asked the still bleary-eyed Elwin.

"Yeah. They get three thousand or so for a Yamaha. You've got to figure about a hundred bucks a horsepower at the marina store. Why?"

"Have you got the money?"

"Why?"

Wakefield spent twenty minutes explaining his plan to Elwin, and finally received Elwin's grudging agreement. Elwin would buy the motor and take care of other aspects of the plan as they had agreed. He admitted that, if they played it carefully, it had a good chance of working, freeing them from the lethal pursuit that now threatened them both. Moreover, they were out of acceptable alternative options. Wakefield gave the keys to the leased Cherokee to Elwin, who roused himself completely, splashed some water into his face, and drove his newly ratified ally to the airport. Wakefield kept glancing behind them, looking for some sign that they were being followed. There was nothing.

With a final call from the airport, just before boarding his flight, Wakefield reached his office in Houston. Thomas, the target of his call, was out to lunch, and Rosie swarmed verbally over his psyche with a thousand questions. Wakefield reassured her in a general sense without really telling her anything. He

236

managed to get clear of her only by interrupting with the fact that he had a flight to catch and had to hang up.

As the jet climbed out over the blazing, arid desert of Baja California del Sur and took a heading for Los Angeles, Wakefield fell soundly asleep from sheer exhaustion, upright in his seat.

40

25 September, Present

The drive north from Albuquerque was a quiet and restful time for Wakefield. The high, barren desert plateau around the city gave way shortly to rising, pine-covered mountains, with long easy curves on the roadway. As he continued to gain elevation north of Santa Fe, the pine forests thickened and occasionally broke ranks to form open, grass-covered parks.

Taos itself was a quaint little village. He cruised the town square once before he headed out to Herb's place, reading the hastily jotted instructions Herb had given him over the phone. As he approached up the gravel driveway, he saw the house, a rambling wood and stone affair with expanses of glass that reflected the boulders and pines around on all sides. Herb came out of the front door of the house as Wakefield rolled the rented Ford to a stop.

"Saw you coming from the bottom of the hill," said Herb. "How was the trip?"

"No problems. I slept most of the way on the flight, and the drive up here from Albuquerque is breathtaking. How do you stand it?" Wakefield gestured at the view.

"We manage. Somebody's got to do it. Come on in and say 'Hi' to Daphne. She's got coffee on."

Daphne welcomed him warmly with a cup of that excellent and unmistakable coffee that only a coffee lover can brew, along with a platter of ham sandwiches and sweet gherkins. Wakefield was hungrier than he would have thought possible, and wolfed down the first sandwich as if starving, washing it down with great slugs of the wondrous coffee.

The remainder of the long afternoon, and well into the darkening night, Wakefield told his astounding story. They took supper cloistered in Herb's nest, a computer room *cum* library *cum* communications center *cum* magnificent view, where Herb churned out novel after novel to pay for all of it.

BRADD HOPKINS

At the outset, Herb had keyed a reel-to-reel tape recorder and set a microphone on the coffee table in front of them. They lounged comfortably in overstuffed chairs covered with Navajo blankets as Wakefield related his tale from the beginning.

Herb's place had the exact feeling that Wakefield had tried to create in his office lobby in Houston, right down to a piney-woods smell. The thought of it seemed like a lifetime past. Herb scribbled on a yellow legal pad from time to time, and asked an occasional question, usually urging Wakefield to greater detail. He seemed to absorb the story with aplomb.

Through the alpine sunset, well into the darkness of the New Mexico night, Wakefield narrated the events and feelings that were at the root of his unlikely visit to his old friend. At the end, Herb invited him onto the deck adjoining his office study for a nightcap. It was nipping cold, and a Turkish moon shone down from a black velvet sky studded with blazing lights, illuminating the open meadow that fell away from the house with light enough to read by. The pines at the verge cast long, distinct shadows across the park. The still air was redolent of pine.

"That's quite a story, Russ," Herb commented quietly as he swirled his brandy to release the vapors. "You realize that there's not enough hard information for me to handle it as an exposé." He inhaled at the mouth of the snifter, then sipped.

"I know. I know. I don't know what you can do with it, but I'd like you to try. The word has to go out, even if it can't be verified."

"Is there any way I can talk to this Richard Elwin character?"

"Not for now. He won't even confirm my story to my attorney. He's scared, and he's known these people a lot longer than I have. Maybe later, if we live that long."

"I'll have to do it as speculative fiction. Names changed to protect the innocent . . . and the guilty," Herb mused thoughtfully. "Might be hard to find a publisher; sometimes they can be a conservative lot, and the story you just told me is anything but conservative . . . I don't see how fiction can suit your purposes. What you really need is something, a forum, like *Sixty Minutes*."

"I'd have to expose myself to do that. These guys wouldn't hesitate to exploit a vulnerability like that. The sequel would probably involve the folks at *Sixty Minutes* reporting my untimely death from accidental causes. Noooo, I don't think so..."

"I'll write it. When can I start?"

"Start now. Tonight, if you want. I'm returning to Mexico tomorrow, and will be, as they say, unavailable for comment. If our plan works, my attorney will call you. Don't be surprised at anything she might tell you. She's on my side, but I am in a

240

position where I'm forced to deceive her. Her call will make a lot of things clearer."

"Listen, Russ. I've got maps in my research library. Let's find out where Navassa Island really is!"

"I'm bushed, Herb. Let's save it for the morning. Where do I bunk?"

"Daphne's made up the spare room for you. We don't get many visitors, 'way up here. Suits me fine."

"Not half as much as it suits me."

BRADD HOPKINS

"I only ask to be free. The butterflies are free."
—Charles Dickens, Bleak House.

41

26 September, Present

Elwin was waiting with the Cherokee at the airport when Wakefield's flight touched down. As soon as he cleared customs and picked up his baggage, they headed straight for the hotel.

Elwin was quiet. He looked significantly at the oversized package that Wakefield had paid extra to bring along, regarding it with what appeared to be sadness. It was in a plain, butcher paper wrapping, bound with yellow polypropylene rope, which made it easier to throw onto the roof rack of the Cherokee. It wouldn't fit inside, and it took the both of them to hoist it, grunting and straining, up onto the roof. Elwin deftly lashed it down.

As they departed the airport for the short drive to the El Presidente Hotel at Cabo San Lucas, Wakefield spoke.

"Is everything ready?"

"Yeah," said Elwin. "Everything but me." Elwin's main resistance to the plan was that it sacrificed the *Mariposa Negra,* which, of course, was one of the things that would make the planned deceit credible. The other part of the plan involved abandoning the Cherokee. They were going to vanish.

"Tomorrow morning, then?"

"Yup."

They remained silent for a minute, the tires humming on the rough pavement. Then Wakefield asked, "What does *Mariposa Negra* mean?"

"It means 'Black Butterfly'," said Elwin.

"Strange name for a boat."

Elwin recited:

*"Eran ayer mis dolores
como gusanos de seda
que iban labrando capullos;*

hoy son mariposas negras."

Then he translated:
"'Yesterday my sorrows were
as silkworms
making cocoons;
today they are black butterflies.'

"It's an old poem by a Spanish poet named Antonio Machado. I chose the name to remind me of the poem, which reminds me of the temporality of all life and existence, about the inevitability of death and change. Somehow, that idea helped me to live with myself, knowing what I know about the Navassa conspiracy, and people dying, and me not telling anybody. I was afraid I would not be believed, and they would kill me if I talked. Still, I needed some tools to manage the guilt. I used tequila, too, when the mental armor rusted through."

"Must have been hard."

"It was. It still is."

"We'll find a way. That's what I've been doing in New Mexico. I have a friend who will tell the story."

"They'll kill him," Elwin predicted bluntly. "He'll have an accident. They have people who specialize in creating accidents."

"I think we've figured out a way to avoid that," Wakefield reassured him. "He knows there is some risk, but he thinks he can pull it off. He..."

"I don't want to know any more. Just let it happen; I don't need to know." Elwin gripped the steering wheel doggedly, starring straight ahead.

They were in front of the hotel, and Elwin dropped him off. "See you tomorrow," said Elwin. "Early."

Wakefield nodded, and watched him as he drove away, headed for the marina. He himself entered the hotel and went to find Sylvia.

42

27 September, Present

They bought live bait at the shabby little stand at the Marina in the pre-dawn hours early the following morning, making sure that the vendor noticed them. Enthusiastically, they greeted Xavier, who was preparing for a charter a few dozen feet away from the slip where the *Mariposa Negra* sat quietly tied against the running tide with a deadly secret in her bowels. They bought beer, and were seen by the clerk in the early hours, joking happily about the fish they would catch this day. The things they truly needed for this voyage were already aboard, stowed out of sight aboard the *Mariposa* during the preceding days by an industrious and secretive Richard Elwin, working unobtrusively at an hour when no other souls were about.

Dawn streaked the eastern horizon with crimson when Richard Elwin, mentally reciting a fervent prayer, touched the ignition key on the flying bridge. Then quickly he glanced aft to where the engine compartment hatch stood open. In moments, Wakefield emerged and gave him a thumbs-up signal. Elwin powered gently out of the slip without warming the engines to temperature. The signal meant that the timer on the bomb was active. The clock on the timing device was running at an acceptable rate, its red block numerals changing with each second. It was unnerving, standing on the deck of the *Mariposa,* knowing that a timer was ticking away the seconds to an explosion directly beneath their feet. Starting the engine had been the hardest thing Elwin had ever done.

The red dawn sky and the somber cast of the westward clouds warned Elwin's weather eye of an approaching storm. The wind was swinging up from the south. The worst storms came from the south. He worried, briefly, wondering if they would outrun it. If they could, it would suit their purposes perfectly.

Timing, now, was everything.

With binoculars from a hotel window overlooking the Marina, a dark figure observed the preparations and the hand signals of the two men loading the craft. He watched with professional satisfaction what he knew to be the final departure of the *Mariposa Negra* from Cabo San Lucas. It was better than he could have hoped. He would get the two in a single shot.

As the small craft cleared the harbor mouth of Bahía San Lucas and entered the Pacific Ocean, he set the field glasses aside and began to pack his few belongings. His work here was nearly finished... it was almost time to go home. It would be relatively easy to perform the last of his assigned duties before leaving. It would look like a random robbery and murder, maybe even a rape. He hadn't decided about that yet. Not that murder was random in Cabo San Lucas; violent crime was rare here, and would be sure to attract lots of official attention. No matter; he'd be long gone before things got hot. *That jerk Wakefield still hasn't got a clue,* he thought to himself. *And the world can certainly do with one less attorney.*

The casual, almost languid preparations for a day of fishing were a masquerade of true intent. When the landmass dropped into the far distance astern, a frenzy of preparation ensued aboard the *Mariposa Negra*. Wakefield broke open the plain brown package he had brought along from his late travels in New Mexico and feverishly began to inflate a small Zodiac rubber skiff with a foot pump. Elwin set the Iron Mike, an electronic autopilot, to which he referred in the old term for the early mechanical steering devices. He vanished into the cabin below, and re-emerged topside lugging a thirty-horsepower Yamaha outboard motor onto the deck. He installed it on the wooden transom of the Zodiac. He tightened the sets, and clipped the safety cable to the transom ring.

He scrambled back to the flying bridge and throttled down to a stop. The two men set the inflated raft over the rail using one of the davits. A number of fuel cans, a set of oars, two large boxes of foodstuffs in waterproof packets, a battery, a compass, and several cans of water were stowed aboard the small craft.

Elwin next scurried up to the flying bridge and dismounted the antenna, the marine radio, and its microphone, and conveyed these items to Wakefield in the skiff. He watched as Wakefield hooked up a fuel tank, primed the fuel lines to the outboard motor, and pulled it to life. It ran fully and smoothly, idling quietly alongside the *Mariposa*. Elwin looked once around the deck, then undid the painter securing the Zodiac to the larger craft. He tossed the end of the line to Wakefield.

NAVASSA

Wakefield peeled away from the beam of the *Mariposa Negra* and steered the Zodiac in circles off the *Mariposa's* stern. There was more chop than he'd anticipated, and the ride was rough. Clouds were darkening the western horizon. To his inexperienced eye, they were distant and innocuous in appearance. There were no other boats in sight. The timer on the bomb had now been running for a little over an hour and twenty minutes.

Elwin went back to the flying bridge, throttled up to full power, then set the Iron Mike to steer a course of 180 degrees, due south. He went aft and donned a life vest, looking wistfully around the vessel one last time before he jumped overboard off the stern. He took in a snootful of seawater, having failed to account for his velocity relative to the water, and surfaced in the *Mariposa's* wake coughing and sputtering, bobbing around like a large, orange cork in the turbulent water.

Wakefield, following in the inflatable skiff, fished the drenched and despondent Elwin from the water. They both watched for a moment as the *Mariposa Negra* bore away from them on autopilot at full power, headed for the open reaches of the Pacific.

"I really loved that boat," Elwin said, and threw up.

Wakefield came about to a pre-planned heading of eighty-one degrees and took the little outboard Yamaha to full power. He steered with a hand compass. On this course, approximately two hundred miles ahead, lay the continental coast of Mexico, and, more specifically, the airport at Mazatlán. They should make landfall in about twenty hours or less, but they were still on the clock. There was one last element of the plan that had to be executed before the *Mariposa* went down.

Elwin hooked up the radio to the battery, set the antenna in a makeshift mounting, and made the necessary connections for everything to work. At precisely two hours after the engines had started in the Marina, Elwin transmitted a distress signal, reporting as his position the calculated position of the *Mariposa Negra* based on her last heading and the speed of the vessel. It had long since vanished from the horizon. He reported an explosion and fire aboard, and switched off the radio abruptly as the Mexican Navy acknowledged his transmission.

At that moment, nearly twenty miles away, the electronic timer on a detonator connected to five pounds of plastic explosive read a row of four identical zeros one instant before the detonator did its job. The *Mariposa Negra* became matchwood and flotsam in a microsecond of flame and fury.

A mushroom plume of explosive smoke and hot gases roiled black, shot through with red as it rolled skyward. Although they could not hear the blast, both of her former crew noted the rising plume from the *Mariposa* astern on the horizon. They were silent. The slapping of the Zodiac's bow on the rising chop and the muffled maniacal scream of the Yamaha were the only sounds in the unrestricted expanse of dull water.

As they turned away from the dying *Mariposa* to face their destination, Wakefield began to chuckle.

Elwin turned toward him in irritation at this rude interruption of his private grief for his beloved boat. He snarled: "What's so damned funny?"

"Toilet paper," chuckled Wakefield. "By god, we forgot toilet paper."

43

27 September, Present

In a small radio room in Acapulco, radioman Carmen Alonso Rodrigues of the Mexican Navy listened as a private vessel some three hundred miles away transmitted a distress signal. Rodrigues answered the call, knowing that he was probably the only one listening to the emergency distress band. There were only four small vessels of the Mexican Navy stationed on the entire western coast of Mexico, and all but one were currently in the harbor. The *Revolución* was anchored off Puerto Vallarta, in the Bahía de Banderas.

The four vessels constituted Mexico's entire naval presence in the Pacific Ocean, and would be the only resources available to effect a rescue, unless the passengers and crew of the distressed vessel were lucky enough to be within range of a foreign trawler. Not that a lot of luck was required; foreign trawlers abounded in these waters. Rodrigues jotted down the coordinates that the distressed vessel had transmitted. His concern grew deeper as the response from the vessel was cut off in midsentence. He rushed from the radio room, a slip of white paper in his hand, to find an officer who could issue the orders necessary to begin the rescue.

The *Mariposa Negra's* EPIRB, Emergency Position-Indicating Radio Beacon, popped undamaged to the surface even as the fragmented hull of the craft slipped beneath the rising waves. It dutifully began the automatic transmission of a coded distress signal. The signal bounced off a satellite orbiting a hundred miles in the sky, and was picked up at a monitoring point. A technician immediately cross-indexed the EPIRB's electronic signature on a computer database. The registry indicated that the vessel in trouble was the *Mariposa Negra,* out of Cabo San Lucas, owned by a Richard Elwin. She was about a hundred miles south of her homeport, in an area that was in international waters according to Marine Law, but well within Mexican territorial waters as claimed by the sovereign government of Mexico. The technician immediately notified his supervisor, who directed him to notify the Mexican authorities.

The call came from the Mexican Naval Central Command in Mexico City within a half an hour, ordering the fastest available vessel based in Acapulco to sea, to the coordinates of the EPIRB, for a search and rescue mission. The vessel would be supported, Rodrigues was told, by a locating search flight from Los Cabos International Airport. The fixed wing aircraft dispatched for the search would be over the last known position of the *Mariposa Negra* within seventy minutes.

Meanwhile, the Commandant of the army detachment outside Cabo San Lucas would dispatch an investigative team to the Marina, to learn what they could about the number and identities of the crew and passengers of the *Mariposa*.

It was with considerable pride that Rodrigues responded to the communication from Central Command by reporting that the *Revolución* would be underway within fifteen minutes. He did not mention his interception of the original message, and the subsequent preparations. Such a short time of response would indicate to Command that the level of preparedness was exceptionally high. It never did harm to favorably surprise one's superiors with unexpectedly high performance. It would surely be noted.

The *Revolución* left her anchorage off Puerto Vallarta under full steam, making sixteen knots in the teeth of a stiffening breeze, against the three-foot chop running before the mounting weather. Her destination was ten hours away.

Humberto Gonsalvo banked his prehistoric Cessna 210 in a wide, sweeping turn around the wreckage floating on a churning sea at the coordinates he had been given. His eyes scanned the field of view for any movement or color that would evidence survivors. He had nearly missed seeing the wreckage in the turbulent water below as he struggled with the controls of the little push-pull two-engine aircraft for dominance over the storm whose clear intent was to blow him out of the sky. This was becoming a nasty bit of weather, and he could circle only a few minutes before he must retreat from the building force of the blow. He radioed the *Revolución* that no survivors were visible amidst the wreckage, and turned his aircraft before the wind, running for land.

250

Captain Herve Madrilla, attended by two regulars toting assault rifles, walked onto the docks at the Cabo San Lucas Marina and systematically began to query every person he could find there about the *Mariposa Negra*. Several had seen her depart in the early morning hours with two men aboard, but it was not until Madrilla approached the *Dama Suerte,* lunging safe in her slip against the brewing storm, that he found anyone who knew the identities of the two men. From a fisherman named Xavier Gallegos, he learned that two Americans had been aboard the *Mariposa*: one a long-time resident of the area, and one a *tourista*. The tourist had a friend, an attractive *Americana,* who was staying at the hotel Solmar. Xavier gave the names of both men but did not know the name of Wakefield's female companion.

Bill Selmack was eating his first leisurely breakfast in the hotel Solmar dining room, although he had been there nearly a week. He'd been watching enough to know that he could set his watch by the appearance of Sylvia Bixler for breakfast. It was much more casual and relaxing, now that Wakefield wasn't around to recognize him. He no longer needed to skulk about to avoid being seen by the man. Now, he could truly relax. Wakefield was with the fishes.

Selmack found himself wishing for a few more days in this place. He needed a vacation and he liked the potential, but Malleck, the prick, had been clear and definite. He was under orders to be on the 2:05 flight, without fail, regardless of the status of his efforts.

Sylvia ordered coffee and ate breakfast, unaware that the man across the room was watching her surreptitiously, unaware that he was planning her death within the hour. She signed the check, and walked back to her room. She would stay only another day, and she felt a mild resentment toward Wakefield for going fishing during their last few hours together in paradise. She berated herself mentally for not allowing their relationship to proceed into intimacy, wondering if that was Wakefield's motive for his untimely fishing trip. Was he doing it to irritate her? If so, she was pleased at her earlier recalcitrance. She would not tolerate such inconsiderate, game-playing behavior from any person in her life, let alone a lover.

Still, that hadn't been her sense of it. Instead, it felt as if Wakefield had something crucial to do. She had an odd sense of foreboding when he'd given her a phone number on a slip of paper upon his return from New Mexico the previous day.

"If anything happens to me, call this number and ask for

Herb," Wakefield had said, handing her the paper scrawled in pencil with a phone number. "Tell him what has happened, and for God's sake, make the call from a pay phone... and don't use a credit card."

"Who is Herb?" she'd asked.

"It's better you don't know. But this is the most important thing you must do if something happens to me." *It's almost as if he's expecting something to happen,* she had thought to herself.

She finished her breakfast and returned to her room. Shortly after she closed the door there was the knock of someone used to authority: three unmistakable and aggressive sounding blows. She moved to answer it, wondering who it could possibly be. The hotel staff, maids and room service people knocked quietly, unobtrusively. Russ was off fishing; moreover, his knock was inevitably the 'shave and a haircut' pattern. This knock was obtrusive, insistent. She opened the door to see a tall, intimidating, dark-haired man, and her mind leapt as she saw guns.

"Captain Madrilla at your service, Señora," said the man in passable English, nodding in a peculiarly formal fashion that was almost a bow. She saw now that he wore a uniform, and the guns that had so shocked her were in the hands of two helmeted soldiers. "I must ask you some questions."

Bill Selmack turned the corner into the hallway outside Sylvia's hotel room in time to see the two armed soldiers enter the room. He turned suddenly, as though he'd forgotten something important. He scuttled out of sight, back the way he'd come, and peered carefully around the corner. The corridor was clear, unoccupied. He settled in to wait for the Federales to leave, lounging casually in the vacant hallway just around the corner, out of sight.

"Are you acquainted with Russell Wakefield?" Captain Madrilla asked Sylvia. He pronounced it "Roosel", and his 'y's sounded faintly like the English 'j'.

"Why? What's going on? Why are you here?" Sylvia wanted some answers and she was showing her irritation at having her hotel room turned into an armed camp. The two riflemen had taken up posts on each side of the door. Their presence was intimidating. Captain Madrilla smelled distinctly of cumin, coming somewhere from the general vicinity of his bushy, black moustache.

"Please sit down, Señora Bixler. We are here to ask the questions. You are here to answer."

252

Sylvia bristled at his brusque, intimidating manner. She found herself on the wrong side of the bench and didn't much care for it. The attorney in her rose to gain an equal footing in their interchange.

"What do you mean, coming in here without a warrant, questioning me about my private affairs?" she demanded indignantly.

Captain Madrilla shrugged, and gestured to his soldiers. One slung his rifle by its strap over his shoulder and approached the defiant counselor. The other dropped his rifle to a ready position. It struck Sylvia that these men meant business, and she was unsure of her rights in the matter. One the other hand, she was absolutely certain that the soldiers had all the guns. Her rights would not stop bullets. It was that simple.

"Señora Bixler. You will accompany us to headquarters, where you will answer the questions we ask. Please come quietly. We will use force if we believe it to be necessary." The soldier moved behind her and produced a pair of handcuffs, which he deftly fitted before Sylvia realized what he was about. She suppressed a moment of panic, a transient urgency to react violently. In reality, it was too late for violence, if it had ever been possible at all. She clammed up and said nothing, amazed at the feeling of powerlessness the handcuffs produced in her. It was horrible.

Another gesture from Madrilla and the soldiers fell in around her, one on each side, grabbing her upper arms just above the elbows. Their grip suggested they weren't afraid to break something. At that instant, Sylvia decided to cooperate.

The soldiers escorted her from the room down the hallway, past a casually innocent-looking man with a pock-marked face and an oddly simian build, who stepped quickly aside to let them pass. They went through the hotel lobby and out onto the street. The desk clerk said something to her as she was being hustled by, but Captain Madrilla drove him away with a threatening glare. He stepped behind his counter in silence, quickly recalling some extremely pressing matter in a stack of billing statements that demanded his immediate attention. Sylvia was placed in a waiting jeep, and whisked from the hotel under armed guard.

Bill Selmack watched as the jeep roared off in a cloud of dust and careened out of sight around a corner. As his quarry moved temporarily out of reach, he shrugged in disappointment, then returned to the front desk to settle his account. He was under orders. He had a flight to catch.

BRADD HOPKINS

"Red sky at morning, sailors take warning."
—Old seafarers' rhyme

"Teach us delight in simple things,
And mirth that has no bitter springs."
—Rudyard Kipling, The Children's Song.

44

27 September, Present

They were in trouble. The Zodiac, fit enough in calm water, was no match for the wind and waves of the tropical storm that caught up with them mid-way across the Sea of Cortez. They began to take water as the little craft skidded down the face of the following storm seas, plowed into the troughs, and tossed high again on the crest of the wave behind.

The motion made Wakefield desperately ill. Elwin, gripped the hand throttle like a vise. He attempted to adjust the speed of the craft to match the crest and trough of the marching waves in a desperate effort to avoid foundering.

After the first of several episodes of vomiting, Wakefield bore his illness stoically and bailed as furiously as his nausea would permit, using an empty coffee can. One particularly violent surge caught him off balance and he fell forward into the stowed gear, bashing his nose on something hard. His nose felt broken, and blood gushed from it. Doggedly, he returned to bailing, covered now with his own blood and vomitus.

Elwin motioned at him. Screaming into his ear in an effort to be heard above the noise of the storm, he instructed Wakefield to cut two pieces of rope and make up lifelines. Wakefield somehow managed it, tying each line to the grip line running around the gunwales of the Zodiac and then around their waists. He was grateful that Elwin had thought of it. To be dumped into this sea now would mean certain death, even with the personal flotation each man wore.

Night fell, manifested only by the further darkening of an already dark sky. The weather continued unabated. Wakefield's arms were fatigued beyond belief, yet he continued bailing. He shivered uncontrollably, cold and wind-whipped, soaked to the very marrow, as did Elwin.

With the onset of darkness, Elwin was steering blind. He had no way of knowing how to make the small adjustments to steering that lessened the effects of the waves that he made during daylight. He tried to listen for the hiss of the breaking crests as they came at the raft from the blackness, but he could not distinguish the noise he sought from the surrounding din of the storm. At the last moment before impact, he would try, usually unsuccessfully, to steer for an easier blow.

The night wore on. Both men pondered their idiotic foolishness in thinking that such a thing as crossing two hundred miles of open water in a Zodiac could be done. They feared, neither daring to speak the thought that they might well pay for their folly with their lives. It was impossible to steer a course, even if the compass could have been consulted. In the dark, with the relentless motion of the raft, it was useless. Their only course lay in running before the wind in whatever direction it chose to blow them.

Eating and drinking were impossible in the bounding craft. Hunger and thirst became their companions throughout the night. Wakefield took a perverse, simple pleasure in the warmth of his own urine running down his leg inside his soaked trousers. He simply couldn't spare a hand to work the zipper. Fatigue set in with a vengeance. Bailing and steering became numb tasks of rote, without human thought. The actions of bailing and steering became numb tasks of rote, without human thought, as if sensibility had departed their world for one with better weather. There remained only the incessant, violent motion of the sea, to be countered in its effects by yet another effort of will, by yet more painful and halting movement of exhausted muscles.

Then, its fuel supply tank empty, the Yamaha sputtered and quit

The first awareness was pink light, then pain... pain everywhere. Wakefield opened his eyes, then snapped them quickly shut against a white glare. He felt none of his body, merely an abyss of undifferentiated pain. With Herculean effort, he rolled over, trying to get away from the light. The act exhausted him, and he lost consciousness again.

The second awareness was a mouth full of salty-tasting sand. The pain had diminished to stiffness, to soreness, hunger, and a driving thirst. He lifted his head and opened his eyes, spitting dryly and sputtering weakly at the sand in his mouth. Elwin lay on the sand, not far away, unconscious or dead. Wakefield couldn't tell. He crawled a few feet and rested. He crawled a few more feet. Finally, he reached Elwin and reached out to shake his shoulder. Nothing. He shook it again and Elwin groaned!

He shook harder, and Elwin opened his eyes owlishly and peered at Wakefield.

"We made it!" he croaked hoarsely. "We made it!"

Wakefield nodded, smiling weakly, his hand still on Elwin's shoulder, too exhausted to move again. Both men looked mutely at each other for a time. Then, Wakefield made a noise.

"Mrrpff," he said, beginning to chuckle. Elwin caught the spirit immediately.

"Hmmff," said Elwin.

Their laughter grew and swelled like a snowball rolling down a hill, and in moments, peals of wild hilarity filled the air. The two men lay in the wet sand at the edge of the Sea of Cortez, laughed uncontrollably together, tears running down their cheeks, until they were again drained. Then they collapsed and laughed some more. It was defiant laughter, laughter born of being alive, of having slipped free when death had held them in its bony grasp. It expressed the unadulterated joy of living humans, pealing like the calls of gulls that soared above the sandy beach in celebration of each breath of existence.

It released the boundless triumph of living humans who had cheated death but narrowly. The laughter faded, with only an occasional guffaw surfacing, bubbling up from the silence. They looked around, turning their heads to see a golden strand, deserted, tapering away in each direction.

"There's the Zodiac!" Elwin cried, pointing. It rested no more than two hundred feet away, lodged with its propeller imbedded in the sand, perhaps ten feet from the waterline.

The men rose, using each other as supports, and staggered toward the rubber craft. Most of its cargo was still in the bottom. They broke out the water first, then food from the plastic packets Elwin had packed. They ate and drank with a curiously delicate, proper demeanor that was almost dainty, savoring the intense pleasure of living. This feeling was amplified, intensified by the underlying demand of their bodies for sustenance. Elwin issued aspirin for their dessert and they washed it down with the precious, wonderful water they'd found.

They rested, absorbing the warmth of the sun.

"Where do you suppose we are?" Wakefield asked finally. He gazed down a long, sandy strand that terminated at low hills in the distance. The ubiquitous cacti of the Sonoran Desert marched down the rocky hills, stopping where the beach sand began. The water was a glassy, golden azure. Gentle waves sloshed calmly at the water's edge, the only sound that could be heard. There was no wind, no birds, no movement. It was getting hot, and Wakefield's skin felt as if it would crack in the heat, dried as it was from the preceding night's saltwater soaking. The only remnant of the storm was a line of debris far up the beach, cast ashore by the highest waves of the night before.

"North of Mazatlán," said Elwin. "We can walk straight east and cut over toward the DF 15 highway in a few miles. Or we can walk south, and cut inland when our water gets low. DF 15 will be closer to the coast then. It's your call."

"What about the Zodiac? Will it still run? We could cruise right down the coast."

"Hadn't thought of that," Elwin admitted, laughing. "Ready to go back to sea, are we?" He cocked an eyebrow, and both men burst out laughing again.

"If we can get it running," Wakefield pointed out, "we won't have to carry our gear."

Elwin hooked up a fresh fuel tank and pumped the bulb in the fuel line a few times to deliver fuel to the Yamaha's carburetor. With considerable difficulty due to their weakened condition, they managed to drag the little boat back into the warm water. To their amazement, the Zodiac's new Yamaha outboard started defiantly on the second pull, as if to spite the beating it had taken in the storm and its unceremonious beaching. They piled aboard, and set off southward along the beach at a moderate pace, just outside the line of gently breaking waves.

Wakefield lay quietly in the sunshine, his head pillowed in the bow. His eyes were closed, but his mind was active. He had gained a new anonymity that would allow him to go anywhere he'd never been before without being recognized. He could assume any identity... he could start a new life. He could be anybody he wanted to be and create his own personal history from scratch.

Then it hit him, clearer than ever before in his life: he *liked* who he was. He liked his life. He had a son he cherished, and the boy's sexual preference was a minor, secondary concern when it was measured against the potential of a full and productive life.

He still owned a share of the biggest, most horrible secret in the world. Some nasty, powerful people had tried to take it all away from him. They'd taken his sister and his best friend; they'd chased him to the end of a continent and forced him to fake his own death. And, by inference, they'd tried to prevent him from ever seeing his son again.

Thomas was all that remained of Susan, and his son didn't deserve his rejection for being what he was—for being *who* he was. As Wakefield thought about it, he became really angry.

Opening his eyes, he bored a look straight into Elwin's heart. And he found there a kindred spirit, a comrade in arms, another who'd lost everything. Elwin's gaze bored straight back at him.

"Let's get those sons of bitches," he said. And with that, their deal was made.

BRADD HOPKINS

45

5 October, Present

"I think she's legit. She doesn't know anything, or we'd have had some sign of it by now." General Donald Brockner gazed out the window overlooking the Snake River in Idaho Falls, his hands flattened across the small of his back. It was the same view General Martindale had enjoyed when this had been his office. "So far, her communications have all been routine."

"Should we yank the phone taps? They're still on her office and her home phone. We're also monitoring her cellular and tracking her credit card account." Colonel Malleck was the only other person in the room.

"No . . . not yet." Brockner's brows knitted to form a single black scowl. "Let's leave them in place for another month or so, just to be safe." It bothered Brockner that there was no irrefutable proof of Wakefield's death, or that of Richard Elwin. That they might have survived was academic. They were a hundred miles offshore when their vessel went down.

Marine reports they'd monitored during the week following Selmack's return demonstrated that no fishermen had been rescued, no bodies had been retrieved.

He was also uncomfortable with another question his field agents had not been unable to answer: Where had Wakefield gone from Albuquerque in the days before his 'accident'. They had tracked him that far. He had rented a Ford at the Albuquerque terminal. So where had he gone? It made no sense, and this bothered Brockner. It offended him, frustrated his need for a tidy, believable closure to the Wakefield Affair.

"So, we leave her alone?"

"We leave her alone. No point in our getting wet if there's not reason for it. Just watch her for a while longer. It's probably for the best that Selmack missed her in Cabo."

"Yes, sir."

BRADD HOPKINS

46

6 October, Present

Herb Hutchinson gazed past his computer screen, watching a Stellar's jay do a thorough search of his patio deck. The bright-eyed little creature flitted from place to place in a frenzy, looking for whatever jays were driven to look for. The blue male, with gray-barred wings snapping in the brittle morning sun and a nearly black crest cocked inquisitively over his work, burrowed his beak into the soil of a potted plant on the railing. He shook his head as he withdrew it from the pot, scattering potting soil and dead leaves about on the decking.

Hutchinson's years in this place had made the jay noteworthy. It was well past the time when most of its brethren had moved to lower elevations for over-wintering, down from the pine boughs of the mountainsides into the oaks of the lowlands and valleys. Here in the high pines at this time of year, this bird was an anomaly.

The jays arrived in late spring when the last snows were melting, amid a tirade of raucous screeches and screams, staking out their territory. Then, things got quiet. They were shy and recalcitrant while they were nesting and rearing their young—usually in a twiggy nest tucked into the darkest recesses of a fulsome pine tree. When the youngsters fledged, they resumed their noisy and meddlesome ways until shortening days and colder nights drove them back down the mountain to relative comfort and abundance.

Herb loved the birds. They were so irreverent and self-centered, so predictable.

He thought about Russ Wakefield's recent visit as he watched the jay.

Either the man was madder than a hatter, or else he was enmeshed in something so bizarre and shocking that it defied belief. Years of putting words on paper, decades of journalistic research, swayed Hutchinson's personal opinion toward the former, as regrettable and unfortunate as it might be. The odds were large in favor of Wakefield having a loose screw.

Still, the premise was intriguing. What if there *had* been a botched test of a germ warfare agent, and the spin-off resulted in an epidemic? What if there was an active cover-up, a conspiracy to preserve the secret—the terrible secret—of the true source of all that death?

On closer analysis, it was less outlandish than it seemed at first view. What of the recently released reports of government agencies feeding radioactive breakfast foods to the unknowing, mentally-impaired children of uninformed parents to measure calcium uptake? What about the Army marching troops through fresh atomic blast areas during the Manhattan Project, to see how well they could fight after being dosed with radiation? What of the legendary testing of viral agents and hallucinogenic drugs on prison inmates? Was their consent informed? Implicitly not, since the need for testing suggested that the scientists didn't know all there was to be known and could not, therefore, competently inform the test subjects of all potential harmful effects, since they were uninformed in that regard themselves.

Hutchinson reached for his Atlas. It was the newest edition of the best Atlas in print, kept on hand for the occasional geographical reference his writing might require. He flipped to the Caribbean, and looked for Navassa Island. Nothing. He checked the index, drawing a blank there as well. The island of Wakefield's story either didn't exist or was so small it wasn't worth noting. There were some pretty small islands in the book: the Dry Tortugas, for example, one hundred sixty miles west of Key West. Less than seven square miles. They were on the map. They were even marked as the site of the Fort Jefferson National Monument.

Making a mental note to check a marine navigational chart of the Caribbean for Navassa Island when the opportunity presented itself, he returned to the computer screen. His screen-saving program had activated and the words "Touch Me and Die!" were parading in red letters across an otherwise blank screen. He killed the display and the screen returned to his current work. He typed another few words into the computer, where a draft manuscript was in progress.

Words and ideas were not coming easy this morning. Herb entertained the notion of knocking off for the remainder of the day to clear his head, to tackle the manuscript later, after his subconscious had had some time to work on it. The tactic usually produced results.

He rose from the terminal. The jay had vanished, off somewhere with pressing jay business. Herb stretched, and walked over to his bookshelves. Somewhere here lying around there was a book about the history of piracy. He'd used it for research some years back and remembered there were some maps and old sea charts reproduced in it. Finally, he found it on the top shelf: "The Spanish Main" was dusty and cracking at the binding.

He found a rag and cleaned most of the dust off the book. He opened it and began to look at sea charts, reproductions from the days of colonial Spain. By god, there *was* an island! On a chart dated 1715, lying halfway between Haiti and Jamaica, lay a small island. The Spanish spelling was 'Navaza', but it was too close to be coincidental.

Somewhere on his shelves, he remembered, there ought to be an older Atlas, slightly better in detail than the newer one he was currently using. He searched for it and found the island, spelled as 'Navassa'. It was listed as a U.S. possession. Two square miles in area. Uninhabited. He checked the date of publication of the Atlas: 1971.

Had they disappeared an entire island? The timetable was right. And there was no reason to delete an island from maps commonly available before the mid-1970s. However, assuming that Wakefield's story was true, there were plenty reasons for deleting it from newer editions. Maybe Wakefield really was onto something . . .

The phone rang, startling him. "Hello?"

"Hello. You don't know me," a female voice began, "but I'm a friend of Russell Wakefield's. He gave me this number. I don't know whom I'm speaking to, or who to ask for, except 'Herb.' Is there a Herb there?"

"Speaking. Herb Hutchinson."

"Do you know Russell Wakefield?"

"Yes."

"My name is Sylvia Bixler. Several days ago he told me to call you if anything happened to him."

"Please, go on. Presumably something has happened."

"Russ is dead. He was killed in a boating accident off Cabo San Lucas. He was with a friend on a fishing boat and the boat blew up. They found the wreckage of the boat a hundred miles offshore, but they found no life raft and no bodies."

"How do you know this?" Hutchinson asked.

"I was there. Well, not really there. They were a hundred miles offshore on a fishing trip. The Mexican authorities arrested me and held me for two days, asking questions about what happened. Finally, they decided it was an accident, or so they said, and they closed the investigation. When they finally let me go from that rotten jail, there was nothing to do but return to the States. I'm Wakefield's attorney and now I must handle his estate. Do you have any idea why he wanted me to call you, specifically, if he were to die?"

"Yes," Hutchinson said thoughtfully, "Yes, I do."

"Well?"

"It's not important, now. But, thanks. Say, where can I contact you after I've had time to absorb all this? It may be important."

Sylvia almost gave him her office number, then reconsidered and gave her home number instead. "I know this is going to sound crazy," she apologized, "but when you call, don't identify yourself. Use a code name. Just a simple code name, and I'll call you back. What will it be?"

"It doesn't sound as crazy as you might think," Hutchinson had caught her caution, emphasized especially in light of his recent cartographic discovery. "Use 'Bluejay'. When I call, I'll use the word 'bluejay' in the message. I think we may have a lot to talk about in the future."

"Mr. Hutchinson... did you know Russ well?" Now that Russ was gone, Sylvia sought out any vicarious contact with him she could find. She wanted to know more about him. The grief she still suppressed was substantially greater than she had anticipated. She'd cared more than she had known.

"Not really. We went to school together, but we haven't kept in touch. He showed up here last week, after nothing but Christmas cards for years, and told me a wild, unbelievable story. He said you'd call, and that would be its proof."

Sylvia now knew precisely where Wakefield had been in those days before the accident while she was stewing in Los Cabos. Had he really been astute enough to anticipate his own death? Was it really an accident, or had the men Wakefield said were trying to kill him finally succeeded? The very thought of the bomb he'd described was anathema to her ordered world. It had been much more comfortable to believe that Russ had misinterpreted a string of random, coincidental events; that he was harmlessly a little off his nut, still stressed by his sister's death. Maybe she'd been wrong.

"We both need time to think," she said at last. "I'm sorry to bring you the news." She broke the connection.

Herb Hutchinson spent the next three days on pins and needles, his mind whirring like a pinwheel in a high wind. He slept little, and was thankful when Daphne accepted his telegraphed request for solitude. He did not come out of his office study, except to attend to the necessities of survival. She'd seen him do this before when he was working on a book.

He read, studied, listened to Wakefield's taped story, reasoned, and inferred. He scratched his head; he rubbed his chin; he tugged absently at his Amish beard. He sat for hours staring vacantly out the window; he paced in the wee hours of the morning, trying to fill in the wide voids between what he knew, what he thought, what he suspected, and what he needed to find out before he could continue. The computer hummed quietly in the corner, neglected but not turned off, as his mind attempted to find a way of doing what he knew he must.

On the morning of the fourth day, he woke with the answer. Remarkably refreshed after a night under an Indian blanket on the sofa, he approached the computer terminal and sat down. With no hesitation, he began to type the words of the novel he would write; the title would come to him later.

As his fingers tripped across the keys, a line of text appeared on the screen, and then another:

"Diabolical, destructive, and criminal were not words that General Thomas Martindale would have used at that time in late 1969, in that place on the west side of the Snake River in Idaho Falls, to describe the activity his command staff was about to perform.
"Had he had been asked . . ."

Nearly two thousand miles away, two nameless American fishermen in a battered Zodiac motored quietly into the dock at Mazatlán. One was badly sunburned from hours of exposure under the relentless sun in the open craft... both were hungry, thirsty, and exhausted. Both shared a terrible secret, and both shared a purpose. Both had survived.

"So?" Elwin looked at his shipmate, raising an eyebrow in inquiry. They'd unpacked the Zodiac, salvaged whatever had any use for them, and had given the rest away at ten cents on the dollar to the owner of a fishing charter service on the waterfront in Mazatlán, subject to his assurance that he wouldn't reveal the source of his good fortune. It was time now to part company.

"Brockner is the place to start. I don't know how yet, but we've got to get to him without getting killed in the process. He knows the truth. I've got to find a journalist, somebody with some juice, who can take the story and run with it—as news, not as fiction. I don't know... I just don't know." Wakefield shook his head from side to side. "What about you?"

"I've got to find a place to stay, and find a way to get my money out of the Banco de Mexico. My mother is my nearest surviving relative; she's going to need help. I'm going to Portland."

"Portland?"

"Suzanne Coletti is there. She'll be happy to see me. We had a good thing once, but I couldn't go back to the States and she couldn't find a future in Cabo. Then I want to pay a visit to some researcher friends of mine in San Francisco. They're looking for a vaccine for AIDS. Perhaps I might be able to point them in the right direction. You'll be able to contact me through Suzanne. Columbia Veterinary Clinic. You? Where will you go from here?"

"Houston. I think I'll take a bus, walk across the border at Juarez as a day tourist, loaded down with sombreros and piñatas, and just climb on a bus. Sylvia can help. I've got to see my son. They both think I'm dead. And I need to collect my resources if I'm going to take on Brockner and his bunch. Meanwhile, I've got a son who needs to know I love him."

"Reach out and touch someone," Elwin said.

"Huh?"

"Call him. Tell him you're coming."

"Yeah... yeah, I will. Right away." Wakefield reached for Elwin's extended hand and drew the man into an embrace. The awkwardness he'd felt at physical contact with males in earlier times was gone now, and he hugged the surprised Elwin in a sincere clinch that managed to convey volumes about the bond they shared. They finished with a handshake, and Wakefield said, "Take care of yourself. I'll be in touch."

"Adios," Elwin responded simply, casting his eyes down to the rough wooden planks on which they stood, then raising them to meet Wakefield's with a clear and forthright gaze.

Wakefield watched Elwin turn and walk away towards the town.

He bent to pick up his overnight bag. It had been with him since his flight from Houston, and it contained, among other things, the copies of the documents he'd discovered in the walls of a crumbling building on a not-so-insignificant island, several lifetimes ago.

With a lightness in his heart, and a spring in his gait, he went looking for a telephone. *I intend to reach out and touch a lot of people,* he thought wryly to himself with quiet determination underneath the self-induced amusement.

But first, Thomas. First, my son.

The brittle sunlight of late autumn streamed through the window of the rattletrap bus and spattered over the occupants as they bounced and banged northward from Mazatlán on a particularly rough stretch of DF 15 north of Los Mochis.

The warm, sour smell of live chickens assailed the nose of Russ Wakefield. He sat, soaking up the frugal warmth of the sun's rays, his eyes closed, looking absently at the red glow that penetrated his eyelids. His body felt abused and battered. He was sore and bone-weary, and was feeling his age. His mind, however, was as clear as a Montana sky.

The dirty face of a small native boy, an *Indio,* peered at him in rapt curiosity from around the edge of a bench seat. The boy's wide brown eyes regarded Wakefield. He was out of place here, this Gringo. Perhaps he would do something interesting. The back wheel of the bus dropped into a particularly nasty pothole with a jarring crash that rattled the windows of the old bus. The Gringo stirred, grunted, but did not awaken. The boy turned away, searching for something else to ease the boredom of the bus ride.

Beneath the closed eyelids of the alert Wakefield, a thought was forming. It grew from outrage, rolling and billowing like black smoke from the *Mariposa Negra* into the clear sky of his mind. It took substance, and formed into resolve as the bus clattered and whined beneath him, bearing him northward to his destiny.

"They have a cure. The bastards have a cure, or they wouldn't have made the stuff."

BRADD HOPKINS

EPILOGUE

Nago Espiridion Uribe watched mutely from the edge of the jungle as the flames licked skyward from his village. Black smoke billowed from the burning huts into the still heat of midday. The others had gone, for this place was now under a curse, sacrificed to the old gods and to be purified by fire.

It was the consensus of the council of elders that the old gods were offended because the Guaymi had turned away from them to the white man's Catholic god. The old gods now wreaked their revenge, and required the sacrifice of the village to placate their anger and their jealousy. There was to be no further contact with the white men or their god.

Nago did not believe the council. He was beginning to suspect that perhaps there were no gods at all. His wife had been taken by the wasting disease, and also his youngest son. His elder son was showing the first signs that he, too, had the wasting disease. Others in the village shared similar losses; no family had been untouched. The funeral pyres had burned brightly for too many nights in the village. Death alone lived there now.

Scientists had been there, white doctors in white coats taking blood from the people, but now the scientists were gone. They had brought no cure for the wasting disease. They were of no more help than the aging Brujo Alejandro, who had secretly preserved and practiced the old ways of healing with herbs and incantations. Nothing seemed to work to stem the tide of the wasting disease. In final desperation, the village people moved away to a new place, torching the old one when the last Guaymi had departed. The spirits of their ancestors had been properly told of the move.

Nago turned silently from the leaping flames. His grief made it impossible to watch any longer. The radiant heat from the angry, crackling fire became uncomfortable and he stepped into the protection of the jungle. Absently, his hand scratched at a small lesion of discolored skin on his neck that he had not yet consciously noticed.

He walked through the hushed undergrowth toward his new home in the new village of the Guaymi. He hoped the gods were satisfied.

POSTSCRIPT

This novel was conceived at Rose's Landing in Morro Bay, California, in late December of 1992. Godparents include several tasty, low-sodium margaritas, and the company of good friends on a cold and rainy night. It started with the questions, 'Where was AIDS before 1980; why did it suddenly appear as an epidemic?'

The wild hypothecation and pseudo-logical analyses that emerged from the roundtable were at least superficially credible, and Courtney Cable, a dear friend and kindred spirit, turned to me and taunted, "Why don't you write a book?"

Warmed to overconfidence on that chilly December night by the glow of alcohol and lively company, and woefully unaware of the depth of the commitment I was making, I said, "I will!" We ordered another round.

The challenge was to look at apparently unrelated facts in a new way. The novel is fictional; of that there can be no doubt. I built the story around facts that are common knowledge, which may give it the illusion of truthfulness. The story is fiction.

The facts surrounding the AIDS crisis—its too-sudden emergence as a threat to the very existence of our society, its failure to approach the initial doomsday statistical projections, and recent news reports of governmental irresponsibility in the realm of research on unwitting subjects (particularly in the area of ionizing radiation effects)—combine to lead to some interestingly credible and disturbingly black speculations about the origins of the disease.

Research for the novel turned up some interesting corollaries to the basic hypothesis. For example, Duesberg's work, cited in the text, is real, although loosely interpreted for purposes of the story. He did indeed lose his NIH grant, but probably not for the reasons suggested in the novel. His findings have yet to find publication in this country, and I'm still not convinced that the reasons are apolitical.

Navassa Island is a real place. It was a navigational marker for the Spanish sails in the New World, and appears on maps dating from 1715. I discovered it as I was trying to answer the question of where might be a good place to conduct dangerous research on germ warfare. It is a U.S. possession, under the control of the State Department, laying between Jamaica and Haiti, accessible by helicopter, seaplane, or vessel easily from Guantanamo Bay in Cuba, and likewise from Florida. Interestingly enough, it does not appear on most maps after 1971, although a 1981 National Geographic World Atlas shows it. I'm sure it's been deleted in some published maps because the island is so insignificant, but it was still in most cartographic publications dated before that time. Coincidentally, early speculations by some scientists and epidemiologists, as you will recall, tentatively placed the origin of the AIDS virus in Haiti, brought into the U.S. by airline flight attendants. Having discovered Navassa Island, the invention of Nago Espiridion Uribe to explain that entry vector was a natural development in the plot.

In the Panamanian village of Changuinola, the Guaymi Indians have an unusually high incidence of what may be an HIV related retrovirus, HTLV-1. Other than among intravenous drug users in the United States, their 9% infection rate is reported to be the highest in the Western Hemisphere. HTLV-1 is not AIDS, but may be a precursor. This fact dovetailed nicely with the exploits of Nago Espiridion Uribe, the Guaymi Indian described in the Augury.

The official theory is that HTLV-1 in these Indian populations must have been present since before the European conquest of the New World, as was syphilis. Still, researchers have yet to establish a source of infection by identifying intermediary steps along a migration path where similar infections in Indian cultures—say in native Alaskans—would indicate that the disease was imported by migrating populations. There are no such contiguous paths to the Guaymi. More importantly, there is no documented origin. HTLV-1 is treated in the writing as an intermediate step between the Simian Immunovirus (SIV) modified by recombinant DNA techniques at Navassa into HTLV-3, which is the definitive form of HIV believed to be the cause of AIDS.

Perhaps the most significant stumbling block to the acceptance of the premise is the issue of the government, and particularly the Army, intentionally testing germ warfare agents on an unwitting urban population. The fact that this did, indeed, occur in the post-World War Two years is documented by Leonard A. Cole's book, Clouds of Secrecy: The Army's Germ Warfare Tests Over Populated Areas (1990), available from Rowman & Littlefield Publishers, Inc., 8705 Bollman Place, Savage, Maryland, 20763. I suggest you read it.

The testing Cole describes in his well-documented work was

largely of bacterial agents, called "simulants", that mimic the behavior of more deadly pathogens. In hearings held by the Senate Subcommittee on Health and Scientific Research of the Committee on Human Resources in 1977, an Army spokesman acknowledged that between 1949 and 1969, 239 populated areas from coast to coast had been *intentionally* exposed to simulant microorganisms as part of a biological warfare testing program.

In 1969, President Richard M. Nixon announced the end of the United States offensive biological warfare program, perhaps with an eye toward setting up a credible position for the United States at the coming 1972 Biological Weapons Convention. There, attending nations reaffirmed their support of the 1925 Geneva Protocol that prohibited the use of chemical weapons. The convention further outlawed the development and possession of offensive biological and toxin weapons. The issue of defensive testing was never mentioned, and the Army has admitted in public hearings that offensive and defensive testing are virtually impossible to distinguish.

Defensive testing may have continued secretly in the face of the presidential injunction, however, partly in response to the reports that Iraq had used biological and chemical agents in its war against Iran, and reports that the Soviets had employed biological agents in Afghanistan. During this period, it is entirely possible (if not probable) that biological 'defensive' warfare research moved into the arena of viral agents. It is a logical progression, given the contemporary scientific advances in recombinant DNA work, in genetic engineering, and in virology. The drive of the military to get a viral agent into the war reserve stockpiles would have been irresistible. Operational testing of viral agents would have required the use of simulants, and there were none. This problem would be solved typically by using a weakened strain of the virus itself.

The Army's 1984 proposal to build in Utah an indoor biological defense testing facility that would allow for testing of genetically engineered microorganisms that cause diseases with no cure suggests that clandestine research may, indeed, have continued in this vein, although the Army has denied it flatly. The plan was abandoned in 1988 because critics prevailed with the ideas that it would be too hazardous to the workers and the public, and would risk violating the 1972 Biological Weapons Convention accords. Cole's information is that the testing was re-initiated in 1986, in spite of all the concerns.

In 1977, Congress passed legislation that required the Department of Defense to notify Congress before conducting any tests that involve biological or chemical agents on human subjects. The premise of Navassa suggests that there may have been a mad scramble to complete any pending tests before the new law took effect, and that such tests might have been rushed to beat the Congressional deadline. An alternative explanation posed in the story suggests that the new legislation might have been a Congressional knee-jerk reaction to the actual loss of control over the hypothetical tests.

That many AIDS-related opportunistic infections are more prevalent and virulent in people with impaired immune systems, such as those who take immunosupressive medications, is a matter of common knowledge in the scientific community, and common sense among the rest of us. Emergence of these opportunistic diseases usually represents the reactivation of quiescent infections that were held in check by the patient's immune system before HIV started destroying T-cells. When the T-cell count drops below its normal levels of around 1,000 per cubic millimeter to levels of between 400 and 200, the first opportunistic infections usually appear. In fact, recently reported research directly correlates the life-style use of amyl nitrite "poppers" with the emergence of Kaposi's sarcoma as a symptom in AIDS patients.

Thus, the colossal blunder which gives rise to the protagonist's troubles was one of failing to assess the effects of the weakened virus when tested on a population with weakened immunities from other environmental stresses. There is a growing body of evidence to suggest that our immune systems are being weakened by stress, drug abuse, chemical pollution, population density (the Deer Island Syndrome), increasing ultraviolet radiation intensity from the polar ozone holes, and other factors as yet unidentified. The blunder becomes somewhat more credible viewed in that light.

Such testing, while possibly unthinkable in this day, could well have been perceived as acceptable governmental behavior in the 1970's; witness the emerging evidence in ionizing radiation effects research during that period which points to some rather cavalier attitudes regarding the sovereignty of governmental needs over individual health effects. Navassa uses this attitude as a vector to intentionally introduce the weakened virus into the population of San Francisco. In reality, the government has been there before. Documented testing of aerosol simulants in San Francisco occurred in 1950, and formed the cause of action in the Nevins case. (Nevins sued the United States in 1977 for damages, alleging wrongful death of his father resulted from simulant aerosols that were used in the testing program described in Cole's work).

Several aspects of technology had to be present for the novel's premise to become credible, and they are. New research in the fields of genetic engineering, recombinant DNA work, virology, and biochemistry indicates that this knowledge could have been emerging in the rarefied atmosphere of high level research laboratories in the late 1960s and early 1970s, long before it entered the arena of general knowledge. Research on the T-2 virus' reproductive process, which paved the way for recombinant DNA research, was published popularly as early as 1964. The application of this knowledge by the medical profession has lead to derivative advantages in human health care at a time when we need them badly. This emerging body of information would have been a matter of acute interest to anyone tasked with germ warfare research during the insane arms race of the Cold War, and the military priorities would have been substantially different from those of the healing institutions in its application.

Thinking backwards, the symptoms and behavior of the AIDS virus, strengthened in virulence and accelerated in progression, would make a germ warfare agent that would carry the potential of being among the best possible solutions to the problems of offensive biological warfare. An agent that destroyed immune system response rapidly would create a wide range of manifestations and symptoms, depending on which pathogens were present in a given environment, and which latent infections were present in each individual, but suppressed by each individual's immune system before it was destroyed by the etiological agent. In a very real sense, it represents a classical approach to warfare; destruction of the enemy defenses must always precede an assault. The thinking requires only its extension from the battlefield to the soldier's body.

I hope the reader will bear with me as I deviate from the path of empirical inquiry for the sake of diversion, and assemble random fact, speculation, and pure fiction at the whim of my muse. As with all fiction, the reader may be required to suspend disbelief to accept the initial premise. After that, all follows in a remarkably believable logic. Any resemblance to reality, or to any person, living or dead, in <u>Navassa</u> is strictly coincidental.

It was during the course of this writing, revising, and editing this work that I discovered my true passion.

B.D. Hopkins
Creston, California. 1994.

BRADD HOPKINS